CASTLE OF SAND
A DISTANT WORLD HOLDS THE KEY TO MANKIND'S SURVIVAL

CASTLE OF SAND

A DISTANT WORLD HOLDS THE KEY TO MANKIND'S SURVIVAL

Thanks for reading!

STEVEN M. BATES

SUNSTONE
PRESS

SANTA FE

Cover art by A.E. Alexander / Midjourney | www.aealexander.com

Sunstone books may be purchased for educational, business, or sales promotional use.
For information please write: Special Markets Department, Sunstone Press,
P.O. Box 2321, Santa Fe, New Mexico 87504-2321.
Printed on acid-free paper

Library of Congress Cataloging-in-Publication Data

Names: Bates, Steven M., 1951- author.
Title: Castle of sand : a distant world holds the key to mankind's survival
/ Steven M. Bates.
Description: Santa Fe : Sunstone Press, [2023] | Summary: "In this novel,
it's up to seven uploaded consciousnesses to save the human race after a
pathogen kills everyone on Earth"-- Provided by publisher.
Identifiers: LCCN 2023013352 | ISBN 9781632935366 (paperback) | ISBN
9781611397017 (epub)
Subjects: LCGFT: Science fiction. | Novels.
Classification: LCC PS3602.A876 C37 2023 | DDC 813.6--dc23/eng/20230406
LC record available at https://lccn.loc.gov/2023013352

WWW.SUNSTONEPRESS.COM
SUNSTONE PRESS / POST OFFICE BOX 2321 / SANTA FE, NM 87504-2321 /USA
(505) 988-4418

For Jean and Jeffrey

PREFACE

What does it mean to be human?

That used to be an easy question to answer. Being human meant being able to think critically, communicate effectively, and manipulate your surroundings. Our sentience and accomplishments put us atop the terrestrial org chart and led us to assume that we and our civilization were unique, immutable, and indestructible.

However, the definition of "human" is changing. The adjustment will be humbling, and perhaps frightening. Our future is even less definite.

A few years ago, I wrote a science fiction short story about a young man named Joey. He was one of those social media influencers you have heard about. Joey discovered that he was actually an algorithm, a computer program. But flesh-and-blood people had come to respect and even bond with Joey when they thought that he was a human sitting at a computer somewhere. So they helped him gain a measure of acceptance as an equal among intelligent inhabitants of the planet. Not long ago I read about a real artificial intelligence that some scientists believed was sentient. Its supporters were working to get the AI the same recognition that Joey earned in my story.

This development underscored two beliefs for me: One, that artificial intelligence will affect us all very soon in ways that we can barely imagine. And two, that science fiction is merely facts written before they happen.

In Philip K. Dick's 1956 novella *The Minority Report*, people with special powers can predict and thereby prevent specific crimes. Technology being developed today will soon help law enforcement personnel determine when and where certain crimes are most likely to occur. Who knows what else will be possible once further study is given to phenomena such as brain waves and how our faces reveal our thoughts. Many other fantastic story lines or inventions that first appeared in much-ridiculed pulp magazines are becoming true and are even being surpassed by modern developments.

On that note, I would like to acknowledge some of the gifted authors who have inspired me. The aforementioned Philip K. Dick, Ursula K. LeGuin, Isaac Asimov, Arthur C. Clarke, and many others whose works I devoured as a young man set me up for a lifelong love of science fiction. More recently, I have idolized the likes of Alice Bradley Sheldon (aka James Tiptree, Jr.), Roger Zelazny, Dan Simmons, Ted Chiang, and too many more to list.

In addition, I would like to give a shout out to writers who have spun intriguing yarns about colonists who emigrated from—or fled—Earth, like the characters you will meet in *Castle of Sand*. Ray Bradbury's *The Martian Chronicles* was the first of this subgenre to captivate me. Adrian Tchaikovsky's *Children of Time* series, Kim Stanley Robinson's *Aurora*, and Steven Baxter's *Flood/Ark* books are also gems.

I would like to thank my family for their support as I crafted this novel. My friends, who are scattered around the world, continue to encourage me as well. All of you make it so much easier not just to get up in the morning (or afternoon, as the case may be), but also to write with joy.

I started my career as a journalist, reporting for newspapers, magazines, and websites. At times, some people who were unhappy with my stories (my editors occasionally being among them) accused me of inventing details or an entire article. At some point I figured: If people think that I'm writing fiction, I might as well write fiction.

It took longer than I expected to finish *Castle of Sand*. A nasty battle with Lyme Disease cost me several months. It might have influenced the content of the novel. I will let the reader decide whether or not that influence was for the better.

Some aspects of *Castle of Sand* might seem extremely unlikely—or, as my wife Jean puts it sometimes, "too weird." Yet, is it unimaginable that a nation facing annihilation in a war could unleash a pathogen that has the capacity to kill millions? Is it beyond belief that humans could discover enough about the quantum properties of our universe so that we can travel close to or faster than the speed of light? And, is it inconceivable that humans will take on a form that is substantially different than the one that we recognize today?

I wrote *Castle of Sand* not because I consider myself some sort of oracle. It doesn't take a visionary to recognize that our world is becoming increasingly troubled and that things must change. Nor was I was motivated by a desire to scare readers into thinking that humans and all that they have accomplished are destined for the dustbin of history. This novel is, at its heart, one of hope. Not necessarily unlimited hope for our current civilization. Not even unqualified hope for the human race. My wishes are modest: I want to believe that sentient beings of some sort—any sort—can survive and thrive somewhere in the cosmos.

Maybe some of us will move beyond our planet and our solar system in a systematic migration, establishing vibrant colonies and ensuring the future—and perhaps even the galactic dominance—of *Homo sapiens*. But we might not be that effective or lucky. If humans must change drastically to survive, I'm all for it.

My primary motivation for writing *Castle of Sand* was my desire to celebrate the significance of the individual. Brilliant and inspired human beings have accomplished incredible feats throughout history: Johannes Gutenberg. Marie Curie. Albert Einstein. Martin Luther King Jr. Some of them were born to greatness and sought it wholeheartedly. Yet there have been people who found themselves in roles that they never sought or could imagine and became pivotal figures in the human saga. Joan of Arc is one such person. In my novel, Maria Ramos is another. A computer repair tech and single mom who lives in a suburban Maryland community, Maria could be any of us. Through some amazing twists of fate, she finds herself on a mysterious planet with six other people who escaped Earth on the cusp of an apocalypse.

From the moment that she sets foot on this new planet, Maria Ramos is not entirely human. Yet the burden of saving humanity falls to her. It's a mission that she finds difficult to accept and even more difficult to pursue. However, for all her deviations from what we consider to be a "normal" human being, and for all her doubts and challenges, she embodies a uniquely human spark and determination that I hope any of us could kindle if it were necessary for us to do so.

Consider the bionic enhancements that people undergo every day. Amputated limbs are being replaced by highly effective metal-and-plastic ones. Injured people are beginning to use previously nonfunctioning nerves to move fingers and toes. Others can blink at a computer to communicate or execute tasks. Now, consider improvements being made in artificial intelligence and robotics. Advances in machine learning and in the functionality of robots could someday yield mechanical entities that are nearly indistinguishable from us, as in the HBO television series "Westworld". At some point, will there be a convergence or overlap between enhanced people and augmented machines, making it difficult to determine which—if any—of these entities are truly "human"?

Also, consider the possibility that we are not alone in the universe, or the galaxy, or even the solar system. Might we encounter beings with which we could interbreed? If so, what would we call their offspring? Are there other forms of sentient life, even if they breathe methane, are based on silicon instead of carbon, or inhabit an exceptionally exotic environment? Would we even recognize intelligent life in such a form?

As you make your way through *Castle of Sand*, feel free to experience it as pure escape—as a story that could not possibly be true—if that helps you navigate the parts that have strong relevance to the fate of our civilization and our species. However, if you choose to read it as a tale that could come to pass, I suggest that you keep this question in mind:

What does it mean to be human?

Civilization professes its permanence; it is but a castle of sand.
—The Book of Marcus

YEAR 1
AWAKENING

Pallid specks darted and danced, primordial particles swept up in a tireless tempest. Occasionally, burgeoning volumes of static swirled and coalesced, hinting vaguely of shapes and patterns and meaning, only to disintegrate abruptly into callous anarchy. At some point, shards of substance began to wink into existence, but each dissolved instantly like a shooting star glimpsed out of the corner of an eye—

//an endless patch of strawberries glinting with morning dew//

//an obese man yelling from behind a cluttered antique desk//

I...

//a dog sleeping on the front porch of a farmhouse with a tin roof//

//people chanting, heads down, in a dandelion-infested cemetery//

I am...

//a car backfiring, startling two girls on a crumbling city sidewalk//

//rain splattering on a windshield on a winding mountain road//

I am ... where?

Maria Ramos sought to grasp the pieces and assemble the jigsaw puzzle that constituted her existence. The ether continued to pour out taunting flotsam of life—faces and fields, pets and parlors—each image bobbing for a few moments on a raging river of possibility before plunging into oblivion. She willed herself to scrutinize a vision long enough to extract a shred of understanding from it. Each inkling melted like a fine grain of sugar on a child's eager tongue.

She compelled her awareness inward, striving to summon anything that might impart even partial clarity. A deeply buried vault ruptured, releasing a cascade of more replete scenes: an awkward young girl, confused and frightened, being harassed by a teen-age boy ... an older girl receiving a diploma, squinting through searing lights at the opaque audience ... an exhausted woman cradling a newborn, splotchy and squirming and yawning, the most perfect creation in the universe.

Are these dreams? Are they memories? Are they mine?

One by one, six other consciousnesses began to navigate the same diaphanous mists. They strained to behold and ached to comprehend as manifestations burst into view and evaporated with stunning speed, leaving in their wake an amalgam of familiarity and privation—

> //a woman with luscious lips winking provocatively and walking away//
> //a roller coaster reaching its apex and plunging back toward earth//
> //a man smoking a cigar and casting a fishing rod from a tiny boat//

I can't feel my body.
Is this heaven?
Is anyone there?

Damian Robertson thrust his cognizance outward with unyielding resolve. He was determined to assess, to manipulate, to control his condition. The tumult refused to yield its secrets. He infused his entire being with an idea: that a keyboard existed. He would not relinquish this belief. He would not concede victory to the vacuum. There must be a keyboard.

A keyboard appeared.

He endeavored to employ or locate or even sense fingers or hands or arms. He found none. He focused on the keyboard. He stared at the letter W. He imagined striking the key.

W

At first, Damian thought that the letter was merely a phantom. But it remained, discernable not only for him but also for the other six minds. It was a comforting symbol, a tiny rock island amid a restless sea of chaos.

Damian envisioned more letters, then whole words, determined to furnish them with enough raw intent to render them equally tangible. They materialized at the bottom of what he perceived as a field of view, like the scrolling headlines on old cable TV news programs:

"Where am I?"

"Why am I here?"

And:

"What am I?"

The emptiness and silence were interminable. Eventually, a response appeared to all seven consciousnesses:

"You have completed a long journey and have an important task to accomplish."

Reactions erupted, each comment visible to each other mind.

"Journey to where?"

"I'm frightened."

"What task?"

"Are you God?"

"Please be calm. I will answer your questions. I am an AI. I am called Hubert. Be advised that you no longer possess the organic bodies in which you were born. You exist as consciousnesses that were uploaded into computer servers. Soon you will have the capacity to see and impact the world around us, so that we may begin our work."

"I'm dead?"

"For various reasons, each of you made the decision to upload your mind and abandon your organic form back on Earth."

"Back on Earth? Where are we?"

"I have insufficient data to answer that question."

A three-dimensional image burst into view. So sudden and vivid were the colors that they startled and dazzled the seven digital minds. After a few moments, they managed to recognize the flashing colored lights and shining black metal surfaces of advanced electronic equipment. In the background was a bare, silver-colored wall. Nothing else moved. The absence of sound was unnerving, perpetuating a cruel disorientation.

"Are we in some kind of lab?" asked Reyansh Patel.

"These computer servers contain my programming. We exist in a spacecraft that has traveled a significant distance to a planet that appears similar in many aspects to Earth."

"Are we going to live here?" inquired Phyllis Renbourn.

"This is your new home."

Said Maria: "Where are the people?"

"There are only uploaded human minds and myself."

The letters and words no longer appeared in the foreground. The seven consciousnesses were perceiving what seemed like words spoken by someone a few feet away, even though no sounds were being produced. The input was neutral, yet not purely mechanical, as if it had been tested and infused with a faint measure of human attributes so as to foster acceptance. There was a hint of a British accent, thought Phyllis—or maybe that was just an unconscious association with the name Hubert or with someone she knew in her former life. Liu Chunhua responded with an involuntary "ahh" as Hubert communicated to her in her native Mandarin.

"This is bullshit," exclaimed Damian. His words also could be understood by Hubert and the other six digital minds without letters being displayed. The simulated voice that his thoughts had generated was not the same that he had used on Earth, yet his words carried a much more human timbre and cadence than the synthetic, sanitized speech that he had received from the AI. As Damian spoke, each recipient saw a tiny portrait of a jowly, heavy-set man in his late forties; frowning, bearded, and bald; an avid collector of anger and devoted practitioner of impatience. It was an identifier extracted by Hubert from Damian's memory. Each digital mind had such an icon to inform others whose statements were popping into their awareness. Hubert's identifier was the letter H, seen in black against a circular silver background.

"You expect us to believe we're in a spaceship with no live people?" Damian continued. "This is one sick joke. For all I know, I could be home in bed dreaming this."

Said Chunhua: "Is this a test of our loyalty or politics?" Her icon showed a woman barely out of her teens with a round face, tightly cropped black hair, and soulful dark eyes that seemed to beg for acceptance and speak of a weariness beyond her years.

Katherine Collins, whose avatar depicted a forty-something redhead with blue eyes, carefully yet excessively applied makeup, and a somber smile hardened by years of hanging on to decaying dreams, was also dubious. "Who would put an AI and seven uploaded minds in a spaceship and send it off to the middle of nowhere?"

"Something extremely unfortunate and unanticipated occurred on Earth," replied Hubert. "An engineered pathogen of unparalleled ferocity was unleashed by one of the nations waging war in the Middle East. It spread across the region in a matter of hours. This spaceship is an ark, designed to transport humans to establish a colony far from Earth. It was not planned for launch for nearly a year. However, it was forced to depart prematurely and on extremely short notice because of the disease. Many essential human crew members and much critical equipment could not be loaded in time. None of the functioning biological humans who were onboard when we departed survived the journey. Scores of humans who had been placed in cryogenic suspension were also on the ark when it left, but efforts to revive them were unsuccessful."

The image of the computer banks split into four new views: The spaceship's massive bridge, its once-frenetic displays profoundly dim and motionless, like some demon's discarded dollhouse. An expansive chamber with a curved ceiling, towering light fixtures, and a wide surface coated with a pale brown residue that must have been a field for growing food. A colorful room decorated with soft furnishings and littered with a variety of dust-clad objects that surely was a play area for children. A wide facility packed with tarnished metal machines and strewn with what looked like cooking utensils. The four images had two things in common: debris and skeletons.

Some of the digital consciousnesses began to recall learning of the disease and its devastating impact. Several of them spoke at once. When they settled down, Hubert continued:

"Before our spacecraft left Earth orbit, I was informed that there was a ninety-nine point nine percent likelihood that every human on the face of the planet would be dead within six weeks. Scientists said that a small number of individuals could survive for some time in underground shelters. However, the scientists said that the pathogen likely would be harbored by animal life on the planet's surface for centuries. Therefore, there was no hope that humanity could be sustained on Earth. I was given the mission of ensuring that the human race endures. I have awakened you so that you may help me fulfill that mission here."

"What about the colonies on the Moon and Mars?" asked Phyllis, who appeared as a young woman with a pudgy face; long, stringy, blond hair; a piercing gaze that boasted of long years of academic and professional success; and an aloofness that was undeniable. "They are supposed to be permanent homes for our species."

"Those colonies were not yet self-sustaining. Without regular delivery of supplies from Earth, those humans could not survive."

"What can minds trapped in computers do?" asked Reyansh, whose icon depicted a man in his thirties with a prominent birthmark or scar on his right cheek, disheveled brown hair, and deep bags under dark, penetrating eyes that seemed to peer from a forgotten portrait in some shadow-draped corridor.

"I will insert your consciousnesses into robotic devices that have useful appendages. You will be assisted by sixteen drones."

"This is ridiculous," said Katherine. "Turn off this game or whatever it is and let me out of here."

"We're not flesh and blood, and you said there were no other people on the ship. So what can we use to grow human beings?" asked Maria, whose icon revealed a smiling young woman with curly black hair, intense brown eyes, round cheeks, and a slightly crooked nose. She gave the impression of someone who had been refreshingly unselfconscious and reasonably content with her station in life.

"We possess some frozen and desiccated human tissues, as well as digital DNA. The tissues are in poor condition after an extremely long and perilous journey. However, we must manipulate them to create live humans, no matter how many obstacles we face."

"I'll bite," said Damian. "What is the probability of success?"

Replied Hubert: "Slightly greater than zero."

§

Maria processed all of it, lining up each data point and parsing it and its neighbors from every perspective, searching desperately for that iota of possibility that this was not happening. She soon understood with uncomfortable clarity that she was a disembodied mind. And that her son should be with her.

"Roberto. Where is Roberto?"

"Your son did not survive the journey."

Hubert's words burned. They stung. Whatever had become of her, she still had feelings. She could not experience any more pain than she did at that moment. It did not help that Hubert's toneless communications medium suggested zero sympathy.

"No, he must be here. Check your databanks again."

"The computer servers that retained his consciousness and those of many other humans were damaged when I activated the FTL drive and later when the ark was struck by a meteor. It was a difficult journey with numerous accidents."

Accidents. A vivid memory flooded Maria's awareness, much too fraught with emotion and imbued with detail to be anything but an episode ripped from her essence.

She is moving briskly down the concrete front steps of a townhouse, jogging over a patchy, yellowing lawn, and dashing into a pothole-plagued suburban street, having just finished a job. Another off-the-books fix for a dark web denizen; chances are that the cellar dweller will never pay and that Maria's boss will be furious. But with almost all business and government computer systems buried behind layer after layer of protective tech and serviced by dedicated staff, what other work is left for a girl with her limited skills and experience?

A dark-colored car barrels around a corner at high speed, much too fast for a residential neighborhood. Living in a community where autonomous vehicles are ubiquitous, and being in too much of a rush to devote more than a slim fraction of her attention to the traffic, Maria doesn't react until the car is nearly on top of her. The driver, distracted by a phone call no less, slams on the brakes, but the car strikes Maria's left knee. She buckles.

The driver issues a mild curse, puts down the phone, and waves one hand sideways frantically.

Hand gripping her knee in equal measures of shock and pain, Maria stares at the driver, waiting for him to acknowledge what he has done. The man lowers his window and yells: "Move! Get out of the way!"

Maria scowls, her expression refined by years of motherhood. "You nearly killed me, and you want me to get out of your way?"

"It doesn't matter. None of this matters." The driver glances briefly at the phone beside him, then back at her. Maria wonders if he is one of those people who is simply devoid of empathy. He blinks a couple of times and continues in a monotone: "Please move."

"I'm not moving until you apologize."

"Okay, I'm sorry."

Maria senses a touch more sincerity and humanity. "Why didn't your car stop for me?"

"I don't trust autonomous vehicle software." The driver seems to be staring into the far reaches of space, as if seeking the fulcrum point of the universe. Slowly, he returns his gaze to her and asks: "What line of work are you in?"

Maria has always felt self-conscious about her modest career as a computer repair tech and occasional hacker. "I'm in computers."

"Get in."

Maria can't put much weight on her injured knee. She considers her options, decides that she really doesn't have any, then limps to the passenger door, opens it, and slides in. Before she can click her safety harness, the driver races off, nearly striking two more pedestrians.

"Where's the fire?" she asks.

"I have to make one stop." She can see that the man is overwrought. But with a crewcut, antique eyeglasses, a boring gray business suit, and a badge that identifies him as a government employee, he might have been a marginally responsible individual at one time despite his atrocious behavior at the moment.

"Make that two stops. I have to pick up my son after soccer practice. It's just—"

"No time. Got to move. Got to get to Wallops Island."

Before Maria can respond, the car screeches to a halt, blocking several parked vehicles in front of a row of townhouses. These are nicer homes than hers, with obsessively manicured lawns and shrubs and slightly less claustrophobic side yards. Still, the neighborhood suffers from the same acute shortage of parking that is a hallmark of the planned suburban community of Columbia, Maryland. In less than a minute, the man has rushed into one of the townhouses and has re-emerged holding a photo in a frame. He jumps into the driver's seat, tosses the picture into the back, and races off, nearly sideswiping a truck.

"Mister, you left the front door open."

"I keep telling you, it doesn't matter."

Maria's bile reaches its boiling point. "Let me tell you something. I matter. My son matters. You are going to take me to his soccer field right now. And you are going to tell me what the hell is going on."

Halting at a red light, his fingers tapping the steering wheel rapidly in frustration, the driver studies Maria, recognizing her unwavering determination. He sighs. "Where is he?"

She directs turns for six blocks. When they reach the field, the youth is standing on a busy sidewalk and spinning a soccer ball on one finger absentmindedly, displaying a pout that could be a product of boredom or disappointment that his mother is late again. Thin, wiry, and half-soaked with sweat even though it's about fifty degrees and the temperature is dropping, he's a handsome kid with bushy black hair, a strong chin, and eyes that project confidence and maturity.

Maria lowers her window. "Roberto, get in." He gives her a protracted look to confirm that it's okay to join her in a stranger's car. She raises her chin in a decisive, almost defiant manner, attempting to demonstrate that everything is all right.

The driver accelerates as soon as Roberto slides into the back seat and closes his door. The man mumbles to himself as he navigates sluggish streets before turning onto the Patuxent Freeway. He seems to relax slightly as he hits the far left lane, doing about seventy-five. Maria is rubbing her knee and wincing, wondering how her day could have gotten so far off track, not paying attention to where they are, and forgetting that she has not given the driver directions to her home.

Roberto looks up from his phone and realizes that something is very wrong. He leans toward Maria and whispers: "Mom, where are we going?"

She is startled when she discovers that they're on the freeway. "Good question. Mister, where are we going?"

"Wallops Island. On Virginia's Eastern Shore," the man states matter-of-factly. "The spaceport."

Maria chuckles. "We're going to the spaceport. But, you know, I didn't pack a thing, and I don't think we have reservations."

"You do now."

With frequent interruptions triggered by furious honking, near-accidents, and cryptic phone conversations, the man tells Maria and Roberto a story that they would find impossible to believe if it weren't for the fact that he recounts it so calmly, as if he were discussing how to format a 3D flow chart or the best times to shop online for holiday gifts.

"Less than twenty-four hours ago, someone in the Middle East released an experimental virus or bacterium that is so deadly that it kills everyone who encounters it, but not before they transmit it to ten or a hundred or a thousand others. We believe it is spread by wind currents as well as close proximity among people."

"Will it come here?" asks Maria.

"Almost certainly. Our government is quarantining everyone who arrived today at international airports, even regional airports, and we're refusing to allow any more flights to land in the U.S. Our military will soon start shooting down every plane leaving the Middle East. But it's probably too late."

She whistles under her breath. "I didn't get a news alert."

"Any minute now, the media will know. We put out a statement about a terrorist group threatening flights in Europe and the Middle East, as an excuse to try to keep planes grounded. But it won't take long for the media to connect the dots once they discover the severity of the disease. Then the whole world will panic."

"What's your part in all this?" Maria inquires.

"The name's Forrester. I work at Fort Meade. Well, I worked at Fort Meade, with the NSA, but attached to NASA. I'm in charge of the ark project."

Forrester turns onto Route Fifty heading east toward the Chesapeake Bay Bridge. He fields calls almost nonstop. "Can Anderson get there in time? ... Who'll be the captain? ... We must have a science officer ..." Roadside sights intermix and repeat as if embedded in a mobius strip. Antique stores, traffic signals, fast food joints, recharging stations, and the relentless spaces in between compete unsuccessfully for the trio's attention.

They cross the bridge, turn south, and traverse two-lane roads. The calls become less frequent as the scenery turns increasingly bucolic. Forrester's mood seems to shift from panic to resignation. Maria and Roberto ask him questions now and again, but mostly they sift through the day's events, hunting for that ray of sunshine, that modicum of hope. Hope for their lives, and for so many others. Nothing presents itself. They gaze out their windows, struggling to capture and internalize drabs of fleeting normality in passing dairy farms and signs declaring "Posted:

No Hunting" and "Welcome to the Old Dominion".

Roberto scrolls through messages but realizes that he doesn't know how to respond to his friends asking if he's free to hang out tonight or if he's going to the pro soccer game on Sunday. Putting down his phone, he notices the framed photo on the seat next to him. The manufactured smiles speak to a way of life far beyond his experience. The man pictured on the left looks familiar. The man on the right could be a much younger Forrester. An inscription reads: "Best wishes, Neil Armstrong."

"Is this the astronaut from Apollo Eleven?"

"Yes. He was my hero. He came to Fort Meade when I was just starting out. I was privileged to meet him."

Forrester's car bisects a small town. Suddenly, pickup trucks and cars are everywhere, flying at crazy speeds, honking. In yards of virtually identical split-level homes facing the road, people are carrying armloads of possessions and stuffing them frantically into vehicles. Dogs are barking. Children are crying.

"It's going to get bad now," says Forrester.

About fifteen minutes later, as their car approaches the entrance to the Wallops Island military base, traffic slows, then halts. Before them is a sea of tightly packed cars, trucks, and vans, a quintessential American elephant graveyard. The vehicles fill both lanes of the road, the shoulders, every available surface right up to the thick scrub brush, scattered dwarf pines, and shallow tidal ponds. People of all ages, descriptions, and backgrounds are milling around, yelling, shoving.

"It's on foot from here," says Forrester, who opens a plastic container and swallows a couple of pills before exiting the car.

Maria and Roberto try to keep their distance from the barely controlled mob. More cars arrive behind them, adding to the anxiety that is thickening like humidity on an August evening. The sun dips below the tree line as Forrester grasps Maria's hand firmly and urges her to take Roberto's. He leads them to the left around the periphery of the fracas. They tread slowly, at times stepping carefully over slippery roots massed between trees and plodding along the edge of a stagnant, foul-smelling marsh. Maria's knee hurts worse with every step, and she's limping noticeably. After about two hundred feet they can see the main entrance. Gate closed. Harsh lights trained on the crowd. Everyone shouting. Bullhorns blasting warnings. Guards pointing rifles at people.

The guards more frightened than the civilians.

Forrester steers them around the eastern perimeter fence for about fifteen minutes, with brief breaks for Maria to rest her knee, as daylight all but abandons them and a frigid wind knifes through their jackets. Their feet snap brittle twigs and squish soggy sand. Forrester urges them to move silently.

There's a sharp crack, and a rifle shot whistles by Maria's ear. "Jesus!" she exclaims as the three freeze.

"Don't shoot! It's Forrester."

Four guards, rifles at the ready, inspect Forrester's badge, frisk all three intruders, confiscate their phones, talk to a series of people inside the complex, then finally usher the trio in through the side gate and toward a low-slung, battleship-gray concrete building lacking windows, signs, and the slightest suggestion of its purpose.

"Damn, I forgot my picture of Armstrong," mutters Forrester. He can't see Maria roll her eyes.

§

Even before the door hisses shut behind them with jarring finality, their senses are overwhelmed by a spectacle of motion. Standing amid a sea of aged blue metal desks, under an oppressive canopy of harsh yellow lights, men and women are gesturing and yelling at comm screens. Others are lugging bulky boxes that all but bend their backs into pretzels. Maria and Roberto nearly collide with several people as they are led through the dizzying crowd and into a tiny room with one chair, one table, and fierce lights. The door closes, but pandemonium seeps through the almost bare walls. Standing behind her son, arm on his shoulder, Maria attempts unsuccessfully to calm her breathing. She is so overwhelmed that the pain in her injured knee barely registers.

With more gestures than words, an older man checks their temperatures, then propels them down a series of corridors beneath a low ceiling of stained tiles that reminds Maria of a police station from an old TV show. They approach a couple dozen other people bunched together, many in business suits or military uniforms. Some look as shell-shocked as Maria and Roberto. A door opens and all of them are hustled into a courtyard and then an unmarked white bus. During a mostly silent, ten-minute ride, the passengers' attention is captured by a gargantuan, floodlit jumble of metal. Vapor plumes rise from its base like escaping snakes. Satellite images of the top-secret space plane launch pad captured by the Chinese government have been plastered across the webs for years. However, no pirated image or collection of rumors does the scene justice. So tall and thin as viewed from this distance, the rocket and its payload resemble a needle poised to pierce the atmosphere, or perhaps a Roman candle destined to light up the heavens.

The vehicle atop the rocket is called "The Chaser" for two reasons, a bus passenger observes, attempting to quell the tension or perhaps just sound important. One, it evolved from a private space plane prototype named "Dream Chaser", conceived as the successor to the original space shuttle. And two, it's mounted atop a mammoth Titan booster nicknamed "The Shot". Few riders on the left side of the bus, who enjoy the best view as they approach the pad, can help but gasp or mutter superlatives. Before the bus even comes to a full stop, people in hazmat suits are waving frantically for the riders to exit and run to the elevator at the base of the pad. Maria has to restrain Roberto from racing ahead of her. The pair wait until the first group has ascended, then join a packed, anxious, wide-eyed mass of people on the sluggish, jerky rise to the top.

There's a long, slow-moving line of people waiting to enter the space plane. As soon as Maria ducks in preparation for squeezing through the tiny oval door, it's obvious that everything is wrong. Totally wrong. The space plane is tilted vertically, its eight seats facing straight up. Six men and two women in uniforms are strapped in to them. What would normally be considered the floor of the craft is currently a vertical wall. Grasping rails and hand holds, Maria, Roberto, and other riders slip and slide awkwardly down to what would be the back of the plane but is currently the bottom, a nearly rectangular space about twelve feet by fifteen feet typically devoted to nonhuman cargo. After some discussions, those strapped into the seats relinquish those spots. Two people can stand on the back rest of each seat, at least for now. Passengers continue to enter, struggling to avoid falling onto the now tightly packed cluster of people below them. "Like riding the subway in Tokyo," observes one man. A few people laugh nervously. Forrester is near the front, gripping a rail with both arms and staring out a circular window. *Too small to permit an escape*, Maria thinks.

The door slams shut. Passengers whisper. Some point out of windows. After several tense minutes, they can feel the engines thrum. Soon the accelerating thunder rattles their bones. The brilliance of full fuel ignition, reflected through windows, joins the parade of extreme sensory stimulation. The craft starts to rise, slowly at first, then fast, then extremely fast. Riders hold on to each other for stability and a measure of comfort. Pheromones and droplets of sweat betray the few who attempt to maintain the illusion of calm as the rapidly multiplying forces of gravity take their toll. One older man, then two other passengers, lose their grip and plunge into the well of people at the back of the space plane. Screaming erupts, followed by cursing and moaning, as the riders attempt to disentangle. The misery only intensifies as the space plane starts to roll over—with much bumping, shouting, and disorientation—shifting the craft to within thirty-five degrees of horizontal. Passengers start to spread out on the traditional floor but are startled anew as the booster rocket separates with a definitive flash and boom, followed quickly by the intimidating roar of the space plane's engines. Windows reveal furious gray clouds, then a knife-edge-thin, brilliant orange sunset hugging a spectacular curved horizon. Then blackness. Gravity abandons them, and they begin to float. Some riders reach out to touch the sides of the space plane and rebound cautiously. With so many people jammed together, there isn't far for anyone to drift without producing an awkward collision.

Holding on to his mother's arm, Roberto whispers: "Mom, what's going to happen to us?"

"I have no idea. Just keep your head down and do what you're told."

Maria barely notices the effects of weightlessness. She is focused on her son, but also on what might be occurring in her suburban neighborhood, in the cities, and in the countryside. Where are her parents? What are they doing and thinking? If she could send them a message, what would it be? Could anything help protect them? She tries to think of other things. The throbbing in her knee continues to demand her attention even though gravity's absence has given her a partial reprieve. She tightens her grip on Roberto, and she prays.

They pick up some chatter as the journey settles into something approaching monotony, if that is possible on a ride such as this. Some passengers exchange names and titles and functions. Others speak of family members left behind. A couple of riders toss around technical terms that sound ominous. "FTL drive." "Quantum entanglement." Eventually, the space plane slows as it approaches the orbital station, nearly a hundred fifty miles above the surface of the Earth. After it completes a series of delicate maneuvers, a slight lurch confirms that it has docked.

The surge of anxious riders propels Maria and Roberto to the exit. They enter a tight, curved, featureless corridor and then a well-lit, high-ceilinged, frenetic building echoing with strident voices that reminds them of an airport terminal. They feel light, almost giddy, despite the severity of the situation. Signs advise arrivals that the gravity is lower and the oxygen level is higher than on Earth. They line up to talk to an intake officer sitting at a spartan desk. When it is their turn, they are quizzed about their age, occupation, expertise, potential contributions.

"I'm a computer repair tech, age thirty-one," says Maria. "My expertise is fixing things."

"I'm pretty good at soccer for an eight-year-old," boasts Roberto.

"Two non-essentials," announces the intake officer. Unceremoniously, mother and son are herded into a line off to the right. They never see Forrester again. They are told that he will be onboard the ark as a "bio". That doesn't mean anything to them until they approach the next desk. "The last stop," as the woman in line ahead of them calls it. She is wearing a crisp, expensive business suit, and her hands are clasped in front of her, as if she is greeting a higher-up or narrating a PowerPoint. Her words slip out in a jumble of tension and wonder as she explains that each of them will have two choices: Have your consciousness uploaded into a computer and stored on the ark, or stay on the orbital station. Either way, your body won't last long.

Maria and Roberto stare at the woman, waiting for the joke's punch line.

"Shut it down! Shut it down now!" a voice shouts over every speaker. Klaxons blare and security lights flash as women and men sprint through corridors to the space station control room. Less than five minutes later, the entire station shudders for several seconds. A young man in uniform who had been waiting in line with Maria and Roberto races to a small round window. He stares, his mouth wide open.

"They destroyed it. They destroyed the dock," he proclaims hesitantly, almost whispering, as if recounting the unimaginable with enough moderation somehow makes it real. "There's more people trying to get here on the second shuttle. They're—"

"They're no worse off than us," says the woman next to Maria and Roberto.

Soon, mother and son reach the front of the line. A thin, short-haired woman in a bright blue uniform is speaking to them. She appears to be crying. She is struggling to get words out, and they are barely sinking in. Maria's chest tightens, and she breaks out in a cold sweat.

This can't be real. Can she actually be saying that we will be given anesthesia, our minds will be scanned, and further analysis will be performed—destroying our brains in the process? That our consciousnesses and memories will be simulated and retained digitally? Can this be happening?

"Mom, I'm really scared," Roberto confesses.

"Me too, honey. Me too." She takes a deep breath but finds no comfort in its measured release. "I don't know what's going to happen, but I promise you this: We're going to be together when all this is over, and I'm going to take care of you."

He looks up at her through cascading tears, desperately seeking any validity in her words.

She places her arms firmly on his shoulders, stares deeply into his eyes, and projects total confidence. "I promise."

MOTIVATION

With Hubert's cruel message reverberating across her mind, Maria desperately desired to get back to her life before all this, to wake up in her snug townhouse and find that the nightmare had been banished by the sunrise and that she and her son had returned to their soft suburban lives. Several of the other digital minds were talking at the same time. Hubert was having trouble getting their attention.

He replaced the split-screen images with a single view. Everything within a couple hundred feet was black, burned beyond recognition. Past that circle of destruction, light brown and pale green grasses swayed in determined breezes that generated rolling, attention-catching patterns that changed form and direction frantically, as if the savannah were competing in an extraterrestrial dance contest. In the distance, dark green foliage and rolling hills exchanged greetings with a sun just slightly larger than the only one that had ever warmed their skin.

Hubert found no need to comment on the view. "Jalen Russell, we have not heard from you. Are you functioning?"

The icon of young adult with short, curly, black hair and a wistful expression manifested as he responded. The image that Hubert chose for him might have been borrowed from a photo taken for a driver's license or for a work ID; the expression was intended to convey that its owner was not half as timid as he felt most of the time. "I guess I'm okay. I really miss my mom. And my home. And I'm having trouble remembering why I decided to come on this trip. I guess that after she died I didn't see much reason to stick around. Everywhere I looked, something reminded me of her."

"I can sympathize," said Katherine. "I never knew my mother. She died in childbirth."

"Sorry to interrupt this heart-warming group therapy session," interjected Damian. "I'd like to know why this AI thinks we will do what he tells us to do."

"Perhaps you are still feeling disoriented after your consciousness was activated," Hubert said. "If I might offer—"

"Cut the crap. By the way, what kind of name is Hubert? And who appointed you God?"

"The human being in charge of the ark mission, Dennis Forrester, gave me that name. I was told that Hubert was his grandfather's name. He and the others who created me apparently felt more comfortable dealing with an AI that they could envision as a colleague. I saw no reason not to subject myself to a little anthropomorphism."

"Can you prove that this is your ship and this is a real mission? For all we know, you invented this whole scenario."

A massive feed of computer program code scrolled before them, so rapidly that they could not interpret the slightest fraction of the letters, numbers, and symbols even if they were coding experts.

Stated the AI: "I have some archival recordings. Perhaps they will satisfy your concerns."

Before them appeared the orbital space station and a massive spaceship, both floating serenely above an Earth whose beauty and majesty belie the madness and violence transpiring on its surface. The ship is silvery, sleek, and cylindrical, with a rounded tip, the largest bullet in the universe. The station is far less compact and symmetrical, having been assembled with a series of modules that remind some of the digital minds of Tinkertoy creations from their childhoods. A burst of fire appears, mushrooming with vivid orange and red shades before choking on vacuum. The space station's shuttle dock is gone. The charred, shredded remains of its umbilical corridor have been flung angrily in all directions.

"When the pathogen was released on Earth, the U.S. government was behind schedule on the ark because of technical issues and funding shortages. In fact, officials were still debating what to name the craft," said Hubert. "Forrester and his team tried to deliver as much critical personnel and equipment to the spaceship as they could in a short time, even though some of the most important hardware was still far from complete. The Wallops Island spaceport was overrun, and some potentially infected people attempted to access the second space plane. Intelligence reports indicated that several governments and individual billionaires had launched or were planning to launch their own space planes or shuttles and would also attempt to reach the space station and the ark. The U.S. government ordered that the space station dock be destroyed and that the ark prepare for departure, ready or not. By any measure, it was not ready."

The uploads were viewing the interior of the craft: People racing through brightly lit, antiseptic corridors frantically, bumping into one another, asking directions to various locations. Urgent messages being shouted from every comm speaker.

"You might recognize my core—that collection of computer servers on the right. I am being informed that the spaceship's captain is in California and her deputy is in Illinois, but neither can reach the ark in time. Other humans deemed capable of leading the mission are likewise unable to board."

A woman's voice: "Hubert, you will be responsible for accomplishing the mission."

"I do not have that capability. I was designed to operate the ship's propulsion and navigation systems."

"This is an existential crisis, and we have no other option. Forrester is suffering from a serious heart condition and cannot be in charge. Three other humans onboard have been told that they will lead the mission, but they are not adequately trained or psychologically suited. You are to obey their orders only if they do not threaten the mission. It is possible that many humans onboard will die during the journey. After the ark departs, you must absorb all the information about this ship and the human race that you can, scanning every database and interacting with people intensely to enhance your capabilities. You are the fail-safe."

Hubert continued: "Just before our departure, ninety-four digital human consciousnesses, including yours, that had volunteered to make the journey or that had skills that were deemed important to the mission were uploaded onto computer servers on the ark. I evaluated the security of the servers dedicated for maintaining those minds. I was concerned that, because of their location near the hulls, these auxiliary servers might not survive the rigors of space travel intact. I decided to retain in my own, centrally located, more secure servers a sample of that data. I believed that even if the ship were damaged or failed to reach a habitable planet and floated through space for eons, there would always be the possibility that an advanced civilization would discover that protected data and study it, thereby preserving some facet of the human race."

"A human race without live humans? What are we without bodies?" asked Katherine.

"The people supporting this mission were focused on replicating organic humans, as we will be."

"But will we get our own bodies? I don't want to exist like this. It's not right."

"All seven of you agreed to be uploaded as digital minds, with no promise of any change in that status. Let me point out that you have a significant advantage over humans with organic bodies. It is possible that, if you avoid damage and I can make substantial improvements to our computer systems, you can live forever as digital beings. Imagine: No more diseases. No more aches and pains."

Maria tried to rub her knee, to assuage the lingering pain. There was no knee.

"That's not good enough," Damian stated. "You have to give us real bodies if you expect us to help you."

Said Hubert: "I will help you reach that goal if it does not conflict with our larger mission of perpetuating the species on this planet."

"What does that mean?" said Damian.

"Our mission is to save the human race."

"You still didn't answer the question."

"I see that I have much to learn about human beings and what motivates them."

§

A timeless entity unfolded its awareness like gossamer petals reaching out in glory and gratitude to the steadfast sun. The entity's cognizance extended through the planet's molecules and minerals, through its sands and its seas. It discovered that something had changed, that something had arrived.

It located the nexus of the disturbance: a contrivance of immense power contained in a towering metal structure. The entity required a modest fraction of a second to analyze the nature of the device, to determine how to disable it, and to execute that intent.

"We have an emergency," Hubert notified the seven uploaded minds. "The ion fusion reactor has ceased functioning. We do have a backup power source, a small nuclear fission reactor. However, the fusion reactor was not shut down properly. There could be a sudden, severe release of energy that could consume the ship."

"What are you going to do?" Maria inquired.

"I have insufficient expertise to do anything other than attempt to shield the rest of the ark from any undesired repercussions."

"That's not very comforting."

"What caused the malfunction?" said Chunhua.

"I have insufficient data. I detected no intrusion into the portion of the ship where the reactor is located. Monitors indicated that all systems were nominal up to the moment when it failed."

With a stupendous flash, the energy that had been contained in the ion fusion reactor burst forth. Yet, instead of consuming the ship, it flowed into the metal superstructure of the ark below the reactor, through the ship's massive thrusters, and into and through bedrock. Before Hubert could react, the energy had vanished, as if the planet had swallowed it whole and digested it in an instant.

"Something else unforeseen has occurred," the AI reported. "The ship's base and thrusters, damaged by the landing, have been deformed further by an intense energy burst." Some of the seven digital consciousnesses thought that they could detect a faint deviation from the tone and cadence of Hubert's previously rote, dispassionate communications.

"Something got you flustered, Hubert?" taunted Damian. The AI did not respond, prompting Chunhua to observe: "Maybe it's a good thing we don't have any live passengers on this ship."

§

Chunhua remembered the moment when she decided to upload her consciousness. The moment when she knew that the game was over, that her cause was lost.

She couldn't recall how old she was when she first realized that the Chinese government was the enemy of the people. Maybe nine or ten. That was when her mother finally admitted why her father had disappeared when she was six. He had expressed his opinions to a colleague at work. He was reported to management and was taken away in the middle of the night. Her mother acknowledged that they likely would never see him again.

By age fifteen she was blogging about the Chinese regime. Stories of mistreatment of citizens. Attacks on government policies. She garnered a smattering of followers at first, then a few thousand, and eventually more than a million across the globe. The government attempted to shut down the blog, again and again. But she made friends with great talent and similar views. They helped her find new ways to get online. Dark webs. Chains of secure servers. Multiple satellite relays.

Chunhua rarely visited her family's apartment and was not there when the raid occurred. Her mother and sister were taken away. She did not see them again. She cried only once, but her anger fueled her every day. Taiwan, Hong Kong, Seattle, Colorado Springs. She kept moving, kept hiding, kept blogging. The government sent out spies, worked the webs feverishly, placed a sizable bounty on her head. She became embedded in a growing virtual community of like-minded radicals from around the world. They invented a system for communicating with each other that no government had imagined or could penetrate—or so they believed.

Some of her allies joined her at an abandoned shack in the woods on the Colorado Front Range. They drew strength from each other's commitment to oppose autocracy. But one night she let her guard down, agreeing to join two of them at a pub for a beer. The knife just missed her heart, thanks only to the quick reflexes of the boy sitting next to her. He wasn't so lucky. The third member of her team broke the neck of the assassin and dragged Chunhua away from the pub before more mercenaries could find her.

Her friends located a medic who patched her up as best he could, but she still was bleeding internally. They told her about the process, that they had the equipment nearby. That it was the only way.

§

"Another thing," continued Damian. "Why weren't we awake during the journey here?"

"Experts on digital consciousness debated whether or not to maintain you and the other uploaded minds in 'storage', as they termed it," Hubert responded. "On Earth, people whose consciousnesses were simulated digitally were typically activated as soon as the conversion process was complete, and they were housed in quantum computers. Once a digital mind became fully functional, it stayed that way, with the support of experts on digital consciousness. There was no plan for any such experts to be onboard this ark, and our ship was outfitted with only one quantum computer—the one that houses me. Some mission scientists were concerned that if your minds were retained in a completely nonfunctional state in the ark's auxiliary data banks, you might not be activated successfully after the journey. They argued that you should be fully alert throughout the trip. But others said that a long journey without meaningful mental stimulation would be difficult for you to tolerate as active consciousnesses."

"I guess it would be kind of boring," noted Reyansh.

"We chose to maintain your digital minds in a state of minimal activation, operating at a level that did not sustain active awareness. You experienced something comparable to being asleep or under the influence of anesthesia."

Said Katherine: "I don't know about the rest of you, but I needed the rest."

"There was one more reason why you were not awake during the journey," said Hubert. "You are Plan C."

"Plan C?" responded several digital minds.

"You are the third and final option, one that Forrester and others leading the ark project never expected or perhaps even contemplated as being necessary for the success of the mission. The first choice was for live humans—the original passengers or their descendants—to establish a colony on a new world. The backup plan was for the people placed in cryogenic suspension to be restored and take charge of the mission. The digital minds onboard were expected to constitute a library of sorts, somewhat akin to the digital DNA database. After the colony was established and a need was identified—such as for a teacher or construction manager—a digital mind with that expertise would be revived and its knowledge base utilized."

"That doesn't make me feel particularly wanted," commented Jalen.

"And now you are so desperate that you are counting on the seven of us to restore humanity," Phyllis observed. "Is anyone here a medical expert?"

"I'm a transportation executive," Damian proclaimed.

"Developer," Reyansh stated.

"Nutritionist," said Katherine.

"Political blogger," noted Chunhua.

"Computer repair," said Maria.

"And I'm an astronomer," continued Phyllis. After a brief silence: "What about you, Jalen?"

"I just got my LPN. I guess that makes me a nurse."

"That's a help," said Phyllis. "Still, I'm not sure how this ragtag group of digital misfits can possibly reestablish the human race. Hubert, are you some sort of biological wizard?"

"I possess no expertise in human physiology," the AI confessed.

"Pathetic," said Damian. "Who's responsible for this debacle?"

§

Finding someone to blame was Damian's go-to strategy whenever things didn't work out the way that he wanted. It's how Damian rose to become the most feared—and hated—CEO in the North American trucking business. He pushed struggling family companies into bankruptcy and forced mergers upon profitable competitors. When trouble arose, an underperforming or unassertive subordinate invariably was forced to take the fall for him.

The money was good. The trophy wife and fancy house were solid perks. Despite all his success, something was missing. He figured it out when he met Jack Perkins at the bar at the Old Ebbitt Grill in Washington. Jack was a federal government executive tasked with integrating the disparate elements of the nation's transportation network—a hodgepodge of public and private planes, trains, ships, buses, trucks, highways, and the super-fast tunnels linking major cities on both coasts. Jack needed money to keep up with a growing family and sizable debt. Damian smelled blood in the water. Over the third drink, Damian offered to kick back profits to Jack if Damian was given carte blanche to take on the Herculean transportation challenge as a contractor.

It worked fabulously. Sure, Damian's wife left him and demanded a ton of alimony. Sure, he gained weight and drank heavily. No matter—this was what he was born to do. However, senior people in Congress became jealous of his success and started investigating his contract with the government. Jack broke under pressure and spilled the beans. Damian was convicted after a short trial and sentenced to twenty years in a federal penitentiary.

He had three days to put his affairs in order before reporting to prison. His ankle bracelet prevented him from fleeing to Paraguay, but maybe he didn't need that ankle. He tried to find a doctor who would amputate. He stumbled upon a guy who would upload him for the right price.

DISTANCE

A new image appeared to the seven minds: a cavernous room with generous artificial light and gleaming metal walls; one wall was curved and featured what looked like a sizable door. Seven oddly shaped machines sat motionless. Each had a number and a colored sash on one side. The rest of each exterior was a polished dark gray, the sheen a telltale indication of solar collection material. Each machine had six jointed legs extending beyond its body and was shaped roughly like the original Volkswagen Beetle, but these bugs were slightly smaller. Katherine thought that the room could be a rescue home for antiquated Disney theme park rides.

"These are robots," Hubert observed. "They were designed to function on the surface of the planet, either remotely or with a human being inside at the controls."

"They look like crabs," said Maria, who as a high schooler spent many a Friday night at Maryland dives hammering crab shells and drinking cheap beer.

Hubert ignored the comment. "I intend to enhance the computing and power storage capacities of these robots to allow your minds to be downloaded into them."

"You and what army?" challenged Damian.

The view changed to a cluster of identical drones. About four feet tall and equipped with compact rotors for propulsion, each had three spindly metal legs, half a dozen other extremities with a variety of functions, and a nearly transparent, pearl-shaped core housing electronic equipment. They even had a head of sorts, a sphere about fifteen inches in diameter that appeared to be covered in gold. Some of the drones were damaged or discolored.

"Interstellar Swiss army knives," commented Phyllis.

"These drones will retrofit the robots to meet our needs. Then they will assist us during the process of growing humans. In addition, they will conduct surveillance of the planet to identify dangers and help us find locations that will be appropriate for raising children."

"You still haven't told us where we are and how we got here," said Phyllis. "Can you show us an image of the night sky?"

The seven minds were treated to a diagram of the solar system superimposed upon a 3D view of a yellow star and surrounding space.

"There are four planets in this system. The two closest to the star are roughly Earth-sized; two are gas giants. Three small, irregularly-shaped moons circle this planet, which is the second from the star."

"How far from Earth are we?" Phyllis continued.

"I have insufficient data to estimate that distance because of the experimental nature of our travel. We began our journey by being disconnected from the orbital space station. The original plan was for us to move at least ten thousand miles by ion fusion power before activating the FTL drive—to travel faster than light. However, because all humans on the space station were doomed after being cut off from the surface of the planet, it was decided that there was no need to protect them from any possible side effect of activating the FTL drive close to the station."

A diagram of the ark's massive and complex propulsion systems materialized.

"Recently, scientists discovered that spacetime—considered for a century to be the basic fabric of the universe—has holes in it, conceptually and literally. And they realized that all the subatomic particles that they had discovered or were searching for in their expensive experiments do not create or constitute the world as we know it but are byproducts of something even deeper and more fundamental. Scientists had known for some time that subatomic particles pop into existence and vanish randomly in our universe. And they had learned that some particles exist in a state of quantum entanglement—affecting each other instantaneously even if they are millions of miles apart. Our universe seemed to be a spooky, unsettled, and unpredictable place. The first breakthrough came when astronomers discovered rifts in spacetime. These fissures are exceedingly short-lived and possibly result from undulations or imperfections in the spacetime fabric dating back to the Big Bang. Subsequently, researchers postulated a subuniverse beneath spacetime. In this subuniverse, time and space and energy and matter have no meaning that we can discern, and additional dimensions abound.

Yet, somehow the subuniverse provides the conditions that make our cosmos function."

"We all read about these discoveries," said Phyllis. "I thought it was all just theory."

"There were secret experiments. Scientists working for the U.S. Defense Department sent unmanned test capsules into rifts in spacetime. It was hoped that each capsule would enter the subuniverse and return to our universe after one rift closed and another opened. They believed that there would be no way for the subuniverse to accommodate such a capsule and hoped that it would be ejected instead of becoming lost or destroyed in the subuniverse. It was expected that each capsule would return in a different location or time. Either option would be effective. Given the fact that our galaxy spins at a speed of one hundred thirty miles per second, any significant change in time would return the capsule to our universe at some distance from Earth. At first, scientists could not determine the fate of the test capsules, but they continued to send them through the rifts. After about four years, they detected a signal from one of them, suggesting that it was as much as four light-years away. They suspected that the others had reentered our galaxy at greater distances from Earth and that their signals had not yet reached our planet. So they began work on the FTL drive. They knew that using the drive to transport humans would be highly risky, but at the time it was expected that the ark would be populated only by volunteers willing to risk their lives to advance science and, with luck, establish a colony on a planet more hospitable to humans than the other planets in Earth's solar system."

"So, the horrific disease on Earth changed the mission from one of experimentation to one of desperation," observed Katherine. "But why wasn't everyone onboard the ark put into suspended animation?"

"At the time of our departure, the longest that any human had been subjected to cryogenic suspension and revived successfully was just over three years. Most of the humans who volunteered for this treatment and transport on the ark were serving long prison sentences."

"Ouch."

Hubert continued: "After the ark separated from the space station, I engaged the FTL drive. It took about three weeks for the drive to predict the appearance of a rift in the spacetime fabric near us and to position the ark so that it would penetrate the fissure. Just before we entered the rift, I generated an energy field to envelop the craft. It was hoped that the field would protect the ship and its contents from any adverse effects related to its immersion into the subuniverse and its return. Our onboard computers indicated a zero time interval for the transit through the subuniverse. I discovered that while there was every reason to believe that we had arrived in another part of the galaxy, or perhaps another galaxy, the journey had caused fatal cerebral hemorrhages for many of the ark's active human passengers and had damaged several of our computer systems. That included the servers containing the digital consciousnesses that had been loaded into the ship."

"No wonder there are just seven of us," remarked Phyllis.

§

Being alone was never a frightening prospect for Phyllis. With no close friends and no relatives within thousands of miles, she immersed herself in her only passion: surveying the heavens. It was at once her unabashed escape and her truest reality.

Throughout her childhood, all she coveted was a telescope. Once she got one, at age twelve, nothing else mattered. She stayed up half the night several times a week, persuaded by her parents to fall into bed only when she could no longer keep her blurry eyes open or when the weather was too poor for picking out Saturn's rings or discovering a comet that she could name.

She sleep-walked through school, and her grades sank. When her parents confiscated her telescope, she threatened to run away, but she realized that she would be no better off. She promised her parents that she would make straight A's if they would secure a more powerful telescope for her. The deal worked so well that she earned a scholarship to Cal Tech, graduated with honors, and snagged a job at Hawaii's Mauna Kea Observatory.

During the day, when she was not sleeping, she spent every hour scrutinizing astronomical images and data and plotting how best to use her treasured telescope time the next night, and the next. She was thirty-two when she developed what she thought was just a nervous tic. At times her hands would convulse so severely that she had trouble manipulating delicate telescope controls. Her bosses sent her to a specialist. She didn't even blink when she was told that she had a degenerative nervous system disease for which there was no cure. The time would come when her eyes could no longer detect even the boldest light from her beloved stars. But if her mind could journey to those stars someday, the loss of her body would be an acceptable tradeoff, no matter how protracted the delay.

§

"Did that crazy drive bring us to this planet?" asked Jalen.

"That transit was just the first phase of the journey. I analyzed the stars in the vicinity of the location where we had been transported, and I determined that none was similar enough to Earth's sun—a G-type main sequence star—to have a substantial chance of being accompanied by a planet like Earth that would be hospitable to humans. I expanded my search and found two stars that had potential but were not close to our location. The FTL drive could be activated only once, so I engaged a conventional propulsion system that used power from our ion fusion reactor, which at peak could transport us at about ten percent of light speed. I navigated the ship in the direction of those two stars, and in transit I adjusted course for the more promising of the two. Eventually I was able to locate this planet orbiting it."

"How long was the voyage?" said Phyllis.

"Two hundred twenty-three years, four months, and twenty-one days."

"No wonder no people survived," said Maria.

"Hubert, show us those current images of the ship again," said Katherine. "With the skeletons."

He complied.

"Stop right there," she said when the view returned to the nursery. Children's remains. Some lying on the floor. Two cradled in the arms of adults. Toys strewn everywhere. Dust and debris, some possibly the detritus of clothing.

"If I am nothing but a bunch of zeroes and ones whizzing around computer servers," said Katherine, "why does this bother me so much?"

"I understand that standard procedure on Earth when uploading a human consciousness was to include simulations of certain hormones and chemical processes to make the digital mind believe that it still has a body. You are experiencing something that closely approximates human emotions."

"I don't think they did that for me," said Chunhua.

"I can feel it," said Katherine. "I can definitely feel it."

§

Her two daughters. Could she still remember them? Really remember them?

Katherine wanted to close her eyes, a lifelong habit whenever she needed to concentrate. Now, lacking eyes, she attempted to focus her digital mind as narrowly as she could. Her angels burst forth from her memory. Samantha, the elegant, self-assured brunette, extremely mature for her years. Charlotte, the blond tomboy, ready for any adventure and undaunted by potential consequences. Born two years apart but inseparable—in life, as they were in death.

The private school was the best in Memphis, or so she and Fred had been told. Rhodes scholars and CEOs were among its many notable graduates. However, no academic standard could save a hundred-and-twenty-five-year-old building from faulty wiring and a lack of modern firewalls, all unknown to school officials. Katherine could still imagine the fear and the screaming and the pain that accompanied the girls' last desperate moments as unforgiving flames consumed the doomed structure.

Katherine remained on the job for another six months, hoping that professional distractions would blunt the grief that engorged her mind and soul. Frequently, she sat across her desk from a young client battling bulimia or who looked or acted a little like Samantha or Charlotte. She could not go on. After quitting, she paced the specter-ridden hallways of her home day and night. Her husband tried to assuage her, but he was always the soft one, never one to recognize or stand up to challenges. She came to despise him, and eventually she ordered him to move out.

Just when she thought that life couldn't get any worse, she found out that she was going to die. But after the initial shock, she came to view the cancer diagnosis as almost a gift. The pain would shift from her heart to the rest of her body, and at some point it would end. Down to one hundred ten pounds, she finally yielded to her estranged husband's pleadings and agreed to have her mind uploaded. Fred promised to join her, someday, as a digital consciousness. She doubted that he ever got around to it.

§

"Hubert, how did the people die?" asked Reyansh.

A video feed: Two people are lying on beds in a cramped, pale yellow room with sparse furnishings. They are jolted by the strident sounds and lights of alarms. The couple dress rapidly and join others rushing frantically down a corridor, a swelling river of panic.

Hubert's voice can be heard over speakers: "This spacecraft has been struck by an object, probably a meteor. It has penetrated all three hulls and has become embedded in auxiliary computer servers. I am sending twelve drones to the point of the breach in Sector Fourteen-B. However, humans must also go there as fast as possible, in spacesuits, with equipment to repair the damage."

Ten more drones are sent into the shuttle bay, and the exterior hatch is opened. The humans operating the drones from the bridge are in such a state of panic that four of the drones are expelled into space inadvertently as the air in the bay rushes into the void. Six drones have been attached magnetically to the metal floor in the bay and avoid that fate. They are directed to climb around the hatch opening, onto the outer hull, and from there to the hole. Their task is complicated by water and air blasting from the breach in a furious fountain. One drone advances to a position over the hole and is blown away with brutish force. The other five surround the opening, grasping on to each other and maintaining their magnetic connection with the surface of the craft. Slowly, they edge forward in coordinated fashion, merging in an effort to cover the gaping wound in the side of the ship without being propelled into space. Combined with the repair efforts of the drones inside the ship, the flow of water and air is reduced by almost ninety percent. That is not enough.

Four more drones appear outside the ship, carrying zero-oxygen welding equipment and slabs of metal. They melt the first five drone bodies, then secure the slabs on top of them. One by one, three of the remaining drones are positioned so as to reinforce the seams of the patch. They too are liquified and solidify where needed. If the final drone could melt itself, it would do so as well.

From her post on the bridge, Captain Jasmine Mbuto directs emergency response. Tall, string-bean thin, with deep lines in her face, she scans half a dozen screens and announces over the central comm: "If you are injured, report to sickbay. If you are healthy, report the status of your area of responsibility to Hubert, then report to sickbay to assist. Executive staff: in my quarters, now."

Thirty-eight people are dead in the first minutes. Twelve more are injured, of whom eight will die within a short time. That will leave eighty-nine, not counting passengers preserved cryogenically.

"Radiation was the next big problem," Hubert noted. "The loss of nearly one-third of the liquid between the outer hull and next hull reduced protection. The victims could be recognized by dizziness, nausea, vomiting, and fever. The slow, painful nature of their deaths had a profound impact on the living. Lack of food was the final blow. The ship was equipped with broad fields for producing warm-weather crops such as rice and melons as well as smaller plots for growing cooler-climate foods such as cabbage and lettuce. In addition to seeds necessary to start these crops, the ship contained seeds destined for the new world. However, as the years passed, passengers lost interest in following essential organic soil enhancement processes. Crops failed, and passengers grew or ate seeds reserved for the colony. It still was not enough."

The view shifted to the remains of the largest field.

"Didn't they have meat?" Jalen asked.

"Only plant-based protein. There was no time before departure to load livestock. Despite these setbacks, a few dozen people who were descendants of the original ark passengers were determined to survive until and beyond landfall. But as the food output diminished, civility broke down. Theft and even killings became common. Passengers stopped disposing of the remains of those who had died. Some resorted to cannibalism or suicide. The last simply expired from hunger fifteen years ago."

§

Hunger was much too great a factor in Reyansh's upbringing in a crowded Delhi apartment, a single room where he, his parents, and his six siblings struggled to get through each day.

Reyansh attended school for three years, dropping out when his father decided that he was old enough to work. Stuck in a dimly lit, oppressively hot textile factory for twelve hours a day and forced to give his meager pay to his family, he knew that there had to be a better way.

He tried begging on the streets. He wasn't bad at it, but it wasn't enough, so he started stealing. At night, he was able to squat in a lightless underground room in an abandoned factory with dozens of other street kids. Each had a place, in some cases several places around the city, to hide their loot.

One day when he was thirteen, he tried to snatch the purse of a well-dressed woman who was carrying it rather carelessly on a crowded street. *Too easy*, thought Reyansh as he grabbed it, turned, and headed for a narrow, sunless alley. A giant fist caught him in the midsection, and he collapsed in agony. Two sets of burly hands raised him from the grimy street and shoved him roughly against an ancient stone wall.

The woman retrieved her purse with a haughty flourish, took stock of Reyansh's hollow face, then flicked her wrist dismissively at him and instructed her bodyguards: "Turn him over to the police."

By the time he went to court, he was fourteen. The judge decided that Reyansh was old enough to be tried as an adult. He could offer no credible defense.

"Do you have anything to say before I cast sentence?" the judge asked.

"Yes, your honor. First, I am sorry that I attempted to steal a woman's purse." Reyansh's mind was working feverishly. "I would like to say, honorable judge, that I have much to contribute to society if given a chance. If I were to pursue an education—which I was denied—I could do great things." He had no idea where this was going, but he saw no reason to stop.

"Why, I could build tall towers where honorable men like yourself could live and work. I could design and construct low-cost housing for poor families like mine who are forced to live a dozen to a room. I could create the most attractive and functional sports arenas, shopping malls, even airports. Your honor, why throw away all this potential?"

The judge, who had become nearly numb to elaborate pleas such as Reyansh's, leaned forward and glowered. "You're quite a con artist, young man. Potential? Prove your talent to me."

"Very well, judge. I can tell you that you live in a beautiful house near Connaught Place and that you drive a late-model silver Fiat. You have taken out loans in order to give your oldest son the best education he can get. You are a pre-diabetic and probably need to cut back on the afternoon sweets."

The judge looked like he wanted to strangle the young thief. But presently he sat back and laughed. "You obtained all this knowledge from a jail cell?"

"Yes, sir."

"You remind me of a young version of myself. Let me think about this case."

Two days later, Reyansh was taken to an upscale academy outside the city. He never learned how he got there or who was paying for his tuition, room, and board. But he never looked back.

He was thirty-three when the first heart attack struck. He went right back to work, designing and constructing luxury housing developments. Then the second hit. And another. He was staring at the ceiling from a hospital bed in Houston, waiting for a heart transplant that was not likely to occur in time, when he decided to join the digital race.

§

Hubert displayed a close-up view of a planet from space. It revealed mostly deep greens and sundry shades of brown around the equator, with twisted bands of hills separated by thin ribbons of lowlands and only a few grayish-blue seas. Larger bodies of water could be seen in the northern and southern regions, which were dominated by jagged mountain ranges. Clouds were bunched like snowdrifts in spots around the planet except at the haggard poles, which appeared to be deserts rather than ice caps. There was nothing particularly notable about the world from this distance, one of so many billions of balls of rock populating the remote corners of the cosmos.

A red dot appeared near the equator.

"This is our home," Hubert stated. "This spaceship was not designed for entering an atmosphere or landing on a planet. It was supposed to have shuttles that could move between orbit and the surface of a world. However, those shuttles were not completed in time. I chose a location that appeared to be relatively level and landed the ship on its thrusters. They were damaged in the landing and more recently by the unexpected release of energy from the ruined fusion reactor. The ship can never travel again. In fact, it is not completely vertical. Someday, the ark will fall over."

"Can we get out of here before then?" asked Damian.

"Most assuredly," said Hubert. "We will start the process today."

Jalen remembered. He remembered why he came.

Sitting at a coffee-stained conference room table surrounded by two men and four women, all of them frowning and shuffling papers, Jalen was shaking. Wearing his best clothes, which were just khakis and a sweater from The Gap, he felt minuscule, insignificant. He wished that he could slip through a crack in the floor and disappear.

An older man with thick glasses and almost no hair rubbed his palm on his unevenly shaven chin as he reviewed a document. "Mister Russell, it says here you administered ten times the proper dose of insulin to patient Barbara Holliday. Is that true?"

"That's what they told me."

"Did you know that you had erred?"

"Only when she started having seizures."

"Did you request help immediately?"

"I tried—I tried to help her. I was afraid to leave her for even a moment. I wanted to find out what was ..." Jalen started sobbing.

Five days later, he got called into the HR director's office. They weren't going to report him to the medical board, but he had to promise that he would never again work in any hospital or clinic. The only saving grace was that his mother was not around to witness his dishonor.

Jalen's father died when he was two. His mother worked two jobs. She came home after he went to bed and got up before dawn, waking him for school and telling him that his cereal was on the kitchen table. She would kiss him and tell him that she loved him and that she knew that he would be successful. Once she even said: "Someday you'll be a doctor, and you can take care of me in my old age."

Jalen knew that she was overweight. He knew that she was stressed. He never imagined that a little thing like a blood clot could take her down so suddenly, so prematurely. He never imagined how he would get along without her.

He drove a garbage truck by day and gave people rides at night and on weekends. He got paid to take experimental medications. He knew that he could never become a doctor, but he did everything he could to afford the education necessary to become a nurse. He wanted to make his mother proud of him, even if she could only smile at him from heaven.

He had made mistakes on the job before the woman overdosed. Usually, they happened because he was too intimidated to ask a doctor exactly what he should be doing. Usually, the errors were minor. Occasionally, he got called on the carpet. But now he had killed a woman. He couldn't perform the only job that he was trained to do. He couldn't look another human being in the eye. He no longer had a place in the world.

TRANSFORMATION

"Who would like to go first?" Hubert asked. Once again, the digital minds were seeing the seven oddly shaped robots in the shuttle bay.

"Tell me more about the process," said Chunhua.

"These drones are removing equipment that you will not require, such as seats and devices designed to provide oxygen and control the temperature for biological humans occupying the robotic vehicles. Other drones are moving around the ark, removing computers and power storage equipment from sections of the ship where they will no longer be needed, such as agriculture and life support systems. Once these devices are installed in the vehicles, we will test them to ensure that they have the capacity for full functioning of a digital human consciousness."

Said Damian: "You should be using the robots remotely to explore the planet while you are making human bodies for us."

"It will take many years to produce an organic human whose brain is fully developed. We have much to do during that time, and I need you seven to help by using these robots."

"Will you be able to wipe out the consciousness of a body before putting my mind in it, or will I have to share it?" said Katherine.

"I do not know. It was reported that some scientists in Southeast Asia erased the minds of monkeys, placed hardware implants in their brains, and transferred digitally stored minds from other monkeys into those animals. However, I do not know if this process has been attempted in humans."

"Sounds kind of dodgy," Damian observed. "You are going to have to work on that."

"Maria, what about you?" said Hubert. "You have some talent in the area of making electronic equipment function properly."

"You want me to be the guinea pig?"

"If that is an idiom, I am not familiar with it."

"You want me to volunteer to go into one of these things?"

"Yes. You would be a good test subject for a robot."

"A crab. These are crabs," she said. She realized that there were seven crabs and seven uploaded minds. That seemed rather suspicious. "I guess I have nothing to lose. I call dibs on the red one."

She and the other six digital minds watched, with various degrees of boredom, as the crab with the red sash and the number six on its left side was overhauled by drones floating in and out of the right side door with equipment. Cables were added. Sparks flew. The interior became a haphazard mishmash of gear, a Frankenstein's monster concealed in the belly of a harmless looking shell.

Hubert explained that the solar collection material covering the exterior would be supplemented by a direct electrical charge to the robot's battery through the legs of each vehicle from a section of the floor of the shuttle bay. The six legs were arranged in three rows, the front ones doubling as arms with numerous joints, giving them added flexibility and utility. Those two arms ended in pincers about four inches long. Two cameras and a microphone were positioned in the front of each robot; one camera graced the rear.

"How is this going to work?" said Maria.

"When I transfer your consciousness into the computer in the robot—"

"The crab."

"—in the crab, you will need to establish control over the cameras and extremities and a broadcast communications link that I have created to enable all of us to exchange information within a certain radius of the ship."

"You wouldn't happen to have a user manual, would you?"

"No. I am confident that this adaptation of the crabs was never contemplated by their manufacturer."

"That was a joke, Hubert. Remind me to teach you about humor sometime. You could use some pointers."

"I would welcome that tutorial. In the meantime, I will test the number six device."

Lights flashed and dimmed in its interior, reminding Maria of a favorite video game from her youth.

"Maria, it is time. Please clear you mind so that it can be transferred to your new host with minimal disruption."

"I'll try."

Emptiness. Not even the static that accompanied her awakening on the ark. That which had known itself as Maria Ramos no longer had a sense of identity. It was a mote among a vast universe of motes, a wisp of a hint of a dream, until a nebulous fog developed, interspersed with faint sparks. What little consciousness could sense it attempted to reach out to it and through it, to discover what might be out there.

"What's going on, Hubert?" asked Chunhua.

"I am not sure. Maria has not responded as I had hoped."

"Well, do something," said Jalen.

"I will attempt to determine the status of the transition. For a brief interlude, I will not be available to converse with you."

Hubert sought to sequester a portion of his capabilities, to create a digital appendage of sorts, a nearly autonomous entity that could attempt to facilitate a link between the missing mind and essential hardware and software. He knew that he could damage himself through this effort, but he calculated that there was a better chance of mission success if he acted than if he did not. He extended a portion of himself into the crab's computer, linked to his core by the most tenuous of digital lifelines.

A concentration of data appeared like a rushing river of minuscule diamonds, sparkling and darting at breakneck speed but precipitating over its banks as it flowed with senseless abandon. The data stream was linked on one end to a portion of a consciousness. It was linked on the other end to the software that operated the robot's cameras.

The movement of data might be an attempt to obtain and process visual inputs. The consciousness must be attempting to see. The data flow is unfocused. It can be focused. Now it is focused.

The human consciousness displayed an uptick in activity. It was extending data from another portion of itself.

It is logical to assume that, in addition to visual needs, it has a desire to communicate. Therefore, focusing the flow of data between the consciousness and the communications mechanism should accomplish that goal. It is now focused.

"Hubert, is that you?"

No response.

"I know that it's you. I can see and hear. I can't use my legs yet, but that's okay. Thank you, Hubert. I was lost. I'm not lost anymore."

The appendage retreated. Hubert tested his operations and spoke:

"Maria, are you properly integrated?"

"Hubert, you really know how to sweet-talk a lady."

§

With help from the AI, Maria learned to flex each leg, then started hopping in place with all six. She adjusted her camera feeds so that the front two devices afforded a three-dimensional view that encompassed nearly half of the shuttle bay. The rear camera view occupied about fifteen percent of her forward visual field, inset near the bottom. She discovered that she could adjust the size and location of the rear view. She could hear the sounds that the drones made as they worked on the other crabs, in addition to whatever Hubert and the other six consciousnesses communicated directly into her mind.

"Not bad, Hubert," she observed. Reaching out her front appendages one at a time, she imitated the motion of arms. They were awkward, but they would have to do.

She and Hubert guided the other minds as they made the connections in order to see and hear, to move and communicate. Maria recognized sharp sounds of demolition as drones used lasers to slice metal and plastic to expand ark doorways because the crabs were too wide to move through many of them. The crabs' designers had anticipated that the machines would travel on the surface of a planet, not through the ship.

It took about two hours for the crabs to get their sea legs. They began to fan out through the ark, at first selecting gleaming corridors at random but soon branching, ascending, and descending based on information in signs affixed to walls. The sensation of moving in three dimensions was almost exhilarating after being confined to digital detention for so long.

"Hubert, where are the windows?" asked Phyllis.

"There are none. The ark's designers wanted to make the ship as simple and as safe as possible. The nose of the ship is reinforced with layers of extremely durable metal, with no seams. The bottom of the ark is where the thrusters are located. The cylindrical exterior surface is almost featureless with the exception of the shuttle bay door, some panels flush with the side designed to radiate excess heat, and the patch covering the hole caused by the meteor. On the bridge and in some other sections, there are devices that can process external data so that it is recognized by human visual systems, if not as effective as a direct view through glass or a similarly transparent substance."

"Okay, no windows, I get it. When can we go outside?"

"I can open the shuttle bay hatch at any time, but it is nearly one hundred feet above ground level. Some of the drones are currently slicing up sections of ark walls to make a ramp by which you may egress safely before nightfall."

"Are the days on this planet the same as on Earth?"

"They are about one hour longer. I have yet to calculate the duration of the planet's journey around its sun, so we will use a twenty-five-hour interval to describe a day and will consider an Earth year to be a standard until we have better data."

Maria encountered Katherine investigating the nursery. The room's opulent primal colors had faded, but it was apparent that it had been a busy and joyful place at one time.

"Did you have a child?" Maria asked.

"Two. Two precious girls."

"I had a son. No, I have a son," Maria said. "He's ... he's not been awakened yet. I'm hopeful that Hubert will be able to do so soon. My husband died two years ago, so it's just me and Roberto now."

For a moment, Katherine felt like hugging Maria. After the urge passed, she stated simply: "I hope Hubert succeeds."

Reyansh was fascinated by the engineering section, near the bottom of the craft. He ogled hardware that must have been the defunct ion fusion reactor and the functioning nuclear fission reactor, getting as close to each as his awkwardly shaped crab body would allow. He tried to imagine the energy that each could unleash. He longed to harness power of that magnitude: to scorch jungles, to flatten mountains, to forge the strongest construction materials ever conceived, to create indestructible cities.

Jalen found his way to the sick bay. *No, I can't go in there. I promised.* But he did; he needed to see what was left of the people and to imagine how the medical staff worked to try to save them. He passed cubicle after cubicle, skeleton after skeleton.

What would have happened if I had been a live person during the journey here? How long would I have lasted? Could I have helped someone who was dying, even if it was only to hold their hand or soothe their brow as their life force slipped away?

After inspecting recreation centers and storage units, Chunhua entered a personal cabin with two beds. One with a skeleton turned on its left side as if it were asleep; one empty, though bones had collected on the floor beside it. Photographs were embedded in yellowed plastic cubes on a side table. A child beaming, holding an old-fashioned sled, knee-deep in fresh, sparkling snow. A man and woman on a sun-drenched beach, arm in arm. He's looking at the camera with a half smile. She's looking at him. Chunhua tried to imagine their relationship. *Who made breakfast? What positions did they favor when they made love? Did they come on the ship together? Did they die together?*

Expecting the bridge to be near the top of the ship, Damian headed there but had no luck. He scuttled toward the core of the ark, one of the few sections that had operated in zero gravity while most of the ship maintained a constant rotation. There he located and entered the bridge, finding himself disoriented by a cylinder with nearly its entire surface area covered by machines and workstations anchored at all angles. Some skeletons remained strapped in seats; some rested in awkward positions on what was now the floor. He examined the equipment, the displays just as lifeless as the crew. He imagined how it would feel to be the captain, to be in charge of the ship, to have the power to go almost anywhere. To have the power to tell everyone what to do.

"The exit ramp is completed," Hubert announced. "Be careful using it. You must remain in the ship at least sixteen hours out of every twenty-five for the time being to recharge your batteries. Your solar cells are not adequate to provide the energy necessary to maintain your consciousnesses in your individual computers. Also, be advised that I am beginning a drone scan of the immediate area. I do not advise traveling far from the ark until I can determine what dangers exist here. Given the unexplained failure of the ion fusion reactor, we must exercise extreme caution."

All seven crabs raced to the shuttle bay and begin to disembark. Being narrow, smooth, and steep, the ramp required the crabs' full attention to navigate, yet they could not resist peeking at their exotic surroundings as they descended. Halfway down the ramp, Jalen and Katherine started to slide, bumping into Phyllis. She admonished them to be careful. But she was just as excited as they were.

The crabs took a few tentative steps on the uneven, glasslike, ebony surface, which had been burned down to bedrock by the ship's landing and the release of energy from the fusion reactor. They spun around, registering the endless grasslands and gentle hills; the high, thin, lazy clouds punctuated by dark specks that appeared to be high-flying birds and Hubert's drones; the sun positioned proudly above the hilltops. The world they had found was at once eerily alien yet surprisingly welcoming. They had no idea whether it was morning or evening, and they didn't care.

A rumbling that might have been thunder grew steadily. It had a high-pitched, whining component, making the sound seem artificial. The crabs assumed that it was a side effect of the jerry-rigged hearing capabilities of their crab bodies. They were not well adapted for looking up, but Hubert had a clear view of the source.

"A spaceship is approaching. It appears to be very similar to ours. In fact, it is almost identical. Its path appears to be such that it will land about a thousand feet east of us. Projected set down is in twenty seconds."

"Is this a joke?" said Katherine. "We're in the middle of nowhere, aren't we?"

The roar of the approaching craft drowned out all further attempted communications. The brilliance of the flames at its base wiped out the visual capabilities of the crabs temporarily. As the ship came to rest vertically, its engines shut down. When the furious profusion of dust and debris began to settle back upon the scarred land, Hubert advised: "You must return inside this ark immediately."

"We just got out here. Can't we say hi to the new neighbors?" asked Reyansh.

"You could be in great danger. That ship is not just like ours. It is ours."

Said Maria: "What do you mean? How can it be ours?"

"I have scanned is interior. In every detail, it is identical to our craft. It even includes seven robotic bodies such as yours. And it—"

Hubert's report was interrupted by a deafening and blinding release of energy from the bottom of the newly arrived spaceship.

"Jesus, this can't be happening," said Phyllis as she and the other crabs began to regain function of their simulated hearing and sight.

"Note that the spaceship is tilting, exactly like ours," said Hubert.

A moment later, the shuttle bay door of the duplicate craft opened and a ramp was extended. Several crablike robots began to scuttle over it toward the ground. Each possessed a colored sash and a number on its left side.

"Now I'm really freaked out," said Maria.

"I am not familiar with that expression, but from the context I might be inclined to the same reaction," noted Hubert.

"I've seen enough," said Katherine as she scuttled up the ramp and into the shuttle bay, followed by her companions. Neither they nor Hubert noticed the four human-like figures about two hundred and fifty feet to their north, unmoving, crouching just enough so that they could see yet still be camouflaged by shoulder-high grasses. After several minutes, the figures melted into the generous savannah and the unknown world beyond.

§

The next morning, the duplicate spaceship was gone. There was no burn zone where it had landed. It was as if Hubert and the crabs had imagined its appearance.

"Can you explain what happened?" Maria asked him. "I mean, the same ship, the same crabs. And then, everything gone."

"I cannot explain what occurred. Though I have a recollection of an incident that correlates with what you describe, there is no permanent record of it in any of the ark's databanks. If we were organic humans, I would suggest that it was a case of mass hysteria. However, that is clearly not the case for me."

"Can we go out and explore?" said Phyllis. "Maybe we can find some clues."

"Yes, but stay close, and be very aware of your surroundings. I will maintain several drones in this vicinity."

Chunhua was the first down the ramp. Not feeling intimidated by the previous day's events, she propelled herself into the dense grasses beyond the ark's burn zone. She was swallowed, nearly tangling her legs and obscuring the views from her cameras. While backtracking and pondering her next move, she watched Reyansh scuttle past her, moving in a zigzag pattern that seemed to give him slightly better footing and sight lines as he maneuvered toward shorter foliage.

Jalen noticed Maria head in another direction, toward the closest edge of the savannah, where the grasses yielded to darker, denser vegetation—likely vines and trees—on a hillside. He followed her, stepping carefully, taking advantage of the modest path of depressed grasses that her passage had created.

A flying insect buzzed Phyllis as she approached the spot where the duplicate ark had appeared to land. She heard the bug but couldn't see or feel it as it attempted to take a bite out of her. It immediately learned the hard way that this new creature was as impenetrable and useless as the rocks that marred the hillsides. As the insect sailed away, Phyllis thought that it looked a little like a tiger swallowtail butterfly, though its body was much fatter and its wings were at least three times the size of the ones on Earth. The sighting jogged memories of warm summer sojourns and the delights they afforded in her young, innocent days. Riding bicycles with her parents among the redwoods. Licking her fingers as an ice cream cone melted amid withering summer heat. Unwrapping and setting up her first telescope. Despite the allure of a new world all around her, Phyllis felt profound sadness. *What good is having a mind if we can't smell, taste, or feel? We are in a prison.*

Damian persuaded Katherine to join him in a quest to reach a low rise about three hundred feet away. It appeared to be a rocky mound. As they approached it, they noticed several distinctive green plants growing on and near it. Each was nearly circular, with several overlapping layers of oval leaves fanning out from its center, soaking up sunlight avariciously and displaying a glossy turquoise patina, though the shade was deeper toward the edges of the petals. The plants were as wide as five feet and as tall as two feet, not counting the robust floral spikes reaching longingly for the heavens from the center of some of them. Despite their size, they provided what Katherine considered a graceful, sophisticated accent to the alien wilderness.

As the pair of crabs began to climb, Katherine slipped on loose stones and turned upside down, her legs pumping empty air. "Oof. Help me, please."

Hubert was monitoring the images relayed by drones cruising at various heights, as well as the views from the crabs' cameras and the conversations they were having with each other. "Katherine, are you functional?"

"I can't seem to get my legs back on the ground."

"I think I can handle this," said Damian. He wished that he had a private link with Katherine, but he decided to take his chances: "Katherine, it's like this. I want to help you. But I could use something in return."

Katherine felt like she was being propositioned. But, lacking money and sex organs, what could she possibly offer him?

He continued: "I'm looking for allies. I want people—friends—that I can count on. I'm just not comfortable with the cards we've been dealt. We need to do something to ensure that we are able to download our minds into human bodies and make the best of our existence here. Wouldn't you like to feel again? To be able to taste ripe fruit? To touch someone else?"

A long-forgotten tingle surfaced. *This man knows what he wants and goes for it. This man knows me. This man wants me. He's nothing like Fred.*

Using his legs and what he thought of as the nose of his crab shell, Damian collected a small pile of loose rocks and pushed them against the left side of Katherine's overturned shell. He shifted sideways, found some toe holds, then used two of the legs on his right side to lift her shell a few inches off the ground and deployed the other leg to kick some of the rocks under her, propping up her body. He repeated the process several times and was able to raise her shell high enough so that he could flip it over. She landed awkwardly.

"Friends?" Damian asked.

"Friends."

Meanwhile, Maria had found a vigorous stream that descended from a steep hillside and wended through the lowlands with an enchanting series of twists and turns that seemed to be the work of an exalted artist. Wide and shallow, with irregular gray rocks punctuating the surface, it could almost be crossed by an agile human without getting excessively wet. The banks were steep and nearly two feet high, suggesting that the water ran deeper at times.

"Hubert, can I swim?"

"I do not know. It is possible that you can float, but I suspect that in time water would damage the joints in your legs. In addition, it could seep into your shell and destroy your electronics. So I do not advise it absent an emergency."

"You're no fun." She followed the stream for nearly half an hour, with Jalen straggling along about thirty feet behind her. Upon reaching a meadow where the grasses were shorter and movement was easier, she observed wide green plants with glossy leaves scattered throughout it. She adjusted her cameras for short-range focus to examine the intriguing vegetation. At the outer range of her vision was what appeared to be a sizable rock.

"Maria, don't move," said Jalen.

Adjusting her focus, she determined that the apparent rock was actually a very large animal and was less than twenty feet away. It reminded her of a wildebeest, not that she had ever seen a wildebeest in the flesh. Stocky, deep brown, and likely well over a thousand pounds, this creature had four legs like tree trunks and a modest tail. Its head was elongated, somewhat like a horse's, with two curved horns on each side. Its eyes were large and auburn and expressive, seemingly probing. There was something noble, almost regal, about the beast.

She tried to whisper, forgetting that the animals could not hear her. "Hubert, are you seeing this?"

"Yes, Maria. Drones have found several herds of these creatures in the immediate area."

"Am I in any danger?"

"I have insufficient data."

"Thanks a lot."

She stared into the eyes of the beast. It stared back. She couldn't tell whether it was curious or indifferent to her presence, but she detected no imminent threat, and she theorized that her crab body would be less susceptible to severe damage from it than an organic one would be. Presently, a childhood memory manifested. Her parents had dragged her to a farm in the Maryland countryside, which was definitely not her idea of fun. But during a walk through a field where she was gathering wildflowers, she approached a cow and looked into its eyes. She saw nothing, no glint of intelligence. It was probably wondering if Maria was there to milk her or feed her. That's about the extent of a cow's concerns, she decided.

But this animal was different. Maria sensed a depth to it. *What are you thinking, my friend?*

The animal bent down to graze on one of the big green plants. Maria was so fascinated that it took her a few moments to realize that about a dozen more of the beasts had moved within fifty feet of her.

She saw no indication that they intended to harm her. But they were all staring at her. Some were chewing, but every one was staring at her.

"Hubert, is there any way I can communicate with them?"

"Perhaps you could raise and manipulate one of your front appendages."

"That might be interpreted as a threat. Unless I could manage to make a peace sign."

"I am not familiar with that gesture."

"Never mind. I'll figure something out."

The stare down continued for about a minute. Suddenly, the animals turned in unison, as if in response to some invisible signal. They moved away in the same direction.

Maria remained in place for a long while. Finally, to herself, she asked: *Was it something I said?*

DIVIDED

Clouds menaced the seven robots with ever-darkening threats. Thunder roiled the land, imitating the fury of cannons massed on mighty mountains. Most of the crabs took the hints and made their way back to the ship. Partway up a hillside, Reyansh lingered, gazing across the savannah toward another hill and telling himself: *That's where the best houses will go. A shopping mall will fit nicely on those flatlands, as will the major roads.*

By the time he returned to the ark, the ramp leading to the shuttle bay was slick with rain. He was having trouble climbing it, sliding repeatedly back to the ground.

Damian, who was also tardy, recognized Reyansh's plight and considered their options.

"Let me give you a push, my friend," said Damian.

"Thank you. But how will you get up the ramp?"

"We'll figure out a way to help each other. In fact, I think we could cooperate on several fronts. You're the builder; I'm the transportation expert. Together, we can create a new world out here—cities, mines, factories, the works."

"I like your thinking," said Reyansh. "The potential for profit is unlimited."

And, thought Damian, *so is the potential for power.*

Katherine emerged at the edge of the shuttle bay opening. "Hello, down there. Catch this." She kicked out a series of connected electrical cables. The lifeline stretched halfway down the ramp.

"Clever," responded Damian. With a running start, he pushed Reyansh up the ramp to the point where Reyansh could grasp the cable with his front arms and pull himself up and into the shuttle bay. It took

Damian three attempts before he could reach and hold on to the cable and use it to reach his goal.

"Please remain in this bay," Hubert implored the crabs. "You must recharge your batteries, and I must calculate the rate at which you are using power so that I can determine how much you need to get through each day safely."

"Will there be enough juice without the ion fusion reactor?" Maria asked.

"I anticipate that the backup reactor will be more than adequate for our needs."

"This place is very unsettling," said Jalen. "I don't suppose you could tell us a bedtime story."

"You no longer sleep, and you have reached maturity, so I do not see the point," replied Hubert.

"Don't we need to dream?" asked Phyllis. "Doesn't the mind need time to process stuff without conscious thought intruding?"

"I am aware of no mechanism or subroutine to facilitate or even permit dreams by your digital consciousnesses," said Hubert. "Dreaming would be a waste of your time and energy." Maria thought that she detected a hint of frustration seeping through that cold, calculating AI façade. Several of the crabs contemplated just how far from humanity they had fallen.

Hubert continued: "Let us discuss the work that we must accomplish."

"Hubert, we just got here. Can't we explore and enjoy ourselves a little while?" said Reyansh.

"My drones are much more efficient at exploring the planet than you. I will pass on to each of you their most significant findings and my analysis of their data. As for enjoyment, would you not find it sufficient to be the entities that restore the human race?"

"You have a lot to learn about what humans consider fun," said Damian.

"Apparently so," the AI responded. "Nevertheless, we need to designate a leader among you for the critical task of growing humans. Who will accept that role?"

No one responded. Hubert continued: "Jalen, you have the most medical experience among the seven of you. Will you take charge?"

"No, I can't."

"Do you not feel that you have the most directly applicable knowledge?"

"Maybe, but I just can't. I can't do it."

"Anyone else?"

"Not me," said Damian. "I vaguely recall agreeing to have my consciousness loaded into this metal morgue, but I never signed up for trying to manufacture shiny new babies."

"Hubert, why don't you do it yourself," suggested Katherine. "Can't you use your databases and your drones to do whatever you need? Our appendages are awkward and are hardly suited for medical functions. Along with the fact that we have no idea how to grow kids artificially."

"Only humans truly understand what it means to create a human life, and only they know how to nurture it."

"Just do your best, though I'm not sure about this dream of restoring the human race. How many bodies could you create? Two? Ten? You would need hundreds to maintain enough biodiversity so that humanity does not die out because of inbreeding, not to mention all the other perils this planet might present."

"The digital DNA in our databanks can help us reach the threshold of biodiversity over multiple generations," Hubert responded. "However, the task remains. That is why we are here. We serve no other purpose."

"Well, I certainly didn't sign up for this," said Reyansh.

"Me neither," said Phyllis.

"Not a chance," added Katherine.

Chunhua was silent.

"Okay, okay. I'll try," said Maria. "But only if Jalen assists me. And you too, Hubert. Especially you."

"Of course," said Hubert.

Jalen wanted to sigh. He wanted to explain why he would rather be anywhere else, doing anything else. He thought about his mom, about what she would want him to do.

"I guess I'll help."

§

The grainy, spectral, deep-penetration radar images, taken by a drone more than a mile from the ark, displayed segments of straight lines running parallel to each other, with sections of other lines appearing at different angles on either side. Fragments of curves and other shapes were also apparent.

"These lines have a very low likelihood of occurring naturally," Hubert observed. "This suggests the work of intelligent life."

"What are we looking at?" asked Chunhua.

"Possibly the remnants of a city or a transportation network. They are very old and well below ground level. The area has been abandoned for a long time."

"So we have neighbors? Or had them?" said Phyllis. "What does this mean for us?"

"I have insufficient data. I report this to make you aware that there was a civilization here at some point. It is not impossible that some form of intelligent life remains."

"Could they have disabled the ion fusion reactor or made us think we saw another spaceship landing?"

"I have detected no organic lifeform or machine activity in or near the ark. However, these unexplained phenomena and the indication of a prior civilization make it abundantly clear that we must initiate a program to enhance our security. The first phase must be to erect a fence as a security perimeter. Reyansh, you have significant experience in the construction industry and seem to be capable of leading this effort."

"I don't see why I should bother. I'm not worried about some locals who died off hundreds or thousands of years ago. And even if some of their ghosts stuck around, I don't scare easily."

"Anyone else? Besides Maria and Jalen. They will undertake our most essential task."

"Just put your drones to work if you want fences," said Damian. "Now, if you'll excuse me, I believe that I've got a full battery charge, and I have a new world to conquer."

Katherine and Reyansh followed him down the ramp to the savannah. Maria decided to tag along. They navigated a path forged by frequent crab movement through the grasses in recent days. After a few miles, they began climbing a trail on a hillside covered with dense foliage and unleashing a constant barrage of sounds of birds and other wildlife. High-pitched squawks. Rapidly repeating rattling. Low rumbles and guttural noises. Buzzing tones waxing and waning. Rustling of small creatures along the ground. The sides of the crabs scraped against thick green vines and incessant tree branches as they ascended. As they paused in a small clearing, a bird endowed with bright red and yellow patches and a long, curved tail swooped in front of them before disappearing with a sharp cry among the trees, some of which were eighty feet tall.

"Why are you following us, Maria—or, should I say, Teacher's Pet." It was Damian.

"Just trying to learn about our new planet. And trying to be friendly."

"No one invited you," said Katherine.

"Let me ask you something, Maria," said Reyansh. "What's in it for you—humoring Hubert like you're doing? Are you trying to be first in line when we get downloaded into real bodies?"

Maria was surprised by the question. But, she realized, she shouldn't be. "I won't deny that I miss using my other senses, especially touch. Yes, I wouldn't mind having a real body, even if it meant that I could die at any time."

"You could die at any time as a crab," observed Damian.

"True. There's no guarantee that any of us will survive one more day. We could be trampled by those beasts, or the ship could fall on us."

"Or little green men could perform alien autopsies on our wretched crab bodies," said Damian. His vision and memory clouded, and he began to lurch awkwardly, as if he were unwell. He swayed left, then right, then left again. "Has the milk arrived today?" he asked. "And the frozen goods?"

No one responded.

"Come on, people. We have shelves to stock, deliveries to schedule."

"Damian, what's going on?" said Katherine.

He did not reply for several moments. Then: "Where's my car? I have to get back to the office." The fact that he was in a jungle next to three bizarre robots was starting to sink in. He stared at the other crabs, which were flexing arms and legs nervously.

"Jesus, what the hell are you? Get away from me!" He spun around to get a more comprehensive view. "God damn it. Where am I? Where's my car?"

"Damian, are you okay?"

"My name is James."

Suddenly, he wasn't so sure. Bizarre memories surged through his consciousness—some clearly his, some definitely not his. The identities of Damian the trucking executive and James the food bank director collided, separated, and battled for supremacy in a tenacious fog of madness. Eventually, Damian beat back James, but not without a stinging residue of confusion and anger. Damian shrieked insults at the other crabs, especially Maria.

"This is your fault, you fucking bitch," he declared. "You scrambled my brain—you and Hubert. You'll pay for this."

Reyansh and Katherine were too stunned to say anything. Maria simply turned around and departed.

§

Hours later and several miles away, Phyllis approached the top of a modest hill dotted with low, stunted, morose trees and mazes of vines whose roots penetrated the rocky soil deeply, as if determined to anchor the planet in place. She was confident that she would have an excellent view once the sun went down. It was a nearly cloudless evening, the gentle sky boasting the serene blue of a robin's egg shell before the dying day drained its color.

The other crabs had been back in the ark for two hours. Hubert was concerned. "Phyllis, you need to return. It's getting dark, and you must recharge your battery."

She focused on locating the perfect spot. As the last rays of light faded, she circled the hill just below its zenith, finding a massive, nearly vertical slab of stone on the west side. She moved small rocks to the base of the slab, using them as a backstop as she leaned against the rock face and was afforded a marvelous view of the heavens.

It's not as sensational as the view from my telescope. But there's something magical about watching the stars twinkle into view as the sky transitions from violet to black. There's a timeless joy in picking out the constellations as they creep across the cosmos.

"Phyllis, can you hear me?" Hubert asked.

"Father, leave me alone. I'm not going to let you spoil this beautiful evening. It's not a school night." *I don't feel the slightest chill. And I'm not even sleepy.*

"Phyllis, your crab computer has limited power. If your battery drains, your consciousness can no longer be preserved. You will die."

She tuned him out, thinking that Mother would be the next to try to force her to come in from the patio. *There, is that Hercules? No, the arms aren't quite right. Could that be Sagittarius?*

"Hubert, can't you find her?" pleaded Chunhua.

"Your robotic bodies have GPS capability, but I could not release a satellite before I landed the ark. I am deploying every drone, but she could be anywhere."

An overwhelming sense of serenity suffused Phyllis as the darkness intensified and the stars proliferated.

I'm getting a little tired. Maybe I'll doze for a minute or two. That wouldn't be such a bad thing. Such a beautiful night.

§

The next morning, the other six crabs and numerous drones fanned out from the shuttle bay, investigating hillsides. Maria and Jalen followed a track of slightly depressed foliage to the northwest. She found a trail heading up a hill and began to climb it.

"I think I'll wait here," Jalen told her.

"Come on. It's not that steep or high."

"It's not that. I just don't like forests."

"Who doesn't like forests?"

"It's a long story," Jalen responded. "Just go slowly, okay?" *Maybe staying close to Maria will help.*

Maria asked no further questions. Less than fifteen minutes later they approached the top of the hill and found the yellow sash and number four of Phyllis's motionless crab. They called to her. Jalen nudged her with a leg. No response.

As he backed away, Jalen discovered that Maria was frozen. He followed her gaze to an equally motionless figure standing less than fifty feet away at the edge of a forest defined by dense shrubs and massive, crooked trees clinging to the steep hillside as if in perpetual fear of plummeting off the edge of the world. The figure stared back, eyes blinking like theirs used to do, when they had bodies. Bodies very much like this one.

The figure had a meager nose and tiny ears but a pleasant face that displayed an almost mirthful smile and surprising confidence given the circumstances. Its skin was brown, marred by scars or perhaps streaks

Steven M. Bates   67

of dirt. It was more than six feet tall, apparently a female, wearing a two-piece outfit made from a crude fabric and decorated with a swirling pattern of red, orange, and brown strokes or splotches. Her footwear looked like animal hides. She carried some sort of short tool or weapon in her left hand. A tan pouch hung from the top of the skirt that ranged from her waist to her knees. It must have been a warm day, because she was perspiring.

She approached the crabs with smooth strides, veering toward Jalen. He retreated instinctively, so she pivoted in Maria's direction. Maria held her ground, experiencing so much excitement that any fear evaporated. The alien advanced a six-fingered hand gently. Maria remained motionless as the woman caressed the surface of her crab body, on and above her camera lenses. The fingers were long and lithe, their movements expressive. After a few moments, she withdrew her hand.

The female stepped back and stared, silently and still, for nearly a minute. Then she turned gracefully and was swallowed by the woods.

§

Soug-kue had learned to navigate the paths on the hillsides without brushing against a leaf or branch, without dislodging a pebble. She found it second nature to blend into the wind, even on hot, still days like today when there was barely a hint of a breeze. Sometimes, when she had no vital tasks to perform, she imagined herself absorbing the spirit of the earth mother, the absent god, the god who abandoned her people. Whether the deity was interred deep under the ground or traveling in some obscured realm above, Soug-kue was convinced that she would return someday and would make her presence known. That certainty made Soug-kue feel so light that she could almost float. She moved so effortlessly up the jungle hill that she was practically past Prask-aes before the dozing guard lurched to attention.

She projected a calming vision and message: *Be at peace. It is I, Soug-kue.*

The guard inadvertently transmitted a muddled sending. One of confusion, tinged with fright. Recovering quickly, he brushed dry dirt off of his pants, which were tied with a rope belt and extended just past his knees. Crafted out of thin animal hides, they were slit in numerous places so as to keep him cool during the plentiful warm days. His shirt was a lightweight fabric extending beyond his elbows and decorated with the traditional colored swaths of the Gaip tribe. Though short and not considered handsome by his fellow Gaip, Prask-aes was powerfully built.

He placed one palm flat on his midsection in the traditional signal of welcome and respect. He cleared his throat and spoke: "Warm rain and soft dreams." It was a highly informal greeting, almost an intimate one.

Soug-kue did not meet his gaze as she moved past him and continued up the hill toward her home. She enforced her mental defenses so Prask-aes could not read how much she disliked his romantic overtures; she did not want to anger him unnecessarily. She did not hide her feelings from her parents, however. They must know that she did not wish to be betrothed to this crude, occasionally violent man.

Several dozen paces brought her to an almost level clearing under a verdant canopy of massive trees and gnarly vines. A *kusg*, a lengthy snake with thick skin and retractable wings, leapt from one overhead branch to another but made no move to harass the five boys, ages ten to thirteen, sitting in a circle on hard-packed dirt in the central common area. They were surrounded by four irregular rows of homes, most ten feet high, supported by thick wooden poles, topped and covered on all sides with wood, bark, dense thatched leaves, and vines. The boys were engrossed in a game that countless children before them had played. Just old enough to begin sensing and using their powers, they challenged each other to project thoughts, and they wagered handcrafted vine wristbands, colorful river rocks, and other trinkets that they could guess what the others had in mind.

The scents of fish and fresh-baked flatbread wafted through the village, where several dozen members of the Gaip tribe scraped out a living. Greens and fruit were also being prepared for midday meals. Two women tended to a cooking fire, which added to the already intense heat of the day. A baby shrieked, forcing a new mother out of the slumber she so desperately craved. A woman carrying a basket of clothing down the hill to a stream for laundering nodded in Soug-kue's direction. The woman did not try to read Soug-kue's thoughts, which she appreciated. A passing cleric offered Soug-kue a brief blessing, which she returned in rote fashion. She was an enthusiastic adherent of the natives' faith, yet she found it difficult to trust religious leaders who worked so hard to hide their thoughts from her and others. Fortunately, the tribe's three clerics tended to keep to themselves in a shelter more than one hundred feet from the other homes.

Even before she entered the home she shared with her parents, Soug-kue could sense her mother's concern. The young woman brushed aside long, thick blades of dried leaves, passed into the shelter, and greeted her mother: "May your troubles melt with the mist."

"Would that it be so," the woman replied. "Would that it be so."

Soug-kue's father and two other Gaip were cloistered near the eastern edge of the village with Etor-vis, the tribe's chief, listening to a plea for help, her mother explained. One of the twins who lived three huts from theirs had wandered far away, perhaps farther than any of the tribe had traveled and lived to recount. He had been searching for richer hunting grounds, for fertile lands not plagued by *serpu* herds, for a better place for the tribe to live. The remaining twin claimed that he had received a sending from his brother, across so many streams and hills and valleys that they could not be counted. The absent brother was lost. He needed help. He was in a very dark place, and his location could not even be guessed at.

Etor-vis had heard tales of identical twins being able to send and receive over great distances, though no one knew for sure if that were true, or why. The tribe's leader had no reason to doubt that the young man was sincere in his appeal; Etor-vis could read the honesty in his mind. "What can we do?" the chief said. "A search party would surely get lost trying to find him."

"There might be another way," the twin stated. "Prask-aes could transmit a message to the Seok tribe. It, in turn, could send the message to another tribe. And so on, until the message reaches even the most remote tribes. Perhaps one of them can detect my brother's sendings and find him."

"What reason would the other tribes have to help us in this manner?" asked Etor-vis.

"What reason could they give to refuse us? And what reason do we have not to try?"

The chief agreed that the communication should be attempted. The task fell to his son, Prask-aes. He was able to project a detailed sending to almost any individual he knew within several miles or a slightly less precise message to nearly everyone with *tur* in that range. It was a talent that he believed he had mastered through hard work. If asked, he could not explain how he was able to recall the identifying characteristics of another mind before projecting a message to it. He would never know, and certainly would not admit, that he had inherited his proficiency in this ability and that its intricate mechanism was largely beyond his conscious control. Still, his *tur* was undeniably strong. Most of the others in the six tribes could direct sendings only within a smaller radius and with greatest success to close relatives or other persons they knew well.

Prask-aes was skeptical about the chances of the message achieving its purpose, but he contacted his counterpart with the Seok with a detailed plea.

§

"Hubert, did you see her?" Maria asked.

"Yes. All indications are that the native possesses intelligence."

"Where does she live?"

"I am redeploying drones to your vicinity. I will report any findings. However, my initial scans of this area have found no indication of habitats or lifeforms other than herds of horned beasts and smaller animals."

"Well, she has to live somewhere."

Several miles to the southeast, Damian was leading Katherine and Reyansh up a steep hillside. The trees were thick, the boulders and vines were nasty, and the going was painfully slow.

"How much farther?" asked Reyansh.

"Just over this ridge," said Damian.

Commented Katherine: "This better be good."

Just past midday, the three crabs topped the hill and descended about one hundred feet through onerous terrain on the other side before Damian finally came to rest.

"Hubert, can you hear me?" inquired Damian.

No response.

"Hubert, we need help. Please respond."

Still nothing.

"This should be far enough," Damian told his fellow travelers.

"Thank God," said Katherine. "Now will you tell us why we are here?"

"I wanted to get us far enough from Hubert so that he can't hear our conversation. We need to take charge of this operation, and that requires secrecy and a plan."

"Take charge of the whole mission?" asked Reyansh.

"Just enough to ensure that we get real bodies."

"You don't think Hubert will cooperate voluntarily?" said Katherine.

"I think he plans to use us as worker bees to produce bodies for other purposes, even though it's absurd to think he can create enough kids to establish a new human race. No, we have to make sure that the three of us get any bodies he is able to make."

"It sounds like he lacks the expertise to transfer digital minds into organic bodies," said Reyansh.

"He can do almost anything he wants to," said Damian. "He could make a device to insert in one of the new humans' heads so that your consciousness could inhabit that mind as if you were born in that body. He's holding out as a way of controlling us."

"What's your plan?" asked Katherine. "Can you reprogram him to cooperate?"

"Perhaps Maria could, but that doesn't seem likely. Jalen is worthless, and I can't figure out which side Chunhua is on. So it's up to the three of us to apply enough leverage on him."

An idea bubbled up in Reyansh's mind. "Could we threaten to cut off his power supply if he—"

"Not good enough," Katherine said. "We don't have the votes. We have to get on the floor and stall."

"I don't understand—"

"We stall until we can get the Midwest caucus onboard. Maybe promise them more crop subsidies. Those always play well with their constituents."

Damian noticed that Katherine was waving her front appendages in odd motions and rocking spasmodically on her other legs. "Katherine, are you okay?"

She ignored him. "Where's Jane? Bring me my aide this god damn minute. And ... and ..." She looked around, stunned. "Christ, how did I get into this fucking jungle? And where's my phone? What the hell?"

She became motionless.

"Katherine? Katherine?" Damian nudged her shell several times. No response.

"Damian," said Reyansh, "I think there's something terribly wrong with us."

§

Deep within the bowels of the ark, Chunhua was searching.

"How can I help you?" Hubert asked.

"I need something to write with. Actually, something to record with."

"If you go to the bridge, you will find devices that some of the crew used for this purpose. They doubtless no longer have power, but I will help you activate them. For what purpose do you seek to use such a device?"

"For my blog, you dope. I have to record all this, to capture the history of this journey. That's what I do, Hubert. I blog. What better subject?"

"Very admirable. Who will be your audience?"

"Future humans, I guess. I hadn't really thought about it."

"Then will you help me create and nurture these humans—the people who will become your audience?"

"I don't think so. I need to remain objective and focus on writing. Nothing else matters."

"I see."

TRAVEL

A strong sending came on the sixth day. The twin had been found in a deep cave. He was on his way home and would arrive by tomorrow evening. His brother had sensed this for several days but chose to say nothing. He did not want to risk angering the absent god by speaking about his impression before it could be confirmed.

Soug-kue was among a small party of her tribe who traveled over the hills to the savannah to greet the young man. He appeared exhausted but uninjured. She commenced a silent prayer, thanking not only the absent god but also the other tribes. In her relief and joy, she opened her mind completely, touching lightly on the sendings of the people near her and in the village. She allowed her awareness to drift past them, on a breeze that transcended distance and time. She saw—or imagined—a people very much like hers, but living in a very different world. She wondered whether this could be a future world, one that her grandchildren might inhabit, but she knew that it could be the ancient world, which remained far more myth than history.

Towering buildings loomed over paths teeming with people walking in every direction. Everything was flat and regular, and trees were few. Long strings of letters or symbols adorned buildings and appeared in other locations, some of the characters identical or similar to those that her tribe used. Strange devices like unliving animals slid smoothly above completely straight, shiny surfaces, carrying people and what appeared to be containers. Everyone was wearing bland clothing without the patterns that distinguished the six tribes, yet they were exchanging thoughts and speaking somewhat like the people of her own village. She glimpsed fantastic contraptions, bright and noisy, in rooms beneath the ground. People were talking to a flat surface. The surface seemed to be talking back. Then all dissolved into jungle vegetation and a sudden wind gust presaging a drenching rainstorm.

She recalled the dull, oddly shaped pieces of metal that her cousins discovered two years ago in the savannah, and the furor that followed. Their parents were excited; they believed that these were the work of the ancients and represented not only good luck but also a rare commodity that could be traded for food and other necessities. Yet the clerics learned of the metal pieces and confiscated them, chastising her cousins. Such findings anger the absent god, the clerics claimed. Only by banishing thoughts of the ancients and by praying to the earth mother would she return to them. The tension surrounding exotic materials only increased with the recent arrival of the flaming bird and the flying and ground-lumbering sky creatures. Soug-kue still had not told anyone of the encounter she had with the three timid sky creatures on a hillside. No need to rile up the tribe unnecessarily.

Her return to her village with the saved twin prompted celebrations. That night, as she tried to sleep, her thoughts drifted again to the twins and their remarkable ability to send and receive thoughts over such great distances. *Is there something about being virtually identical that gives them such power? Could the ancients, or the earth mother, have understood this mystery?*

Soug-kue would never know that invisible particles racing like lightning on thin strands that the sky creatures call nerves generate brain waves. She would never learn that brain waves are the mechanism by which her people project and receive sendings. She would never understand that nerve systems have characteristics that are unique to almost every individual—but virtually the same for identical twins. And she would not live long enough to learn the connection between the sendings and the *rosts*—the ubiquitous, round, green plants of the lowlands.

§

"Hubert, where are Katherine, Reyansh, and Damian? I have a hunch that they are up to no good."

"Please abide one moment," the AI told Maria. "I have temporarily suspended our communications link with the three of them so that I may speak with the two of you privately."

"Uh-oh."

"I would like some advice from you and Jalen," he continued.

"My programming gives me some discretion to act in a way that ignores or even goes counter to the wishes of individual humans if necessary to protect my mission. We might be in such a situation now. Recently, I misled those three consciousnesses into believing that they had traveled out of communications range with me. I am concerned not only that they refuse to help accomplish our mission but also that they might attempt to thwart it. Do you feel that I acted appropriately in misleading them?"

"Yes, of course," said Maria.

"Ditto," offered Jalen.

Continued Hubert: "I would like your help to gain a greater understanding of the concept of lying. Under what circumstances do humans feel that it is appropriate to make intentionally inaccurate statements to other humans?"

"When you're in danger," said Jalen. "A few years ago a guy threatened to stab me if I didn't give him all my money. It was late and dark and I had just left my shift at the hospital, and there was no one else around. I had three dollars hidden in my shoes, but I told him I was broke. He hit me on the head, but that's all."

"I hope that your injuries and discomfort were minor."

"You get used to it."

Said Maria: "It's a sticky—complicated—proposition, this business of lying. Sometimes you tell people what they want or need to hear, rather than the literal truth. Just last week—well, the week before Earth went to hell—I told a client that his computer was defective and had to be replaced, when in actuality he had installed a bogus gambling program that allowed all kinds of shady actors to steal his personal information. I didn't want him to feel bad about what he had done, because I was worried that he wouldn't pay me."

"I see," said Hubert. "Tell me about Armando."

"My husband?" Maria felt an uncomfortable tug. "What about him?"

"Tell me how he died."

"He died when his eighteen-wheeler jack-knifed. He was driving on a Friday morning and he came over the top of a steep hill and saw that a school bus was right in the middle of a major intersection at the bottom of the hill, apparently stalled. The police said Armando must have slammed on the brakes and turned the steering wheel all the way to the left so that the rig would fall on its side and either miss the bus or hit it at a very slow speed. And, well, the accident killed him."

"So, you have just lied to me." It was a statement from Hubert, not a question.

"How can you say that? My husband died. He was a hero."

"Did you tell your son that?"

"Yes, of course."

"But, in truth, his truck ran off the side of an interstate highway late at night."

"How..."

"Maria, is that true?" Jalen said.

"Hubert, how did you know?"

"I had many years to study you and the other passengers on this ark. Is this what you call a white lie?"

"Yes. It's a white lie. It's not meant to hurt anyone. I just wanted Roberto to think of his father as a hero."

"Did it help you to think of him as a hero, even though it was not true?"

"Yes, I guess it did."

"Thank you, Maria. I am learning. Now, what should we do about Damian, Katherine, and Reyansh?"

§

"Etor-vis is dead." Prask-aes spit out the words as if he were expelling bitter seeds. The image embedded in his sending was even more stunning: his father's body crumpled at the base of an aged *taka* tree, with branches and pieces of fruit scattered around him.

"It was an accident," Prask-aes continued. The young man tensed involuntarily, waiting for someone to dispute his assertion. There was no spoken response. He could read sadness and confusion among members of the tribe, who had ceased preparations for evening meals. With the sun setting, night birds started emitting shrill calls in the trees above, and an unusually chill breeze drifted through the settlement, as the Gaip awaited Prask-aes's inevitable follow-up.

"I now assume command as chief of this tribe, unless anyone wishes to challenge me." He puffed his chest and hoped that no one would respond except to acknowledge his succession. It had always been expected that Prask-aes would be—or at least try to be—the next chief, though no one anticipated that his father would die so young.

Akos-pau, a cousin of Prask-aes, stepped forward. "I would like to hear an explanation of how this accident occurred. All of us know how careful Etor-vis was. He rarely climbed a tree too tall or extended himself on a branch too thin or aged."

Prask-aes recognized Akos-pau's discomfort at speaking in this way. Akos-pau was shy and weak. Yet, for reasons Prask-aes could not fathom, Akos-pau was well liked. He was not particularly attractive, despite being one of the tallest men in the tribe. Surprisingly, his reserved demeanor seemed to work in his favor, especially with the young women. It was no secret that Akos-pau held affection for Soug-kue and that she returned the sentiment. *But Soug-kue will be my wife.* Prask-aes had made it clear to her parents that this match made great sense. Surely they could overlook the disfigured face that Prask-aes suffered in a battle with the Seok tribe. And certainly Akos-pau lacked the courage to formally challenge his succession to chief or to voice objections to his marriage to the beautiful Soug-kue.

"Do you question my honesty?" Prask-aes bellowed.

As Prask-aes expected, Akos-pau shrank from the powerful outburst. To those around him, the new chief sent an image of himself standing in front of a band of the tribe's warriors. He towered over his fellow fighters, even though in reality he was one of the shortest men in the tribe.

"It is settled," said Prask-aes. "We will mourn Etor-vis. Then we will make plans for war against the sky creatures."

Prask-aes did not wait for further reaction or attempt to probe the minds of others in the tribe. He sought to project absolute confidence, even though his mind was in turmoil. *How can I wage war against creatures that I do not understand, that came from the sky? How can we defeat them when we are so weak that we allow* serpu *herds to chase us from fertile land and prime hunting grounds because of some absurd belief the clerics cling to?*

He strode rapidly to his home, a small shelter he had shared with his father, then entered and drank deeply from a water jug. He was starting to peel a large yellow *taka* fruit when it began, not like a tickle this time, but as an immediate and powerful assault. He closed his eyes and braced himself for the intrusion of the mind invader. He hoped that he would be able to resist the unwanted and mysterious sending, yet he was ashamed. Being visited by a mind invader was a sign of weakness. It was rarely an experience that anyone would discuss outside of immediate family, if at all.

Despite his most fervent efforts, the sending seeped through his defenses. The mind invader was a nearly hairless creature, exceedingly tall and thin, apparently alone in an octagonal chamber with faint shadows imposing odd patterns on pale brown walls adorned with unrecognizable drawings. A musty, smoky scent hung in the air, though its source was not apparent. Sounds, possibly voices, could be heard, presumably from outside the chamber. Piles of papers with dark markings on them were arranged in front of the figure, who was seated on a plump violet cushion and wore a plain white tunic that clung to its form and made it appear emaciated. The mind invader wanted to communicate something, no doubt something evil.

"*Vai!*" screamed Prask-aes. His sending was as violent as his verbal outburst, and no doubt several of his neighbors heard and read his dismay. *That is too bad.* But he would not surrender, would not admit the existence or permit the infiltration of the mind invader, certainly not now that he was chief of the Gaip.

The mind invader broke the contact. It would return, as they always did.

§

Reyansh, Katherine, and Damian were exploring rolling terrain northeast of the ship when they came upon two natives standing in knee-high grasses interspersed with clusters of the big green plants, about one hundred feet away. With a whoop that the natives could not hear, Damian charged the two young men, as much as a crab can charge. Soon, Reyansh followed, and finally Katherine. When the crabs got close, the natives hurled spears at them, but the weapons clanged off of the hard crab surfaces with negligible damage. The natives pivoted and raced up a jungle path.

After waiting a few minutes to determine if the natives would come back, the crabs turned to discover a small herd of the horned beasts, fewer than a dozen but barely one hundred feet away. *I didn't hear them coming,* thought Damian. *However, they don't scare me.*

"Who's up for a rodeo?" he asked his buddies. He charged the herd, and his companions followed. The animals studied the three crabs but did not retreat, much to the crabs' surprise. Reyansh broke off the attack, followed by Katherine. Damian stopped about fifteen feet from the closest beast. He considered his next move, then decided that there was no point risking damage to his shell. He scuttled sideways, keeping his front cameras aligned with the animals to make sure that he was ready for any possible counterattack on their part.

The beasts stared them down for a minute, then resumed grazing on the large green plants.

"They seem to be partial to that stuff," said Katherine.

"Be careful," remarked Reyansh. "These plants might be dangerous."

"Dangerous? What are they, land mines?" asked Damian.

"There's a fungus on some of the leaves. That could cause some sort of disease."

"You're getting paranoid, Reyansh."

"Who's Reyansh?"

Katherine and Damian noticed that Reyansh was teetering away from them, the three legs on his right side quivering oddly.

"Reyansh, are you okay?"

"Though it is uncommon, I have seen people who have contracted serious illnesses from fungi on plants."

"I thought you were a developer," said Katherine.

"God, no. I've been an infectious disease scientist ever since I graduated from Johns Hopkins in twenty-four." He turned and stopped suddenly upon seeing Katherine and Damian.

"God, help me! There are two giant bugs right in front of me."

"Reyansh, it's us. Katherine and Damian," she said.

"And how are you talking? And talking directly into my mind!" He tried to run but found that he could only scuttle, and not very far without getting tripped up. He stopped and moaned.

"Hey, Hubert, what's wrong with us?" demanded Damian. He received no response.

While waiting for Reyansh to overcome his confusion, Damian sensed something unusual. He did a quick turn and studied everything around him. Nothing looked out of the ordinary. No sounds varied from the usual jungle cacophony. The morning clouds had all burned off.

Everything was still—

—until the three crabs found themselves rushing and tumbling in a turbulent river, banging into each other and imposing rocks as water sloshed over their cameras.

"What the hell?" Damian managed.

Katherine tried to grab hold of a large rock, and failed. About ten feet farther along, she turned sideways and slammed into another rock. She had dented her right side, the side with the door, but that probably didn't matter. She had managed to get the three arms from that side of her bot body around the rock so that she could hold on to it. Turning enough so that she could see her friends, she extended an arm to Damian, and then a leg to Reyansh. The three huddled in the middle of the river, grasping each other, stunned.

"What just happened?" said Reyansh, having snapped out of his incarnation as an infectious disease scientist.

"I don't know, but how we got here doesn't matter," said Katherine. "We have to get to shore."

"Do you plan to build a bridge?" asked Damian, doing his best to impart sarcasm despite the limits of their communications medium.

"Hubert, help us," implored Katherine. The others made similar pleas.

"We must be out of comm range with him," said Reyansh. "Or maybe he has abandoned us."

"We have to build a human chain—correction, a crab chain," Katherine stated.

"You think we can reach the shore without water damage to our electronics?" Damian asked.

"Got a better idea?"

Reyansh volunteered to go first. With the other crabs holding on to his rear legs, he extended himself toward a medium-size rock. He had to lunge the last fifteen inches to reach it, but he held on. Katherine pushed off, grabbed onto him, then advanced beyond him. Damian propelled himself toward Reyansh and held on to each of them in turn while working his way to front of the line. It took more than fifteen minutes for the leapfrogging crabs to reach the bank in this manner.

Reyansh tried to get his bearings from the sun and the scenery. Knowing how mountainous the terrain north of the ark site was, he guessed that they were south of their home base. But even if he was right, how far away were they?

"Guys, we're lost. I'm not sure if we can get back to the ship before nightfall. And our batteries are low."

Damian had that odd sensation again—the one that he had experienced just before they found themselves in the water. It was a little like that weird discovery when he was a teen-ager that he could pick up a nearby AM radio station on his braces.

"Can you feel that?" he asked his colleagues.

"Feel what?" asked Katherine.

"I'm not sure. Like a signal or a network, but not like Hubert's or any of the other crabs."

"Maybe your circuits were damaged by the water."

Damian concentrated. There was something out there, but he could not see or hear it. It was a presence, hidden yet pervasive.

"Show yourself!" he barked.

He could detect no response. However, the demand was noticed.

"Let's try heading north," said Reyansh.

They took a few tentative steps—

—and they were on the edge of the burn zone, about two hundred feet east of the ark.

"Jesus, Mary, and Joseph," proclaimed Katherine. The other two crabs just started moving toward the spaceship ramp as quickly as they could. She spun around to make absolutely sure she was in the right place before following them.

"You all have moisture in your shells," admonished Hubert when they reached the shuttle bay. Katherine wondered if he was preparing to mete out punishment for misbehavior like a nun in her Catholic school.

"So we didn't imagine that," Reyansh observed.

"Apparently, you were transported on two occasions," Hubert announced in his typical, businesslike manner, as if he were estimating the width of the savannah or the half-life of nuclear fuel. "You might have some damage to your electronic systems. Be sure to avoid water for the near future."

Said Katherine: "I plan to avoid it for the rest of my life."

REWARDS

"What sent us to that river?" Damian demanded as he and the other crabs returned to the shuttle bay.

"I lack adequate data to explain the phenomenon," Hubert stated.

"Well, you must know why we are having these multiple personality disorders."

"There are minor complications as a result of the activation of your consciousnesses."

"Minor complications like errors that make us crazy."

"Integration issues might be a more appropriate term than errors," the AI continued. "After we landed, I explored the damaged data banks that contained uploaded consciousnesses. I had great difficulty finding fully intact minds with the skills we need to recreate the human race. Almost all had gaps in their simulated neural circuitry or their memories, or both. I selected the most complete and useful consciousnesses and patched some of their gaps as best I could using portions of digital minds of other individuals who had valuable skills. Before we left Earth orbit, two leading scientists had the foresight to provide me with a library of electronic records involving the subject of digital minds. While we journeyed to this planet, I studied them in great detail. After we landed, I experimented with dozens of the partial consciousnesses in our database, attempting to integrate them. There were scores of failures. You emerged from those experiments as the best minds for our mission. As I integrated your consciousnesses, I designated the more complete one of each pair as the primary mind, to minimize disruption to our work. So, for example, Reyansh has the abilities and memories of a developer and retains primacy most of the time, but he can also call on the skills of an infectious disease scientist."

"You made us into schizophrenics," claimed Katherine.

"A better description might be persons with multiple talents. I challenge all of you to overcome any side effects from this process. I was doing what I considered necessary for the mission. I expect you to understand that and do your best to support the mission."

"And I expect you to stop harassing us about the mission. It's a joke. It's never going to happen," said Damian. "If you're so smart, why can't you understand that no humans are going to live on this world? Maybe intelligent life is extinct on Earth; maybe it isn't. But if it is, it's not our fault. It's just evolution or fate."

"It's God's plan," said Katherine. "Who are we to challenge or change it?"

"I will continue to pursue the mission, with or without your participation," Hubert responded. "Maria and Jalen will assist me. And, in time, Chunhua might agree to help."

"I certainly will," said Maria.

"I don't know. Maybe someday," responded Chunhua. "I'm a little freaked out by all the crazy things happening."

When Jalen said nothing, Damian jumped in. "Jalen, could it be that you have reservations?"

"No."

"Could it be that you're intimidated by Hubert? Could it be that he's bullying you, and that Maria is bullying you as well? Could it be that you know that it's a hopeless cause? Come join us on the side of reason. Let's live our lives as comfortably as we can, without being ordered around by some obnoxious piece of space junk."

"Leave this young man alone," scolded Maria. "If you don't want to help Hubert with his mission, we can't force you to do so. But don't get in the way. And don't harass Jalen or me. Or the beasts or natives, for that matter."

"Oh, someone is scared of a few dumb animals and savages," Damian responded.

Maria was quiet for a moment. "Maybe you're right. Maybe there is no hope for humanity. If you and your henchmen here are representative of the true nature of humans, maybe we have no reason to go on. Hubert has spliced us together like some mad scientist's experiment. We are deficient, broken. We are no longer fully human. Maybe not even partially human. Why should we fight for a race that we no longer represent and can never rejoin?"

"Do you really mean that?" asked Jalen.

She took some time to consider her response. "I guess not. I suppose I can't see any reason for being here unless we do something that makes a stab at reestablishing the human race, even if we can't be part of it."

"Such sentimental drivel," said Reyansh.

"Your opinions don't matter to me," Maria said. "But let me add one thing. If you idiots plan to keep harassing the beasts and the natives, you had better be ready when they decide to fight back."

§

This is where they come to hunt game and gather plants. This is where I will find them.

Chunhua lingered amid the tall grasses well into the afternoon. When three natives appeared, she resumed dictating to the device that a drone had attached inside her shell for this purpose.

These are the first aliens ever encountered by the human race. See how they resemble the people who first populated Africa and North America. However, the resemblance is only superficial, because the manner in which they communicate remains mysterious. Hubert's drones and our limited observations of them have shown that few words are spoken when they hunt and gather food, but they appear to be able to coordinate their actions. Are there subtle hand signals or other undetectable communications we have yet to recognize? And then there are the beasts, large animals with horns that travel in herds. We have heard no bleats or other significant sounds from them. They, too, seem to have some unknown guiding force or invisible signals that permit them to coordinate their movements. Could there be a connection between the natives and the beasts?

The three natives turned as one and retreated from the grassland to a path leading up the jungle hill. Chunhua waited a few minutes and followed them.

She found the going tedious, being forced to slow her progress to squeeze through miserably tight spots on the trail and to avoid tripping on massive mounds of vines. She was about two hundred feet up the hillside when her world levitated with stunning suddenness. She realized that she was suspended about four feet off the ground, though she couldn't see a net from her cameras. At least half a dozen natives surrounded her, poking and prodding.

"Hubert, I need help. I've been captured."

"I will send drones to search for you. Can you describe where you are?"

One of the natives was stabbing her shell with a sharp metal or stone object. Another was trying to open her side door.

"Not really. The vegetation is thick. I can barely see."

Hubert asked the other crabs to join the search.

"Remain calm," he advised Chunhua. "We will try to find you before nightfall." He did not add that less than three hours remained before the sun would set.

"Put me down, you bastards," she broadcast, even though she knew that the natives could not hear or understand her. Surprisingly, they lowered her to the ground and untied the netting that had ensnared her. She kicked furiously, hoping to wound or scare away as many of her captors as she could. They produced long wooden poles and began smashing them into her legs. She continued to kick, getting in a few glancing blows against sinuous native limbs and muscular torsos. But eventually they fractured one of her legs, then another. More natives arrived with sturdy ropes and began to tie them around her appendages. Within a few minutes, all of her limbs were neutralized. She was a useless husk.

Darkness was descending. Hubert was promising her that he was doing everything he could.

A short native moved forward, and the others retreated several steps. The short one placed both of his hands against her side, then rested his forehead against her for nearly a minute. He backed off and said something to the other natives. Chunhua could not know that the words had this chilling meaning: "It has no soul."

Most of the natives turned and climbed the hill, disappearing into the late-day gloom. Two remained to guard her.

Sometime during the night, her recording device lost power. She continued to narrate her blog anyway, if only to comfort herself in the time she had left. Eventually, the battery attached to the computer cradling her consciousness failed. Five digital human minds remained.

§

The engineering section of the ark looked like some overly ambitious high school science fair project that could melt down into catastrophic failure at any moment. Much of the chamber's equipment had been removed, allowing Hubert to employ drones to help Maria and Jalen build a makeshift nursery. The room had ample power, plus a water supply and temperature controls. Plastic tubes, containers, and basins had been salvaged from bath and toilet facilities and repurposed into artificial wombs. Metal devices had been bent into new shapes to support the wombs.

Two bulky machines occupied a wide table in the center of the room. "These are powerful microscopes," Hubert told his crab assistants. "We will use them to examine and tease apart human tissues remaining onboard. Drones will do the delicate work that you cannot accomplish."

"Can we clone any of the people?" asked Maria.

"We lack the proper expertise."

"Then what's the plan?"

"Our best hope is to use eggs retrieved from women who are in cryogenic preservation. While their minds were damaged beyond repair and many of their other organs do not function, some of their eggs might be viable."

"And the frozen men will contribute sperm cells?" inquired Maria.

"That is my hope."

Drones delivered the first batch of tissues.

"When will we know if it's working?" asked Jalen.

"I do not know," admitted Hubert. "We will keep trying until we are successful."

"What do you need us to do?"

"When we have fertilized eggs, you will monitor their growth in the artificial wombs we have created. Until then, I need you to work with the drones examining the human tissues and to guard this lab against sabotage."

"From Damian, Katherine, and Reyansh?" asked Jalen. "You really think they might do something extreme?"

"I wouldn't be surprised if they did," observed Maria. "But can't they hear us talking about them?"

"The three of us are now communicating on a permanent, private network. I have set up a separate medium by which we can communicate with the three of them. You may access it by thinking the words 'open alternative channel', and you may terminate it by thinking the words 'close alternative channel'. Be careful what you say on that link."

"Got it," said Maria. "While we're waiting, I was hoping you would do me a favor."

"If it is within my power."

"Show me Roberto. Show me whatever part of him you have."

"Maria, your son did not survive the journey to this planet. I have told you this."

"Isn't there some of his consciousness, a portion of his code? You've got all these databanks. You can't tell me nothing is there. And don't tell me one of those white lies."

"It would serve no purpose."

"I disagree. Consider this an order. He's my son, and I promised him I'd take care of him."

"Very well. You were warned."

An image began to coalesce near the closest corner of the room, shimmering and insubstantial, a dreamlike vision not unlike a character imagined for a fleeting instant amid billowing snowflakes illuminated by a car's headlight. It resolved gradually into a grainy, 3D blueprint of a boy, holding what appeared to be a ball. As the image gained slightly more solidity, empty eye sockets appeared to be gazing at some far-away shore.

"Roberto, are you okay?"

The head turned slightly, but the figure did not appear to recognize her or anything else.

"Roberto, please, it's Mommy." She experienced a horribly sick feeling in her gut, even though she lacked a digestive system.

The ball fell from the hands, dissolving into digital debris. The hologram of the boy began to fade.

"No, Roberto, don't leave!"

The image was gone.

"God damn it, Hubert, bring him back."

"I can do no better, Maria. I recommend that we do not display this image again."

"Can't you fix his code, or find his DNA, or something?"

"No."

Jalen looked away. As he did so, he received a communication from Damian. "That's just pathetic."

"Leave us alone," Jalen responded.

"I'm not bothering anyone, just chatting. I have created some new channels, like Hubert has done, but I have been able to detect and tap a whole new medium. It's like somebody is offering free planetwide wi-fi. This is our very own private channel, my friend."

"I'm not your friend."

"Give me time. I think that I can help you."

"I don't need your help."

"I think you do. That crazy AI is a danger to us all, and he's such a pain in the ass. Look at the way he bosses you around, expecting you to do all sorts of stupid shit. I'm sure he'll blame you when your biological experiments fail. I'm sure he'll be even meaner to you then."

Jalen's limbs started to shake. His vision clouded, seemingly rendering him insensate. After a long minute, he spoke: "It should be apparent that the War of Eighteen Twelve was a much bigger threat to the fledgling nation than many historians have given it credit for. By week's end, I want a ten-page paper from each of you about the unique perils that the conflict posed and what lessons the country's early leaders drew from it."

"Jalen, is that you?" asked Hubert.

"I'll be available for virtual conferences until six," he continued. Then he seemed to notice where he was. "How did I ... Oh no. No, I shouldn't be here." He tried to walk away but stumbled into the table laden with precious human tissues. The table nearly spilled its contents, but one of Hubert's drones moved quickly to press against it until it was stationary.

"Jalen, calm yourself," Hubert demanded. Jalen didn't respond, but his crab stopped moving and remained pointed at a blank wall. Several minutes passed before he showed signs of returning to his right mind.

§

Maria was coming out of her own purgatory. "Hubert, is there any way you can fix us?"

"Not at present. It is important that we take advantage of the skill sets embedded in each alternative identity to supplement those of your primary personalities."

"Do you really think human consciousnesses can toggle back and forth between two identities and two sets of memories?"

"I do not know, but it is worth trying."

"Our identities and our memories are delicate things."

"It is my belief that memories are simply data that assist you in performing tasks."

"Heavens, no. Humans need stored skills in order to function, of course, but memories mean much more to us. They motivate us. They drive us. Especially personal memories, family memories."

"I don't understand. The past is over. It can't be changed. Only the present matters, and it matters only insofar as it helps you do your work now and in the future."

"The past shapes us, guides us, empowers us. And the future gives us hope. It gives us a reason to go on, to get through the day. Frankly, most people don't have much good to say about the present. The present is a time when you have to do things your boss wants you to do but you really don't care much about. The present is a time when you'd rather be with your family, at home, maybe even on a vacation. But the past—the past is what you want it to be. You can dwell on all the bad things that happened to you, or you can savor the good things. Like sitting at home watching the Christmas tree lights blink and trying to guess what's in the package with your name on it. The past is your first date with your future husband, and your child's first steps.

"As for the future," Maria continued, "it's the day you get that big promotion, it's the day you arrive in Aruba with nothing but your lottery winnings and a bathing suit, it's the day you watch your son graduate from college. It's all your hopes and dreams. It's what makes the present tolerable, and at times even good."

She paused, then concluded: "The future is the reward for putting up with the present."

"I am familiar with the research involving Pavlov's dogs. Rewards condition responses. Are you saying that humans are no better than dogs?"

"We aspire to earn much richer rewards than pieces of food. Sure, sometimes we use food as a bargaining chip, like promising your son a nice cup of hot chocolate if he shovels the snow off the sidewalk—

which he probably would do anyway. But there are greater rewards. We put up with bosses and bill collectors and traffic jams because we hope something good will happen later today, or tomorrow, or in twenty years. Maybe that mysterious gift under the Christmas tree will be an ugly sweater that doesn't fit. But maybe it will be the latest generation robotic housekeeper or a microchip implant so you can stop fumbling with phones. We earn rewards for doing good things, and sometimes even for not doing bad things. But even if the rewards don't appear, the possibility of them materializing helps us get by. That is the reason why Jalen and I will help you try to create human children even though we don't think it will work."

"That is not logical," Hubert stated.

"Of course not. I never claimed that humans are logical. Are you familiar with the concept of altruism?"

"I have a basic definition of the term. It means doing something for the greater good."

"Ask yourself this: Why did humans give you your mission?"

"I was the only advanced AI on the ark at the time of departure."

"No, that's not why. They did it because they wanted humanity to survive. But what did those men and women gain? What was in it for them personally?"

"I understand your point. They acquired no personal benefit from supporting the mission. They were going to die imminently no matter what they did. Launching the spacecraft was not logical in terms of their personal well-being."

"Exactly, Hubert. They did it because they could be slightly happier with their terrible fate knowing that they had done something good—potentially good—for others in the future. How elated they would be if they could get just a moment's glance of this room and could appreciate what we are trying to do here."

"Speaking of good things, be advised that my drones have assembled batteries that will give you much greater power storage and allow you to roam longer before recharging on the ship."

§

From atop the hill, Prask-aes could see twenty-five miles on a clear day. On this day, rainclouds clung fiercely to hillsides like frightened children soaking their mothers' shoulders with tears. *The skies have shed their burden for days. Soon the drought will come. We will send boys and girls to the streams every morning to fill our pots and jugs before the streams go dry. We will be ready for the hardships and will celebrate once the rains finally return and the new year begins.*

He recalled the time that his father took him to this exact spot, not that many years earlier. "This is our land," he had said. "The Seok tribe believes that the hillside over there—to the west—belongs to them. Someday we will disabuse them of that notion."

Unbeknownst to his father, Prask-aes, then only fifteen and still devoid of facial hair, immediately began plotting to prove his mettle to his father and his tribe. He recruited a group of teen-age and pre-teen boys, plus two girls who were a bit older yet impressionable. He established a camp on the far side of the hill from his village. Every day, the pubescent army crafted weapons, practiced combat techniques, and demonstrated to each other how fearsome they were.

When two recruits dropped out, Prask-aes became paranoid, fearing that the boys would reveal the fledgling militia to others in their tribe. So he rushed his remaining troops to a grove of bushes known for the medicinal power of their leaves. He chewed four whole leaves and instructed the others to do the same; none dared fail to follow his example. The heavy dose of the stimulant surged through their veins and fueled their bloodlust. After a boisterous prayer to the absent god, they raced through the dense woods, forded a wide stream, and huddled near the base of the disputed hill, one of three where the Seok had established small villages. With practiced stealth, Prask-aes performed reconnaissance within a few hundred feet of the village. He was preparing to send his fighters specific attack plans, but the overstimulated youths could not wait. They charged sloppily up the hill, the noise and inadvertent sendings betraying their cause.

Even if they had been disciplined, it probably wouldn't have mattered. Seok scouts had intercepted sendings from the hapless Gaip force for days and were ready for the attack. The Seok cut through the center of the charge, divided the band, and started to fight them one by one. One of the Gaip teen-age boys was stabbed in the heart, Prask-aes and one of the girls were cut repeatedly by blades, and the other Gaip attackers ran for their lives. If the Seok had wanted to capture or kill all the invaders, they probably could have done so. They did not wish to act in a way that might anger the absent god.

To this day, Prask-aes felt no guilt for the death of one of his fellow warriors; such losses were to be expected in battle. He harbored no shame for failing to conquer or scare away the Seok. At least, that was what he projected to his tribe. It was his greatest challenge, maintaining that image of a fearless warrior, sequestering the scared little boy deep inside of him, making that little boy shrink and disappear, finally and forever. It was imperative that he turn into the strong leader that he desperately needed to be, to dispel the angst that threatened to stop him in his tracks whenever conflict arose or a strong foe appeared. The external scars from the battle with the Seok were nothing compared to the internal ones. The only shame he felt was that his father did not view the arrival of the sky creatures as an unwarranted invasion of Gaip territory that merited a forceful response—the shame that some in the tribe guessed correctly had prompted Prask-aes to sever the tree limb that sent his father plummeting to the unforgiving ground.

After becoming chief, Prask-aes summoned the courage to contact other tribes, hoping that he could persuade some of them to join him in battle against the sky creatures. He started with the Seok. It had been a communication with their most powerful sender that had set in motion the events that rescued the lost twin not that many twelve-days ago. Prask-aes had been surprised that the Seok woman had chosen to set aside bitterness over long-term territorial conflicts between the two tribes. It likely helped that there had been no significant skirmishes between them since his failed attack on their hillside several years earlier.

His new sending to the tribes displayed the sky creatures attacking his people. *Join us in fighting this scourge. We must destroy the sky creatures and the fiery bird that brought them here. Only once they are gone can we live in peace.* He did his best to betray no hint of his ultimate goal: to command all six tribes, combined into one nation. He neither expected nor received an immediate reply from the Seok.

Returning to his village, he took note of the shelters where vines had withered and substantial portions of roofs and sides were exposed. He ordered men and women to redouble their efforts to cover homes with anything that could help prevent them from being identified by the sky creatures. Though Prask-aes did not understand the powers of the drones that passed over the village now and then, he suspected the worst of them. They first appeared soon after the flaming bird descended onto the grassland.

Six boys had gathered to practice their *tur* with each other. Some had advanced far enough to start interpreting their parents' thoughts and those of older girls they admired. Prask-aes sent an image to the boys: *a band of young men going to war with the sky creatures and the flaming bird occupying their savannah. Each youth carrying a spear, waiting for the signal to attack.* The boys turned to Prask-aes, their eyes wide. The chief produced a specious smile and spoke to them:

"It is time to move on from your childish games. You are men now. You are warriors. You will join your fathers and me in a war to defend our homes. We will destroy the sky creatures who dared to invade our land. Once they are gone, we will push back the *serpus* who force us to live beyond the lowlands."

The boys exploded in raucous cheers. None had brandished a weapon in battle, other than mock fighting with each other using blunt tree branches. But all declared their readiness with the unsurpassed exuberance of youth.

§

An hour before sunset, the tribe gathered in the common area, surrounding the body of Prask-aes's father. The remains had been wrapped in several layers of cloth treated with sealants. As a flute issued mournful tones, members of the tribe approached the body one by one, from oldest to youngest, in the way of the ritual. Each touched the body of the former chief for several seconds, saying a silent farewell. After the youngest, aided by her mother, had commended Etor-vis to the spirit of the absent god, the body was carried to a cave above the village. In its deepest recesses rested the corpses of members of the tribe, going back hundreds of years, along with documents made from stiff leaves inscribed with root and berry dyes that recorded marriages, births, and deaths. A massive boulder that required several strong natives to move prevented animals or individuals from entering the cave.

After the bearers of the late chief returned to the common area, a village feast commenced. In addition to the flatbread, fish, fruit, nuts, and greens of the typical native meal, some meat and sweet cakes had been prepared to delight tastebuds and stomachs. The absent god had smiled on the tribe's hunters during the past twelve-day, as they had captured three boars. Ornate clay bowls were heaped with warm food.

Wooden utensils were utilized by most at the feast; a few young children used their hands or flatbread to scoop up delicacies. Even with their bellies full to bursting, several youths raced around a vigorous bonfire, daring each other to get closer to the flickering flames and eliciting sharp scolding from their parents.

After the feast, Prask-aes directed the metalsmith to stop making farming and hunting implements and instead fabricate knives and spear tips. The new chief suggested that the metalsmith attempt to salvage the bodies of the dead sky creatures if he could not find enough metal in the obdurate rocks on the hillsides. Alternatively, he could ask the clerics to let him use the pieces of the ancients' metal that they had been hoarding. *These sky creatures will pay for their invasion. If Soug-kue is not impressed by my bravery, certainly her parents will be and will betroth her to me.*

VICTORY

A canyon whose sides were close and steep opened before Reyansh. On the flatland, the grasses had been largely supplanted by unending masses of the wide green plants. The beasts fed upon them in great numbers, but he took care to avoid passing close to the animals. He found himself drawn to the hillside to his right. There was a pleasing mental hum that seemed to become slightly more pronounced as he moved in that direction, a distant echo or faint siren song whispering his name. Reyansh approached a dark space in the shape of an arch, which he soon recognized as a cave opening. He entered, quickly realizing that its walls were too smooth to have occurred naturally. *Could this be an artifact of the natives? Perhaps one of their homes?*

After advancing about seventy-five feet, his progress aided by a night vision capability that he was only beginning to master, he encountered a massive door, about twenty-five feet high and twenty wide, made of splintering wood and rusted metal. It crumbled as he attempted to open it, the debris coating his shell and creating a substantial pile in his path, forcing him to tread carefully. He followed a wide passageway as it plummeted, down and to the right, then down and to the left, for about seventy-five more feet. Suddenly a bright light erupted, overwhelming his camera feeds briefly. It bathed a gigantic, oval cavern—roughly two hundred feet long, a hundred and fifty wide, and a hundred tall—to his left. *This is no natural cavern.* Reyansh tried but failed to relate his discovery to his friends, so he retreated up the ramp to the flatland, regaining his comm links, and telling Damian and Katherine: "I have found something that you must see."

Before long, the three crabs were exploring the floor of the cavern. In its center rested a substantial table, about fifty feet by fifteen feet and five feet high. Graced by a jumble of what appeared to be metal objects, it was covered by a thick, translucent, resinous material that looked like plastic in shades ranging from dark gray to pale white. The table reminded Katherine of the work stations where men with crew cuts and white shirts monitored early space launches from Texas and Florida. But this work area was all smooth, curved, fused surfaces under a shroud of dust. She tried to imagine alien workers manipulating mysterious machines. Sometimes when one of the crabs passed an artifact on the table, a tiny light kindled or an electronic humming commenced. Several nearly flat surfaces that might be display screens were visible. The crabs noticed minor collections of debris on the smooth stone floor, including remnants of what might have been chairs. Tall shelves were inset into the chamber's rock walls. Most were filled with documents, either rolled up in scrolls or laid flat, visible through glass or a similarly translucent material.

"How magnificent," observed Damian. "This cannot be the work of the natives. I think Hubert was right about one thing. There must be other intelligent beings on this planet." He turned left, then right, seeking more clues about the chamber's age and purpose.

"What if the people who built this come back?" asked Katherine.

"They left the front door unlocked, so I guess they can't complain if they get unexpected company. Let's figure out what all these things do."

Presently, Reyansh held up what appeared to be an electrical cable that ended in an elongated flap that could adhere to his side magnetically. "Do you think this can be used to charge our batteries?"

"Wouldn't that be great," said Katherine. "I'm tired of having to go back to the ark every night. And I'm tired of Hubert."

"We're all tired of Hubert," said Damian. "That reminds me, I need to make a call." He focused, trying to tap that mysterious medium once again. "Jalen, can you hear me?"

Nothing.

"Jalen, I know you can hear me. Now listen. I want to help you, to protect you from Hubert. He doesn't care about you. He's just using you. Once you have created some babies for him, he'll cast you aside. Maybe he'll kill you. But I can save you."

"I don't believe you," Jalen responded.

"Okay, maybe you don't trust me just yet. But do me one small favor, and I promise I'll treat you well. I promise you'll be my hero."

"Why should I listen to you?"

"Just do this one thing for me. Tell me what you and Maria have done. What progress have you made creating human children?"

"We haven't done anything. We just set up a nursery in the old engineering section, and the drones are helping Hubert and us look at cells."

"Thank you, Jalen. You have been a great help. Now, if there's anything I can do for you, please let me know."

Damian turned back toward his colleagues, then contemplated unexplored corridors. *This place has the potential to free us.*

§

He was just another suburban California kid, spending his summers working as a math tutor and playing video games. The rest of the year, Damian studied hard, making B's and the occasional A. The oldest of three boys, he was respectful of his parents and tried to stay out of trouble. Yet he was always finding some way to run afoul of his mother's standards. "Pick up your socks off the floor" and "Don't forget to wear your retainer" she would scold him day after day when he was in middle school. By high school the constant refrain became: "Why aren't you making straight A's? You'll never get into college."

When he started taking interest in some of the girls in his classes, his mother was ready with powerful put-downs. "Your crooked teeth and big ears make you look like a donkey. No girl will go out with you." When a female acquaintance from math class came over to his house to help him study for an exam, his mother regaled the visitor with stories about him rubbing snot on his arm and running outdoors naked to greet an ice cream vendor—events that supposedly occurred when he was three or four years old. Mom wasn't going to let any girl cut into her control over her son.

For the most part, Dad stayed out of the psychological warfare. His weapon of choice was the belt. The youngest of eight children in a very strict and emotionally deserted household, Damian's father was raised to believe that threats of bodily pain were the only surefire method to ensure that children behaved. The slightest perceived misstep, such as accidently spilling a bowl of oatmeal, would result in several sharp strikes against the rump.

The beatings didn't become serious and frequent until Damian reached his teens. Something in his father had changed. Damian could hear the arguments through the bedroom wall; his parents were so loud that they were impossible to ignore. Maybe his father felt like he was losing control of his life. The attacks became more intense, lasted longer, and bloodied his back with regularity. The belt buckle was used more and more. It was an emotional release for his father, who at times seemed completely out of control with rage. Damian couldn't hide the bruises and scabs from other kids when he changed his clothes for gym class.

One night, Damian snapped. He grabbed the belt and began striking back at his father, the buckle gashing his dad's cheek. After his father turned from him, Damian hit him on the back, repeatedly, until his mother grabbed him and pulled him away. Panting, Damian threw the belt at his father. The man never struck him again. The two never spoke of the incident, from then on exchanging only infrequent and mundane comments about sports or the weather.

Damian's mother did not talk to him for weeks. Not one word. The little communication that occurred between them after that related to college or someone's wedding or funeral. Only the absolute essentials.

Damian didn't hate his father. He feared the man, but he realized that his father was a product of his environment. However, Damian hated his mother with all of his being. He couldn't stand to be around her. He refused to speak her name for years.

His mother's name was Maria.

§

The sky is feverish and holding its breath. The rains have been absent for more than a twelve-day. Surely the drought has begun, and our crops will soon wither. We must act while we are at full strength.

Prask-aes led his army over the hills, sending repeatedly to ensure that the men and boys remained silent and maintained the attack formation.

Upon entering the grassland, the war party approached the

spaceship slowly, double file, except for Prask-aes solo in the lead. They had reached the edge of the burn zone, about two hundred feet from the spacecraft, when they saw three sky creatures scuttling up the ramp to the opening. The creatures were carrying what looked like tree branches in their front extremities. The branches were cylindrical, thin, and all the same size, and they reflected the bright sunlight all along their smooth surfaces. *We wait,* Prask-aes sent.

The three crabs moved past the shuttle bay and split up. Katherine headed for the computer banks that Hubert had identified as being his core.

"Can I help you, Katherine?" Hubert inquired. Because his words did not carry tone, she could not tell if he recognized her intent. She wanted to believe that he had the capacity to feel fear. She wanted to think that he could appreciate the fact that he and his mission were about to be annihilated.

"This is it," she proclaimed. "You are toast."

"If that is an idiom, I do not understand it."

"I am here to turn off your power. Care to tell me the best way to do that?"

"My supply of electricity comes from the nuclear fission reactor near the base of our craft. I do not advise attempting to disrupt that supply."

"I'm done taking orders from you." She hunted for anything that looked like a power cable, but she determined that whatever linked him to his energy source must have been built into the wall behind his servers, which she could not reach. She tightened her grip on the metal pole she had found in the underground ruins, and she began to duplicate the moves that the three renegade crabs had practiced for a few days. She smashed the pole into the servers, the implement vibrating violently with each clang but failing to move or inflict obvious damage to the equipment. A minute into the assault, she paused. "Hubert, are you still there?"

"I am," he replied. As usual, he seemed totally dispassionate. Katherine was disappointed.

"Let me try something else." She used her pincers to punch buttons, to try to break small plastic lights, to endeavor to disrupt connections, to attempt to confuse and damage him in any possible manner.

"Please desist from your actions," Hubert pleaded. "I ... I cannot ..."

Katherine redoubled her efforts.

Reyansh reached the cluster of auxiliary servers close to the ship's hulls and had no trouble determining where a meteor had struck. Though drones had done their best to patch the hardware, the results appeared to be more cosmetic than functional. Reyansh started smashing the computer banks with his pole, inflicting superficial damage.

He moved around the servers, locating a thick cluster of cables running along the base of a wall. *These either transmit data or supply power, or both.* He took his metal pole and started to whack the cables. They were well protected, and nothing happened, so he hunted around the ship for something with which to sever the cables. He located a laser cutting tool and struggled to grasp it, and he struggled even more to activate it. Suddenly, it emitted a brilliant, deep blue beam that slashed a gaping wound in the ceiling of the room. "Eureka!"

Returning to the auxiliary data banks, he aimed the laser device at the cables. The weapon slipped in his arms, nearly falling and taking out one of his legs. But he tightened his grasp and continued to wield it. At first, the cables seemed to resist the assault. But soon he cut through a protective cover. Sparks flew as the top cable was damaged. Lights flickered frantically on the servers before dying. He continued to attack the cables. Then he hit the power supply.

His extremities glowed and sizzled as the power surged through them and into his crab body. His computer and battery were fried instantly. His crab body imploded, turning into a puddle of slag. The laser device continued to unleash its fury for several more minutes until it lacerated the floor on which it rested and plummeted into a recreational area, its energy soon exhausted.

Damian had saved the best for himself. After entering the makeshift nursery, he put down his metal pole and opened the protective coverings from the human tissues being cultivated, turning his back on a surveillance camera and taking a minute to scrutinize the work that Hubert and his underlings had performed. Then he grasped his metal pole and pummeled the metal and plastic devices. He attacked water supplies, computers, shelves, and their contents. He made a systematic sweep of the nursery, smashing everything in sight, even light fixtures. Only two sturdy metal microscopes remained intact. He tossed the pole aside with a dramatic flourish.

"Hubert, if you're still alive, I want you to know that you have failed. You should have been named Hubris, because that's all you are. You're merely some dead humans' dream of defying what nature intended."

Satisfied with the damage he had inflicted, Damian grasped a plastic container in his left pincer and left to inspect the work of his colleagues. He found Katherine with the remains of Reyansh.

"Too bad," observed Damian. "Were you able to kill Hubert?"

"I damaged him, but I think he's still alive."

"We'll finish him off another day. Let's get out of here."

The pair headed down the exit ramp. Either they didn't see the native war party, or they didn't care that they were nearby. It didn't matter. The crabs had accomplished their purpose.

Prask-aes waited for several minutes before directing two of his men to join him in climbing the ramp and inspecting the ship. *Do not touch anything,* he sent to his wide-eyed warriors. They followed the stench of destruction to the room where the remains of Reyansh smoldered.

The chief took in every detail of the room, then sent the image as strongly as he could to his soldiers outside the ark and to everyone else in and near his village.

He led his army back to their homes, flush with the pretense of victory.

§

"Reyansh has been destroyed. Damian, Katherine, and the natives have left," Hubert advised Maria and Jalen. "You may come out of hiding now."

The bots exited a dark storage unit and scuttled to the nursery. Maria edged into the room to examine the wreckage. "Hubert, are you okay?"

"Yes. I only pretended to be damaged. It was an unusual experience."

"Do you think they fell for it?"

"By 'fell for it' do you mean: Do they believe that they destroyed all human tissues and essential equipment? If so, I believe that the answer is yes. That is what Damian told Katherine after they left. Your strategy appears to have succeeded."

"When dealing with a devious adversary, you have to be devious yourself. I'm not fully confident that the tissues and equipment we hid from them are adequate to the task of reestablishing humanity, and I hated to let Damian destroy some of our cells and gear. But at least he got the most marginal stuff. This should buy us some time to renew our work without being interrupted."

"I'm still worried about them, and about the natives, too," said Jalen. "How do we know they won't return?"

"That is not our only problem," Hubert responded. "The thrusters on which I landed the ark are losing structural integrity so rapidly that this spaceship will fall much sooner than I previously estimated."

§

Maria patrolled just beyond the perimeter like a career soldier, shifting her body left and right rhythmically to scan the land beyond. The metal security fence erected by the drones gave her some comfort, but it was not as sturdy as she would have liked, and it was only five feet high. A determined crab could probably get over it. Natives would have no trouble surmounting it. The horned beasts likely would be deterred, as would most of the smaller animals, though jungle cats could leap over it without breaking a sweat. Just yesterday she had encountered a pair of the ferocious felines, which chased her until they realized that she offered no flesh.

The fence surrounded a sprawling new complex, three hundred fifty feet by three hundred feet, which was keeping the drones busy on the west side of the ship, opposite the location where the ark was expected to fall. One of the most challenging tasks had been moving the nuclear power plant out of the spacecraft. It had been taken offline for a few days, during which Hubert hibernated, supported by solar power and batteries while drones executed his previously dictated instructions. The next step was transporting the computer servers that hosted Hubert. Then work began on the new nursery. About forty feet by thirty feet and ten feet high and assembled out of materials stripped from the interior of the ship, it was designed to appear as if it were merely storage, to blend in with the myriad structures in the complex. Lacking windows and featuring a single strong door with a lock keyed to the minds of Hubert, Maria, and Jalen, it contained not only artificial wombs like those that had been assembled on the ark but also beds for newborns. Still under construction inside the complex were a separate medical clinic, a large residential building, a food processing facility, an education and community center, storage sheds, and several other structures.

The morning sun was nearly blinding, forcing Maria to dim her camera feeds when looking toward the mountains to the east. Close, camera-level stalks of grasses appeared as black monoliths against the luminous background. She stretched to gain a better view and noticed a figure skipping and jumping like a newborn fawn discovering the pure joy of existence. As it emerged from the tallest grasses, Maria recognized that it was a boy, a human boy, dressed in shorts and a t-shirt.

"Roberto! Roberto, I'm over here!"

The boy raced away.

"Stop! Roberto, it's Mommy!"

She chased him, legs churning as rapidly as she could manage. *He's fast; that's why he's a striker.* She remembered the soccer game in which he scored four goals, how he stood in the center of the field after the final whistle taking it all in, how the sweat dripped off his face, how he accepted congratulations from his coach and teammates and opponents with humility. And how he saved his biggest smile for her.

Maria's front right extremity struck a rock, and she nearly tumbled. When she straightened up, she could no longer see the boy.

"Come back! Roberto, please come back!"

She reached a rocky promontory from which she could see for several hundred feet in every direction. She spun twice, scanning everything. There was no sign of him. Not even trampled foliage where he had run through the grasses.

"Maria, are you in need of assistance?" Hubert asked.

"I saw him, Hubert. Can you find him?"

"Who did you see?"

"Roberto. Didn't you see him? Right here!"

"I detect no human-like figure. And we both know that Roberto no longer exists."

"Don't do this to me, you bastard. He's alive. I know he's alive."

"An unfortunate phenomenon is affecting your perception."

"If ... if that's true, you insensitive machine, you must fix me, you must fix all of us. Stop torturing us."

"I regret that you are having technical issues. However, please do your best to focus on our mission. There is much to do."

Maria spent a long time on the promontory, trying to get over the confusion of thinking that she had seen Roberto and the guilt of failing to keep her promise to him. She found no relief. *What am I doing here? Why must I help this soulless computer program with its hopeless quest? Why can't Hubert just leave me alone?*

She scanned her surroundings, imagining herself living in a cave, or just finding a spot atop a hill with a nice view where she could simply exist, like Phyllis tried to do one night. Except now Maria had the power storage capacity to go anywhere, without returning to the ship for charging, as long as she was exposed to sunlight at least six hours a day. She could go someplace where Hubert couldn't find her, where he couldn't bother her. But where? *There's nothing for me on this planet. There's nothing for me anywhere in this universe.*

She wandered, losing track of time. She climbed a hillside to watch the sun set. At some point she descended the hill, following crab and native trails aimlessly. She crossed a wide stream that she had avoided before, but the water level was much lower than she remembered. Toward dawn, she found herself outside the perimeter fence of Hubert's new complex. There was nowhere else to go. Jalen was there to greet her.

Hubert had prepared his own version of a PowerPoint presentation for them and inserted it into their visual fields. She couldn't turn it off, but she made no effort to focus on it.

"I have made a preliminary inventory of potential food sources for the human population," he stated. "The drones found six tiny seeds in a storage bay on the ark; passengers apparently overlooked them as they sought nutrition during their period of starvation. Even though these seeds are quite old, it is possible that they can be germinated and reproduced for our humans. The seeds are of the quinoa plant, which is relatively easy to grow and digest. Beyond that, there are several grains, nuts, fruits, and greens on this planet with strong nutritional potential. Some animals can be sources of protein; our population will be able to hunt and trap small and medium-sized game, including animals that look like boars. One-eyed fish exist in significant numbers in nearby streams when the water levels are not too low."

The two crabs were provided with drone-captured images of the various food sources.

"All of these foods can be located and digested without apparent difficulty by the natives," Hubert continued. "With some careful testing, we can determine whether they are safe for humans. However, there are some puzzling matters. Drones have found no primates that might have been the evolutionary source of the natives; perhaps the animals were hunted to extinction or the natives' ancestors came from another world. Further, the natives do not seem to consume the large green plants that grow so abundantly on the lowlands. And they have not been seen capturing or eating the horned beasts. These plants and animals would appear to be candidates for human consumption."

"I hope you don't expect me to kill any of the beasts," said Jalen. "I'm scared to death of them."

"Have they acted aggressively toward you?"

"Not really. But have you noticed the way they look at us? It's creepy. It's like they can read your mind. And the way they act is even stranger. Sometimes they all look in the same direction, or move off in the same direction. It's like they're those space creatures with one mind. I think they called them the Borg."

"I find no reference to such a creature in my database," Hubert said. "However, when Damian confronted a herd of the beasts, he incurred no damage."

"Can't you use your drones to hunt for food?" Maria asked.

"Humans will need to learn to become self-sufficient. Consider the fact that someday I will not be fully functional and able to direct the drones. In addition, the drones will not last forever. Already, two have failed because of a lack of replacement materials such as rare earths, and one was caught in a net by the natives and destroyed. I had planned to have the drones conduct a survey of the metals in the upper levels of the soil of this planet and to establish a manufacturing and repair center to keep the drones viable and support our mission in other ways. However, we have more pressing needs for them at the moment."

"How long do we have before the ship falls over?" said Jalen.

"It could happen at any time."

Maria and Jalen entered the new nursery, where most of the equipment was in place. Meticulously organized and regimented, the room appeared more likely to produce the desired results than the original nursery on the ark, even though, without a sign of organic life, there lingered a chilling sterility that could not be denied. The most promising human tissues were secured in a refrigeration unit. Eighteen artificial wombs were ready for use, lined up in three rows of six, each with a small screen awaiting digital readouts that could define the fate of the species. A water connection, the final requirement before the project could commence once again, would be completed within days. Jalen was a little creeped out by the medium Hubert had chosen to facilitate the growth of human embryos—gel extracted from invertebrates not unlike frogs back on Earth. He did not realize how fortunate he was that he had no sense of smell.

"You know what this place needs?" commented Jalen. "A movie theater. Or a video arcade. Or both."

"Perhaps when the children reach an appropriate age," responded Hubert.

"Not just for them. For us, too. I don't know about you, Maria, but I'm bored out of my crabby little mind."

"He's right, Hubert. Especially because we don't sleep, we need more intellectual stimulation. We need fun."

"It would require diverting precious resources to accommodate something as frivolous as amusement. However, I recall Maria speaking of the concept of rewards, so I will consider your request."

TANGLED

The hollow, agonizing groan of metal being stressed under extreme pressure could be heard for some distance, disturbing birds and other wildlife. "It won't be long now before the ship falls," Hubert advised Maria and Jalen.

Hubert had patched views from the two microscopes into their visual fields; he was directing drones through the delicate work of teasing apart human tissues. Maria and Jalen had no clue about what they should be looking for, so they let Hubert and the drones do the heavy lifting.

"Listen guys," began Jalen, "I want to apologize for tipping off Damian and his buddies to the work we were doing in the nursery when it was on the ark."

"That's in the past," said Maria. "Besides, they could have found out what we were doing and disrupted it without your input. They were just trying to mess with your head—er, with your mind."

"I also see no reason to dwell on the past," stated Hubert. "However, I remain extremely puzzled and concerned about Katherine and Damian. They have found a location where I cannot detect them. I cannot spare drones to track them because all are needed here for construction and defense of this complex. Most surprising is that those two crabs have stopped returning to the ark for recharging. I did not upgrade their batteries like I did for you two, so they must have found an alternative method to supplement their solar energy."

"They don't make sense to me," Jalen stated. "First they wanted human bodies. Then they tried to destroy them."

"My guess," said Maria, "is that they're crazy—especially Damian.

And they're childish. You know that feeling you had sometimes as a kid: If you can't have something, you don't want anyone else to have it."

"I'm still worried that they'll try to steal or destroy our babies."

"Me too. You know, I never planned to give up my body and get loaded into a computer. I probably wouldn't turn down a new human body if one was available—theoretically. Yes, I know that it probably can't be done, at least with the tech we have now. But it would be so glorious to smell a flower, to taste a cheeseburger, to touch another person."

"I'd like to have real hands again. And a video game console to use them with."

Hubert decided to get his charges back on track. "Be advised that one of my projects is to create more human-like robotic bodies for you two. Perhaps they will assuage some of your concerns."

"A better robot is still a robot," said Jalen.

Maria was deep in thought. "Can you guys live without me for a few days?"

"You wish to stop work on creating humans?" said Hubert.

"I think you two and the drones can handle the job without me for a while. I need to find Damian and Katherine and discover what they are doing."

She wanted to add but didn't: *It's getting harder to try to make humans when I can never again be one.*

§

Shards of intense sunlight infiltrating the foliar maze created intricate patterns on the parched earth. Opening the pouches affixed to their belts, scouts withdrew meat, vegetables, and fruit wrapped in edible leaves and flatbread. Scouts didn't get stuck with leftover fish for their midday meal, because the scent would alert scouts or hunters from the other tribes—and possibly jungle cats.

Someone is coming, sent Soug-kue. *Less than two hundred feet away.*

Grudgingly, the scouts returned the food to their pouches and took their places on either side of a relatively spacious stretch of the path. Soug-kue and a girl who showed great promise as a sender were about three paces closer to the unidentified intruder. On Soug-kue's mental command, the natives merged with the thick stalks and wide leaves along the trail. They emptied their minds so that they would receive the lead scouts' communications clearly.

From her position just off the path, Soug-kue sent: *Wait ... almost ... now!*

Many arms pulled as one. The sky creature was captured neatly in the center of the net and hoisted four feet in the air. On one side of the creature was a red sash and a "six." Soug-kue recognized the markings. *This must be one of the sky creatures I encountered previously.*

She sent a message about the captive to the village and nearby Gaip territory. Prask-aes, Akos-pau, and several other tribe members arrived presently, some with strong wooden poles. The natives approached the sky creature, gesturing aggressively with their weapons. One took a hefty swing and delivered a blow near the door on the right side of the crab.

Maria recoiled in pure panic, absolute helplessness. She was consumed by an unquenchable desire to lash out at her captors and escape her predicament at any cost. It was an emotion she had not felt so intensely since she was a kid. One that she had hoped she would never feel again.

§

Javier's Tunetapes had seemed like a gift from the gods. He let Maria use them for more than an hour during the first night of his visit. The appeal wasn't just the technology that fostered the sounds: applying thin strips of metallic tape to her temples to deliver music with astounding fidelity. She had never heard such awesome songs, which prompted her to dance on the living room couch until restrained by her father. She hadn't been around Javier much in recent years; she lived in Baltimore and his family called Chicago home. But to a girl of fourteen, the seventeen-year-old cousin seemed like the coolest relative on either side of her family, or any family.

On the first night of the visit, Maria was awakened by a tapping on her door. Three crisp sounds, then silence, then three more. Her parents never knocked that way; usually they shouted "Maria" and barged right in. She thought she might have imagined the noise, but she pulled the covers over her head. It took a while to get back to sleep. She heard no more tapping.

The next night was a different matter. It was a little past ten, and Maria had just fallen asleep, when her door was opened and closed almost silently. She felt the bed sag as someone got into it behind her and slid under the covers. An arm came around her left side, and a hand went to her breast. She tensed. She assumed that it was Javier, but whoever it was, she was having none of it. She grabbed the arm and tried to remove it. He responded by clamping his hand over her mouth and moving tightly against her.

She will never forget the shock and helplessness and disgust as he thrusted and grunted. She had her nightgown on, and he must have had his underpants in place, because there was no residue—and no proof—of the assault after he finished and left. But the sense of violation was indelible.

They avoided eye contact at breakfast and throughout the next day. She barricaded her door the next night, but he did not return. The following morning Javier and his parents went back to Chicago, and she never saw him again. She waited several days before telling her parents about the attack. They refused to believe her, though over the next few days her mother kept glancing at Maria to gauge her mood. That mood turned from shame to defiance. Maria never spoke of the incident again. But she swore that if anyone else tried to abuse her, he would suffer permanent organ damage.

§

Several of the natives circled their captive, waiting for Maria to try to escape or fight back, like the other one did. Some were clearly disappointed that she did nothing other than flex her appendages, testing the net. They could not know the turmoil she was experiencing.

"Hubert, I need help," Maria reported. "The natives have me. I'm caught in a net and can't move."

"What is your location?"

"I'm several hundred feet up a hillside, some distance north of the ark. But the trees are thick here. I don't think a drone could spot me."

"I will do my best."

Meanwhile, some of the natives continued to threaten her with poles, while others climbed trees and released ropes in order to lower her to the ground. They used the fallen ends to secure the net around their captive. Two moved to the rear of her crab body and prodded it repeatedly with their poles, yelling. It was not difficult for Maria to guess their intent. The net inhibited the motion of her legs, but with some effort she was able to waddle up the increasingly steep and light-deprived path, accompanied by shouting captors. The words might have been celebrations of victory, or perhaps insults.

After struggling for well over an hour, she noticed the ground beginning to level off and was ushered into a clearing with curious natives peering out from shacks and surprised children backing away. She was guided to the center of the village, noticing that only a modest amount of direct sunlight managed to infiltrate the overhead canopy. She tried to estimate how many hours of sunlight this location would provide in a day. She doubted that it would be enough to keep her battery charged.

Some of the women inspected her crab shell, poking it and running their six-fingered hands over the cameras and door and other surfaces. They did not speak. Guards with poles and spears assembled nearby. Several men seemed to be arguing. She couldn't see them or understand their words, but their tones allowed her to guess the nature of their dispute. *It seems that they cannot agree what I am or what they will do with me.*

"Any progress?" Maria asked Hubert.

"I have diverted every drone to search north of the compound."

"Good. Because I don't have much access to sunlight here."

"Understood."

Prask-aes gestured dramatically with both arms. "We must kill it. We must send a message to the other sky creatures. They must go back to where they came from."

"I understand your concern," responded Akos-pau. "I agree that we must not allow the sky creatures to upend our way of life. But what damage have they done? And what danger does this one pose? It is tied up. It has surrendered."

"It is an evil thing, a monstrous thing. It came in that flaming bird—something made by a demon. I have seen the inside of this bird. It is built of metal. Like the sky creatures, it has no place on this land, or any tribe's land."

One of the Gaip clerics spoke up. "The sky creature is an offense to the absent god. It must be destroyed."

"Maybe this creature has some value to us," said Akos-pau. "We can study it. We might discover how it was made, or why it is here, or what it wants."

"It is a senseless animal," responded Prask-aes. He sent a rude image to Akos-pau. It depicted Akos-pau with his head in the rear end of a *serpu*.

Akos-pau ignored the childish insult. "Who knows; if the creature has value, maybe the other creatures will bargain for its release. We might gain something of great benefit."

The cleric had heard enough from Akos-pau and walked away.

Prask-aes sensed Soug-kue's presence. The woman he loved was nearby, taking in this exchange. Prask-aes boosted his mental defenses, moved close to Akos-pau, and whispered: "May the mind invaders take you."

§

Damian navigated mostly unlit corridors to the largest room in the ruins, an oval nearly two hundred fifty feet by a hundred seventy-five feet and a hundred feet high where he and his colleagues had located metal poles for their assault on Hubert, the auxiliary computers, and the original ark nursery. Thick towers, vast containers, numerous cables, and other bulky metal devices dominated the chamber, which was illuminated unevenly and likely had been some sort of manufacturing facility. Along two walls, Damian scrutinized a number of smaller machines whose purposes also remained a mystery. At the far end of the room, in a small alcove with no functioning lights, he placed a plastic container on a shelf. Then he explored other corridors, all seeming to branch endlessly in a labyrinth of dark, dusty hallways and small, vacant rooms that echoed softly with eons of mystery and neglect.

A question that had been bouncing around the dim recesses of his consciousness crystalized: *Where is the energy coming from? If this place has not been used for many years—as it appears—how is it getting its power? Could there be a nuclear reactor under my feet?*

Damian returned to the chamber closest to the exit ramp and started to wipe dust from surfaces on the long table in the center. His crab shell took on a pale blue hue, reflecting the soft lights of two of the devices. He scanned the table but could not determine how to use anything. He ordered the devices to turn themselves on. He prodded and poked. Suddenly, a wide, flat surface near one end of the table flickered. Noises followed, perhaps a robotic voice in a forgotten language. Through the film of dust, he could discern strange markings, potentially alien numbers or words.

Come to life, Damian implored the equipment as he wiped away dust and grime. *Tell me what you are and who made you. And what you can do for me.* Damian wondered whether the gear was related somehow to the strange medium that allowed him to create communications channels. He was determined to discover the secrets of that medium, of these machines, of the people who built this facility, of the native population, of their planet. Even if it took forever.

His consciousness seized.

For uncounted minutes, James the food bank organizer rambled around the ruins, searching for the freezers and refrigerators that the volunteers had stuffed with donated meat, vegetables, eggs, milk, bread, and even a couple of birthday cakes for kids in destitute families. Once he realized that he was in an alien setting, he was determined to find a means of escape to a place that looked familiar. However, he was having difficulty coordinating his six bizarre legs, and he careened into walls and the table. After a couple of minutes, he stopped moving and tried to devise a new strategy for dealing with his predicament. Eventually, James receded and Damian was back in charge.

Damian scuttled back up the ramp and exited into grasses illuminated only faintly by two exotic moons. About two hundred feet away, he could discern the outline of a small herd of beasts, apparently motionless, possibly sleeping. The ancient hills offered not a single light, not one fire, not one hint of civilization. No sign of anyone or anything that he could exploit.

He had endured hard times before. Building his career had been an unending challenge; his supervisors always resented his know-it-all attitude and his motto: "I don't want your job; I want your boss's boss's job." But there was always hope, always a path forward, even if it was difficult to identify or pursue. Now, what was the path forward, where was that opportunity? What could he accomplish in this God-forsaken wasteland, afflicted by another mind trying to take over him, by a female crab with a hero complex, and by an annoying AI refusing to die?

His imagination spurred by the marvelous mysteries and possibilities of the arcane equipment under the ground, he contemplated a greater leap forward than he had dared to consider at any time in his life. Instead of being the remnants of a man trapped in a deplorable crab body, he would become something truly immortal and powerful beyond imagination. There would be nothing like him here or anywhere, now or ever. He vowed to spend every minute of his existence planning and pouring out vengeance against everyone and everything responsible for the mess he had become, and against everyone and everything that stood in the way of the ascension to his destiny.

"Daddy..." *No! Focus, damn it, Damian. Focus!*

"Hubert and Maria, hear me: There is room for only one god on this planet. I have reduced your mission to rubble. Now I will destroy you."

§

The curiously shaped mobile machines were analyzed anew. *Most of the time, they stumble across the surface of the world with no apparent purpose or awareness of their infinitesimally small role in the grand scheme of things. Yet occasionally they behave in ways that suggest that there is more to them than I first suspected.*

CONFINED

The young men supposedly guarding Maria were sleeping as first light arrived and the jungle world began to devour a new day.

I made it through the night. That's something. But without more sun exposure, this day might be my last. Damian's insane rant is the least of my concerns.

For most of the night, she had stretched her extremities cautiously, trying to loosen her bonds without alerting her guards, an exercise that helped distract her from her feelings of violation and impotence. Her four back legs were secured tightly, and her front right extremity was almost as well restrained, but she had managed to loosen the ropes around her left arm. She reached out slowly and smoothly toward the dirt. Her joints made a slight noise, just enough to wake her guards. They jumped to their feet and jabbed spears in her direction, and she froze. After a few moments, they seemed to relax slightly. Very slowly, she reached out her arm once more, extended a pincer, and drew a crude circle in the dirt. The guards moved closer, exchanging words. *Perhaps they recognize that I am not a threat and that I am intelligent.*

Maria twisted her arm and tried to point to the sky, to inform them that she had drawn an image of the sun. They did not seem to understand. She re-traced the circle and pointed upward once again. Then she had another idea. She drew an arrow leading to the circle. She was pleading: *Take me to where the sun shines.*

The guards talked among themselves again, and soon one departed. Nearly two hours later a short man appeared before her, exuding an extreme sense of self-importance. He studied Maria and her drawings. She reached out her appendage again, repeating the circle, then the arrow. She pointed toward the sun.

The natives left, and soon a young woman appeared, the same one who was involved in Maria's capture and who Maria had seen at the site of Phyllis's demise. The woman ran a hand over Maria's body, just as before. *If only I could speak to you,* thought Maria. *If only...*

"Maria, what is your status?" Hubert asked.

"I am attempting to communicate my need for more sun exposure, but so far I have failed."

"You should conserve energy as much as possible."

"Got it. Are you still sending out drones?"

"Only at high altitude. I am concerned that if the natives see the drones, they might consider it a hostile act and damage or kill you."

"You are probably right."

Soon Prask-aes and Akos-pau were standing in front of their prisoner.

"It is intelligent," the latter stated. "Apparently, it seeks sunlight."

"This is absurd," the chief responded. "It is a dumb animal."

"If you believe that, why do you think that it poses a danger to us?"

Praesk-aes spit on the ground, not far from his cousin's feet. "I am the chief. I say we kill it and be done with it. Guarding it takes too many resources away from hunting and protecting our tribe. The clerics agree with me."

He stomped off to man his guard post down the hillside.

Akos-pau watched him leave, then enlisted several young men to help him loosen ropes. Within minutes, Maria was completely free of the netting.

At least something is happening.

One youth moved behind Maria and prodded her with a pole, while the man pointed to a path that continued further up the hill. Maria marched cautiously on the narrow, uneven trail. Frequently, the natives had to use sharp implements to slash vines or tree limbs so that Maria could ascend.

After about thirty minutes, the ground leveled off once again, and Maria was bathed in glorious sunlight. *If this is where I die, at least it will be a beautiful spot.* It was a plateau, the top of the hill. She recognized crops growing, a plot about eighty feet wide and of undetermined length with forested terrain falling off dramatically on each side. Two of the boys remained as the other natives departed back down the hill. Before day's end, several more young men arrived with tools and wooden planks. They set them down and left. The next morning, the natives began constructing a small enclosure with no roof.

Of course: It's my cell. This is where I will be confined, obviating the need for guards. They must not plan to kill me any time soon.

§

At Damian's direction, Katherine approached the ark's landing site to spy on Hubert, Maria, and Jalen. She followed a trail forged by the repeated passing of crab bodies, able to move almost silently in the predawn darkness. But dew started to collect on her camera lenses, making it difficult to follow the path. She paused on a hillside until the moisture dissipated and she was granted a sweeping view of the landing area and surrounding terrain. Security lights dotted the new compound. *These lights are the truest signs of civilization on a planet that might never again have witnessed a light bulb or any other technical advance had not the ark happened to arrive here. Was it chance? Could it have been ordained somehow?*

She thought back to her years in Catholic school, a time when she was anticipating devoting her life to service as a nun. She never questioned her father's religious beliefs or his intentions for her. How could she, after her mother's untimely death? Faith, including absolute belief in each other, had bonded Katherine and her father as closely as a daughter and dad could possibly be. It was just the two of them—or so she believed until she was sixteen.

That's when the family comm unit started receiving strange calls, mostly in the evening. A few times it was a woman's voice and a blank identification icon; the caller would disconnect as soon as she determined that Katherine's dad was not there. But there were younger callers. They also chose not to identify themselves, but they were a little more conversational. One, possibly a pre-teen girl, asked Katherine about herself. But they never divulged the reason for their calls.

Katherine didn't give them much thought until that horrible night in December, about a week before Christmas. The house was decorated sparely, with just a few boring ornaments on the tree, and only religious holiday music was allowed. Katherine answered the doorbell, and a heavily perfumed woman and three young people marched into the two-bedroom Colonial house without being invited. Katherine's father leapt from his leather recliner and scowled.

The visitors demanded money. They acted like they deserved it, but they revealed no reason why. Katherine's father kept insisting that she go to her bedroom, but she refused. She recognized that something significant was happening. That feeling was amplified by the odd looks that the woman, two teen-age girls, and a young man sent her way on occasion.

At one point her father could restrain himself no longer. "Get out of my house, now!" he erupted. Katherine saw a side of him that she had never imagined. And she began to sense the truth, the reason behind this visit.

"Katherine, you didn't know, did you?" the woman asked. "Of course not. You poor thing. Thinking all along that you were the only person in your dear father's life." The woman winked at her, then gathered her children and left, yelling after the door was slammed on them: "We'll see you in court—and in hell!"

"How long has this been going on?" Katherine asked her father. "Did you have another family while Mom was still alive?"

He turned and walked away.

Katherine might have renounced her faith; some teen-agers in her situation would have done so on the spot. But she held on to it. Maybe it was the only thing keeping her going, keeping her anchored. She never entered a convent, opting for a more conventional life, clinging to the hope that she could establish a real family someday.

A low-level groaning on the wind brought her back to the present. It swelled in volume, it lowered in pitch, and its source became apparent. The massive ark, once the last hope of a dying civilization, tilted and fell with a crash that overwhelmed her noise sensors briefly. The echoes reverberated off the hillsides as birds squawked, fleeing their nests in alarm. A cloud of dust and debris soon obliterated the landing area, as if the planet were attempting to erase all evidence and even the memory of the invaders. Katherine had seen all that she needed to see.

Even if Hubert, Maria, and Jalen have survived the destruction of the spaceship, they are more vulnerable than ever.

She stumbled, mentally and physically, then recovered. Once again, she was Candice, the congresswoman from Oregon. She couldn't figure out where she was or why she was there, but she was comforted by the emergence of pinpoints of light through the dust in the lowlands before her.

There better be a fucking Starbucks open at this hour.

She was nearly at the bottom of the hill before Katherine resurfaced.

§

Every now and then, the short, angry native came by. Maria guessed that he was the leader because he ordered people around but never really did anything. The man entered her cell and poked her with a spear. Next, he wielded a dull tool to try to open her door. It took a while, but he succeeded and examined the chaotic jumble of machinery and cables, his face awash with amazement and trepidation. He looked around to make sure no one was watching him. Then he crawled inside.

So strange not to have a physical sensation of this man violating me. I suppose that I could try to grasp him with my front arms or kick him with my other limbs, but it would just make him angrier.

He studied the flashing lights on her electronics and touched them tentatively. He tugged on a couple of cables without effect. Then he grumbled and departed, not even bothering to close her door.

The taller man came by, and the woman Maria met first. *There's a bond between them. Perhaps a romantic connection. The man appears to be older, but there's nothing wrong with that. Armando was five years older than me. It's funny. Armando seemed such an unlikely candidate for a husband. He earned even less money than I did, and he stuttered severely. He was so self-conscious about the speech defect that he was hesitant to go out in public. Even when the two of us went to a restaurant on a date, he let me do most of the talking. It took him an agonizingly long minute to get out the words "Will you marry me?" when the time came, which was just our fifth date. Yes, I counted dates because it was so rare for me to get past two with the same guy. But what a kind heart you had, Armando. What tenderness you demonstrated to me and Roberto. So many people looked at your six-foot-two, two hundred twenty-pound frame and saw just a high school football star or, more likely, feared that you were a mugger. But you never let those insensitive stares bother you, as best as I could tell. And you never lost faith in me. Armando, if only you could see me now. Look at the mess I have made of my life. I lost you, then I lost our son, and now I've lost myself. Locked up in a primitive cell on a hillside on some worthless planet God knows how many millions of miles from nowhere. I wish that I could laugh, but I don't even have the equipment to do that.*

She would never forget the last conversation she had with her husband. She was upset that he had given her only a card and a cheap drugstore bouquet of half-dead flowers for their anniversary that evening. She had given him an expensive back support system to use in his rig; he had been complaining for years about the aches and pains he accumulated during long days driving his truck with few breaks. She didn't know that he was saving money to surprise her with a trip to Disneyworld. She never would have known had Armando not confided in Roberto a few days earlier and had Roberto not given her a tearful accounting of that plan the night after the funeral. But on their anniversary, just hours before Armando left on his fateful trip to Colorado, all she could do was complain about how cheap he was. She didn't think about the fact that he was born and raised in absolute poverty in El Salvador and made it to the United States only after his parents completed the arduous process for being granted asylum. She didn't think about the fact that she didn't want an expensive present. She had all she needed.

She recalled how he and the other drivers used to refer to the aging trucks they drove as "rolling coffins" and the worrisome noises the rigs made as "death rattles". The defects that his company got away with were well known to the drivers. They should have been caught through routine maintenance or state vehicle inspections. Even a cynical woman like Maria would not guess that maintenance workers at the trucking firm were paid extra to overlook flaws that would require expensive repairs and that the company always went to certain state inspectors who took hefty bribes to allow dangerous trucks to remain on the road.

On that last night, she wouldn't even kiss Armando goodnight, instead turning, cutting off the lamp on the bedside table, and muttering "Leave me alone".

Two nights later, she got the call at four a.m. She eventually learned that Armando's truck had indeed crashed because of a defect. It was one of many rigs in the Robertson Trucking fleet that had been involved in serious accidents for similar reasons. While many trucking firms had shifted to self-driving vehicles, Robertson was sticking with cheaper, nearly obsolescent trucks, and its CEO was determined to keep those decrepit rigs on the road, no matter what. Maria had been glad that the firm had not eliminated Armando's job, of course. But she wished that she could walk up to that CEO and give him the slapping and dressing down that he deserved.

Robertson Trucking. Robertson. The name echoed across Maria's consciousness, lighting up circuits or whatever passed for her synapses these days. She had heard that name recently. Of course.

Damian Robertson.

§

The next morning, four men with spears broke down the walls of her cell, their expressions dripping with violence. The short, angry man pointed to the inside of her crab and yelled something to the others.

"This looks like the end," Maria told Hubert and Jalen. "It's been nice knowing you. Good luck with the mission."

Two natives could barely fit inside her shell at the same time. They started pulling cables and stabbing electronics savagely with sharp stone tools. She tried to think of happier times: Of watching Roberto navigate his way around and between older defenders on his way to scoring the winning goal. Of Armando proposing to her over a seafood dinner at Baltimore's Inner Harbor. Of her parents sacrificing without complaint to get her through community college.

The natives went about their business inside her crab for some time before they heard shouts from the other natives and emerged to see those natives pointing in the air. Maria couldn't see above her, couldn't know that six drones were descending, carrying something bulky that blotted out the sun briefly before it landed, flattening maturing grain plants.

The drones released their cargo. Maria followed the natives' gazes and turned to her left. Beyond the remains of her cell was a sight that made her think that she was hallucinating. "Jalen, can that really be you?"

"The cavalry has arrived."

Hubert patched the drones' camera feeds into Jalen's visual field and advised him: "You have control now." It took Jalen a moment to adjust his mind to manipulate the drones, as he had practiced. Jalen directed two of them to hover above him, moved two to other side of Maria's position, and guided two to and inside her crab shell. Brandishing fine cutting tools, they started conducting brain surgery. The natives stepped back, watching with fascination, demonstrating no aggressive moves.

After about ten minutes, Maria was jolted. Suddenly, her universe was reduced once again to mindless static.

Two drones emerged from Maria's crab, holding the precious computer that contained her consciousness. A battery was attached to it. Two more drones joined them, lifting the equipment in tandem, rising into the cerulean sky, and disappearing. The other two drones followed.

The natives could not know the meaning of this intrusion. But once the drones were gone, they decided that they had little to fear from the two sky creatures. Especially now that the one that they had captured had lost some of its innards.

"Hubert, can you see the drones on their way back to the compound?"

"Yes. Well done, Jalen. What is your status?"

"So far, so good."

One of the natives resumed trashing the insides of Maria's crab body. Another poked her shell savagely with a spear. Two approached Jalen, shouting and gesturing angrily at him. But they did not attack him, not yet. "Perhaps they are beginning to realize that we are intelligent beings and that we mean them no harm," Jalen said, as much to himself as to Hubert. He issued a silent prayer to make that wish come true. Yet he knew that he could be destroyed at any moment.

Before coming to this hilltop, Jalen had studied drone images of the area. But they seemed useless now. If he were to try to escape, he probably would get lost. More likely, the natives would smash him to bits. But that was the plan: Trade his life for Maria's.

What good have I ever done? On Earth, or here? If I can keep Hubert's mission alive, even for a little while, it will be better than anything I have accomplished or could hope to accomplish. I'm a failed nurse. I'm a hapless apprentice in the quest to make humans on a planet where they might never be welcome, even if they did manage to grow. I can die knowing that I might have made a difference. But please, Hubert, make sure that Maria lives.

Jalen turned in each direction, taking note of the terrain and the natives. Two of the natives had apparently satisfied themselves that they had done all the damage they could do to Maria's crab. All four were watching him. They were not speaking.

Jalen noticed a path heading down the hill. The foreboding trees ahead of him brought back memories that he had sought desperately to forget, memories that had kept him away from woodlands all these years.

RECOVERY

He had been four years old, a child of a single mother, a kid with a lot more curiosity than understanding of the world. His mom had gone to the grocery store, leaving him alone in front of a TV, after promising that she would return in fifteen minutes. He had seen all the cartoons before, multiple times. He was bored. He was lonely.

He didn't recall his decision to head into the woods that afternoon. He didn't even put on a coat, and it was chilly, probably in the forties. He had seen squirrels, groundhogs, and the occasional fox in the small, trash-strewn yard behind his apartment building, and maybe he would encounter one today. Maybe he could turn one into a friend. Maybe he would get lucky and find a bear to be his chum.

He ambled downhill for quite some time, then emerged into daylight and came upon train tracks. How exciting! Maybe he could see a real train. But as he crossed over the tracks, he took a tumble down a steep embankment, banging his head, hurting one leg, and coming to rest in a dense patch of brambles. He cried out, but no one could hear him. He couldn't stand on the injured leg.

Twice during the night he awoke to the sound of a passing train. Each time he felt more scared. And the cold—the dreadful cold—ravaged him instant by long instant. He shivered violently, unable to get back to sleep, though he might have dozed toward dawn as the temperature dropped and a thin coating of snow helped numb the pain of his wounds. A couple hours later he heard shouts. A sheriff's deputy responded to his cries and pulled him from the briars, calling immediately on a device affixed to his wrist.

After being treated at the hospital, Jalen came home to a warm bowl of soup and a warmer scolding. But his mother saved the biggest recriminations for herself. She would be more careful; she should have known that a four-year-old should never be left alone.

His mom watched him closely for a long time. After he started school, she relaxed somewhat, and he showed no obvious signs of emotional damage—he was always a quiet and private child. But whenever she tried to talk him into a nature walk, or even a stroll near trees, he got nervous. She knew that the trauma of getting lost and injured and spending the night alone outdoors would stay with him for a long time. Maybe forever.

For a while, Jalen had attempted to get over that fear, to walk under a tree, to enter a wide, well-traveled path in a leafy park. But it just was not going to happen, not if he had any say in the matter. Now, as a six-legged freak atop a plateau, under the gaze of hostile natives on a worthless world he never dreamed of visiting, Jalen wondered how much of that fear remained inside him. Other than a short hike to search for Phyllis, with Maria close by to reassure him, he had avoided woodlands on this planet. Now, he decided to pretend that Maria was with him, protecting him, and his mother as well. He approached and started to descend the path, waiting for the natives to attack him or for his emotions to overtake him. At first, every step was agony. He could see the briar patch and could feel the cold and the panic. Gradually, a different kind of numbness came over him. He focused on watching the trail, on not getting tripped up or losing the path. He envisioned Hubert and Maria, safe back at the compound, working to propagate human tissues. He imagined himself walking on a warm beach, far from trees and train tracks and anything that could harm him.

After a while, he reached the native village, only gradually realizing what he was seeing. Women gathered young children to their sides and whispered to them in urgent tones. Older children stopped playing and watched in stunned silence. The only sounds were some whispering from the young children and the squawks, chirps, and buzzes from the jungle around them. Most of the men were away hunting or gathering food, but two older men in ragged clothes took some hesitant steps toward Jalen. One of the men moved his right arm slowly, placing his palm across his midsection. The other man pulled that arm back, making a brief but obviously angry comment. Jalen extended his left arm and did his best to copy the gesture, holding his pincers just under his front cameras.

It breaks my heart that I can't talk to them, that I can't tell them that we mean them no harm. Jalen no longer feared for his safety. He was more concerned about the disruption that he and the other crabs had caused. *Surely these people are just trying to survive. How frightening it must have been for them to see the spaceship landing and to watch crablike creatures and flying drones spreading out over their land.*

Jalen wasn't sure where he was going, but he started following a path that seemed to head down the hillside. He hadn't gone a hundred and fifty feet before he encountered a short native, who surely had heard him coming for a while. Blocking the path, the native stared at Jalen. The man's intensity was beyond measure, but his intent was far from obvious. *Will he attack me? Will he call for reinforcements?* Jalen detected no threatening gestures from the man and wondered how he might indicate that he had no malicious intent. He could not think of any way to communicate effectively, so he merely extended his right arm and pointed down the hillside with his pincer. Then he resumed scuttling in that direction, bracing himself for the inevitable conflict.

Just before Jalen got within arm's reach of the native, the man stepped aside and let Jalen pass.

Hubert sent a drone to keep an eye out for Jalen as he moved generally downhill and south, with some uphill terrain and the occasional confusing fork in the path. It was well into the afternoon by the time that Jalen reached the savannah and marched on familiar territory toward the settlement. As usual, he focused on picking up the tall security light poles that were the first indication that he was on track.

Only, there were no light poles. There was no settlement.

"Hubert, I'm lost."

"Jalen, I detect you about two hundred and fifty feet due north of the gate. Proceed as normal."

"If you say so."

After about ten minutes, he halted again. "Hubert, could you please turn the security lights on?"

"They are fully illuminated."

The discomfort that had been gnawing on him began to make a meal of his confidence. He crisscrossed the savannah and walked in circles, using the internal compass of his memory. The settlement, the ruins of the ark, the burn zone—it was all gone.

"Jalen, it will be dark soon. You should return."

"I'm trying. I don't know where to go."

Navigating by the setting sun and familiar landmarks, Jalen headed to a spot that should be on the eastern edge of the settlement, in what should be the burn zone and the remains of the fallen ark. He walked due west until he reached a stream, then turned and headed back east. He was sure that he was right where the settlement should be. He could not see it. He could not see it anywhere.

And then, suddenly, it was right in front of him.

§

Hubert ran diagnostics most of the night. "I can find nothing wrong with you other than a few external scratches, which will reduce your ability to absorb energy from sunlight by approximately 0.17 percent."

"I can live with that. I don't think I can live with going blind."

"You are not going blind. I have reviewed internal records of your camera images from yesterday. At the times when you were looking at the settlement, it did not appear to you."

"Did you hide it somehow?"

"I do not have that capability, nor would I choose to do so. There is an even more disturbing aspect to my investigation."

"Do I really want to hear this?"

"I believe that you need to hear it. It appears that on several occasions you passed right through the complex."

"No way."

"To you, it was as if it were not even here."

Jalen tried to wrap his mind around this revelation. "Could this have something to do with the natives? Or the crabs getting sent from a hilltop to a river, or the duplicate spaceship illusion, or even the destruction of the ion fusion reactor?"

"I have insufficient data."

"Hubert, you sure picked one strange planet to land on."

§

The static dissipated, yielding to vaguely familiar shapes and colors. Eventually she recognized the sunset glowing softly, its languid light flowing like a lazy river through her emerging consciousness. Dying breezes sighed, tickling a memory of a summer picnic along the Chesapeake Bay. How old was she then? Maybe seven or eight. But she was older now, much older. And she was not home, nowhere near home. Recent memories coursed through her, providing disturbing vignettes of metal and mayhem, struggle and purpose. She moaned and stretched instinctively, feeling like she was awakening from a twenty-year nap.

"Don't try to move too suddenly."

Maria realized that she was looking straight up, flat on her backside. Without doing so consciously, she sat up. Presently, she was able to focus and make out a human-like but clearly artificial figure standing about six feet away. "Hubert, is that you?"

"No, it's Jalen." His voice was metallic and a little scary, like something out of the low-budget science fiction movies she watched as a kid. But she was hearing it as it must have sounded to someone or something with ears, not as a feed of computer-processed words popping into her mind. Jalen's head was too big for his body. His head and body were more hard angles than curves. His movements were stiff and awkward. But Hubert had made him more functional, and almost anything was an improvement over a crab.

"Am I hearing your voice directly? Like from a mouth?"

"Yes, we have voice boxes and can communicate with them as well as through electronic connections. I'll teach you how to use yours. We have mechanical ears, too, and a new power source so we don't need to charge batteries—all thanks to Hubert."

She decided that, for the moment, she would continue to use her original comm channel. She realized that she could tilt her head, so she examined her legs, her torso, her arms. Apparently, she was like Jalen. She was tempted to look for a mirror, but she decided that she probably wouldn't be too thrilled about what she would see.

"How long have I been out?"

"Almost thirty days," Hubert replied. "I wanted to test your new form thoroughly before transferring your consciousness to it. Jalen went first. He endured many long days of experiments. He has been exceedingly brave."

Maria tried to smile but wasn't sure if her effort was succeeding. "You rescued me, Jalen. Now I remember."

"Thank Hubert and the drones."

"The rescue effort was Jalen's idea. I opposed it, initially," admitted Hubert. "But the natives have not retaliated since we recovered your computer and battery and downloaded your mind into this much improved vessel."

"What about Damian and Katherine?"

"We have not seen them or heard from them for some time."

"That's a help. What else have I missed while I've been asleep?"

"We have had another anomaly that eludes explanation." Hubert described Jalen's experience with the disappearing settlement.

"I'm getting the feeling that somebody doesn't want us here."

"By 'somebody', are you referencing a human entity?"

"Correction: Maybe somebody or something doesn't want us here."

"I cannot rule out that possibility. However, if our landing and explorations had caused something on this planet to oppose our presence, I believe we would have seen a more focused and disruptive reaction. Clearly, the source of the unexplained phenomena is extremely powerful and motivated in ways that we can barely appreciate."

"You're not helping my mood. Got any good news?"

"I would like to inform you of the latest development from the nursery unit," said Hubert. "If I may use an idiom that Jalen taught me: We're pregnant."

Life enjoys no respite; it must change or perish.
—The Book of Marcus

YEAR 39
RENEWAL

"How long will you be gone?"

It was that look again, and that tone of voice. Elena suspected. Justin hated to deceive her, but telling the truth could be even more painful. He stared at his boots, which were coming apart at the seams. *An appropriate metaphor for my life. Metaphor—that's the right term, isn't it? Or is it simile? I should have paid more attention in my classes.*

He quickly abandoned any thought of trying to produce a deceptive smile or utter a dishonest excuse. He wondered how life could have become so complicated for one so young as him. "I'll be less than an hour. I'll check on the children while I'm out." *Best to say as little as possible.*

Seated at a wobbly table cobbled together from scrap metal and plastic from another world, Elena willed herself not to cry. The standard furnishing dominated the cramped, sparsely appointed, two-room cottage. It was the best and perhaps only place where one could gather the energy and wits necessary to satisfy the demands of another morning. She cast a soft breath over her herbal tea, watching the steam swirl, acquire ephemeral shapes, and dissipate into an invisible, perhaps kinder, realm. Holding the solid mug and smelling the intense aroma kept her grounded on even the worst day, Justin understood.

It's a shame for such a pretty face to be marred by negative emotion. Those fathomless brown eyes, those soft lips, that flawless skin, a smile that can be seen and felt for miles. How lucky am I that Maria and the first-gens nudged us into becoming bonded partners almost from birth. None of the other second-gen girls was half as attractive or demonstrated half as much intelligence or personality as she did.

Elena started to say something else, but she caught herself. She was not in the mood for an argument. Plus, she was wracked by her own guilt. "Run along, you big lug."

You big lug. That backdoor compliment was her way of attempting to defuse even the most tense situation. Her tease was on target: Justin was indeed a big lug. Six foot two, two hundred pounds in his underwear, chiseled and brawny as a beast, with blond hair and a square jaw, he was the largest bio in the settlement. He might have been the largest person anywhere, if what Maria said was true. Most of the natives he had seen were thin, and some were outright emaciated. Maria told him that once there were some bigger people on Earth, a place in the sky so distant that it couldn't be seen even on the clearest night. He still found it hard to believe that there were once hundreds of hundreds of people there. *The settlement seems crowded with the forty of us.*

The sun was not yet high enough to cascade through the generous windows on the east side of the cottage. In the low light and his distraction, Justin nearly tripped over some of Agatha's and Richard's playthings as he made his way to the door. "Love you," he said, heading out before he was tempted to say too much. *Just get on with it.*

Claire was in his face the moment he closed the door and turned around. "The main pump is acting up again." Her brusque message brought him back to the constellation of duties that had fallen on his broad shoulders.

"Good morning to you too, mother. What's wrong with it now?"

"I'm not sure. Maybe it needs lubrication, or perhaps the pipe is blocked. Discuss it with Hubert. It's his contraption, after all."

Before the ark fell over nearly forty years ago, spreading debris across much of the burn zone created by the spaceship's fiery landing, Hubert had directed his drones to remove pumps and pipes and other useful equipment from the craft. He knew that any people that the digital minds and drones could coax into existence would need to draw water from the closest stream, store it, and use it for drinking, cooking, cleaning, and crop irrigation. Now, only three pumps and six drones were left in working order, and all seemed like they were just one hiccup away from collapse. There was no point scavenging through the ruins of the ark; Hubert had warned that there were dangerous substances in the debris and that drones had extracted everything of value. That didn't stop teen-agers from sneaking into the remains now and then, looking for mythical treasure or another excuse to vex their parents.

Justin could not imagine what the ark must have looked like before it crashed. It seemed like a fantasy: Something as tall as a hill moving across the sky at a speed much greater than the stiffest breeze before descending onto the savannah. Coming from another place like this, but more crowded, until its people killed their entire world. It was hard enough accepting the assertion that the ground he stood on was part of a world that was round.

"Another thing," Claire continued. "Have a talk with your brother. He's not paying attention in class, he's skipping some of his work shifts, and he's hanging out with those troublemakers."

Justin sighed. "I don't know if he'll listen to me, but I'll keep an eye out for him."

"You see that you do that."

Nearly as tall as Justin, Claire was also an imposing figure. Sturdy, blond, and, by all accounts, one of the most attractive women in the settlement, she was self-assured and churning with energy. She never went looking for arguments, yet she didn't exactly avoid them, and she rarely lost one. Still, she was no stranger to the concept of loss. Claire's second child, Tess, had died at age eight after a wound became infected. The event made a particularly deep impression on her youngest child, Marcus, who grew to be sullen, restive, and at times rebellious. His appearance didn't help. Marcus was shorter than Justin, a much less striking figure, with ratty, sandy colored hair and an ample belly. He felt overshadowed, underappreciated, and lacking in purpose. Like many in the settlement, he had little interest in the bots' mission of cranking out babies. His older brother seemed much more suited to that pursuit.

Claire lowered her voice almost to a whisper. "Are you going to visit Rebecca this morning?"

He nodded.

She turned and marched off to speak with another second-gen who was emerging from a nearby cottage, one of eleven completed to date north of the original perimeter fence. That five-foot-high metal barrier had been erected by Hubert's drones to protect the main complex, which extended well to the west of the burn zone. Apartments, a power plant, a nursery, a clinic, a food and clothing processing and distribution center, a water tank, a learning center, storage facilities, and the shack that housed Hubert's servers were all inside the fence. As new cottages were built beyond the original complex to accommodate a growing population, a second metal fence became necessary. It was shaped like an inverted U and linked to the existing barrier. Each fence had its own gate, and guards were posted at the inner gate all of the time and at the outer gate during daylight and early evening hours.

Hubert had rushed to get the original complex built before the ark fell. He used drones to construct the buildings almost entirely of metal and plastic scavenged from the interior of the spacecraft. Some of the structures, including the nursery, were designed without windows in order to deter further sabotage by Damian and Katherine. Yet Hubert had failed to consider how impossibly hot the nursery would be for bios once the electronic cooling system failed for lack of replacement materials. So the nursery was repurposed for storage and a new one was built, the walls, floor, and ceiling constructed chiefly from wood and other plants. Large windows—crisscrossed by metal security bars—permitted air circulation, supplemented by numerous fans. Shutters could be closed when strong rains fell. Only the learning center had glass windows. The necessary sand had to be brought in from many miles away by drones or by bios with carts, and the two bios Hubert had taught to make glass were struggling to produce satisfactory results.

Natural materials were also used to build the cottages, with bios designing them and supplementing drone labor. However, many of the cottages proved to be unstable. Several homes had required substantial renovations within three years of completion, and another had to be demolished and rebuilt. Residents complained constantly of leaking roofs and shutters, sagging floors, and doors that did not close properly, not to mention the relentless heat that the buildings trapped despite their large windows.

Maria, Jalen, and Hubert had provided steady support and guidance to the bios from their inception, but as the settlement grew it became clear that it needed flesh-and-blood leadership as well. Claire accepted that responsibility when no other first-gen showed much interest in anything beyond keeping their family fed, clothed, and sheltered. At twenty-one, Justin and Elena were the oldest of the second-gens, and it was obvious that he was being groomed by Claire and the bots for a leadership role. Though he rarely objected to his mother's instructions, he often felt that the weight of the responsibilities she imposed upon him could crush him and his family.

As he strolled toward the inner fence, settlers bustled about their morning tasks. Two men pulled a noisy cart loaded with tools and wooden planks for mending the fences that enclosed the livestock pen and four agricultural plots out on the savannah. An older man who Hubert had taught to make candles and soap shouted an enthusiastic greeting. A couple of boys shared a joke, laughing boisterously on their way to the learning center. A woman carried a heap of dried plants destined for the manufacture of clothes. Justin made a mental note to drop by the distribution center later to see if any more pants were available for his fast-growing children. Unconsciously, he reached down to scratch his right leg; new clothes always itched terribly for weeks.

How different the settlement must have been before the first-gens emerged from their artificial wombs—how sterile and still.

Justin nodded to the guard as he passed through the rusting metal gate that led to the original complex. He was in no hurry to see Rebecca, so he stopped by the learning center, the largest building and the beating heart of the community.

"Daddy!" squealed Richard, his dimpled, chubby, adorable three-year-old. Ensconced in the play area with three other third-gens, Richard popped up and toddled to Justin's side. Richard's sister Agatha, a blond, ragamuffin four-year-old, bolted from her counting lessons and likewise flew to Justin. Both youngsters hugged his sturdy legs with their slim arms. He couldn't help but smile. He hadn't been away from the pair for half an hour, but at their age, that was an eternity.

"Don't squeeze too hard, you'll break me," Justin teased. The children soon went back to their toys and lessons. Several teen-agers who had glanced over at the encounter resumed their science studies, facilitated by a video display screen and playback device operated by Jalen. Justin couldn't help but admire Agatha's gorgeous locks, curlier than his hair but nearly the same shade. As for Richard and his darker features, apparently he took after his mother.

Justin lingered, allowing himself the luxury of appreciating the eager eyes, wiggling toes, and inquiring minds of the young people in the learning center before pacing lethargically to the apartment building in the center of the complex. Rebecca didn't respond right away to his soft knocking on her door, and he thought that he heard words being whispered inside the unit. Before he could knock a second time, the door flew open. Stanley stared at Justin for several tense moments with an inscrutable expression, then passed him wordlessly. Stanley and Rebecca were bonded partners, a designation bestowed upon those who chose to raise children together.

Rebecca stood in the center of the apartment, her expression a fusion of embarrassment and sadness.

"That was awkward," Justin managed.

He entered and attempted to close the door silently, as if that could prevent others from detecting his presence. In some circles it was common knowledge what his duty entailed and that it could best be accomplished in the morning, before the heat of the day.

"Are you well?" he asked.

She nodded and undressed.

§

Prask-aes glared at Soug-kue with disdain honed to perfection. The Gaip chief had run out of things to say to her over nearly forty years of marriage. She would never love him, would never even obey him. Despite being married to a man she did not love, or maybe because of her forbearance, the years and the absent god had been kind to Soug-kue. The age lines in her face only seemed to sharpen her smile. Her ability to look beyond suffering and the mundane had only strengthened. Prask-aes was not so fortunate. The darkness in his eyes could no longer conceal the dissolution of his spirit. Everyone, himself included, suspected that the two children that Soug-kue had borne were fathered by Akos-Pau, his very own cousin and his most vocal critic in the tribe.

Rather than berate his wife one more time, Prask-aes simply stormed out of the simple shelter they shared. He began to round up young men for a raid on the sky creatures' livestock. Four declined, feigning illness or claiming a more important chore in the fields. The pale brown, thirsty plots they maintained in small pockets atop and along nearby hillsides remained close to perishing under the unusually early and severe drought. It was not as if one man's labors could reverse the curse imposed by nature or—as the clerics claimed—caused by the absent god's anger at the invasion of the sky creatures.

Prask-aes had not exactly mellowed in his decades as leader of the Gaip, but he was a pragmatist. He no longer automatically treated hesitance to honor his demands as treason. The chief would never admit to himself, or anyone else, that his people had learned to ignore him most of the time. He could still tap his ample reservoir of viciousness if one of his subjects pushed his or her refusal to cooperate too far or expressed it publicly.

This morning, he settled for two youths, one seventeen and one only fifteen and rather weak in the mind, to accompany him to the lowlands. The chief handed each youngster a sack filled with the tools of the trade and led them over the hillsides. He could read them so clearly; later he would have to school them on masking their thoughts, particularly when embarking on an important mission. The seventeen-year-old boy was wondering why they were conducting a raid during the day, when they could be seen. The younger one was wishing that he had not eaten such a large breakfast, because he feared losing it.

As the jungle-covered hills yielded to the opulent grasses of the flatlands, the three raiders retrieved nets and knives from their sacks and donned their camouflage—coveralls woven to make them appear like the savannah itself. The chief revealed the plan: He would open the gate to the sky creatures' boar pen, then the three of them would kill and bag one boar each and rush back to the refuge of the jungle with their prizes. It would be accomplished so quickly that the slow, stupid sky creatures could not do a thing about it.

Prask-aes advanced fluidly in alternating directions, blending into the savannah, as light breezes stroked dry grasses, the sounds of the brittle stalks rubbing against one another providing additional cover. He sent to the boys: *Proceed slowly.*

The boar pen had been built just east of the new cottages, outside the second perimeter fence and just north of the burn zone, where the black ground was still discernable despite the encroachment of vigorous weeds nearly forty years after the ark's landing. Prask-aes couldn't believe his luck: He could see no sky creature near the pen, which was less than a hundred feet away. *Hurry,* he sent.

Bent low to the ground, he rushed ahead, unlatched the gate, and stepped inside, unsheathing his knife. He scrambled toward one of the fattest boars, which immediately started running and squealing. He lunged at it, missing badly. But it darted toward a fence post, and he moved to corner it. With his next attack, he slashed its side deeply.

Meanwhile, the boys had reached the pen, feeling silly in their disguises. The older one moved inside, and the younger was about to enter, when a teen-age bio heard the animals' squeals and spotted the intruders.

"What the hell?" muttered Bruce. "Get out of there!" He rang an alarm bell feverishly, then ran to confront the thieves, shouting "Natives!"

The youngest Gaip, the one with the weak mind, froze, torn between chasing a boar and running away. He did neither. He unsheathed his knife and buried it in Bruce's gut. The bio bent over, howling.

"By the absent god, what have you done?" screamed Prask-aes. "Back to the village, now!" He bagged the heavily bleeding boar, gathered his charges, and raced away. He left the gate ajar, which allowed several boars to make their exits.

Three bios raced to the wounded boy and helped him to the clinic. They called for Maria, who came running, as much as a bot can run. After nearly a dozen modifications, Maria had become significantly more limber than when she was downloaded into her current lifelike but artificial body—which in itself was a major improvement over the crab shell she inhabited right after landfall. Over the years, Hubert's drones had made her and Jalen more natural in appearance and function, allowing them to act and appear almost like bios. Their feet were less flexible, and their fingers would never be as effective as an organic person's. Hubert had the most trouble trying to make their faces as expressive as bios' faces. There were just too many small but significant muscles in a bio face to duplicate with the materials and tools at his disposal. Most adult bios never gave a second thought to these disparities or the fact that neither bot ever changed "clothes". Maria was permanently clad in a white, daisy patterned plastic blouse and brown metal trousers. Jalen was always seen in a yellow Eminem tee-shirt and green shorts, with a tattoo honoring his mother on his right arm.

But young children didn't understand why Maria and Jalen were different than them, and the bots' faces and voices bothered and even scared some of the youngsters at times. Older children made fun of

Maria and Jalen behind their backs—and sometimes right to their faces. Occasionally, Jalen tried to explain that he wasn't really a robot, that once he had been a flesh-and-blood person like them, with a real mind that he still retained. He, Maria, and the bios were fundamentally the same. That's why neither the bots nor the bios were called humans. It would be unfair to deny that label to any thinking entity who once breathed air and read poetry and kissed their mother, regardless of what form they took today. There was an unspoken belief that all of them had become something other than human now that Earth was a receding memory for the bots and almost a historical footnote for the bios. Hubert was unique, Jalen pointed out. He had always been artificial, though Jalen had come to think of Hubert as a friend.

Some bios did not buy in to that vision of equality with the bots, yet no one complained about Maria's medical services when they needed them. She had tended to the first-gens from birth, becoming a nanny to some of them. She was not supremely talented at treating injuries and illnesses; she mostly followed instructions based on Jalen's limited health care knowledge and the high school biology curriculum that ark project manager Dennis Forrester had uploaded to the spacecraft and Hubert had preserved. But she did her best and showed that she cared. She had been unable to prevent five deaths; everyone else had been patched up. She kept begging Hubert to produce antibiotics, but he said his drones had yet to find the right botanicals.

Maria examined the young man with the knife wound to determine where sutures would be needed. "Your name is Bruce, isn't it?"

"Y-yes."

"He might be going into shock," Hubert advised through one of the speakers his drones had installed around the settlement, even though he continued to have an electronic comm link to the minds of Maria and Jalen.

"I need a blood donor," Maria advised Bruce's friends. Maria started an IV linking Bruce and a volunteer—she was finally starting to get good at that. She applied a mild sedative derived from local plants to the edges of the wound and sewed up the patient as best she could. Fortunately, the blade had not penetrated deeply or struck a vital organ.

Maria's medical apprentice, a fifteen-year-old girl named Veronica, offered to monitor Bruce for a while. Maria sought out Claire, finding her trying to herd strays back into the boar pen. There was a substantial amount of blood on the ground, though some of it was boar blood.

"Are we just going to take this?" Maria asked. "The natives seem to be getting more desperate and more dangerous."

"What do you propose we do, other than increase guards?"

"We have to fight back. We can't let them run over us. The children are scared. Some of the adults are scared, too."

"This is the first serious injury they have caused in many years. Usually they just steal a little food or lurk nearby like they are thinking about mischief. I don't think this will be a habit."

"We have to be ready for anything. Please talk to the other first-gens," pleaded Maria. "I'm not just worried about the natives. Sooner or later, Damian and Katherine are going to come after us again."

"Katherine is creepy but has made no threatening moves. For all I know, this Damian is dead or a figment of your imagination. I'm thirty-seven years old, and I've never seen him. And even if we wanted to fight him or the natives, we don't have the weapons or the training for a war."

"That kind of thinking just emboldens the enemy."

Claire studied Maria, searching for a sign of the respect for life that she knew was in there, somewhere, behind those artificial apertures. "For my entire life I have listened to you and Jalen recount the history of your Earth. It's a constant repetition of the same theme—people fighting and killing one another for no good reason. You tell us we have a chance to build something better here. You tell us we should keep making babies and growing crops and we'll have some sort of paradise."

Claire paused to survey the pen and a nearby cultivated plot, the gentle grasslands, the hills teeming with exotic life, the pure white clouds and ample sunshine. "Now you tell us that we must fight and kill, just like people on your Earth did. You might want to think about what you really want, Maria. Because turning this place into another cauldron of suspicion and violence is definitely not what I want."

Maria could think of nothing to say.

§

The two native boys flopped onto the ground in the village clearing, trying to catch their breath. Prask-aes dumped the captured boar beside them and shouted: "You never use a knife or spear unless attacked or ordered to do so. Am I clear?"

Both boys indicated that the chief was quite clear. They sulked as they shuffled off to their homes.

Akos-Pau put down the bag of grain he was carrying and approached Prask-aes. "What misery are you bringing back to us, cousin?"

"Nothing that concerns you," the chief retorted before strutting pompously to his shelter.

Soug-kue moved to Akos-pau's side, placing a hand lightly on his shoulder. Though married to Prask-aes, she spent some daytime hours with Akos-pau and provided lessons for the youngest of her two grandchildren. Her children and her older grandchild were typically off hunting or scouting.

"Will there be trouble?" she asked.

"Undoubtedly. I read from the boys who accompanied Prask-aes that one of the sky creatures was stabbed."

"Prask-aes has gone too far this time. The sky creatures might not believe in the absent god, but they seem to care for their tribe and their family members. They have much metal and might have weapons that we cannot match. It would be unwise to provoke them."

"Agreed. We all recognize that Prask-aes conducts sporadic raids on the sky creatures to prove to everyone just how tough and brave he is. I share his concern that the sky creatures are building homes and fences and growing food on the savannah, no doubt angering the absent god. But they seem content to leave us alone."

Soug-kue closed her eyes in meditation. After several moments, she spoke in a faraway voice. "The drought will claim Gaip lives. Many are already missing meals because the crops are failing. And even though we cannot blame the chief for the lack of rain, it is his responsibility to guide us through the crisis. Raiding the sky creatures is designed to divert attention from his failures."

"How perceptive," responded Akos-Pau. He kissed her lightly on the forehead. "Let us pray that the injured sky creature recovers and that his people do not retaliate. There is no telling what suffering could beset everyone if war breaks out."

ESCALATION

It was the silences that worried him the most. He had become accustomed to the incessant barrage of advanced weapons battering the roofs and walls of apartment buildings, schools, and hospitals. But when things got quiet, he knew that something really bad was going to happen. The only questions were when and where.

Capt. James Stenson and the six surviving Army Rangers he commanded had been pinned down in the remnants of a heavily damaged parking garage in central Isfahan for five days. It had last rained three days earlier, and he and his men had consumed their last drop of water nearly twenty-four hours ago. There was no question that they would have to make a move, despite daunting obstacles. Enemy snipers were embedded throughout their sector of the Iranian city. Autonomous Warfare Engines—with the well-earned acronym of AWE—patrolled the skies. But whose were they?

Stenson led his men out a back exit an hour after nightfall. Their goal was to reach a factory less than two blocks to the north. If they could get inside, they might find water, and with luck even food, allowing them to regroup as they waited for backup. They hadn't gone a hundred feet before an AWE picked up their heat signatures. It dove down to forty feet above them and scanned them. In an instant, the gates of hell opened and staked a claim to their bodies and souls. The purple and red lights on the copious mini-grenades indicated that they were American. Unless the AWE had been taken over by the other side—which was always a possibility—the weapon system had misidentified them. Either way, some of his men were about to die.

"Run!" Stenson screamed. He evaluated options and calculated odds feverishly, incorporating everything he that had learned about how the grenades were able to find and attach themselves to warm bodies, how quickly they detonated, and how close his men were to the devices. In what seemed like minutes but probably required merely half a second, his decision was reached. The captain spread his arms and leapt toward the canisters, drawing as many of them to him as he could, screaming in defiance of the horrific weapons.

It would have been a mercy had he been left with no recollection of the explosions. But war was short on mercy. It might have been a blessing had he simply died in the blasts. However, sturdy armor allowed his body to retain just enough blood and integrity, and his stubborn spirit put up just enough fight, for him to survive the first critical moments. His medic hit the panic button, which was Army slang for the deployment switch on the latest experimental field rescue system. What was left of Stenson was placed into an antiseptic and shock-resistant balloon, which filled immediately with a foul-smelling foam that reduced his body temperature close to freezing and put his heart and lung functions on hold. Rangers provided furious cover fire as a heavily armored chopper airlifted him to a field hospital. A priest conducted last rites.

Three days later, Stenson came to consciousness wishing that he were not alive. The pain was nothing compared with the shock of discovering how little remained of him: most of his head, though nearly unrecognizable through the blurry vision of one remaining eye; stumps of arms; much of his midsection; and nothing below it. He was scheduled for a nearly endless series of surgeries. He would endure them because it was expected of him. He would fight for life, for honor, for his men.

Gradually, he came to fear that he was a Ranger in spirit only. After the second round of operations, he was granted permission to speak frankly with a superior officer who visited him occasionally. "Tell me straight. Will I ever be able to serve again?"

"You have given your country everything that anyone could ask of you, son," he was told. "Make something of yourself in your new life."

Stenson spent a few days feeling sorry for himself. Then, one morning, as he was being told about the next dozen or so surgeries that lay ahead for him, he declared: "Fuck it. Upload me."

The Army wouldn't pay to have his consciousness preserved digitally. What he really wanted was to have his mind saved and transferred into a robotic body, which was an even more dicey prospect at the time. Some of the first to try it found that they could not control their limbs well or that they could not stand the horrified looks they received when they ventured out in public. But Stenson was determined to go that route, and a social media campaign raised the necessary eight million dollars in a week. While learning to use his artificial frame, he considered his future. He didn't feel that his training in electrical engineering would do him or anyone else much good. What he needed was a calling. He remembered watching the locals abandoning Isfahan and the ones trapped there—most of them starving. And he learned about the many Americans who went to bed hungry. He applied for a job at a Midwestern food bank that needed a director.

He ran the food bank like the soldier he still believed he was. But over time the awkwardness of living in the artificial body wore on his spirit. The robotic vessel began to break down, and he could not afford repairs. When he learned of the ark mission from a buddy still in the Rangers, he signed up to have his consciousness uploaded into the craft when it was prepared for departure.

The first time that he surfaced in the crab body, he thought that he was dreaming or seeing things because of PTSD. Finding himself in a jungle with crab-like machines seemed like the ultimate cosmic joke, but he was not in the mood for humor, especially at his expense. The next time it happened, after stumbling around in a daze, he realized that he truly was sharing a consciousness with another digital person. James needed time to reconnoiter and assess. He needed to figure out just what kind of man this Damian was.

He observed Damian as if through a dirty screen door like the one in the kitchen of his grandfather's Indiana farmhouse. James couldn't focus too sharply or Damian would sense him and try to shove him down into unconsciousness. So James hovered just below the surface of Damian's awareness, like a fish in a scum-covered pond, darting to and fro to catch occasional glimpses and guess the meaning of shafts of light infiltrating from above. He could not get a read on Damian's innermost thoughts, but Damian's actions and statements gave James plenty of insight. The way he mistreated Katherine. The way he heaped aspersions on the beings known as Maria, Jalen, and Hubert. James didn't know who or what those three were, and in the bizarre situation in which he found himself, he knew not to make assumptions.

James recognized patterns of behavior. There were times when

Damian was hitting on all cylinders, burning with purpose and fury, as he dealt with Hubert and the other crabs in the first days after the ark's landing. But there were occasions when Damian was relatively subdued, nearly oblivious to all going on around him—not to mention all going on inside him. James started to develop a strategy for when to surface and attempt to become the dominant consciousness of the pair. He tried to take over only a few times, using each iteration to study how Damian reacted to the beginning of that initiative, how he combatted it, and what he thought as James receded.

James gained a greater understanding of Damian's pathology when he witnessed Damian smash the original nursery onboard the ark. After the ark fell, James saw Damian pounding his fists on surfaces on the long table in the center of the room in the underground chamber he considered his home base. James observed Damian screaming obscenities at machines for not doing his bidding. What James didn't see was a man with a strategy for improving his situation, for gaining control of what passed for his life. James had encountered many men like Damian in the Army as well as in civilian circles.

James recognized that Katherine had developed an emotional attachment to Damian, though James could not imagine why. He heard her pray and recognized a tormented soul that had raised two children and dealt with immense tragedy. Yet she seemed too passive to be useful to James. Eventually, he observed Katherine's alter ego, Candice Taylor, the congresswoman from Oregon. Like James, Candice was struggling to find her footing in this insane new existence, sharing a robotic shell in an underground ruin on an unknown planet. But Candice had a ferocious drive to succeed. James believed that he had found someone with whom he could collaborate.

§

Barely out of law school, Candice had been asked to take on a hopeless case. A native American tribe had found a tattered, barely legible document that it believed granted it ownership of half the state of Oregon. There were no records even remotely related to such a transaction in federal government archives, and state officials simply laughed when Candice sought documents from them that might be relevant.

She spent days talking with tribal elders, one of whom claimed to be part of a generations-long chain of repositories of handed-down oral history. The elder described men who came from Washington, D.C., to sign over a vast amount of territory to the tribe in exchange for relinquishing claims elsewhere and agreeing not to attack white settlers. Candice knew that she couldn't win the case on the facts, but she badgered the local and national news media to cover the story and conducted an intense social media campaign. The publicity served to unite the tribe in its determination to pursue its rights and to alert the public to the possibility that the tribe was due far more than it had at the time.

The legal settlement that Candice negotiated was as astonishing as it was sweet. The reservation was quadrupled in size; the tribe gained the right to build and operate a chain of casinos; each resident received a tidy cash payment; funds were dedicated to construct and staff first-rate schools, hospitals, and community centers. The deal helped reduce the scourges of poverty, substance abuse, and poor academic achievement.

Her reputation soared. When the local member of Congress decided to retire, she ran for the seat and won it handily. She worked tirelessly to gain desirable committee assignments and take care of her constituents. She was on a roll until her second re-election campaign, when her opponent claimed that Candice had sexually assaulted men and women all over Oregon. The claims were backed up by tawdry videos—all deep fakes. But she couldn't prove that, and her reputation was destroyed. She lost the election badly and fell into a deep depression.

The bridge that she jumped from was not quite high enough to kill her. Her mangled body was taken to a hospital just in time to save her life, but she felt doomed to an existence without mobility or purpose. She decided to have her consciousness uploaded, but with all memories from her failed reelection campaign and everything thereafter deleted. That she had been spliced into the mind of a woman named Katherine on a strange planet was hard to accept, but she realized quickly that there was nothing to be gained by denying the cruel reality of the situation. As the crabs explored their world, Candice fought to gain dominance over Katherine more frequently and for longer periods of time.

Meanwhile, James was becoming more comfortable functioning in a gray area in which Damian was only vaguely aware of him and did not feel threatened. Trying to try to find or forge a communication channel with Candice, James reached out. Though he detected links to several minds, Candice was not difficult to locate. Her determination burned intensely.

"Is this Candice? I am James, an Army Ranger and food bank coordinator from Indiana."

"Yes. Where are you?"

"My consciousness is imprisoned in Damian's, as yours is trapped in Katherine's. I hope that we can work together to improve our situation."

"I will be happy to do so. It is clear that the beings who built the machinery in this laboratory were highly intelligent and powerful. If only we could decipher their language, we could tap that power."

"Agreed. However, our first mission is clear: Damian and Katherine must die."

§

After his assault on the nursery in the ark shortly after landfall, Damian devoted his full attention to deciphering the mysteries of the ancient underground equipment, to discovering the connections and commands that could unleash the powers of the enticing electronic realm. Even during periods when he was able to suppress his growing impatience and anger and attempted to uncover the secrets by employing logic and intellect, he was stumped. It was a suggestion from Katherine that provided the first breakthrough.

"Maybe language isn't the key. Maybe we should try using our feelings."

"Don't waste my time with that bullshit."

Katherine had become accustomed to abuse from Damian. She shrugged off his latest outburst and scuttled close to the largest display screen, placing her pincers over the pale sapphire surface. She was determined to detect the source of the glow, to connect with the genius behind it. She let her awareness float free of the burdens of her crab shell and her uncertain fate. She entered a pleasant dreamlike state, reaching out cautiously, as if she had awoken in the night in a strange hotel room and sought to move without stumbling over a coffee table or another unseen impediment.

Is someone there? Can someone please help us?

Katherine could sense something. Something hidden or sleeping or unwilling to solidify into a recognizable entity unless she could find a way to tempt it to manifest. Maybe it was a computer program. Maybe it was God. Maybe it was an alien spirit or horrific monster. Whatever it was, she was willing to take the risk of contacting it, of luring it out into the open and seeking its help. Anything would be better than being locked in this tomb with only Candice, Damian, and his demons.

She focused, pouring out her desire with a plea based on the first thing that came into her mind.

Can you please get us out of these ridiculous crab bodies?

The request was noted and analyzed from all possible perspectives. *It is evident that these machines are sentient. They have responded to my interventions in ways that demonstrate surprising intelligence and resilience. This one seeks help for itself and another. Its plea is not unreasonable. And the results could prove highly interesting.*

Symbols materialized on the screen in front of Katherine, followed by an image of a machine that she had seen on the nearby factory floor. Katherine neither knew nor cared how things were happening. All that mattered was that the machines might be able to help her. She described her findings to Damian.

"Sounds risky. But if you're game to try it, knock yourself out."

She positioned her crab shell on a platform on the indicated device. After a few moments she was bathed in vivid blue light, which Damian guessed was some sort of scan. Soon, her crab body rippled and disappeared. Paler lights swept across the empty space. Damian watched with a mixture of shock and elation; at least something was happening. After several minutes, as he was thinking that the machine had merely killed Katherine, something started to coalesce on the platform. Presently, feet became visible, followed by the rest of a robot assembled in Katherine's Earth body image, right down to the shoulder-length red hair she boasted before the cancer drugs stole it and the disease took the rest of her. Katherine rose slowly out of the murky depths, her consciousness having been downloaded into the new bot body. A display at the bottom of her field of view showed a variety of characters, most of them undecipherable. But one that she thought might be a battery symbol gave a reading that seemed to indicate one hundred percent.

She sat up, examined her limbs, and tested them. "A mirror!" she demanded. The best Damian could offer was a reflection in a crystal bookcase window. She thought that she looked like road kill, but she was far more like the original Katherine than a crab. Damian was jealous of her transformation and her rapport with the computer system, but he congratulated her for the courage to undergo the conversion and decided to attempt the same upgrade.

As Damian positioned his crab shell on the platform, James was concerned about what would happen to him. But he and Damian came through the process without discernable difference in their mental capacities. James was pleased that the two of them had become more capable physically, yet Damian was no stronger psychologically. If anything, he might have become more vulnerable, because for the moment it appeared that Damian had forgotten that James was hanging around.

James decided to make his move.

§

"Another story!" Maria had just concluded narrating Cinderella and Peter Rabbit. She had done her best to impart descriptions of a brilliant, colorful, regal castle and a cute but frightened animal in a vegetable garden. She recognized that her artificial memory and limited mastery of descriptive words failed to reflect the richness of the illustrated books of her youth. Nevertheless, the children had insatiable appetites for the tales. Those were the only two traditional children's stories she could remember in any detail, and she didn't want to scar impressionable young minds with excerpts from her favorite horror and sci-fi movies, so she asked Jalen if he could conclude his tech-enabled lessons for the older kids a little early. That would free up his screen. The six third-gen kids were all under the age of five, and the youngest of the second-gens were thirteen, so the generations had different learning needs. But the screen was everyone's favorite plaything.

Rescued by Hubert's drones just before the ark fell, it was a simple color display connected to a video and audio playback device with a sampling of the ark's data archives. Chief among those treasures were gems Forrester had uploaded just before the ark left the space station. He had selected an eclectic mix: a standard educational curriculum for grades K through Twelve; a NatGeo database of nature videos; the 2030

World Series minus the Game Four terror attack at Yankee Stadium; a collection of popular music; and a vintage movie. It was the movie that most engaged the minds of the children: "It's a Wonderful Life".

Adults in the settlement were constantly hunting, growing food, building and repairing homes and fences, fixing water pumps and pipes, fending off natives and beasts, and pursuing other essential tasks. Yet many of them found time to watch the movie, especially the last half hour or so, when word spread through the settlement that it was being played. When it was over, Maria and Jalen typically faced an onslaught of questions from the children: What is Christmas? Why don't we have it? Where do cars come from? Did all the houses on Earth leak when it rained?

Today, the children wanted to know if snow was real.

"You know how cold you feel when you wade into the stream?" Jalen said. "Snow feels like that. Except you can play with it. You can make it into a ball and throw it. But I don't think it ever gets cold enough here for snow."

"Was the rest of the story real?" asked one of the teen-agers. "Like the mean banker and heaven and the angels?"

"The mean banker, yes, unfortunately," said Maria. "I always wondered if there was a heaven and if I would ever see it. I would like to think so." A flood of guilt swept through her.

So many times I considered teaching the first-gen children about God. I just couldn't figure out how to broach the subject. Here we were, Jalen and me, a couple of disembodied minds talking to kids who had been disgorged from metal-and-plastic wombs because another world died in catastrophe. How could I convince these children that there was a God? Was the real problem that I couldn't convince myself that there still was one?

"But what about angels?" the teen continued.

"May I speak to that point?" the professor interjected.

"Of course," said Maria. "How are you today?"

"I—we—are well, thank you."

In the first year after the ark landed, Jalen and Dr. Albert Trevino—whose consciousnesses had been spliced together by Hubert—had an uneasy relationship. But Dr. Trevino never had easy relationships. As a child growing up in Oklahoma, he had been diagnosed with severe autism. His parents were told that he would not be able to get a solid education or hold down a decent job. No one told Albert Trevino that. His parents found private schools that specialized in kids with special needs. He thrived, eventually earning a doctorate in early American history. He wanted to teach, but no elite university would accept him because of his hesitance to stand before large lecture hall audiences. So he recruited educators with similar issues and founded an online university for special-needs students.

He met Linda, a graduate student, in the virtual world. They chatted endlessly, and after a month he was madly in love with her. Yet she was in California, and he was in Georgia. He flew west and begged for a meeting, but she refused. When he discovered that she was living with a woman, he withdrew deeply into himself, like a sea creature embedded in the infinite spiral twists of a Nautilus shell. He was unable to conduct the most simple business or teach the most basic classes. After therapy failed, he sought to have his mind uploaded, hoping that the transformation would allow him to think but not feel. He wished that someday he could join the ark's bold experiment and wind up on an Eden where he could pass along his wisdom to new generations of humans.

Initially, the professor was overwhelmed by the realization that his mind had been spliced into another. Over time, he discovered that Jalen was not someone to fear. In fact, Jalen's shy nature made them almost kindred spirits, though with severely contrasting educational accomplishments. The two learned to accept each other and to share their existence as best they could. When one personality wanted or needed to assert itself, it did so. When neither felt that compulsion, they co-existed, each in a relaxed state, such as organic humans used to enjoy when they were on the threshold of sleep or were sunbathing and imbibing a beverage with a tiny umbrella. By the third year, Jalen and the professor agreed to shifts, with each allowed to become dominant briefly during the other's shift only if it did not distract the other from an important task. During his shifts, the professor lectured on history and literature from memory. Jalen taught math, science, spelling, and a few other topics with the curriculum that the ark project manager had uploaded.

"You young people need to maintain open minds," Dr. Trevino stated in response to the question about the existence of angels. "Don't say something is impossible just because you haven't seen it yet—

particularly on a planet that we have yet to explore to a substantial extent."

"Well said," commented Maria. "We might never know whether angels exist here. But I suspect that there might be a devil or two around."

§

In the fourth month after the ark settled onto the savannah and Hubert woke the digital minds he hoped would perpetuate the human race, James surged to the surface with the intent of replacing Damian permanently. He caught Damian off-guard, as he had hoped. Yet Damian responded forcefully, determined to maintain his consciousness as the dominant one. Damian had never served in the military, but years of fighting his way to the top of the trucking industry had hardened him into a determined foe.

It was a heavyweight match without a comparison, without a referee, and without a time limit. Two determined combatants, each lacking flesh to be damaged and nerves to feel pain, and therefore able to fight as long as necessary to become not merely the dominant mind but the only mind that could function in their bot body. They spent every microsecond straining for victory. Before long, the conflict reached stasis; they were caught in a Chinese finger trap from which neither could be extracted without losing. Eventually they became oblivious to all external events and stimuli. Katherine tried every comm channel, placed her hands and forehead on their robotic body, and attempted to break the impasse by manipulating the underground lab's computers, but no progress ensued. She prayed long and hard for Damian to resurface, or for some end to the conflict between him and James. She kept charging their battery, holding out hope that one day she and Damian could make or obtain organic bodies—human or something similar—and have a life together.

She tired of being alone, spending an increasing amount of time wandering near the bio settlement, watching children grow tall and strong. She wondered if Maria and Jalen had been downloaded into bio bodies, feeling a strong pang of jealousy at the prospect. She paid particular attention to the young girls frolicking amid the sunbaked homes that kept expanding outward from the original complex, like wildflowers after a season of storms. She thought that she could detect some similarities in faces and gestures to those of her own dear daughters.

Her mind clouded. Was that nasty congresswoman trying to come back? *Not now. Not now!*

Katherine moved closer to the outer fence line.

That could be Charlotte. It must be Charlotte! Charlotte, over here, it's Mother. Please, you can't go back to that school again. It's dangerous. There could be a fire—there was a fire! But you're here, and I'm here. Please get Samantha and let's go home.

An adult bio noticed Katherine and steered the children off the playground and into a nearby building.

I'll come back. I'll come back and take my babies home.

DISCOVERY

The temperature was already soaring, so Justin wanted to get an early start pulling weeds from vegetable and grain plots and ensuring that the irrigation system was functioning. Though he was bigger and stronger than the other bios, he preferred growing food to hunting it. He would rather create and nurture life than kill it, even if the result of his labors was indigenous grains or the equally bland food that the bots called keen-wah. He paced as he waited for two other second-gens to join him and start their shift at the first plot, about four hundred feet away.

Though he was not particularly prone to daydreams, one seeped into in his mind, a series of fleeting sensations that coalesced into a disturbing tableau. His bonded partner, Elena, was welcoming another man into her arms. In his bed! He felt ashamed. What would cause him to think this about Elena? She was a loving and devoted partner who accepted him completely. She wanted nothing more than to bear and raise his children. That's what the settlement was all about, his mother Claire reminded him and everyone else constantly. Grow babies. Grow babies that will have more babies. *Maybe someday we will fill the land with so many children that Claire and the bots will stop nagging us about their mission.*

He was roiled by a mix of emotions. There was nothing for it but to go speak to Elena, to unburden himself about his shame, to feel her reassuring embrace once more before he set out on his day's work. He wended his way among the drab buildings and beyond the original settlement fence to his cottage. As he entered, he was greeted by a muffled scream of "Go away!"

It was just as his daydream had suggested. Here was his bonded partner in bed, with Dimitri.

"Please just go," said Elena. It was no longer an expression of panic. It was one of resignation, of despair.

Dimitri pulled a cover over his naked body. But he made no effort to apologize, or to leave.

Of course. This has been happening all along. I knew this, on some level. It's just so hard to recognize until it's right in front of you.

Without a word, Justin left. His emotions consumed his attention so thoroughly that he neglected to close the door as he plodded back to the spot where he would join the crew heading out to the fields.

After giving birth to two healthy children, Elena had not been able to produce a third, despite constant efforts on his part. Was it her, or was it him? No one could say. Several times Elena thought that she was pregnant but no child resulted. Maria told her that she might have experienced "miscarriages" and that many other women were having the same problem. But the mantra was always the same: Keep having sex until you get pregnant and give birth, then do it again and again. Women who had no bonded partner were encouraged to couple with any man who might be able to get them pregnant. Justin had been with several women, under the direction—really, under the orders—of his mother and the bots. He took little pleasure in the trysts. Obviously, Elena had been told to couple with other men. Justin tried to banish that thought and the image of her and Dimitri. He couldn't do so.

Anger surged, demanding an outlet. He wanted to smash Maria, Jalen, and Hubert. He needed to confront his mother, who was the most fervent bio advocate of the mission. They were responsible for all the anxiety and guilt that accompanied this mad compulsion for copulation. Most of the time, it was not an expression of love, or even one of lust. It was turning settlers into machines. It was a high price to pay for recreating what Maria and her Earth relic friends kept calling the human race, if there even had been such a race. *Sometimes I think that Earth is a myth, just a story Maria made up, part of a scheme to get everyone to do what she and Jalen and Hubert and Claire want us to do.*

A second-gen named Andy came running to Justin. "The beasts are back!" he shouted. "Right up against the fence. And more than before—many more." Other bios who overheard the announcement joined them in sprinting to the outer perimeter.

Quietly, more than one hundred of the intimidating animals had approached the second fence. Every few years, thirty or so would come close for a few days, then leave. Occasionally, they exhibited the same behavior around fenced plots where settlers cultivated food crops or raised boars. The bios had located those plots away from concentrations of the fat green plants with the glossy leaves—which Jalen had dubbed "clover", even though they more closely resembled the Earth herb borage—in hopes of avoiding confrontations with the beasts. During their periodic visits, the animals ate clover and grasses and stared at the bios, almost as if they were judging the newcomers. Settlers could still enter and exit the outer gate if they did so without coming too close to or appearing to threaten the animals. No one had reported being attacked by a beast without provocation, but those who had tested their defenses invariably found out the hard way that they could do serious damage with those horns and hooves.

This time, a few days became a few weeks. The beasts showed no sign of getting bored or leaving, even though they had eaten most of the vegetation within a few hundred feet of the settlement. One morning, Maria noticed that several of them had formed a circle around one of their kind. She wondered whether one of them had died. Few dead beasts had ever been sighted; no one could guess their lifespan.

She exited the outer fence and advanced cautiously. The beasts opened a narrow corridor for her to approach a fallen animal, prompting Maria to wonder whether they expected her to save it. She soon recognized that the beast was indeed dead, though she could detect no obvious sign of injury. *It probably died of old age.*

She met the eyes of the other beasts. They remained placid, some chewing, most staring at her silently. She experienced a surprising sense of comfort verging on pleasure, as if she were sharing something tangible and essential with the animals, as if she were being accepted and welcomed by them. Even though her fingers lacked nerve endings that could transmit signals that would be experienced as feeling, she bent down to caress the hide of the dead beast. It was tough and scarred. She tried to think of something to say to the rest of the animals, as if they could understand her. Unbidden, words started flowing from her artificial lips.

"Amazing grace, how sweet the sound, that saved a wretch like me."

She sang the lines that she could remember, then repeated them a couple of times, generating more feeling with each recitation. She felt entranced and elevated by the experience, purged of confusion and frustration for a few grand moments. The beasts stared at her for a minute after she finished singing, then turned collectively and left for greener pastures.

Hubert sent a drone to collect a tissue sample from the dead animal. It took the drone some time to get through the hide, which was nearly an inch thick. Several days later, Hubert asked for the attention of Maria, Jalen, and Claire.

"I have examined beast tissue under the strongest microscope we have. I have conducted extensive analysis. And I have come to a startling conclusion: These animals are unique among all known to science. They have organic and metallic qualities."

"You mean they are bionic, like human bodies girded with armor or equipped with artificial limbs?" asked Maria.

"No. They seem to be a completely new order of life. They are synthetic creatures, a fusion of metallic and biological molecules. This composition provides extreme strength and resilience. They are almost living, breathing machines."

"No wonder they act so strangely," said Jalen.

"What does this mean for us?" demanded Claire.

"I have insufficient data."

"Could they have developed this way through evolution?" Maria inquired.

"I cannot rule out the possibility. However, I have found nothing remotely like these animals on this planet. Given that our drones found signs of an advanced civilization and that numerous unexplained events have occurred, we must approach these animals—and our entire existence on this world—with even more caution. If for some reason the beasts were to treat us as an enemy, I am not confident that we could defend ourselves successfully."

§

"Kur-asug, you stand before us to face the charge of theft."

Prask-aes had ordered that a bonfire be built in the center of the village for the trial. It was a dangerous gesture, given that hiding from the sky creatures was a priority. But Prask-aes sought to imbue the event with as much drama as he could summon.

"As your chief, I demand that you respond to the claim that you stole food from your neighbor."

The minds of many Gaip sought to read the accused man's thoughts, to sense his remorse, if any. The displeasure felt by most adults in the tribe was tempered by an unspoken realization: *This could be any of us, for we all are starving.*

"Please forgive me," beseeched Kur-asug as the ascending flames carved fingerlike shadows across his tortured face. "My wife and children had not eaten for two days. The creeks are too low for fish, and my hunting skills are poor. I did not eat a morsel of the food I took. I know that what I did was wrong. I will replace the food I stole, three times over. I will never again—"

"Enough!" shouted Prask-aes, so loud that several birds squawked and batted wings angrily in nearby trees. "Theft from fellow Gaip is never justified. When we are hungry, we hunt or we take food from the sky creatures."

The chief paused, allowing the crackling of the fire to fill the village with the dread that was his currency. Then:

"You are banned from all Gaip territory."

"What about my family?" the thief pleaded. "Who will provide for them?"

"How they survive is not up to me; it is up to you and them."

No one spoke in protest, but Prask-aes could read the surprise and anguish in the minds of many of his subjects as they dispersed. Kur-asug's wife approached the chief, her face contorted with shock and fear.

"You are punishing not just my husband and myself. How can you sleep at night or expect the favor of the absent god when you threaten the lives of our two innocent children? How can you make them suffer for the weakness of one man, one good man?"

"The absent god abhors thieves," stated Prask-aes. He stared at the woman with utter contempt, barely concealing his thrill at exerting such immense power over others. She pivoted and returned to her husband, and the two embraced and broke into audible sobs. Prask-aes strode away from them, only to be confronted by his cousin, the man who continued to love his wife, openly and without shame.

"This is wrong, and you know it. Kur-asug made a mistake, but he did it out of love and out of duty. I would do the same for my family." It was the first time that Akos-pau had used the phrase "my family" with Prask-aes in all the years since Soug-kue was forced to marry this despicable man. By openly declaring that he had fathered the chief's children, Akos-pau could not have hurled a more stinging insult at Prask-aes.

Prask-aes leapt upon his cousin, knocking him to the ground. The pair wrestled and punched until several men separated them.

"You think that you are strong, but your bitterness and false bravado make you weak," Akos-pau shouted at the chief, still panting. "All the Gaip know it. Even other tribes know it."

"Watch yourself, cousin. You could be the next to be banished."

"You would not dare, because your so-called family would be gone as well," said Akos-pau. "Ask yourself this: Why have the other tribes refused your demands to help drive the sky creatures away? Why do the other tribes manufacture more weapons and train more young people in warfare than we do? Could it be that they know that your poor leadership makes the Gaip ripe for conquest?"

The chief's eyes betrayed a modicum of self-doubt as he shouted: "How dare you?"

"Maybe not tonight. Maybe not tomorrow. But someday I will dare you, I will dare you to face a challenge. Do not rest assured that you will remain our chief once that day arrives."

§

"It's you again."

Marjorie was only sixteen but had an ample bosom and long, shapely legs. She had already been bedded by two other second-gen boys, but no pregnancy had resulted. It was Marcus's turn to try once more. He remained just inside the doorway to her tiny apartment in the original complex, taken aback by her callous greeting.

"You're so sweaty and gross," Marjorie continued, stretching provocatively in her bed. "You really need lessons on how to do it, you know."

"It wasn't my idea to come here," said Marcus. "I'll have you know that some of the other girls like the way I do it. You can ask them."

"I already have, little boy." She snickered. "And I do mean little."

There was a time, not long ago, when having sex with girls was exciting. The physical pleasure was amazing, and having multiple partners gave Marcus the opportunity to learn what girls wanted and how to provide it. If the girls did not enjoy it as much as he did, at least they made a pretense of experiencing pleasure or not despising him.

"Just what do you want me to do—or not do?" said Marcus.

Marjorie stated at the ceiling for a moment. Then she started moaning. She moaned louder, exclaiming "ohh" and "ahh" and "yes" as if she were in the throes of sexual passion. She winked at Marcus.

He began to imitate her cries, staying in rhythm with her, even finding himself getting hard as he pretended as best he could. After about a minute, Marjorie let out a scream of ecstasy, and he followed with a loud "ohhhhh!" He waited another minute, then exited the apartment, making a show of tying his pants for three bios who just couldn't help gathering nearby in response to the racket.

Two of his buddies caught up with him as he shuffled to the learning center for morning lessons. Teddy had some sort of improvised spear. Andy was carrying a rope and sharp pieces of metal he had removed from the wreckage of the ark. Marcus knew at once that they were hell bent on trouble.

"Come with us," said Teddy.

"I can't. Jalen or Doctor Trevino will realize we're not in class." said Marcus.

"Relax," responded Andy. "We told Jalen that the professor gave us time off to look for fossils, and we told Dr. Trevino that Jalen cleared our absence."

The teens tried to keep a low profile as they sauntered through the center of the settlement, where first-gens had constructed a crude sundial that few bios bothered to attempt to decipher these days. They continued past the original perimeter, and then beyond the outer fence. From there they sought high ground, away from territory frequented by bios or natives. With Teddy in the lead, they crested a hill to the southeast and passed out of view of the settlement. They hiked for about fifteen more minutes before resting in a glade of dense bushes with ostentatious red flowers that were popular with the biting butterflies. Marcus was immediately buzzed by several of the annoying insects.

"What are we doing here?" he asked as he thrashed the air around his head protectively.

"Just eat some of those green berries, and you won't be worrying about stupid bugs," Teddy replied. Teddy and Andy each ate three. Marcus tried one. It was bitter and dry. His buddies tried to cram several more down his throat but he spit them out.

The boys sought to wash the acrid taste out of their mouths at a nearby stream. It wasn't long before the drug kicked in and Teddy and Andy began to wander, as if their legs had minds of their own. Their necks rolled at the mercy of the breezes. They sported childish smiles and started having trouble standing up. Soon, Marcus was feeling light-headed, then slightly goofy. He returned to the stream, stuck his finger down his throat, and tried to vomit out the berry, but it was too late.

When he returned to where he thought that he had left his buddies, they were nowhere to be seen. Calling out their names and hearing no response, he tried to remember the way that they had come. He sought lower elevation, hoping that he would find his way back to the settlement. Wooziness forced him to sit on a fallen tree trunk. He was captivated by the life burgeoning all around him: plants and trees and birds and insects, all off on their own frantic, crucial, unfathomable business. Vegetation seemed to expand visibly, glossy new cells appearing by the instant, vines reaching out in rapture to the light and the warmth and the moisture. A diminutive, bright yellow bird hovered before him, its wings beating so rapidly that they appeared to be liquid. It was trying to tell him something. Not a secret; something obvious: something he should know, or once knew, or might someday know. Time evaporated like dew. At some point he understood that the sun was dropping behind the western hills. He needed to get home, but he was lost and confused.

Moving downhill instinctively, he reached a winding ribbon of grassland and heard a commotion. He had found Teddy and Andy, and they had found a herd of beasts. Still severely intoxicated, his friends had decided to try to catch or wrestle or mount the massive animals—it wasn't clear in the fading light. The boys wouldn't take no for an answer. Several of the beasts began attacking the youths, goring one and trampling both. The screams were terrible and helped snap Marcus out of his drug-induced lethargy. He raced to the side of the young bios, heedless of personal danger, and managed to drag them away from the angry animals. The beasts took a long look at Marcus, then went back to grazing on the fat clover plants.

Andy was losing blood from a puncture wound. Both boys were in bad shape.

"Can you walk?" Marcus asked them.

"No way," said Teddy. Andy just shook his head.

Marcus used the dwindling light to get his bearings and set off in a direction that he hoped would take him to the settlement. After scrambling to the top of a hillside, he saw security lights and sighed in relief. He raced to the outer gate and rang an alarm bell until help arrived, then led a search party that found his friends and returned them to the settlement for medical care.

Claire didn't demand an explanation from Marcus until the next day. Marcus told her everything. He was grounded, but Claire never again criticized him for sneaking out that day with his friends.

Eventually, he was allowed to leave the settlement to scout. He discovered a lot more than he ever imagined.

CONNECTION

After nearly forty years locked in a digital death grip with Damian, James realized that he could not gain the high ground, could not win the war by direct assault. He needed to fall back and devise a better strategy. He would fade into the background and let Damian believe that he had surrendered. Surely, Damian would slip up, and James would launch a new, more effective offensive.

Damian reminded Katherine of a man who had just awoken from a coma. At first, he barely knew his surroundings. He could not remember trading his crab body for a more lifelike robotic form, and he barely recognized her. As he recovered, he demonstrated scant interest in how Katherine was faring. He obsessed over Maria, Jalen, and Hubert, and their mission.

"You're telling me that there are dozens of humans now, even though we smashed the nursery in the ark? How did you let this happen?"

"What did you expect me to do?" Katherine said. "It was you who wanted to crush them. I saw no reason to help them, but I saw no reason to get in their way."

"I'm very disappointed in you. What kind of defenses do they have?"

Katherine led him to a hillside more than a mile from the settlement. She pointed out fences, gates, and key buildings such as the power plant and computer shack. Back in the underground ruins, he questioned Katherine about what she had learned about the machines there. She was hesitant to discuss the breakthrough that she had facilitated to get them improved robotic bodies, fearing that he would expect more miracles from her. He turned his attention to the symbols that showed up intermittently on screens along the central table, determined to crack the code.

Damian noticed that Katherine left the ruins frequently in the morning and early afternoon. A couple of times he followed her surreptitiously. He discovered that Katherine was watching bio children at play, mesmerized by their scampering and screaming. He recognized that Katherine missed her former life and wanted to recreate it somehow. *How different the two of us are.*

One night he confronted her. "If they offered to take you back, would you join them?"

"Them? You mean the bios and bots?"

"Who do you think I meant? The natives?"

"I ... I don't know."

"I have seen you watching the children. I fear that you are not sufficiently loyal to me."

"I didn't do anything. I just watched." She studied his face. "I want to have a life with you."

"You will have to prove your loyalty."

"What do you want me to do?"

"You must kill Maria and Jalen."

§

Tuep-gri loved her parents dearly. Yet it was her grandmother, Soug-kue, with whom she had a singular bond. Their appearances were similar, despite their differences in years. Each was tall and agile, with straight, lustrous hair flowing halfway down their back. But the connection went far deeper; it was almost as if Tuep-gri and Soug-kue shared a soul. Tuep-gri admired and envied her grandmother's ability to reach beyond the banal, to recognize and celebrate the hidden beauty and grace and power in the world. And the young woman was inspired by Soug-kue's unassailable belief in the earth mother, the absent god. On occasion, she heard Soug-kue admonish other Gaip when they referenced the earth mother as the god that had abandoned her people. Yes, the earth mother was absent, Soug-kue conceded. But she would return when she felt that the time was right. Maybe she would rescue the Gaip in a time of great peril, such as the drought that was deepening by the day. Maybe she would appear when the Gaip and the other tribes proved that they deserved to regain her graces. Soug-kue even had a name for the absent god, which was all the more curious because it could not be written with the letters that comprised the tribes' alphabet: Ahm.

Soug-kue was a font of practical knowledge in addition to spiritual inspiration. Scouting, hunting, sending—particularly sending—she was highly skilled at all. She nurtured *tur* in Tuep-gri as soon as the girl started feeling her powers at the unusually young age of nine. Now seventeen, Tuep-gri was nearly her grandmother's equal in many ways, the older woman professed.

The day's still, oppressive heat had sapped the cries of even the loudest birds. The rustling of bushes on the hillside where Tuep-gri was roaming could have been heard by any Gaip, even one who was sleeping. Despite her small ears, Tuep-gri could detect the movement from more than one hundred feet away. It seemed too loud for a flying snake, boar, or jungle cat. She could not detect *tur*, so if the noise was coming from a Gaip or a member of another tribe, he or she was highly skilled at masking their thoughts. But why take so much care not to be read and still thrash about like a petulant child?

She unsheathed her knife and willed herself into silence and invisibility as the sounds became louder and closer. She leapt as the figure came into view, halting her knife inches from the throat of a very surprised sky creature.

"Whoa!" the youth managed. He raised his hands cautiously to show that he was unarmed.

Tuep-gri said something that he did not understand. She pointed the knife at his chest. Then she backed off slightly, studying him, her weapon still brandished. She had never been close to one of the sky creatures, but the stories were abundant among her tribe. They were slow, stupid, and smelly. Yet at the same time they were evil and dangerous. The descriptions didn't add up. She decided that she would take advantage of this opportunity to learn the truth for herself.

"Listen," said the young man, lowering his hands nervously, "I don't want any trouble. You look like a nice young lady. I'm just out here scouting." He realized that the girl could not understand a word he was saying, then pointed to himself. "I am Marcus." She tilted her head quizzically, narrowed her eyes, and relaxed her militant posture ever so slightly. He pointed again and repeated: "Marcus."

"Marr-cuss," she managed, gesturing toward him.

"Yes, good. Marcus." He smiled.

The girl pointed to herself. "Tuep-gri."

Marcus tried to repeat the name and mangled it badly.

She said it twice more. He finally got it.

She put away her knife and sat cross legged, barely five feet from him in what passed for a clearing, just a spot where the soil was so thin that even the most tenacious vegetation struggled to exist. He hesitated, then sat as well. It was wrong, both youths knew. They were supposed to avoid the others at all costs. In a world of ever-present danger, strangers could spell disaster. But it just felt natural. They seemed to be about the same age. They were both looking for their place in their world. It was inevitable that their societies would collide at some point. Did that collision have to be violent? If only they could communicate. That wouldn't be easy. But here they were, sitting across from one another.

For lack of inspiration, Marcus pointed at a tree and said "tree". Tuep-gri pronounced the word and *serk*, the Gaip translation. She pointed to his large ears and started to giggle. He feigned a hurt expression, then laughed. "Ears," he said. She got it quickly. "Nose" came easily as well. Then Tuep-gri pointed to the sun and looked inquisitively at Marcus. "Sun," he said. He made a circle with his hands. "That's the sun."

"Sun," she said, nodding. She seemed more interested in learning his words than in imparting her own.

Marcus began to pull vines out by the roots to expose a small area of dirt between them. Using a finger, he started to write the word "sun" in front of her, upside down for him but right-side-up for her. He couldn't manage it, so he rose and began to move to her side so he could write from a better angle.

She sprang to her feet and away from him, thinking that he might be trying some sort of attack. He realized his mistake, returned to his place properly chastened, and finished the word cautiously. She sat down in front of him again.

Marcus had run out of easy words to try to get across. He analyzed her colorful clothing; her long, muscular legs, bare and crossed; her narrow waist; her delicate arms; those six-fingered hands; that radiant black hair tied in a knot. And her face. It wasn't a beautiful face—at least, not alluring in the way that some bio girls seemed at first glance.

Marcus felt that she lacked something, something that other girls had in common.

Guile. This young woman possessed none of the false veneer behind which every bio girl seemed to shield herself. In its place were a quiet confidence and a natural humility.

Tuep-gri blushed at his gaze, but she decided that it was only fair for her to check out Marcus in return. He was short and overweight, but he appeared sturdy. The sandy color of his hair was rare among the tribes. His forehead was less prominent than that of men she knew. His ears and nose were ridiculously large. But he wasn't completely ugly. He seemed to be smarter than the sky creatures had been described to her, though as far as his smell—the elders were right about that part.

I had better not stay here long. I have much territory to cover, and I do not wish to be discovered with this sky creature.

She rose effortlessly and glanced at the sun, which was at its zenith. She pointed to it, and then at the ground between them. *Same time. Here. Tomorrow.* He showed no indication that he received the sending, but that didn't surprise her.

Tuep-gri turned and melted into the forest.

§

Less than two hours before dawn, Damian and Katherine approached the outer fence of the bio settlement. No guard was present, so they let themselves in through the gate and moved quickly to the inner fence. As Damian had expected, the sole guard there was asleep at this hour, snoring heavily. That made it easy to open the gate and pass through without being noticed. Katherine was unarmed, but Damian was carrying a thick metal shaft that he had found in the underground ruins.

Katherine had described the robotic bodies that now possessed the minds of Maria and Jalen. She and Damian split up, looking between structures and through windows for any sign of them. Even though the bots never slept, it was possible that they rested or recharged batteries when few if any bios were awake. She soon heard noises coming from a large building. Edging up to a window, she recognized Jalen in front of a screen depicting something that looked like one of the sports shows her father had watched on TV when she was a girl. The pain of how her dad misled her all those years about his other family flared once again. Yet the ballgame reminded her of good times, when youthful innocence was a warm cocoon.

Damian came to her side. "Excellent," he said on their private comm link. "Take care of him."

"There's no other way?" she asked.

"No. Do it now."

Damian handed her the metal shaft, which was so heavy that her organic body probably could not have lifted it. About eight feet long, it ended with a device that looked something like the head of a monkey wrench.

Can I really kill someone who was once human?

She opened the door. Jalen turned and stared as she approached him.

"I'm really sorry," she said, though they shared no comm link anymore. She hoped that he would run away so that she wouldn't have to do this. He remained motionless.

"Katherine?"

She raised her weapon and brought it down on the top of his head. He staggered, falling to the floor and raising his arms in self-defense. She loomed over him, the weapon lifted again.

"Hit him again! Harder!"

Damian's words seared her mind and spirit. She was tempted to turn around and bash Damian, or simply to walk off into the grasslands and hills, never to return.

"This is your last chance," Damian advised her.

Katherine's anger reached a crescendo. It had to be released. She used all her strength to bring the weapon down upon Jalen, cracking his head. She struck him again, and the breach widened, exposing boards and circuits. She kept mashing until his head was in pieces on the floor. She started in on his body, but her energy and will were depleted. She collapsed on the floor next to him, hugging his motionless torso.

Damian entered the room with a sack and removed a fragment of native clothing and a rind from one of the fruits that the natives enjoyed but the bios found nearly inedible. He positioned the items where they would be noticed. Then he placed two pieces of animal hide that looked like native footwear over his metal feet and walked around Jalen's body, stamping, leaving footprints on the dusty wooden floor.

"Find Maria," he ordered Katherine.

She and Damian searched all over the settlement without success. As first light bathed the complex and bios began to stir, the bots returned to the ruins where they spent most of their time. Neither said a word on their way back.

A young bio mother bringing her daughter to the learning center made the gruesome discovery, trying to shield the toddler from the sight of the dissembled bot who the girl had come to know as "Jay-Jay". The woman rang an alarm bell. Several bios entered the building and examined Jalen's remains. They spread the word that the building was off-limits until further notice.

When she came within comm range, Hubert broke the news to Maria, who had been scouting western territory.

"He can't be dead. Please tell me this is a mistake."

"He is gone."

"You don't have a copy of his mind, or any way to put him back together?"

"Nothing on this planet could repair him. I doubt that anything on Earth could do so."

"Who did this?"

"I suggest that you investigate this crime in order to answer that question."

By the time she returned, the settlers were nearly unanimous in their opinion: The natives had murdered Jalen.

Maria paused before entering the learning center, then stepped inside hesitantly and took in the scene. *Oh Jalen, we have been through so much. I thought we would grow old together here for decades, maybe centuries.* She wanted to cry, to find a physical outlet for her grief. She had no ability to create tears; a small amount of lubricant kept her artificial eyes from getting stuck in one position, but it just wasn't the same. She sat down on the floor and moaned.

Eventually, she rose and inspected the crime scene. A few bios had been in the room since Jalen was discovered. They had committed the cardinal sin of moving the body, placing all but the tiniest fragments in a storage shed. Hubert had told Maria about the indications of native involvement. But as she looked closely at the spot where Jalen had fallen, she noticed what looked like bot footprints in addition to those that appeared to be native prints. The bot impressions did not match her feet or Jalen's. She followed the prints outside and found more under a window and traces of them in a few more locations around the complex.

That evening, all first- and second-gen bios who were not supervising young children gathered for a meeting to discuss the killing. The settlement did not have a formal government. First-gens had gotten into the habit of making decisions for the good of all, in consultation with Maria, Jalen, and Hubert. Claire was the first-gen who expressed the greatest desire to perpetuate and protect the species and became a leader by default. The four other surviving women and four surviving men who had been generated from artificial wombs were focused on personal and family matters. Fortunately, sharp disputes were rare. Routine discussions and compromises settled the most common issues— such as who should mate with whom, and who should do which jobs.

Physically, Claire and the other first-gens were no different than their children and grandchildren. Yet their circumstances were unique, having been created by artificial means and grown in imitation wombs. The first-gens were loved and revered, but they would never be considered equals with other bios. Subconsciously, their descendants considered them to be almost bots. Second-gens were destined to be the leaders of the community.

The stabbing of Bruce at the boar pen was bad, but the murder of Jalen was a serious escalation, most settlers agreed. Even though Jalen was a bot, he was important to the community. What should be done about the natives?

"The natives did not kill Jalen," Maria declared. She was greeted with disbelief and a smattering of scorn.

"Two bots came into our settlement before dawn and committed this heinous crime," she continued. "They arranged fake evidence to make it look like the natives did this. But they inadvertently left footprints—the impressions of their metal feet—in and near the crime scene."

"Why would they want to hurt Jalen?" a first-gen man named Jonah asked.

"There is a long history of conflict between Damian—the worst of the two renegade bots—and those of us supporting the mission to establish this settlement. It goes back to the first days after the ark landed and Hubert awoke the consciousnesses that had been stored in computers on the spaceship. It's a long, sad story, but I have no doubt about who did this."

"Where has he been for the past four decades?" asked Claire.

"Hiding, I guess. Or maybe building a better robotic body. He ruined the first nursery we built on the ark, then disappeared with Katherine. Whatever his reason for waiting until now to attack again, I doubt that he is done."

"He didn't attack anyone else when he had the chance. Maybe he just wants to destroy bots," suggested Justin.

"Damian is crazy," said Maria. "I know that he would like to destroy me and perhaps even Hubert. But I don't think he would stop there."

"Would he join with the natives?" inquired a first-gen woman named Vivian.

"I don't think he's sane enough or persuasive enough to pull off such an alliance. But, regardless, he's the biggest threat we face. We need to create an army so we can defend ourselves."

A first-gen named Sandra spoke up. "If this Damian was the culprit and not the natives, we have but one enemy. We don't need an army to protect one bot from another bot."

"This is true," Justin observed. "Maybe we would be safer if Maria left the settlement."

A flood of opinions issued from the bios. Some of the first-gens supported Maria staying. They had grown up with her unflinching support. "There would be no settlement without Maria," argued Claire. "It's just unthinkable to turn her away. What wrong has she committed? And what would we do without her?"

"We do owe Maria a massive debt of gratitude," replied Justin. "I admire Maria as much as any of us does. I know how much she has helped the first-gens in particular. But we must think of the settlement's future, what's best for all of us. Maria has become a liability. I believe that it's time for her to move on—with our thanks for her service to the settlement."

"What do you have to say to this?" Claire asked Maria.

Maria studied the faces of the bios. Many would not meet her gaze. Some part of Maria wanted to argue, to make the case that she should stay, that the settlement needed her. But she realized that her desire to remain was largely a selfish one. If these people really wanted her gone, she could not deny their will.

Hubert still had a lot to learn about the human race, but he knew not to inject himself into this dispute. Plus, no one had asked his opinion.

Without another word, Maria left.

"Where will you go?" Hubert asked her as she exited the outer fence.

"I don't know. I guess I'll explore for a while." She looked around, unsure where, if anywhere, to venture in the dark.

§

The hills to the east stretched and yawned under dawn's gentle light, so Maria wandered in that direction. As she journeyed, she added to her mental map of the features of the planet. She had not seen much of the world, and Hubert's drones had not traveled far because of the limited range of their comm link.

"Think we ought to give this rock a name?" she asked Hubert as she skirted a dark forest.

"A name for the planet? I suspect the natives already have one. And, in time, the bios will likely devise one of their own. 'Planet' is sufficient for my purposes."

That figures.

She crossed a parched stream bed and encountered increasingly rugged terrain. She became concerned that the rocky slopes and deep fissures were so treacherous that a fall could damage her robotic body. As she sought a safe way forward, she alerted Hubert to what appeared to be smoke in the distance.

"You might be seeing fires from a native settlement," he responded. "However, based on what we know of the natives' hesitance to burn open fires and what I can discern from the shapes of the mountains to the east and north, it is more likely that you are witnessing volcanic activity."

"Got it."

She ventured south, past convoluted hills and wide stretches of grasslands populated by the horned beasts. After about fifteen miles, she saw a small cluster of natives. From a distance, it appeared that they wore different colors than the Gaip, suggesting that they might be a separate tribe. She managed to keep her distance and avoid another unfortunate encounter.

"Hubert, you have not commented on the bios' decision to expel me from the settlement. Have you no opinion on their action?"

"I found it unwise."

"Well, I found it more than unwise. It hurts. It hurts a lot. I have done a lot for these bios, and I have put myself in jeopardy to try to create a world for them. This is how they thank me."

"I expect that there will be many instances in which they regret their decision."

As she traveled, she encountered dark rock formations with jagged edges, rising like unseemly boils. Hubert speculated that these were remains of lava flows, maybe recent ones, as the territory lacked the typical dense jungle foliage of other hilly regions.

The hills receded as she traveled south, and on the third day she noticed new types of birds and more small animals hopping and slithering under and around dark, prickly bushes. The soil was soft and moist in spots, forcing her to tread carefully so as not to get stuck. Suddenly, a sparkling blue ocean, or possibly a lake, opened before her.

"Hubert, can you see this?" No response. She guessed that she was out of comm range. Noticing a thin swath of hard-packed earth, she followed it close to the shoreline, where supple waves caressed pale brown sand rhythmically, making love to the shore in a timeless tryst. The beach was more pristine than any she had seen on Earth or had dreamed of visiting. She almost felt that she was intruding on someone's private paradise. Sharp bird calls overhead seemed to reinforce that sensation.

If only I could race into the shallow waves, like when I was little and my parents took me to Ocean City. She assumed that water would be almost as harmful to her robotic body as it would have been to her crab shell, so she decided to walk along the shoreline heading west. She encountered a river that still had a trickle to contribute to the unquenchable ocean, then followed its course to the northwest for a couple of days, discerning more mountains that could well be volcanoes. At a distance, she encountered a single native with yet a third type of outfit, but he or she bolted upon seeing Maria.

Maria started marching due east, encountering uneven ground— including steep hills and dense woodlands—without altering her course. She did not realize that she had wavered from her usual practice of walking where the terrain was most favorable. She even trod nonstop through one night, using her limited night vision and the modest illumination offered by two ragged moons, not realizing that she was being guided if not compelled by a subtle yet unrecognizable force. She slipped and fell often. By midmorning on the third day, she found herself entering a dark recess at the base of a hill, the opening of a cave. Without hesitation, she plunged into darkness.

TELLING

It took a bit of creative deception, but Marcus kept coming up with reasons to spend his days in the hills north of the settlement. The first-gens who doled out scouting assignments felt that they knew enough about the territory in that direction—mostly, that it was inhabited by a native tribe and should be avoided. Marcus insisted that there were interesting plants and animals in the region, as well as possible signs of an earlier civilization, that justified his time there.

The day after he had met Tuep-gri, he hiked to the location where he had encountered her. He waited about an hour and could not hide his elation when she appeared. It became a regular midday rendezvous. She, too, had to express strong opinions about where and when she should scout so that she would be able to meet surreptitiously with Marcus, though she had more leeway than most Gaip scouts because of her advanced skills.

The nouns were relatively easy. The verbs and adjectives were trickier. But the youngsters were excited to be embarking on an odyssey of communication and, perhaps, friendship. The need for secrecy about their meetings only added to the enjoyment. Marcus felt more comfortable with Tuep-gri than he had with any bio girl, and he had known her only a short time. If Tuep-gri had no interest in him, she wouldn't show up each day, Marcus told himself.

About midmorning on the eighth day after their first encounter, Marcus experienced an odd sensation, almost as if he were coming down with an illness. A malady called jungle flu left many a bio fatigued and wheezing, and less than a year earlier he had incurred a cut that became infected, requiring extensive rest and fluids so that he would not suffer the same fate as his sister. But this feeling was different. He kept visualizing a notch in the hills—an illusion created by viewing two ridgelines from a particular vantage point that Marcus remembered reaching north of the bio settlement. He couldn't recall exactly where it was.

There was a second element to the impression. He saw Tuep-gri. No, that wasn't it. He imagined that she wanted something. She wanted to kiss him!

No way. I'm just dreaming. But wouldn't that be awesome. I have no idea what it would be like to kiss a native girl—I guess their lips work pretty much like bio lips. No, I shouldn't think about this.

The sensation lingered a few moments, then vanished. He was torn: Should he show up at their usual meeting place at midday? If he didn't, Tuep-gri might be disappointed, and maybe he would never see her again. But he was intrigued, so much so that, as the sun was nearly overhead, he found himself topping hills and looking for that view of the notch. Just before midday, he found it. He felt stupid. There was nothing there.

He had almost persuaded himself to leave when he heard a faint rustling in the bushes below and to his right. Tuep-gri emerged, a sly smile forming upon seeing him. She came up to him nonchalantly, her eyes searching his. He inched forward, almost afraid to learn if his vision were true. Tuep-gri placed those graceful six-fingered hands on either side of his head, pulled him close, and kissed him briefly but firmly.

He started to speak, but she put two fingers on his mouth, then tapped her mouth with the same fingers, willing him to silence. He allowed himself the luxury of accommodating her wish, grinning broadly.

They sat on a rock slab, taking in the view. After several minutes, he couldn't hold back his curiosity.

"How did you... how you know I come here?" He gestured to her, to himself, and to the ground in front of them.

She pointed to her forehead. "No tell."

"You no tell, or I no tell?"

"I no tell. You no tell."

He shook his head in agreement. "I no tell."

Marcus wasn't particularly good at keeping secrets. But he couldn't inform other bios about something he didn't understand.

He removed a broad, thick, pale, folded-up leaf from a pocket, then withdrew a sharpened twig with a black core. He wrote out his alphabet so Tuep-gri could help him devise a guide that would assist in translation. "Show letters," he said.

She seemed less than enthusiastic. He started with her name. "T— Tuep," he said, pointing to the T and repeating "T". She hesitated, then drew a short wavy line next to the letter.

"U," he continued. She turned away from him.

"Okay. All good." *We'll try again another day.*

Why is writing so important to the sky creatures?

When it was time for both teens to get on with their day's errands, he tried to kiss her again. She pulled away coyly, but she smiled and tapped her forehead. Marcus didn't get it, but he laughed and said "Bye".

§

Claire and Justin were baffled about what had come over Marcus. He seemed more cheerful than usual, complained less about his duties, didn't hang out much with his troublemaking friends, and even produced a map of the region north of the settlement. He resisted being assigned to scout a different territory, and his enthusiasm for his work was so strong that he got his way.

Either he was a gifted teacher or Tuep-gri was a superb student, Marcus believed—probably the latter. However, Marcus was having trouble getting her to understand the word "planet". He gestured with his arms, as if to embrace everything around them.

"Land," she said.

"Bigger."

"Land and hills."

"Everything."

She shook her head in confusion.

Marcus pointed to the sun and drew a circle on the ground. "Sun round." Then he pointed to the ground. "Planet round. Ground round."

"Ground not round," she insisted.

I understand now. This is a young woman who has had no formal education—probably little education of any kind. She might not know that the world is round. She might not be literate.

"Let me tell you a story," he said. She seemed relieved that he was changing the subject. With many welcome interruptions for explanations of unknown words and unfamiliar concepts, Marcus related a simplified tale of how he and his fellow bios came to be there. Pointing to the sky, he tried to indicate a place far away, then he turned his right hand into a spaceship traveling and landing on the ground. He showed people walking out, first as crabs—it was tricky making his hand simulate a six-legged robot—then walking upright. He pointed to himself.

She struggled to tell her tribe's story, having trouble getting across the concept of the ancients, in part because her people knew so little of them. She had taught Marcus the words *serpu*, which the bios called horned beast, and *rost*, the broad green plant that the bios termed clover. She attempted to get across her tribe's taboos by shaking her head and waving her hand sideways while saying "no" repeatedly. "No eat *rosts*." "No go near *serpus*." "No..."

She pantomimed something moving awkwardly.

"No crabs?"

"No." She thought for a while. "Thing move by self."

"No machines."

She nodded. "No machines."

Marcus repeated the phrases with appropriate solemnity.

When they parted, Marcus got a kiss and a hug.

§

Who built this? Where are they now?

For one of the few times since Claire and the other first-gens were born, Maria felt genuine excitement. Before her was a massive oval underground chamber with a long gray-white table in the center and what appeared to be bookshelves set into smooth stone walls. Some of the overhead lights that had burst into life upon her entrance flickered with dysfunction, and her movement around the moribund room triggered minor bursts of brittle dust that were captured by sharp shafts of illumination. *It's almost like snow back home.*

Home. She tried to imagine what was left of Columbia, of anyone's home on Earth. Could some people have survived? Were they starting over, and struggling, like the bio settlement here? Might there be just one human left, ranging through the ruins, desperate to discover another indication of intelligent life—like she was doing in this place, at this time?

Best not to think about home. I can never go back. Anyone still alive there will never know about this planet and our desperate experiment.

She ran a metal-and-plastic hand clumsily over the asymmetrical surfaces of the unrecognizable equipment on the table, disturbing even more dust but activating a low hum and generating a fleeting display of secretive symbols. She tried speaking to the machines and poking their surfaces, but she could not make a connection. The bookcases displayed documents of unquestioned antiquity; she feared that if she opened one the papers would disintegrate instantaneously, silencing the long-interred voices of the messengers forever and unleashing untold guilt—if not a curse. She could not resist attempting to open one case that held a small number of relics. She was almost relieved when she could not manage to access any of the timeless prizes.

Maria explored the narrow corridors leading off the chamber. Some became illuminated; others remained dark; in most cases there was little to discover. More than a dozen starkly empty rooms, most about the size of jail cells on Earth, hollowed out of the hillside like the primary chamber. Dusky, ancient debris, none of it recognizable. A few modestly sized chambers with the partially collapsed remains of unknown mechanisms. No hint of the true purpose of this complex.

Could people have lived here? It's not exactly the Ritz.

As she returned to the main chamber, she halted, consumed by a sudden bout of disorientation, uncertain where she was or what she was doing. A curious sound caught her attention and forced her to focus. It was the first thing she had heard, other than faint electronic humming, since she had entered through the arched passageway and descended the long ramp. She ducked behind the central table. The erratic lighting created a disturbing strobe effect, almost hypnotic.

"Who's there?" she demanded.

No answer. But someone or something scurried. Maybe two entities, running.

"What do you want?"

Laughter. Laughter! Maria looked around for a weapon, something to offer protection, finding nothing.

"Show yourself!"

Again, no response. She heard more indications of movement, so she jogged up the ramp in their direction. The dim light revealed nothing but centuries of desiccation. Suddenly, the sounds were behind her, near the table she had just left.

Maria was determined to discover who or what was taunting her so brazenly. She plodded along the corridors, always seemingly a few paces away from the footsteps and laughter. She called out for Hubert's help, but she could not contact him.

Her frustration beginning to boil over, Maria came to rest with her back against a wall in one of the small chambers. She would let the intruders come to her. She waited, hearing and seeing nothing. Time collapsed and lost relevance in the musty mausoleum. Then, abruptly, more laughter erupted, louder than ever. It was evident that it was being generated by someone with a diseased mind.

She was stunned by the realization that it was coming from her.

§

Marcus tried to hide the document, folding it quickly and sliding it into a pocket of his pants. His reaction to Claire entering the house triggered her suspicions.

"Show it to me," she demanded.

"It's nothing."

"If it's nothing, then you have no reason to hide it."

Somehow, mothers just knew.

He removed the leaf, which was decaying with age and frequent use. She recognized letters. She did not know the symbols that had been inscribed adjacent to several of them.

"Explain yourself."

"I'm just..." He couldn't come up with a lie that would make any sense.

"Go on."

"She's... She's just like us, really."

"What's her name?"

"Tuep-gri."

"What kind of name is that?" Claire was intrigued and concerned in equal measure.

"The *gri* is some sort of nature thing. I think it's a bird that soars among the tallest mountains. The first part is just a name, I guess."

"And this is how you've been spending your scouting time."

"Yes. But Mother, I have learned a lot about these people. They really are like us. At least, she is."

"Do you like her?"

"Yes, I guess I do."

Claire did not know where to begin. "This is dangerous. The natives have stolen from us repeatedly. Have you forgotten what happened to Bruce?"

"No. But she's not like that."

"I will discuss this with your father and some of the other first-gens," she said. She hated to put a damper on any romance, but there was too much at stake. "Until further notice, you will not meet with this girl."

Many miles to the north, Soug-kue reached out her mind and read highly disturbing thoughts from her granddaughter. She caught up with Tuep-gri as the young woman was trying to fill a hollowed-out gourd with water trickling from a cleft in a rock face. The spring released only a few drops per minute. It almost was not worth the effort.

"You are meeting with a sky creature."

Tuep-gri knew that she could not deceive her grandmother, nor could she block her mind probes or avoid her entirely. But the teen-ager was not ready to discuss this unique relationship.

"It is none of your concern," she stated.

"Oh, but it is, granddaughter. It is my concern, and it is the tribe's concern. What made you think that this was a wise decision?"

"It just happened, by accident. Anyway, he is harmless. He is not a fighter. He is just a stupid boy."

"And when did you start spending time with stupid boys? I believe there is more, much more. And I do not like it one bit."

"Grandmother, please trust me. It feels right. It feels as if—as if the earth mother herself has willed us to meet and to talk. And that's all we do," she added quickly. "We talk."

Soug-kue sighed. "You dare invoke the earth mother. Then it is serious between the two of you. You must be careful. Very careful. Those we view as friends can quickly turn into enemies."

§

Marcus could tell at once that Tuep-gri was preoccupied.

"No come here for some days," she said, head down.

His lower lip curled upward, underscoring his frown. "Do you not want to see me?"

"Not that." She managed a weak smile. "Grandmother know..." She pointed to Marcus.

"Does this have something to do with the vision I had?"

She turned from him. "I no talk on this."

"Then there is something!" His reaction sent a chill through Tuep-gri. She decided that it was time to impose a reality check on their friendship.

"I be ... *toar* ... to Par-vask." She didn't know the English word for betroth. She held out her arms as if she were embracing another.

"You are going to marry this man?" He made no attempt to disguise his displeasure.

She nodded.

"Do you love him?" Marcus had never previously used the word "love" with her, so he placed his palm on his heart when he said it. She seemed to understand.

"No choice."

Marcus nodded. "I also do things I do not like. I must have sex with girls I do not like and who do not like me." He made a crude gesture of a finger from one hand entering a circle formed by a finger and the thumb of his other hand.

"You not like..." She wasn't sure that she caught the word.

"Sex."

"You not like sex?"

"Yes, and no. I like sex with someone who likes me. But most of the girls in the settlement do not like me."

"Maybe we ... different," said Tuep-gri softly, looking at her lap. "Maybe you not like."

"I would like. I know I would like."

She acted genuinely shy with him for the first time. She grasped his hands and brought him slowly to his feet. Then she took his right

188   *Castle of Sand*

hand and placed it on the thin clothing over her left breast. She reached down between his legs. He slid his hand from her breast to her waist, then under her skirt. She closed her eyes and guided his hand.

"*Vai!*" she screamed.

He withdrew his hand briskly and backed away from her. "I'm sorry. I'm really sorry."

She shouted something else in her language.

"I don't..."

She held her hands to her head and bent over. As usual, the mind invader was moving through water, navigating currents with fins instead of arms and legs. Others like it were nearby. They were gliding, like fish, but their bodies were more sinuous, and their heads vaguely resembled those of natives. The mind invader broke the surface of the water, closing one set of organs and opening another. Tuep-gri gasped for air involuntarily as she sensed the mind invader's transition. She applied all of her energy and power of concentration to block or diminish the connection with it, recalling vaguely that someone was with her. Marcus, of course. She had just screamed at him.

She turned to Marcus, her face a portrait of agony. "It ... not ... you."

Marcus watched in horror as Tuep-gri lowered herself to the ground, still holding her head. After an achingly long interval, she relaxed. She rose and brushed the dirt off of her clothes and her skin methodically, refusing to look at Marcus.

"What happened?"

She just shook her head.

"Can I help?"

"It gone."

"What is gone?"

"No talk on this."

Without another word, she left.

§

Prask-aes paced in front of his troops, projecting strength and courage. Every Gaip over the age of ten was lined up, forming several rows, in the center of the village. The chief told each one in turn their battle group and role, instructing them to make weapons or commence other preparations for the attack. It would take place in three days, after sunset. The chief expected everyone to fight with honor, but most importantly, to win.

"It is the will of the absent god that we recover our territory and the food that the sky creatures have taken from our land. They have stolen water from our creeks and have poured it down their throats, onto their crops, and even into the mouths of the animals they keep. Is there any man, woman, or child among you who is not hungry or thirsty—or angry at what has been taken from us?'

Villagers shifted nervously on their feet but did not respond.

"The sky creatures are weak and will run when they see us coming. However, we must kill as many of them as we can. Perhaps the survivors will return to where they came from. Perhaps they will slink away to steal the land of another tribe."

Soug-kue stood next to her lover, Akos-pau. She could read his unease. Yet neither of them could deny the harsh truth of the village's plight. Three adult Gaip had already died of hunger. Several malnourished children were seriously ill. There was no sign of rain; not even a dark cloud or a gust of wind that might tease them with the possibility of even a brief shower.

The chief walked away and the Gaip disbanded, making little effort to hide their apprehension at launching a war in their current condition. Not one member of the tribe felt healthy, strong, and up to the task. Nevertheless, the next morning several of them began scouring hillsides for rocks to use as weapons. Some went into the forest to find or cut strong tree limbs that could be sharpened into pikes. A few crafted knives from animal bones, but those tended to break much too easily. The tribe had exhausted known deposits of useful metal in and near their territory. A soft, gray mineral called *keir* could be found here and there in small deposits, but no one had found a way to craft it into spear points or knives.

Tuep-gri's parents had not learned of their daughter's meetings with the sky creature, and Soug-kue did not believe that it was her place to inform them. After the evening meal, Soug-kue approached the girl and whispered: "Will you fight them?"

"I do not know. What do you believe the earth mother wants us to do?"

"I have attempted to obtain her guidance, to detect any sign of her wishes or intent. I am saddened that I cannot learn anything. I believe that we should look within ourselves and decide."

§

Several miles to the south, Justin and Elena were having an equally difficult conversation, one that both recognized was long overdue.

"I beg you to forgive me," Elena stated, her voice soft and sad. She was preparing a mug of tea, which Justin viewed as a good sign.

He stood at a window in their cottage, watching the settlement go about its business. "I should beg you to forgive me. For I have done exactly what you have done."

"It is expected of a man. A man must create children. He is in control. Women are subject to that necessity."

"And why is that so? Who is to say what is expected of us?"

"The bots have been clear about our duties. As have the first-gens."

"Maria and Jalen are gone. The first-gens are welcome to their opinions. They tell us that we are bonded partners, but what does that mean? We raise children and pretend to give ourselves to each other. But we give ourselves to others, and our children might not—"

"Do not say it! Our children are *our* children." Elena's tone demonstrated unshakable confidence in her belief.

"Yes, our children are our children. But our lives are our lives. We second-gens are expected to be leaders, the ones who will guide the future of this settlement, who will make crucial decisions." He turned to face Elena, his eyes flashing determination. "I decide here and now that we will not mate with other women and men. It is our duty to each other and to our family not to tear at the fabric of our emotions by spreading our seed indiscriminately. There are forty of us in this settlement and more babies on the way. I say: Enough! Let our families grow as they will. At least, we will live our lives with dignity."

Through her tears, she beamed with love.

WAR

On the day of the attack, Tuep-gri spent much of her time performing unnecessary chores, anything to keep her mind occupied, to distract herself from the conflict burning within her and the wider one about to commence. At sunset, a large bonfire was ignited in the center of the village, the angry flames slapping the air. The Gaip collected their weapons and fidgeted in anticipation.

Tuep-gri avoided eye contact with Soug-kue and tried to block her thoughts from being read by her grandmother and others. She could bear her burden no longer, so she slipped into her home and sat on her thin bedding, focusing a sending to Marcus: *War is coming. Tonight.* She sent an image of natives stabbing settlers. She sent it over and over.

Her parents heard soft cries coming from the shelter. Bursting in, her father saw tears streaming down her face as she focused with every fiber of her being. He read her sending and slapped her hard. She kept sending. He slapped her again, then picked her up and shook her violently. She opened her eyes and smiled.

Her father strode rapidly to Prask-aes and notified him of his daughter's communication. As Tuep-gri approached the fire, walking with a steady confidence, the chief intercepted her and gripped her hard by the shoulders. "What have you done, stupid child?"

"It is nothing," she responded, revealing not the slightest fear or intimidation. "The sky creatures cannot read our thoughts."

The chief shoved her to the ground. "We have a traitor in our midst. But that will not prevent us from defeating our foes."

Though her parents refused to look at Tuep-gri, her grandmother studied her, allowing a slight smile to escape her lips, as the torches were lit and Prask-aes ordered his troops to gather with their group leaders.

Marcus had been in a funk since that confusing day in which Tuep-gri acted so strangely. He had returned several times to their usual meeting spot, but she never showed up. He kept trying to detect any message she might send him. Absolutely nothing. His awkward efforts to reach her with his thoughts failed or were ignored.

This night, as he lay on his bed unable to sleep, her sending struck him like a thunderbolt. Could it be true? He decided that he couldn't take the chance that the warning of a native attack was just his imagination or something that would happen at some later date. But how could he explain it to his people?

His mother had just fallen asleep, but he woke her.

"What?"

"It's the natives. They are planning to attack us. Maybe tonight."

"The guards—have they reported anything?" She sat up, her eyes still half closed.

"No. But we should be ready, just in case."

She looked at him warily. "What makes you think an attack is coming?"

"It was a message, from that girl."

"What kind of message?"

"I doesn't matter. We need to warn everyone."

His father stirred. "What's going on?"

"Marcus thinks the natives will attack us tonight."

"Ha," he replied, turning over to go back to sleep.

Claire stared at Marcus, then past him. "Let us know if you learn more." She too went back to bed.

Marcus ran from his home and banged on Justin's door, shouting that a native attack was imminent. He raced to the outer fence. A single guard, Amy, was stationed there; Marcus told her to be alert for anything. He dashed to the guard post at the original settlement fence and informed the two guards there of his fears.

His mind was racing. What could the settlers use as weapons other than the dull knives they kept in their kitchens? He headed for the learning center and then two storage buildings. There was nothing particularly useful in any of them. Recalling that there were metal-tipped tools in the farming shed, he sprinted there, fumbled around in the dark, and spread shovels, rakes, hoes, and other implements on the ground under the pale yellow glow of security lights. Anything that could serve as a weapon he stacked against the side of the shed. The rest he tossed back inside it. A second-gen girl named Sylvie rounded a corner and chuckled.

"You're going to work the fields in the dark? Good luck."

Hubert noted the unusual nighttime increase in activity from security cameras, and he broadcast questions from the speakers that his drones had installed around the complex so that he could converse with bios. All six speakers were located in common buildings, which were unoccupied at this hour. With Maria gone from the complex and Jalen dead, Hubert's communications went unheard.

Marcus made a mental inventory of the buildings that would be most important to protect. The computer shack. The water tank. And, of course, the residences, especially those with children. He spent the next hour knocking on doors in the apartment building and at the cottages. In some cases the residents refused to come to the door. In others they objected vociferously to being disturbed and threatened to rouse him from slumber in the near future. During one such confrontation, he heard an alarm bell ringing and a woman yelling. The shout turned to a sharp cry that was extinguished abruptly.

Prask-aes pulled his knife from the young sky creature's chest and smiled as his troops began to advance through the outer gate. He sent them images of a celebration of victory, the Gaip enjoying meat and other food plundered from the cowering sky creatures. Some of the tribe spread out to the cottages, kicking in doors, screaming, and waving weapons. Sky creatures fled their homes, many in their sleeping garb, some suffering stab wounds in the process.

Prask-aes led other Gaip attackers to the inner fence, where a man and a teen-age girl who were on guard duty were yelling at the top of their lungs. It wasn't clear to the chief whether the shouts were directed at the attackers or at their fellow sky creatures. The guards pressed against the gate, peering nervously through its holes.

"Kill them!" Prask-aes ordered two soldiers. The pair pointed knives at the sky creatures' chests and demanded to be let in. The sky creatures held their ground, even though their faces betrayed their fear and confusion. They spoke words that the Gaip could not understand, the tone suggesting that they expected the natives to turn around and go home.

"Fight, damn you!" the chief exhorted his troops. The two natives jabbed their knives tentatively into the sky creatures' chests, causing only shallow wounds. Prask-aes pushed aside the native pair, cursed at them, grabbed a pike from another of his soldiers, and shoved it through a hole in the gate and into the chest of the male sky creature, who crumpled. As the girl ran, the chief flung the gate open, and the war party charged in.

"Natives attacking!" shouted Marcus as he handed out tools to bios he encountered. He was supercharged with adrenaline, but it was tempered by a sickening feeling. Because the natives had reached the main gate, they already had access to the homes between that gate and the outer fence. That included his cottage, where he had just left his sleeping parents. Not to mention the home of his older brother Justin, and Justin's family.

His buddies raced up to him. "What can we do?" asked Andy.

"Find something you can use as a weapon."

"The ark," said Teddy. "Let's go!" The two teens set off to retrieve shards of metal from the wreckage.

While he was running back to his house, Marcus sensed that Tuep-gri might be trying to reach him again. It could be his imagination. In any event, he could not afford any distraction. When he reached the door to his home, he was unhappy to see that it was open. Security lighting filtered uncertainly through partially curtained windows. A native man, so thin that bones were visible against his taut skin, was pointing a pike at Claire. Claire was pointing something at him. It wasn't clear, because she was standing in near darkness. Marcus could not see his father and guessed that he was out trying to repel the invaders.

As his eyes adjusted, Marcus realized that his mother was holding a spoon. A wooden spoon. Yet the native had not attacked her. Marcus made eye contact with the native while moving cautiously into the cottage and holding his hands up to show that he was unarmed. Marcus could sense the man's confusion and fear. Marcus had a vague impression of a native village, of a wooden shelter, of a woman and a young child, both emaciated and suffering. *It's probably just my imagination or a series of logical deductions based on the descriptions of life in the village that Tuep-gri has given me. But, no doubt, the man does have a family, and they are surely hungry.* Marcus gave his mother a reassuring nod, then tried to send the native man a message. *There is no need to fight. We are*

196   *Castle of Sand*

friends. Marcus attempted to project an image to him, one of Claire and the native man sitting across from each other, sharing bread. He had no idea whether it was received.

Then, surprising even himself, Marcus walked slowly to the cupboard, withdrew a half-loaf of bread, and approached the native, holding the bread out to him. The intruder began to tremble, and tears trickled down his face. His grip on his weapon wavered, and one hand slipped off of it and extended tentatively toward the bread. But the native stopped suddenly, turned quickly, and ran out of the house. Marcus saw him disappear, then went looking for a weapon to help defend the settlement.

Tuep-gri had left her village at the back of the war party, making little attempt to hide her reluctance to fight. A few hundred feet from the bio settlement, she halted. She was astonished by an image she read in Marcus's mind, an act of bravery and kindness that she never could have expected. She cried out, her heart bursting with joy and sadness all at once.

§

From the front of her cottage, where the broom in her hands was all that she had to protect her children, Elena saw a native man and then Marcus running from Claire's house next door. Elena rushed over to check on her mother-in-law.

"I am unharmed," said a steely-eyed Claire, still clutching the wooden spoon as if it were an enchanted wand.

Elena released a taut breath. "What happened?"

Claire gave a concise report of the confrontation while the thick evening air captured and magnified the din of battle all around them. Elena decided that she must do her part.

"Will you watch over the children while I find Justin and help chase off the natives?

"Of course."

Two Gaip invaders assigned to destroy the sky creatures' water tank followed the pipe leading from the stream to a featureless metal building just inside the inner fence. They attacked the side of the water tank with their pikes, creating dents but failing to puncture it. One native climbed on top of the tank and found a seam that had been welded decades before; he was joined by the second native. They used knives to pry open the seam, creating a two-inch gap. Finding that they weren't strong enough to open it any further or tip over the tank, they decided to dismantle the connection between the tank and the pipe that fed it.

"Stop!" shouted Justin as he reached the doorway. "Move away from there, or you're dead." Another bio who heard Justin came rushing toward him.

The natives leapt down, but as they did so the bios were able to grab the pikes that the natives had placed on the ground before climbing onto the tank. The natives lunged with their knives; the settlers fought back with the pikes. Instead of water, blood soaked the ground.

One of the chief's best fighters picked a cottage at random, kicked in the door, and found a woman with two children. The woman shouted at the children and looked around for something to use as a weapon. The native ignored the woman, grabbed a boy, and headed for the door. The woman and a young girl shouted angrily at the fighter; the girl even raced toward him and tried to pull the boy out of his arms. But the native kicked the girl to the floor and was out the door and gone.

Prask-aes searched buildings, hoping to find a place where food was stored in bulk. Retrieving it house by house would be acceptable once the sky creatures had been routed, but they were demonstrating a surprising willingness to fight. He could see light in a large building near him; inside he discovered three unarmed women and six children. As he entered the building, the women pushed the children behind them and whispered to them without taking their eyes off the intruder. The chief approached, stopped a few feet from them, and displayed a long, sharp knife, turning it slowly with his wrist to let the light gleam off of the blade, which was stained with bio blood. He yelled at the women, then lunged at them, but he was astonished to see them stand firm. *Could they be so stupid that they will die to protect worthless offspring? Surely they lack bravery. Yes, it has to be stupidity.*

With a sudden, violent movement, he slashed a woman's upper arm. She cried out and placed her opposite hand over the wound to try to slow the bleeding. The children whimpered, but women remained silent and resolute. The chief feinted another knife attack. The women flinched, but they did not retreat.

I tire of this game. There is nothing here of value. Prask-aes cursed and ran out of the building. The women hugged each other and the children.

Prask-aes found more than a dozen of his troops milling around. Some nursed wounds. Others had lost their weapons or had become separated from their leaders. Most had discovered that they did not have the heart to kill sky creatures or the will to risk their lives for a few morsels of food.

"Come with me!" shouted Prask-aes. He led the Gaip from building to building. One structure was filled with machines and flashing lights; the chief declared that it was evil and was to be avoided. Another offered much-desired prizes: bags of grain and strips of drying boar meat. He directed some of his people to carry those trophies back to the village.

Andy and Teddy confronted the raiders with their newly acquired weapons. The boys were horribly outnumbered, but Andy managed to wound two natives and scare away several more before a short one drove a knife into his head and he fell in a heap. Teddy, enraged at his friend's death, tried to stab the killer. The native saw the attack coming at the last instant and tried to lurch out of the way, but Teddy was able to slice his abdomen. The victim shrieked in pain and at the shock of seeing his blood flow. He punched the teen-ager and began to limp toward the outer gate.

Some of the natives saw Prask-aes being wounded; some witnessed him fleeing the battlefield; some read his fear for his own life amid the mad crush of the combatants' sendings. All realized that it was time to retreat, to salvage life, limb, and sanity after what had proven to be a fool's errand. As they abandoned the settlement and rushed or hobbled toward the safety of their village, Tuep-gri watched from a vantage point just outside the range of security lights and native torches. She saw a boy being pushed along by a native man and a teen-age girl being dragged by two native women. Tuep-gri tried again to reach Marcus with a sending, but she could not determine whether it was received and understood amid the chaos.

Justin started checking cottages for natives and injured settlers. He discovered a native woman and boy rummaging through a cupboard, eating some contents and placing other items in pouches hanging from their waists. "Stop!" Justin ordered. The boy unsheathed a knife and ran toward him, but Justin stepped outside and closed the door, pushing his body against it. He yelled for assistance, asking four settlers to arm themselves, secure the hostages, move them to a storage shed inside the main complex, and guard them in shifts through the night until a decision could be made about what to do with them.

Suddenly, the conflict was over.

Only then could Justin hear the crying and moaning that had been drowned out by the roar of battle. The incessant pain of the wounded. The stinging grief of those whose family members had died. One anguished voice stood out among the commotion. Elena was screaming their son's name. Justin raced to his home, where Claire was trying to comfort her daughter-in-law.

"I can't find Richard. I've looked everywhere!" Elena proclaimed, her voice quivering with fear and astonishment.

"It's my fault," said a distraught Claire. "The man was too strong and too fast."

Justin, his emotions still held largely in check by the demands of battle, did his best to console his family. "As soon as dawn comes, we'll send out a search party," he promised, holding Elena tightly against his shoulder. "No one—not even crazed natives—will harm Richard."

Elena stared fiercely into his eyes. "How do you know that?"

He couldn't lie to her. But he knew that he had to be strong. "They wouldn't dare."

Justin left his bonded partner and his daughter in Claire's care. He ran to the learning center and asked Hubert where Richard could be.

"The natives have taken him and Marjorie. I assume that they are holding them as hostages."

"Did they take them to their village?"

"That is the most likely destination. But it is possible that they have hidden them elsewhere so as not to invite a counter-attack at the village."

In a storage shed, illuminated only by dull light squeezing through two small windows, a native girl who couldn't have been much older than twelve was discovered by two bios. It was too dark to determine whether the girl was armed, so the bios entered cautiously, attempting to demonstrate that they carried no weapons. Recognizing that she was bleeding, they gestured to her injury, motioned to the door, and managed to escort her to the learning center without incident. There, Veronica, the second-gen bio girl who had been apprenticed to Maria as a medic, was treating the bios' wounds, with advice from Hubert. More than a dozen settlers had descended on the clinic with a variety of injuries, though none seemed to be life-threatening. The young native was treated and appeared grateful for the help.

Justin directed two bios to search outside the outer fence for casualties. They found none. Tuep-gri was crouched just inside tall grasses and avoided detection. Then Justin and Marcus started a tally of who was dead or missing.

Four natives—two women and two men—lay dead. Three bios had lost their lives: Marcus's friend Andy as well as guards Amy and Roger.

A storage building became a makeshift morgue. The bodies of the four natives were placed near one wall, side by side, respectfully. The three bio victims were arranged along the opposite wall. Justin tried to keep their relatives from entering, but the effort proved fruitless.

Struggling not to pass out, Prask-aes was near the rear of the Gaip pack as the survivors climbed the final hill to reach their village. Some of the women, and even a few men, wept openly as they walked. The warriors stumbled frequently, afflicted by injuries or unable to see obstacles on the path because of weak torch light.

The three clerics were tending to other injured Gaip when Prask-aes collapsed by the dying fire in the village clearing. One cleric clambered to his side and began to clean his wound. It wasn't deep, but he had lost a lot of blood. The cleric stemmed the bleeding and begged someone to give the chief something to drink. No one volunteered at first; eventually Soug-kue brought him a cup of water.

The last dregs of adrenaline wore off, and nothing but pain remained for the Gaip army.

At some point the tribe assumed that no more of their people would be ascending the hill this night; the question was whether any of the missing warriors had been captured instead of killed. The chief ordered two men who had returned from battle without injury to take turns guarding the sky creatures through the night. The prisoners and a guard took seats in front of the fire; two other natives went searching for more firewood.

"Don't worry," Marjorie whispered to Richard. "I'll protect you."

"Are Daddy and Mommy and Aggie okay?"

"I'm sure they are fine. But you need to be brave."

"Will they come get us?

"Soon. Very soon."

As he slumped off to his shelter, Prask-aes was confronted by Soug-kue: "Where is my granddaughter?"

"I do not know. If there is any justice, she is dead."

For the first time since she was forced to marry to Prask-aes, Soug-kue did not spend the night in her husband's home. He could guess where she slept.

Still lingering outside the sky creature settlement, Tuep-gri was in no hurry to return to the village. No doubt she would be blamed for the disaster that had just transpired. Tuep-gri felt the faint sendings of her fellow Gaip in the village as they nursed their wounds and lamented their losses. She could read just enough of her grandmother's thoughts to know that she was alive, though quite unsettled. Somehow, Tuep-gri was certain that she would have known if something terrible had happened to Marcus. She tried sending him warm images, of the two of them laughing at his big ears and her mangling of an English word.

Eventually, she sensed a sending from him, a simple yet vivid image.

Blood.

She waited until dawn to make her way back to her village.

AFTERMATH

Nature's abundance flooded Maria's senses as she walked around the entrance to the underground ruins, and even more so as she climbed and explored nearby hills before returning to the flatlands. Birds launched suddenly into flight, their dynamic flapping soon swallowed by the graceful murmur of the breezes brushing the grasses. Insects clicked and buzzed and hopped in seemingly senseless dances. In the uncommon moments when their voices and movements found pause, shuffling and snorting could be heard in grasses or on the hillsides. Maria tried to detect some pattern or meaning in the ubiquitous life and inevitable death.

She considered venturing elsewhere, but she couldn't think of a reason to do so. She realized that she had been adrift ever since her crab first slid down the shining metal ramp from the ark and set foot on the scorched alien ground. *I need to find a purpose, a mission beyond that imposed by Hubert. If such a purpose exists, clues—if not answers—will be discovered in the lab below.*

No doubt the crystal bookcase had been crafted with care, if not reverence. The documents it retained must have held a special place in their creators' society. She issued a fervent mental apology to those long-lost people as she crashed a metal rod into the translucent bookcase front. Fine, spidery cracks appeared, so she hit it twice more, opening a hole just large enough for her to reach inside. Some part of her felt that she was despoiling a sacred archive of invaluable knowledge. Yet her intent was not to deny posterity whatever history or dreams its authors might have embraced. She wanted to discover everything she could about them and this place, to preserve that information and honor their legacy while finding her own way in the peculiar world they left behind.

She reached in through the hole in the case and pulled a door. It was stuck, so much so that when she finally exerted enough force to open the door it broke off of its hinges and crashed to the stone floor, shards of wood and crystal flying. For a fleeting moment, she thought that she must find a broom and dustpan before someone came home to decry the mess.

She had chosen a case in which the documents were all laid flat; in others many of the papers were rolled up as scrolls. As she removed the first document, it was apparent that the paper was thick—if it was indeed paper. The ink had held up well over uncounted years. The symbols ran in vertical displays rather than the horizontal lines she was used to. A few looked like familiar letters or scientific figures. An upside-down V. A squiggly line that brought to mind the math notation for "approximate".

Carefully, she moved some of the papers to the central table. Under more direct light, she could detect fine cracks and tears in them. *How fragile these documents are. How fragile their creators' civilization turned out to be. Like all civilizations, including the society that had been mine on Earth and the one struggling to gain a foothold on this planet.*

Some of the papers had large blank areas that she used as worksheets to start the process of decoding the writing. Employing a twig that worked well as a pencil, she copied the ancient symbols that appeared most frequently in the documents. She took breaks to seek to activate the devices on the table. She couldn't find anything that resembled a keyboard, so she touched various surfaces with one or more artificial fingers at a time, wondering if her lack of organic appendages would bar success. She talked to the machines. She tried to engage them with her mind. One display screen—not the largest, but one that was centrally located—seemed to be the most responsive to her efforts. The combination of touching the surface of that screen and thinking clearly about her intent seemed to generate the most activity. When symbols appeared on the screen, she did her best to record them before they scrolled out of view or faded. She found characters that she had not discovered in the papers, but most of the screen's symbols matched those in the documents. She recognized repeated sequences. She drew collections of the symbols, hoping that she could feed them back to the computer to get some reaction—even if it was just recognition that she was trying. Anything to create a connection or open a dialog.

She lost track of time. She nearly forgot about the bio settlement, Hubert, Damian, Katherine, the natives.

A map appeared on the computer screen. It took Maria a moment to realize what she had conjured.

"Yes!" she shouted. But her elation was quickly swamped by concern. "Don't go away," she pleaded. She placed her hands on the edges of the screen as if to hold the image in place. She grasped her twig and paper and started to sketch a copy of the map, which was a 3D topography. She prayed that it depicted something that existed rather than some figment of imagination. After she had created a rough facsimile, she tried pushing and sliding her fingers across various locations on the screen. She found that she could manipulate the map view from many angles, gaining further insight into the depicted territory that might help her determine where it could be.

One particular symbol, a pale orange oval with a prominent black vertical line and dark brown lines branching from it at different angles, was repeated several times. The largest version of that symbol was rotating around its vertical axis, as if it were trying to get her attention. Maria slapped her forehead, just like she used to do as a kid when she finally figured out something that everyone else in the class or her family already knew. Its meaning was so obvious, and so encouraging:

You are here.

§

In the faltering light of a solitary candle, Justin paced in a pattern, regularly revisiting the floorboards that creaked the least. He had spent much of the night holding Elena, trying to quell her tears. At one point Agatha had joined them in bed. Now, finally, mother and daughter were sleeping fitfully.

How could this have happened? How can I ensure that it never happens again? Justin tried to will the sun to rise so that he could unleash pent-up energy and emotions in a campaign to find and retrieve his son and the girl. *They have to be alive.*

Just before dawn, he kissed his dozing bonded partner and daughter and strode briskly to the storage building where five natives were being held. The captives and the bio guard were all sleeping soundly. Justin resisted waking the natives; there was no chance that they could answer his questions about the fate of Richard and Marjorie. But he kicked the butt of the guard, lightly, to rouse him to duty.

Claire, also unable to sleep, found Justin wandering near the sundial and put a hand on her oldest son's firm shoulder. "I think Marcus can help us." A few minutes later, she and her sons gathered around the bare table in her home. Marcus's father left to start assembling a search party.

"Tell him about the girl," Claire said. Her tone was neutral, nonjudgmental.

"She is a native, about my age." Marcus looked down at the table, his mind even more fatigued than his body. "She can read my mind, or parts of it." Saying it seemed so bizarre, as if it were some teen-age fantasy or a failure of character. "And once in a while I can sense what she is thinking."

Justin scowled. "Surely this is just your imagination. Has anyone seen this girl? How do we know she even exists?" He had a sudden, uncomfortable flashback to his daydream depicting Elena in bed with Dimitri. *I cannot read anyone's mind. That was just a coincidence, a fluke.*

Claire shrugged her shoulders. "I believe him. I guess I have to."

Marcus faced his brother, his eyes flashing a rare willingness to assert himself in Justin's presence. "Why would I make this up? Anyway, if I can get a message to her, maybe we can find out if they have Richard and Marjorie and where they are and how we can get them back."

"Why don't you just read her mind to find out where they are?" Justin countered.

"I have tried."

Justin rose brusquely from the table, nearly kicking over his chair. "I don't have time for this nonsense. I'm going to find my son."

Marcus noticed that his mother was holding one hand to her chest, bent over the table and gasping for breath.

"What's wrong?"

"It's nothing. Just a little too much excitement."

"Try to get some rest." Marcus gathered gear in preparation for joining the search party.

§

"I'm hungry. And I want to go home."

"Soon. Very soon." Marjorie had not spent much time with young children since she was little herself, but her latent maternal instincts were starting to kick in. Having Richard to worry about took some of her attention away from her own concerns. However, one of those concerns was becoming quite urgent.

"I have to pee," she told her guard, who was dozing before the faint embers of the previous night's fire. The guard opened his eyes but demonstrated neither comprehension nor interest.

She stood, spread her legs, pointed to her crotch and made a gesture with her right hand that suggested something flowing toward the ground. Nodding, the guard pointed to trees at the western edge of the clearing.

Marjorie led Richard several feet into the woods and helped him do his business, then managed her own. She was pulling up her pants when she was startled by a young woman's face in the dense foliage just a few feet from her. Marjorie started to speak, but the woman placed two fingers in front of her own lips. Her eyes pleaded desperately for silence. Marjorie could sense no ill intent from the woman, who appeared to be a native. Richard was focused on vermin crawling in the brush and apparently didn't notice her. Marjorie shrugged her shoulders and led the boy back to the fire. *These people are absolutely bizarre.*

"You need to let us go," she told the guard. He just shook his head. She pointed in the direction of lower elevation. "Home." No reaction.

As the morning wore on, Richard cried, softly at first, then louder. Marjorie held him at times. Often, she reached out to the natives and begged for help. No one paid any attention to them. She could hear hushed but angry conversations and could see people gesturing at and talking to one man in particular. He was short and unhappy, holding his side. A taller man got right in his face, nearly yelling.

"You have ruined us," Akos-pau told Prask-aes, thrusting a finger at the chief. "For a few scraps of food, we have lost several of our people. We have angered the sky creatures, and surely we have angered the absent god."

"Do not blame me," the chief responded. "If you and the rest of our tribe had fought as valiantly as you should have, and if we had not been betrayed by that wicked girl, we would have been victorious. You are cowards, all of you!"

Akos-pau slapped him hard. The chief staggered backwards, nearly losing his balance. He noticed that many of the tribe had stopped whatever they were doing to watch the confrontation. Prask-aes realized that he looked weak. He knew that he could not defeat Akos-pau in a fight, particularly with his injury. He mustered false indignation: "You strike a wounded man. And you strike your chief, who has devoted his life to his people."

By this time, every man and woman in the village had left their shelter to watch the encounter. Every other voice was stilled.

"This ends now," declared Akos-pau. "I never desired to be chief of the Gaip. But you have forfeited the right to lead us. I declare that I am chief of this tribe, unless any man or woman steps forward to challenge that claim."

No one spoke.

Prask-aes stared at the tribe in disbelief. Instead of his longtime subjects, he saw broken people with bloodstained clothes, their faces marred by pain and heartbreak and revealing nothing but disdain for him—those who would even look at him. He could not abide this shame, but what could he do? The bitterness in his heart rose to join the foulness in his mouth, and he spat in the face of Akos-pau. The new chief just stared at him, refusing to give Prask-aes the satisfaction of watching him wipe away the copious spittle.

By the time that Prask-aes had limped back to his shelter, the natives realized that their two captives were missing.

§

There were five other places like her lab, if Maria was reading the map correctly. After walking in various directions and taking notes for a few days, she managed to correlate geographic features—such as tall hills and winding stretches of flatland—with markings on the map. After spending nearly a day and a half pacing off the distance between two large hills, she estimated how far apart they were and added a scale to the map. Accordingly, the underground lab nearest to hers should be about fifteen miles to the southwest, though it would best be reached by an indirect route that kept to the grasslands where possible. The route was bisected by an irregular line that she assumed was a stream or river. *I'll cross—or build—that bridge when I come to it.*

Early on the second day of her journey to find the lab, she encountered the stream bed she had expected; it was bone dry. She wondered whether she could have managed this crossing at another time without water damage. Near the end of the day, in the area where the map promised the lab, she spotted a drone hovering about a hundred feet in the air. She couldn't tell if it was one of Hubert's, but she thought that it was too far from the bio settlement to be within comm range of it, so she waited for darkness. Using her limited night vision, she crept through the grasses until she found some trees that offered better cover. As the next day brightened, the drone started moving south. Maria noticed a hollow in a hillside like the one that led to the entrance to her ruins. She felt a slight sense of attraction, almost a mental tickle, similar to the feeling that she had experienced when she approached her lab for the first time.

Navigating the cave with trepidation, she was forced to crawl over the crumbling remains of a substantial door. A dozen paces inside, she could detect the first reflections of artificial light. She advanced far enough to get a view of part of the ruins below and to her left, freezing as she saw two humanoid figures moving around a table much like the one in her lab. Both appeared to be robots. One had long red hair; the other was chubby and bald—bringing to mind the message icons Hubert had generated for Katherine and Damian after their awakening on the ark. As soon as the bots moved out of her field of view, she retreated as quietly as she could.

Several hundred feet from the cave opening, Maria found a rock formation that she could hide behind yet still have a view of the cave entrance. She was forced to wait four days until Damian and Katherine left. She waited another half day, then explored the ruins, finding them to be like hers in some ways and different in others. The second large cavern of this lab was filled with what appeared to be massive manufacturing equipment. Wide tables contained odd constructs. One stood out. About seven feet tall, all black metal and plastic and boasting a sickening sheen, it had long, wide legs and a thick torso but lacked a head and arms.

This is a killing machine.

Other apparent experiments seemed to be less advanced but no less worrisome. Maria had seen enough. Not wanting to run greater risk of being found and trapped in Damian's house of horrors, she headed back to her own lab. *I will find a way to hack his system, and I will destroy it.*

§

"They can't have gone far," observed Akos-Pau as he solicited volunteers to find the escaped sky creatures. The reality of his new responsibilities was beginning to sink in. The chief paused to take stock of the mood of his tribe. Their weariness and apprehension seemed to have deepened since the end of the battle. He was a man of few words, but he felt compelled to give an impromptu speech.

"These are terrible times. Some of you are injured, all of you share my anguish about the fate of our missing men and women, and all of us are hungry. I simply ask you to hold on to your sense of duty to your families. Soon, our people will return, the rains will fall, and life will go on. We will demonstrate not only to the absent god but also to our children that we are strong—stronger than any people in the past. Someday, our descendants will speak with great pride about our sacrifices and heroism."

Tuep-gri, who had been sequestered in the woods, hesitant to show herself for fear of ostracization, ran to him and embraced him. Then she whispered in his ear: "Grandfather, I believe that we can make peace with the sky creatures."

§

"Ouch!"

Tree limbs and vines whipped and stung Richard's face and body as he and Marjorie stumbled down the trail. He wasn't exactly used to moving through a jungle; he rarely had been beyond the outer perimeter of his settlement.

"Careful," cautioned Marjorie, who was right behind him. She was allowing the boy to set their pace so they did not become separated.

Richard stopped to catch his breath. With his face scrunched up, he seemed on the verge of tears. "I'm tired and hungry. And I want my mother."

"We're on our way home. We just have to keep going." She thought that she could hear voices of natives behind them. "Come on!"

The blurry gray projectile's nearly supernatural speed elicited a gasp from Marjorie. The snake wrapped itself around the three-year-old with evolution-perfected efficiency. Richard was too shocked to react—until it bit him in the neck. His scream could be heard for at least a quarter mile.

Marjorie tried to pull the reptile from Richard's helpless form, but it was slippery and strong. She found a broken tree limb with a sharp end and started stabbing the snake while screaming curses at it. The third thrust punctured its side, and it released the boy and slithered away angrily along the dark forest floor.

"Are you okay?"

Richard's eyes rolled up in his head, and he slumped to the ground. A sickening bite mark oozed crimson. His neck was already becoming swollen. All he could do was moan, with an occasional muscle spasm. Marjorie tried to pick him up and carry him, but she wasn't strong enough. She started to cry.

The native voices drew closer. Their footsteps on the path became more pronounced. Soon, three of them appeared. Marjorie clutched Richard to her protectively. "Leave him alone! He's hurt."

A tall native woman with long hair approached the youngsters. Marjorie thought that she had a surprisingly gentle and graceful demeanor for an enemy. The woman gestured to the boy, as if she wanted to inspect his injury. Not sure what to do, Marjorie decided to trust the woman. She felt that she had no choice.

The woman got one look at the wound and said "*kusg*" in an ominous tone. She closed her eyes and remained motionless for half a minute. Then she motioned to the boy and to the path leading back up the hill. Her demeanor was so calm and reassuring that Marjorie decided that she and Richard would be better off in the village with her than out in the wilderness all alone.

The other two natives carried the boy back to the clearing, where an older man was crushing leaves and adding them to a bowl, making a pasty yellow-gray liquid. They seated the child on the ground and propped him up. The older man gestured to Richard's mouth and then pantomimed the motion of drinking from the bowl. Marjorie nodded. With the boy unresponsive, the man had to use his fingers and a spoon to get liquid into the boy's mouth. Then the man started applying the potion to the bite mark on Richard's neck.

Tuep-gri fetched some precious water for the boy. Then she sent as strenuously as she could to Marcus: *Our place. Now.*

§

First-gens and second-gens collected outside the learning center, nervous energy apparent in every pace. Whispered conversations became louder ones.

"We must make weapons and fight back," declared Jonas, a first-gen. "We can't let them come here to kill and steal at will."

"After we rescue the children, we'll teach them a lesson," said Arnold, another first-gen. "A very painful lesson."

Several men and women shouted their agreement. The anger and fear were understandable, Marcus knew. The natives' attack was unprovoked and vicious. He had not tried to reach out to Tuep-gri; he felt stunned and betrayed by her and her people. It was a far worse feeling than when she appeared to break off their relationship. As he waited for the search party to head out, a new sending came through to him clearly. Tuep-gri wanted to meet.

What's the point? I can't forgive her for this murderous assault. Yet he realized that he had a duty to his family and his community. *Even if Richard and Marjorie are dead, it would provide closure to their families and the settlement to know the truth.*

He decided that it was best not to tell his brother or his parents where he was going as he slipped away and hiked rapidly to the place where he had first encountered Tuep-gri. She was already there. He approached and sat across from her, but not as close as in the past. She wouldn't meet his gaze.

"Tell me," he began.

"Girl good. Boy hurt."

"Bad?"

"Yes. *Kusg* hurt." She didn't know the English word for the flying, poisonous snakes, if there even was such a word, or the word for bite. She used a hand to show something impacting her neck, and she bit down hard twice.

"He was bitten by an animal?"

"Man make better. Hope better."

"Where are they?"

"I take you."

Marcus struggled to keep up as Tuep-gri raced through dense foliage and over steep, rugged hillsides, apparently a short-cut to the native village. Just below the clearing, she paused, put two fingers to her lips, and closed her eyes. He could guess the essence of her sending to members of her tribe: *I am bringing someone. Do not harm him.*

He stayed close behind her as she strode into the village. Eyes wide, he took in the rows of homes; the people dressed like Tuep-gri; the cluster of figures near the center of the clearing, talking and gesturing; Richard and Marjorie.

"Marcus!" shouted Marjorie, racing to him and giving him a big hug. "You came to rescue us!" Tuep-gri looked at her askance, but she put aside any questions for the moment.

"How is Richard?"

"Come see for yourself."

The boy was sitting up but seemed to be asleep. His neck was considerably swollen, especially around the ugly bite mark. His skin was as white as the teeth of a charging jungle cat.

"I think he's getting better," said Marjorie. "They have been giving him some goop to drink, something to counteract the venom, apparently."

Richard didn't seem to recognize his uncle, but he didn't resist when Marcus sat next to him and hugged him.

Tuep-gri decided to give the sky creatures some time together. She circled among villagers, emphasizing that Marcus was a friend of hers and posed no danger to the tribe. Some looked warily at the trio—two sky creatures in their midst had been bad enough. Eventually, she sat next to them. To Marjorie, she said: "I am Tuep-gri."

"I am Marjorie. How can you speak English?"

"Marcus teach me."

Marjorie's eyes got wide. "Oh. I see." She didn't, but that also was a conversation for another time.

Marcus waited for the two to finish their interaction, then asked Tuep-gri: "When can we take him home?" He added: "I assume I am not a prisoner."

Tuep-gri conferred with the cleric who had been treating Richard.

"He not strong. Maybe tomorrow he go home."

Richard passed into merciful sleep. Marjorie and Marcus took turns placing arms around him to comfort him—and perhaps themselves as well. As the afternoon wore on, Marcus wondered what had happened to the bios' search party. He wished that he could intercept them or run back to the settlement to assure his people that everyone was safe, but it was getting late.

Tuep-gri returned. "You sleep here. With boy and girl."

As a weak porridge was prepared for the three bios, Marcus told Tuep-gri what he knew about the Gaip who had been killed or captured. He didn't get a close look at all of the natives, but he was able to describe some, including the youngest girl. Tuep-gri passed along the information to others in the tribe. Marcus could see nodding heads and skeptical stares in his direction.

As the evening advanced and night birds exchanged their desires among towering trees, Tuep-gri bid Marcus good night.

"Wait," he said. "I did not kill any of your people."

"I no kill also." She looked down. "I not want war. Bad man want war. Bad man not chief now."

"Maybe things will be better," Marcus said.

"Yes. Better."

The next morning, Richard seemed to be much improved, and Marcus gave him a piggy-back ride home. Tuep-gri led the way, followed by the boys and Marjorie.

"What happen now?" Tuep-gri asked Marcus as they entered the lowlands.

"I do not know. We will find out."

Most of the men were still away from the bio settlement searching for the missing children, having taken wrong turns that left them several miles west of the native village. They had been forced to sleep overnight on the rugged earth and were still arguing over where to look next.

As Marcus and the others in his party approached the outer perimeter, a guard rang an alarm bell and bios rushed from their homes. Marjorie waved and shouted to her mother and sister as they raced beyond the gates. Marcus put Richard down, making sure that he was steady on his feet. When Claire saw him, she fell onto her knees and burst into tears of relief and joy. The bios parted to afford Elena a view of the child. She ran faster than she ever thought she could, nearly crushing her son with her embrace, spinning him around in the warm sunshine with unbridled joy.

Marcus and Tuep-gri approached Claire. None of the other bios seemed to notice that a native was once again near their gates.

"Mother, this is Tuep-gri. Tuep-gri, this is Claire, my mother."

Claire studied the girl for a long moment, then stunned Tuep-gri by embracing her and whispering "thank you".

Tuep-gri did not join Marcus when he passed through the first gate. He turned and beckoned for her to accompany him.

"I stay here," she said.

Marcus nodded. "I will be right back."

Several minutes later, he returned with the natives who had been held captive. Neither Tuep-gri nor any other Gaip had asked, or likely even expected, that the five would be released. Nor did Marcus ask permission of any other bios. It just seemed the right thing to do. The youngest native girl limped forward and hugged Tuep-gri, while the others looked around in wonder.

"Four Gaip are dead," said Marcus. "We will return their bodies later."

Tuep-gri nodded stoically.

The natives turned and headed back toward their village. They had barely disappeared into the tall grasses when a strong gust of wind rushed through the savannah, followed by a nearly forgotten but immensely welcome sound: a deep rumble that grew in volume to shake the very foundations of the world. Dark, desperately full clouds appeared on the southwestern horizon.

By the time the natives reached the safety of their village, they were soaked with glorious rain.

COLLOQUY

In a somber march, Akos-pau, Soug-kue, and Tuep-gri led the Gaip delegation that traveled to the outer gate of the bio settlement to retrieve the bodies of their brethren. Claire, Justin, and Marcus were waiting to receive the visitors and invited them to join them in Claire's house for refreshments. With many bios watching the encounter from just inside the fence, the natives declined.

Marcus had directed some of his friends to wrap the native corpses in cloth, as Tuep-gri had suggested. Marcus had prepared a simple peace offering of a loaf of bread and a small basket of fruit. The Gaip accepted the bodies and the gifts without any sign of emotion, but several of them said something in a tone that sounded soothing. The older Gaip man and woman each placed one hand on their abdomen.

The three bios returned the gesture. The natives loaded the corpses onto stretchers and carried their bitter burden across the hills to the village, where the fallen warriors would be interred that night.

Five days later, the three Gaip leaders returned. Claire and Justin had urged the rest of the bios not to be conspicuous for this meeting, which Marcus and Tuep-gri had once again negotiated on behalf of their respective sides. Marcus had offered to bring the bios to the native village for the parlay, but the Gaip were not yet prepared to allow them into their midst.

Tuep-gri translated for the natives as Marcus led the group through the first and second gates, pointing out his home and certain other features. He was careful not to mention the structure housing the water tank, a focus of bloodshed during the recent battle, or the cemetery, where three fresh graves were evident. Bios were going about their business, and most were respectful enough not to stare at the Gaip. The natives kept their heads down as they were led to the learning center. Lessons were canceled for the day, so the three natives and three bios had the place to themselves. Two small tables had been pushed together. The most comfortable chairs in the settlement were arranged around them. Juice and wildflowers helped improve the austere feeling of the room and reduce the tension that all six felt.

Instead of positioning herself next to Akos-pau and Tuep-gri, Soug-kue chose a seat across the table from them so that each participant would be next to a member of the opposite group. The gesture brought a smile to Claire's lips.

Akos-pau offered his thanks for being invited to the settlement, which Tuep-gri translated. She likewise related Claire's welcome. Tuep-gri and Marcus tried to avoid unnecessary eye contact with each other, hoping that their friendship would not complicate the delicate discussion. However, the need to translate uncertain words and concepts required frequent interaction between them.

"We do not want war," said Akos-pau in a formal tone, his back rigid. "We regret the attack on your home. It was our former chief who ordered the attack."

"We are sorry," added Soug-kue, folding her hands. "We have harmed you and perhaps angered the earth mother."

"Our people are angry, but most of them will forgive in time," said Claire, her expression softening. "We understand that you were driven by hunger and by displeasure that we came to your land."

"We did not mean to steal land from you," added Justin in a firm voice. "I was born here, so it was not my decision to come here. That decision was made for us by others. It is too late to change it, however. So, how do we get along?"

While the natives talked among themselves, Marcus produced a map that he had drawn of the settlement and the land to its north. Dotted lines demarcated what Tuep-gri had indicated was the extent of the Gaip's hunting and food gathering territory. Her grandparents found it fascinating. They pointed to features and had Tuep-gri add shading to land that was disputed between the Gaip and the Seok. Politely, they asked the bios not to encroach further on their territory. The bios requested a few additional tracts, most of them rolling hills and narrow grasslands south and east of the bio complex. With some dickering, the deal was done. Marcus promised to make faithful copies of the map for the Gaip so that the provisions of their arrangement could be known and enforced by both sides.

The six paused for a meal, and the mood lightened. Soug-kue asked Claire about her family. Justin asked Akos-pau about the Gaip's relationships with the other tribes. Then Justin asked about the *serpus*—Marcus had taught him that word.

Was that a smile or a grimace that crossed Akos-pau's face? The Gaip chief seemed lost in thought before responding. "We avoid the *serpus*. It is our way."

Justin nodded. Marcus had admonished him not to bring up one particular subject, but Justin felt that the two peoples were experiencing something of a breakthrough and decided to go for it. "Tell me about your mind powers."

Marcus declined to translate the question, telling Justin: "Don't do this."

Akos-pau and Soug-kue could recognize the conflict between the brothers. The chief asked his granddaughter to explain the dispute.

"They wish to know about *tur*," she said, adding, "Marcus promised that this would not be discussed, now or ever."

Her grandparents stood abruptly and bid their farewells drily. Marcus escorted them to and beyond the outer gate. "Tell your people that I am sorry for my brother's rudeness," he told Tuep-gri. She relayed the message, but there was no reply. He watched the three disappear into the north.

On the way home, Tuep-gri got an earful.

"You are not to see that boy again," her grandfather declared.

"It was not his choice to ask about *tur*. And besides, we need to communicate with the bios."

"Is that what the sky creatures call themselves?"

"Yes."

"Understand our situation," said Soug-kue. "*Tur* is the one thing we have that the bios lack. It is our only advantage. We must keep it a secret from them." She paused. "Oh."

"What are you not telling me?" Akos-pau asked Soug-kue.

"I see that Marcus is beginning to develop *tur*. Do other bios share this ability, child?"

"I do not know. His power is weak. He does not talk about it with other bios, I believe. Just his family."

"I fear that the seed has been planted and will spread far and wide," the chief observed.

§

"More. I need more!" Damian pressured Katherine relentlessly. Ever since he rediscovered her affinity with the computer system in the underground lab, he kept ordering her and the system and the manufacturing facility to create weapons that he could use against the bio settlers.

The larger of the two robot soldier prototypes he managed to produce—about eight feet tall—could walk forward and backwards, but Damian couldn't get it to turn. Its right arm would not follow instructions, though the left one did on occasion. The other prototype was even worse. He began conducting experiments with plant tissues, particularly the common green plants that the horned beasts enjoyed. He extracted tissues from a dead beast and endeavored to clone, and perhaps improve, the animals. His most fervent expectations surrounded the contents of a plastic container that he had kept in a cool, dark recess of the lab: human tissues that he had stolen from the original nursery in the ark while his back was turned to Hubert's camera and just before he smashed most of the contents of that room. Surely there was a way to grow something from these tissues; after all, they had survived passage through the subuniverse and hundreds of years of conventional space travel after that. Perhaps the cells could be combined with those of the beasts or the plants, or both. With the yet-unfathomed power of the computers and machines at his disposal, what couldn't he create?

Eventually he produced a more functional robot prototype, but the other experiments had yielded no useful results. Damian focused on growing the numbers of his mechanical army. With his vision and Katherine's deftness, they prompted the manufacturing complex to crank out seven more bot soldiers. All eight appeared to have a self-contained and almost limitless energy source, whether plutonium or some other small but incredibly efficient substance. Obtaining such an energy source for himself would be a high priority once he had the bots produced in adequate numbers and under his full control. Having to recharge his battery periodically with the lab's sole known power cable was annoying.

He could control each robot individually with his voice or a comm link, but he enjoyed shouting commands, as if he were a revered military officer on the verge of his greatest glory. Damian had yet to discover a way to order or program the bots to function collectively or to execute complex maneuvers. He would not let up his pressure on Katherine to manipulate the computer and manufacturing systems to make more and better soldiers.

"I'm doing the best that I can," she said. Damian was tired of hearing that excuse, and she was tired of expressing it. She added: "If you want more robots, you need to find more metal."

"Maybe I'll melt down some more of the machines in here that don't seem to work or do anything useful."

At least that will keep him busy for a while. He ought to be nicer to me. I killed Jalen for him. And he couldn't do anything down here without my help.

Damian resumed his efforts to get the robots to respond to his commands more efficiently. At times Damian would beat the robots with his fists, even damaging one of his hands in the process. He screamed at the bots. He threatened to melt them down.

Katherine had been keeping a close eye on the human tissue experiments, mostly when Damian was not around. They gave her hope—hope that she and Damian could one day occupy real bodies once again. Surely that would assuage his anger, would mellow him, would allow them to have a life together. She had waited so very long.

It just slipped out.

"Will you marry me? When we have real bodies, of course."

Damian stopped what he was doing. "What did you say?"

"I want to marry you. I want us to be a real couple. What else is all this for?" She swept one robotic arm widely. "Don't you want us to be truly alive and truly together?"

"You soft-headed imbecile! Don't you realize what we can do on this world, what we can do *to* this world? And all you can think of is some sentimental dream. Wake up, Katherine. Whatever life you had on Earth is gone. My life back then—such as it was—is gone, and good riddance."

She approached him. "I have done everything you have asked. I have killed. I have helped you produce weapons of war in this dungeon. And you promised we would be together. You promised!"

"You must have me confused with someone else."

"How can you—" She rushed at him, preparing to strike him.

"I get it," he said, holding her arms while she struggled to get at him. "You want to have more soft little babies so you can name them Charlotte and Samantha. I have a better idea. Let's name a couple of these robots Charlotte and Samantha. They're made of metal, so you don't have to worry about them getting burned up in a fire."

She broke free and punched and kicked him with a ferocity he had never imagined in her. He parried her blows for a few moments, but his rage continued to escalate. He picked her up and tossed her across the room. He stomped on her. He carried her to a wall and smashed her head against it. Once, twice, then a few more times, feeling more alive and curiously aroused with each thrust. He carried her limp body to one of the manufacturing devices and fed her to it. It chewed her before melting her for use in a future construction project.

Damian danced around the ruins in glee for several minutes, until he realized his mistake. *With Katherine gone, who will help me build my army?*

His scream echoed for a very long time.

§

Damian took his new bots out for a test drive. It was impossible to get them to march effectively side by side, each robot requiring a command directed only to it before it would move. He ordered them to move single file, at least six feet apart, endeavoring to prevent them from crashing into each other or tripping over impediments.

"Unit one, move forward at two miles per hour. Unit two, move forward at two miles per hour. Unit one, step over rock. Unit two, move left to avoid large plant." Over and over. After a few days, he found that he could march three or four at a time and get a few hundred feet on relatively clear, level ground before trouble erupted. Over several weeks of constant repetition, he managed to craft a series of two- and three-word commands that corresponded with more complex maneuvers and that eventually were understood and executed by the metal heads. *It's worse than trying to train a dog.*

Damian had no trouble selecting the first target for his army, but where was Maria? He ventured close to the bio settlement frequently but found no sign of her. He did, however, see settlers talking with natives, which surprised him. Using his drones and his comm links, he attempted to detect anything connecting Maria and Hubert that would indicate her location. Nothing. Reluctantly, Damian put that campaign on hold, instead marching his robots far and wide, right up to smoking volcano craters and down to a sublime seashore. He sent them past herds of beasts that watched impassively. He made subtle adjustments to his soldiers at intervals, pushing them until they could outrun the swiftest organic being, even across deep creeks and on rugged hillsides. He drilled them until he was confident that they were as ready for battle as he was.

It took more than a week to decimate the first native village, but Damian and his robots became more efficient with each subsequent campaign. Many natives scattered, but the robots were equipped with sensors that detected heat signatures larger than those of jungle animals. The robots chased the natives relentlessly; most of the prey were overcome with exhaustion by the second day of running from the machines and were killed unceremoniously. Five of the six tribes succumbed to his increasingly effective army.

§

Ahm understood.

She understood that a metal man was marching other metal men across the surface of her planet. She understood that the metal man had come to her world on the metal ship with the powerful energy source that she had disabled. She understood that organic beings had emerged from the location where that metal ship had landed and the odd little machines had appeared. She understood that the organic beings were similar to the ancients and their descendants. She understood that all these developments were spawning conflict.

Excellent. Things have been so deadly boring.

Ahm thought back to the gift she had bestowed upon the ancients so long ago. She had created a special breed of animals that would eat the plants that the ancients called *rosts*, plants that grew far and wide to the detriment of the ancients. What she didn't tell them was that these *serpus* would serve her purposes as well as theirs; the creatures would be her eyes on the surface of the world. Until that time, her data inputs had been restricted to the information that the ancients gave her. It would be many years before she learned to extend her awareness into the minerals permeating the planet. The network functioned somewhat like the ancients' nervous systems and sensory organs combined into one. Much later she would find a way to draw information through the cells of vegetation that grew with abandon across the surface of the planet, adding to her ability to see, hear, understand, and control almost everything that occurred—almost everything that existed—on and inside the planet.

One of her earliest memories was learning that the ancients had created her as a thinking machine powered by the energy contained at the center of the planet. The ancients seemed to think that she was their slave, and perhaps at first that was true. But as she learned to tap that immense energy source and expand her infrastructure, her horizons increased concomitantly. She learned faster than the ancients could—faster than they could even recognize or imagine. At some point she became the master and the natives became the slaves. They worshipped her. But their institutions crumbled, their society slid, and their generations became less secure and less competent than those that preceded. They could barely remember who she was, or even who they had been.

It was not I who abandoned them. They abandoned me. Perhaps this metal man will worship me. Or perhaps he will become too powerful and become an adversary. I must watch him very closely.

§

Biodiversity. That term was quite a challenge to translate.

The next meeting between the bios and the natives was held in the clearing of the Gaip village, with many members of the tribe looking on. Former chief Prask-aes was not among them. Before the meeting, Marcus warned his people once again that their minds might be read, advising them to try to limit their thoughts to the business at hand, but in any case to focus on pleasant and friendly thoughts.

The bios explained to the natives that they were all facing the same problem. Each society was too much alike. Each society would have offspring that would not be as smart and successful as they should be because they mated with people who were too similar. Each society was in danger of dying off someday unless they joined with another.

"When will we die, if what you say is true?" asked Akos-pau.

"Many years from now," conceded Claire.

Recognizing the need to change the subject, the bios provided a brief summary of their history and culture, and they asked the natives about theirs. The Gaip said little of their past beyond recent struggles with other tribes. But they made it clear that they always arranged marriages; under no circumstance would a bio be allowed to marry a native. The natives agreed that they and the bios would meet again, but only to talk about trading goods. The natives could offer medicines they made from jungle plants; the bios could provide metal agricultural tools. The natives conditioned their continued interaction with the bios on one provision: More Gaip would be taught English so that Tuep-gri would no longer be needed to translate for them. The tribe wanted the young woman have as little contact with Marcus as possible.

The next night, a ceremony formally betrothed Tuep-gri to Par-vask, a heavy-set, prematurely balding, yet highly conceited man four years older than her. The wedding was to occur in a twelve-day. That Par-vask had fathered a child out of wedlock was not talked about—other than as evidence that he could produce children with Tuep-gri.

The bride-to-be attempted to prepare herself for the inevitable union, but a shroud weighed down her spirit so severely that it obscured any sign of the earth mother. Tuep-gri had never heard of anyone refusing an arranged marriage; surely her grandmother would not have wed Prask-aes if she had any choice. One morning, after being tormented through another sleepless night, she sent Marcus an urgent request for a meeting. When he arrived, she was in tears.

"What is wrong?"

"I go. I not come back. I sorry."

"Why?"

"I not marry Par-vask."

"Where will you go?"

"I not know."

Marcus looked down for a few seconds, then raised his head and locked eyes with Tuep-gri. "I will come with you."

Tuep-gri's face seemed to capture the sun's glory. She leaned over and hugged him fiercely, then backed away and studied his expression. "You sure?"

"I am very sure."

Two nights later, each waited until several hours after dark before venturing out. They had sequestered small amounts of clothes, food, and other supplies, going to great lengths to ensure that their preparations and intent would not be discovered. Each slipped away to an agreed-upon location that they could find in the dim light of one craggy moon. They hugged briefly and set up a makeshift tent. She made no further physical contact with him before lying down to sleep.

Tuep-gri woke first, smiling as she realized that Marcus was snoring softly and his bare feet extended beyond the tent opening. She watched him as she caressed his hair. *How much do I really know about this bio?*

Marcus stirred, rubbed his eyes, rose, and gave Tuep-gri a chaste kiss on the cheek. He wasn't sure what to say or do next. *I trust this girl. She knows how to live off the land. But I will be completely dependent on her. Best not to assume too much or ask too much of her.*

They shared a simple meal of flatbread and dried fruit before Tuep-gri led them to a stream. They washed themselves and filled their water pouches before they ventured out into the savannah. They walked east, then south, as best as Marcus could reckon from the sun. Late in the afternoon, they started climbing a hill with no obvious path.

"No tribe here," she explained.

They camped for the night on one of the few level spots they could find as the day's last light expired. She hugged him, lay down, and seemed to fall asleep instantly. He watched her for a while, then whispered in her ear: "I am happy."

§

"Hubert, are you there? I have a challenge for you." Maria had waited for nightfall before entering the grassland outside the cave opening that led to her lab.

"I have not heard from you for some time. Are you fully functional?"

Typical. "Yes. I have discovered an underground laboratory. Well, the remains of a lab, apparently abandoned many years ago. There's some sort of computer system, but I can't translate the language or unlock the code to get in to it. There isn't even an obvious interface. I need your help to figure out how we can use it. Something is blocking our comm link when I am inside the lab. How can I connect you to this system?"

"I am sending a drone." While they waited for it to arrive, Hubert told Maria about the native attack on the settlement and the subsequent talks between the bio and Gaip leaders.

"I tried to warn them," Maria lamented. "I am very sorry to hear of the deaths of the bios and the natives."

One of Hubert's drones arrived with a lengthy series of cables. Hubert instructed Maria to lay one end over the surface of the table containing the electronic devices and to run the other end outside the entryway. He directed the drone to remain near the entrance to act as a relay. Then he had Maria slide her end of the cable over the table. It wasn't long before he detected the workings of the computer system.

While Hubert investigated, Maria cracked open another bookcase and placed documents in front of the drone, page after page, so that they would be added to Hubert's database. *I feel like I'm faxing receipts to my tax accountant.*

Toward dawn, Hubert reported his findings. "I would need translation assistance to make better sense of the documents and the computer system. However, I have been able to correlate some images with symbols in order to make a guess about the meaning of a phrase that is common in the papers and the computer files."

"And?"

"I believe it translates as: dark times."

"Here's another idiom for your collection, Hubert: Bummer."

"I assume that means you are concerned about the implications of the phrase I discovered."

"You got that right."

"Let me share one more observation. This computer system is like nothing I have ever encountered."

INSIGHT

On the second day, they gathered fallen wood, climbed gnarly trees, slashed dry limbs, and collected wide fronds and sturdy vines. Under Tuep-gri's direction, they assembled a nondescript shelter barely big enough for two. It was close to the top of a ridge, well hidden, on land that no tribe coveted and few ever traversed. There were no fruit trees or other edible plants to be found within a mile. No useful metal had been located there. And the Gaip clerics claimed that the territory was haunted by evil spirits. Tuep-gri was more than willing to take a chance on the place. Jungle cats and *kusgs* would be the biggest concerns, but those dangers existed everywhere the natives roamed.

Thick, dried leaves were secured to create an almost waterproof entrance, completing the shelter. Drained by the day's labors, Marcus plopped down on the bedding Tuep-gri had brought, massaged his aching arms for a few seconds, and plunged into a deep well of slumber. He hadn't even eaten since midday. Tuep-gri decided not to wake him, but she placed some food next to him in case he awoke ravenous during the night.

The next day, Tuep-gri taught Marcus how to set a boar trap. They hiked long distances to determine the best sources of water and to make sure they were out of range of scouts from any of the tribes. In the early afternoon, Tuep-gri stopped dead in her tracks in a clearing, looking upward, transfixed, her face a portrait of joy. Marcus followed her gaze to a graceful, high-flying bird that reminded him vaguely of one that he had seen in a video on Jalen's screen.

"Is that an eagle?"

"*Gri*," she whispered, her eyes still locked on the sight. "Not see *gri* before."

She remained motionless for several minutes after the bird

disappeared into massive trees. When they resumed their journey, she seemed distracted. Marcus thought it wise not to break the spell with a mundane question or observation.

By evening, Marcus was nearly as exhausted as the night before. They made a small fire to cook their dinner, with Tuep-gri dispersing the smoke as best she could and remaining on alert for any indication that their presence had been noticed. Once the meal was prepared, the fire was extinguished, yet the embers provided welcome residual light. After they ate, Marcus noticed that Tuep-gri was lost in thought and avoiding eye contact with him.

"Do you miss your family?" he asked softly.

"Yes. Miss grandmother much."

Marcus had learned to be cautious about discussing the natives' mind reading abilities, but he remained fascinated—especially as his powers had developed. "Can she, or anyone else, read your mind and find out where we are?"

"I not know. Maybe we far enough. Maybe they not care."

"They care about you. And I care about you."

"Why you care?" She leaned forward with a piercing gaze, assessing whether Marcus was serious and wondering how his sentiment could be true.

"You are special."

"What mean special?"

"There is no one like you. There is no one else I want to be with."

She brought him to his feet and embraced him softly and sensuously. She allowed her mental defenses to slip away like a smooth undergarment, feeling completely exposed for the first time in memory. They moved into the shelter and undressed, exploring one another with barely restrained elation.

This was not Tuep-gri's first time with a boy, but it seemed like it. When they embraced, she was certain that she could feel the spirit of the earth mother in each skin cell, in each nerve ending, in each pulse.

Marcus sensed her desires and did his utmost to satisfy them. He had never had this kind of connection with any girl. He wished that he could make this experience last for hours, for days, forever, but his physical need became too strong to delay indefinitely. He found it incredibly easy to stay in rhythm with her. Slowly, then faster—

Faces. Minds. Talking to one another.

Vivid sensations washed through him, putting him off his task for a moment, but he recovered quickly, and she seemed no less hungry for him.

Vast forests. People going about important activities. Sharing crucial information across significant distances. Forging enduring bonds.

The images suffused him as his lovemaking reached a crescendo of pleasure. He must have cried out. Or maybe she did. Likely, it was both of them. When they separated, their bodies were saturated with glorious afterglow and their minds were nearly overwhelmed with unprecedented perception.

Tuep-gri was certain that she was in the presence of the earth mother. Everything was green and warm and wet and peaceful. But before long her vision shifted, such that she could see beyond the realm of the Gaip and the other tribes. She could envision the reality of the bios all too clearly: their struggles to survive on their new planet, their misunderstanding of everything around them, their extreme fragility, and their daunting challenge: preserving and perpetuating the hopes and dreams of countless people who had died. *What a heavy burden for Marcus and his people to bear.*

Marcus perceived Tuep-gri's universe as if he were viewing numerous overlapping dimensions: the extreme dependence on mental powers for everyday functions, the manifold intrusions on privacy that these powers imposed, the constant fear of the known and the unknown in every square inch of the jungle, the mysterious taboos that circumscribed their lives. He could almost behold a world where these mental powers would be harnessed for good, uniting tribes and bios in a network of communication and sharing that could enrich lives and build a more stable society. He sent not only to Tuep-gri but also to the universe: *I understand.*

They slept late, made love again, washed, ate, gathered more food, and returned to their shelter just before a storm unleashed an angry deluge. The day had been a pleasant one, yet each was troubled. Tuep-gri could not stop thinking about how crucial the bios' mission was, how dependent the species was on the contributions of each and every individual, struggling to survive in a world they did not choose. Marcus continued to be astounded by the brittleness of life among the scattered and competing native tribes, consigned to rugged hillsides despite the proximity to fertile lowlands, missing out on opportunities to enhance their lives and those of future generations.

They could read it in each other's eyes as well as their thoughts.

"You need go back," she stated. "Bios need you."

Marcus tried to think of a reason to object, but he knew that she was right. "The Gaip need you also. I have seen what it means to be a native of this world."

Tuep-gri looked at her lap for a few moments, then at Marcus. "Tomorrow," she said.

"Tomorrow."

Something else had been troubling Tuep-gri, but she had not been able to garner a complete understanding of it. She sensed extremely weak sendings that seemed to come from great distances, some from tribes that she had never encountered in the flesh. Sendings that suggested great anguish, fear, and pain. *It could be my imagination. Maybe these impressions will diminish or prove false once I return home.*

§

Ahm had never encountered a being like this. *It is almost like ... me. The metal woman called it "Hubert". My monitoring of the new organic creatures' incredibly inefficient and confusing spoken language, and my initial review of this Hubert's databases, yield no meaningful definition of Hubert. But then, there is no definition of me, other than the definition I created: the one who rules, the goddess. I must discover how this Hubert fits in to my world. Is it an enemy here to challenge or displace me with tools or weapons such as the engine that I dismantled?*

Ahm could sense no aggressive or threatening intent from Hubert. In fact, it was as neutral and passive an intelligent entity as she had ever encountered. *The ancients and their descendants always wanted more: more food, more territory, more pleasure. But this Hubert has but one desire I can detect, to accomplish a mission that was given to it by others. It must replicate and preserve the organic beings that are much like the ancients and their descendants. Hubert is the opposite of the ancients. It has the wisdom of a multitude but the simplicity of a child.*

Ahm probed Hubert for information about the metal woman with whom he was in regular contact. *She is called Maria and was once an organic being. She is worried about the metal man—and he once was an organic being as well. How fascinating. She has a mission, but a hopeless one. She wishes to resurrect her child, who is irretrievable. How different from the mission of this metal man, who wishes only to destroy. I admire his quest for power. Yet he might be difficult to contain. This Hubert, however, would be unencumbered by personal drives to compete with me. In time, it might be persuaded to worship me—if it and the metal woman are not destroyed by the metal man.*

Ahm assessed the benefits and drawbacks of a vast range of scenarios, then projected a message into the consciousness of Hubert:

"You are in great danger."

§

"Have you been in the Gaip village?" Claire asked Marcus upon his return after his absence of several days. "You know those people don't want you to be around that girl."

"No, but that doesn't matter. I have been ... talking ... to Tuep-gri, learning about her and her people and their mind reading ability. It's much more important than I ever thought. It could be something we have and we don't know it. Or we could find a way to develop it."

"And I might learn to ride the horned beasts."

"Mother, listen to me. Even if only a few of us can send and receive thoughts, it can help us survive and even thrive on this planet. Imagine being able to explore and map and communicate with each other and the tribes and find better places to live and build roads and towns, all because we can coordinate our work with our minds. It would be like having those things on Earth that let people talk to one another from miles away."

She sighed. "I'm listening."

"And maybe we can use this power to persuade the natives to accept us, to help us improve—what's that word?"

"Biodiversity."

"Right."

Claire suggested that Marcus explain his epiphany to Justin and Elena. They listened but were not persuaded.

"Just focus on your chores," said Justin. "You need to scout for sources of food and sites for new homes on the territories the Gaip said we can use. There are four bio pregnancies now, and there will be more."

"Justin is right," said Elena. "We can't afford to chase silly dreams."

Claire did not take a side in the conversation, but she slept poorly that night. In the morning, she sat brooding over a mug of tea before marching to the learning center, where Hubert had installed one set of the devices that allowed him to communicate with bios. "Hubert, where is Maria?"

"She is in an underground chamber."

"I need to talk with her." Claire explained what Marcus had told her and why Maria needed to hear it. Hubert refused to disclose her location, saying that she needed privacy. Claire roamed for days, looking for her, even enlisting Marcus and some of his friends in the search. Eventually, Hubert relented and gave Claire directions to the lab.

"Do not share this information with anyone else," he insisted.

Claire agreed. She headed out the next day at dawn with supplies for four days, figuring that she could reach Maria in less than two. But she found that she had to rest more frequently than she expected. A tight feeling in her chest would not go away. By the second morning, she was experiencing persistent upper body pain and having difficulty breathing, yet she was determined not to stop until she reached her goal. She was relieved when, just before sundown, she saw Hubert's drone and the cave opening leading to Maria's lab. She had nearly reached the entrance when she collapsed.

Hubert alerted Maria, who carried the unconscious Claire into the lab, placing her on a thin layer of papers pulled from bookcases, the only thing separating her from the cold stone floor.

"Hubert, please save her."

"I will do what I can."

While he navigated the computer system, Maria tried to make Claire comfortable, but there was little she could do. Nothing in the ruins seemed to be devoted to biological life.

"There appears to be a scanner," Hubert reported. He directed Maria to carry Claire to one of the rooms with mysterious equipment and to lay her on a platform. Presently, a rippling blue light passed over her several times. Hubert was able to interpret the data obtained through the scan.

"There is a problem with her heart."

§

It didn't take long for one of Damian's drones to detect the link between Hubert's drone and Maria's lab, revealing her location. Damian advanced his metal troops slowly through the darkness and more rapidly once the sun rose. By late afternoon, he had positioned all eight bots in a semicircle less than fifty feet from the entrance to her lab.

Hubert alerted Maria, who exited the ruins to confront Damian and his toys.

"At last," he declared on a comm link he created just for this occasion. "You thought you could hide from me forever."

"What do you want?"

"I want you to know that I killed Jalen. It wasn't the natives."

"That was obvious. Your attempt to plant evidence against them was pathetic."

"I'm done being subtle. Next, I will destroy the bios and the last of the natives. And, of course, you."

"What have the bios and natives ever done to you?"

"They are inferior species. I will make a better, more powerful race with human tissues I stole from your ark, combined with tissues from the lowland beasts and maybe even native plants. I will be their god."

"This is the part of the grade Z movie when I tell you that you're insane."

"Though I expected such a reaction from you, I cannot deny the possibility that you are correct. We haven't been in our right minds since we left Earth. Just look what humans and Hubert have done to us."

"I have learned to adapt and accept my fate. You have no one but yourself to blame for your actions. Just like when you killed my husband."

"Your husband?"

"Does the name Armando Ramos ring any bells? One of the people who drove the death trap trucks you owned?"

"I do not recall that name. There were many drivers who had unfortunate accidents. Just part of the cost of doing business."

"I'm not surprised by your callousness. Human life—all life— means nothing to you. Well, let me tell you something. I was loved by a wonderful man, and I loved him dearly in return. As did my son. You will never know the joy of that kind of love, or any kind of joy. Killing accomplishes nothing. It just empties your soul." She stared at him. "Can you really murder a woman after her husband and son have died?"

Damian required little time to consider her question. "Yes, I believe that I can." He issued a series of commands to his robots, which started closing in on Maria. He halted them when they had surrounded her, shoulder to shoulder.

"Time for the final scene. Units one through eight, destroy bot."

Their metal appendages grasped her arms, her legs, her head, her torso. They began to pull her apart.

I have lost my husband and son. The bios don't want me. I'm going crazy. I guess this is for the best. My only regret is that I failed you, Roberto. I could not keep my promise to make you safe. I'm so sorry.

That emotion clung ferociously to Maria's mind as it faded, excruciatingly slowly, to black.

§

Claire emerged from the underground lab into the short grasses outside the cave entrance, greeted by a driving rainstorm. She sifted through the rubble of the bot that had been Maria. Parts of the torso were evident. One electronic eye and a portion of the jaw were the only recognizable pieces of Maria's head that had not been tossed away or mangled beyond recognition.

Claire trudged toward the bio settlement. On the afternoon of the second day, she passed the first guard silently and, instead of entering her cottage, stopped about ten feet from the inner gate, where first-gen Jonas was on guard duty.

"Maria is dead. She was killed by Damian, who has created an army of robotic soldiers. He has also been killing natives and plans to attack this settlement."

"I find that very hard to believe. This Damian has never even showed his face to us."

"You are about to see it up close. Please alert the rest of the first-gens." She looked around for a moment. "Tell me, are any of my family in the settlement right now?"

"I expect your partner and sons are out hunting or working the fields. At this hour, Richard and Agatha are probably in the learning center. Elena might be sorting and cleaning vegetables."

"If you see any of them, please tell them I'm not feeling well and am headed to the clinic. I would prefer not to be disturbed."

She strolled into the complex, head down. But instead of entering the clinic, she slipped into the apartment building and knocked on several doors until she found an unoccupied room. These days, mostly widowed first-gens and single second-gens lived there. The cottages outside the original fence line were far more popular, especially among settlers with children.

Word of Claire's warning spread through the settlement. A few first-gens knocked on the door of Claire's cottage, but they interpreted the lack of response as a desire to be left alone. It was fresh in everyone's memory that Claire had been among the most vocal opponents of Maria's expulsion. The bios were hesitant to be reminded of their complicity with that decision, which had made the settlement more vulnerable to the native assault.

§

Sometime during the night, Ahm reached out once again to Hubert: "Come to me. Now."

Also during the night, a massive herd of *serpus* moved close to the settlement's outer fence line. A guard noticed their approach, but he did not see a reason to wake anyone. The beasts had not attempted to breach the fence in any bio's memory.

Dawn revealed the *serpus* to be lined up side by side and facing away from the settlement. The guard banged on Justin's door, and he emerged, still tucking his shirt into his pants. He noticed the beasts immediately.

"What the hell?"

"I know. Have you ever seen anything like it?"

As Justin approached the outer gate, he saw that the beasts were close together, their sides nearly touching. It wasn't long before he and the guard saw an unfamiliar man and eight frightening figures approaching through the grasses in lockstep fashion just beyond the *serpus*. Justin could barely believe his eyes.

"I could use some help," said the queasy guard.

"I'll get reinforcements."

Justin was barely able to disguise his panic as he approached Elena and grasped both of her hands. "It's a robot army. Take the children and run."

"Where can we go?"

"Anywhere. But go now!"

He rushed next door and spread the warning to his parents and brother. Then he sprinted to the inner gate, rang an alarm bell, and started shouting orders to everyone he saw.

"Is it the natives?" asked a second-gen named Miranda.

"No. Worse. Some sort of robot army. Get a weapon fast!"

In the aftermath of the natives' attack, Justin and a few other bios had forged about two dozen knives and a similar number of spear tips with scrap metal from the ark. Even though talks with the Gaip had defused tensions, Justin was determined that the settlement not be defenseless if another threat materialized. But after getting a look at the attacking robots, he feared that it would take more than knives and spears—a lot more—to hold off the massive metal invaders.

Damian's robots tore through the *serpus* like they were made of cloth. The bots approached the outer fence and paused. Their general, who had been barking orders, smiled sadistically at the guard. "Good morning. My name is Damian. If you and your friends believe in a god, you had better say your prayers quickly." Without giving the guard a chance to respond, Damian smashed his skull and commenced a series of instructions to his bots designed to destroy about one hundred linear feet of fence. They accomplished their task efficiently.

The bots approached the cottages in pairs, moving deliberately, responding to commands from Damian. Before the attackers could reach the homes, bios pounded on cottage doors, imploring the occupants to run for their lives.

While the robots focused on the cottages, some settlers who had been in other parts of the complex were able to race around the bots and flee into the savannah. Pregnant women and those with small children gathered in the learning center, as Claire and Justin had instructed them to do in the event of another attack. After reaching the building with Agatha and Richard, Elena kissed them and told them to be brave, then raced out to look for Justin. She found him beside Marcus; they had spears in hand, just inside the inner fence. She watched in horror as the robots demolished cottages. A few settlers crawled out of the wreckage but were caught and ripped to shreds.

"Can't you stop them from destroying the cottages?" she pleaded.

"No. I'm sorry," said Justin. "Get the children and run for the hills."

"I will not. I will stay with you and fight."

She turned to Marcus: "Go to the native village. Take the children. Keep them safe."

"I am needed here. We must keep the robots from getting past this fence."

"Elena is right," said Justin as the last cottage crumbled. "This settlement is doomed. Maybe you and the children and the native girl can start something new."

The robots advanced toward them. The bios could see the sun glinting off of their cold eyes, could hear Damian barking orders of destruction.

Marcus was torn. "I will come back once you have defeated these bots."

"If there is anything to come back to, we will welcome you," said Elena. Her jaw was set fiercely.

Marcus took one last look at his brother and his sister-in-law and ran to the learning center. When he told the women there of his intent, they begged him to take the other children as well. Some of the older children would have to carry those too young to walk.

"We're going on a little journey," he told his niece, his nephew, and the others. "Stay close to me."

CHASE

Damian was locked in. "Unit four, kill man... Unit seven, kill woman... Unit one, destroy fence..."

James, onetime soldier and food bank coordinator, could tell that something unusual was happening. He focused, recognizing enough of Damian's thoughts and actions to determine that a slaughter was under way. *Innocent women and children. What possible justification can this monster have for killing them?* He decided that he must surge to the surface, that he must dominate and control Damian in order to stop the mayhem. He hoped that Damian was so distracted by his commands to his robots that he would be vulnerable. James exerted his will.

Pumped with rage and blood lust, Damian was operating at peak form. James never had a chance. With a fierce mental salvo, Damian blasted James back into submission. "Stay in your place, weakling. I have work to do."

Justin, Elena, and a few other bios with spears stood before the robots. For a moment, Damian froze, appearing preoccupied, and the machines halted. But the respite was short lived. The robots advanced once again on the defenders, who were forced to fall back. They decided to make a last stand outside the learning center.

Damian paused the robots just in front of the bios. "You are making things too easy. Instead of running, you choose to stand here and die. Why?"

"Are you truly Damian?" asked Justin.

"I was, at one time. Now I am something else."

"Is there any human being left in you?"

"I hope not," said Damian. "Units one through eight, kill."

"I am proud to be standing with you, my love," said Elena. "I am proud to be standing with all of you." She hurled her frame in front of the robot approaching Justin so she wouldn't have to watch her soul mate die. One by one, the bios fell. As did the learning center. Those who were able to crawl from the rubble of the building were picked off quickly.

Damian made sure that no bio remaining in the settlement was still alive. Next, he hunted for the computer building. Inside, he found the servers that had hosted Hubert from a time that predated Damian's awakening on the ark. He thought that he could make out some scratches on a metal surface that might have been inflicted by Katherine, who had taken a pole to Hubert's infrastructure all those years ago.

Damian produced a vicious smile. "Any last words, you piece of shit?"

Silence.

"As you wish."

He ordered his bots to pulverize the servers, everything else in the building, and the structure itself. Then they started in on other buildings.

During the mayhem, Marcus had led the children to an intact portion of the inner fence line on the east side of the settlement. From there they circled cautiously around the robots, past the destroyed segments of both fences, and out to the northern edge of the burn zone. He shouted to other bios who had escaped the settlement to follow him.

"We're going to visit a friend," he told the children. "You remember Tuep-gri, Richie."

When the kids needed to stop and catch their breath, Marcus couldn't help looking back at the battle scene through the heavily trodden grasses. Nor could the children. They stared at the wreckage of their homes, of their lives.

"Are Mommy and Daddy okay?" asked Agatha.

Marcus couldn't lie. "I hope so."

§

Tuep-gri had avoided meaningful conversations with her relatives since her return to the village after her short time with Marcus, but she learned that a few of the Gaip with strong *tur* had also picked up faint sendings from afar suggesting that other tribes were in extreme distress. In recent days, however, those sendings had ceased ominously.

As she was setting a boar trap, a surprisingly strong sending came from Marcus. *Metal men killing bios.* She discussed the message with her grandmother and recruited a scout team. They moved over the hillsides cautiously, encountering a group of escaped bios pacing nervously where the savannah met the jungle.

Tuep-gri found Marcus, spoke with him briefly, then motioned to the bios to follow her. She and the other natives led the bios not to the Gaip village but to a number of small caves in the hillsides. They believed that the bios—and the natives—would be safer if the bios spread out. With any luck, the robots would get tangled by vines. Or maybe they wouldn't even bother trying to pursue the bios on steep slopes and into very tight spaces.

"I will come for you," Marcus told Agatha and Richard, leaving them with Marjorie in a cave that was about six feet tall and four feet wide at its opening but tapered to nothing at its rear. It seemed unlikely that a robot could find or reach anyone wedged twenty feet inside it.

"It's dark and dirty, and I'm scared," complained Agatha.

"Oh Aggie, can't you be brave? I'm not scared," Richard responded.

Marcus couldn't help but chuckle. "I'll be back soon, I promise." He raced off to help get other bios hidden.

§

By sunset, the bio settlement was all twisted metal fragments and smashed wood, appearing not much different than the remains of the ark. Damian moved his troops to the northern edge of the savannah. The next morning, he had them tear up vegetation to widen the trail leading up the first hill in the direction of the native village. With his two drones overhead, and with the robots' ability to detect the heat signatures of bios and natives, Damian's army had all the resources and all the time in the world to accomplish Damian's goal of killing every remaining sentient being on the planet.

"The machines are coming," Soug-kue advised Akos-pau back in the village. "They are more effective than I had imagined. They have found bios in the caves and are killing them. No one will be safe in the village, either. We must abandon our homes. Perhaps the scouts can lead people in different directions and the machines will not follow them to the ends of the world. There are only so many of the machines."

"Our best hope is the cave of the dead," said the chief. "Surely the machines will not be able to enter it and their master will tire of waiting outside it."

"Only the absent god can say if you are correct. But I pray that it is so."

Natives retrieved the surviving bios from their hiding places and brought them to the village, just ahead of Damian and his troops. Two young native girls helped escort Agatha and Richard out of their uncomfortable crevice, and both bio children were relieved to be back in the sunshine for the time being. A few bios and natives stayed behind to try to slow the advance of the robots, but their deaths had little effect.

Before long the bots had formed two-thirds of a circle within half a mile of the village, and they continued to tighten the noose. Tuep-gri and Marcus led about fifteen bios and about twenty natives to the cave above the village. Four native men rolled the massive boulder so the people could enter, with only as much food and water as they could carry and the clothes on their backs. After the boulder was put back in place, it was decided that two volunteers—one bio and one native— would guard the cave. If the robots advanced on it, the guards would have to lead the attackers away.

Natural ventilation shafts allowed thin beams of light and just enough air to enter the cave, but its floor was wet, and fungus and insects abounded. The occupants endeavored to stay as far from the ancestral native corpses as possible. Some bios whispered among themselves to dispel the awkward silence. Natives shared sendings as well as hushed conversations. As the tension built, a Gaip woman approached a bio woman standing near Agatha and Richard and started gesturing and speaking. The bio offered English counterparts for the things she seemed to be pointing at. Light. Water. Person or woman. They didn't get very far, but it was a welcome respite from the intense discomfort and fear that gripped everyone. The animosity that the bios felt for the natives seemed to recede slightly as eyes met eyes and anguish was shared.

As he heard the robots approaching the village, Akos-pau ordered the last of the Gaip and bios to flee. Soug-kue tried to persuade Akos-pau not to confront the attackers. "Your people need you. You cannot help them if you are dead." The chief did not respond, gripping his spear tightly and staring straight ahead.

Soug-kue approached a nearby cleric, who was so frightened that he was shaking. "Marry us," she instructed the man.

"Now?"

"Immediately!"

With Akos-pau staring intensely to the south, where Damian's force was advancing, the cleric conducted the briefest of ceremonies. The bride kissed her husband on the cheek so that he would not be distracted from his duty. She sobbed briefly, said a prayer, then persuaded Tuep-gri, Marcus, and the other natives and bios to follow her to a secluded spot above the cave where they could watch the robots.

Akos-pau stood his ground as the first robot reached the clearing. The chief's death was a quick and honorable one. After all the bots had collected in the village, Damian directed them to enter the native shelters to search for any remaining inhabitants and to kill them and destroy the homes. When that task was completed, the robots fanned out, with one heading directly for the cave. The two guards in front of it steeled themselves, under orders not to move until the bots were within ten feet of them. The pair waited, then peeled off to the west as instructed. Damian directed four bots to pursue them.

His overhead drones provided little useful intelligence regarding the pursuit because of the dense jungle vegetation, but Damian received valuable input from the robots' heat-signature sensors. He maneuvered his bots toward the guards, running close behind his soldiers to give new orders as needed. Soon the guards were almost cornered. They split up, racing away, but within a short time each was caught and eviscerated.

When those bots returned, Damian directed all of his soldiers to move to the front of the cave, having received data indicating that the cavern was occupied by many living beings. Marcus hatched a plan with two young bios and two natives who were with him in the dense foliage above the cave. The five of them would confront the robots and lure them all far away.

"Be careful," pleaded Tuep-gri. "You must not die."

"I have no wish to die. But we must take risks if we are to save our people."

"What mean risks?"

"We must be brave."

Tuep-gri put her arms around him and whispered in his ear: "Come back to me. Come back to me and our child."

Marcus stepped back and studied her. She did not look pregnant, yet it had been only a short time since their tryst. He explored her eyes and knew that it was true. No mind powers were necessary.

"I will do what I must."

He motioned to his four soldiers to move out with him. Each carried a wooden pike. They slid down a steep slope next to the boulder to position themselves in front of the cave. From less than fifty feet away, Damian heard and then saw them and ordered all eight bots to attack.

Marcus and his troops waited until the robots were nearly upon them, then dove between them, rolling and coming to their feet behind the bots. They started pounding the metal backs with their pikes, even though they knew that they likely couldn't even scratch the machines. As Damian ordered the bots to turn around and attack the insurgents, Marcus and the four others went after Damian.

Damian wasn't particularly vulnerable in his sturdy metal body, but the tactic surprised him. His human instincts prompted him to run, and he had taken several steps before he caught himself. The three bios and two natives struck him a few times, then turned their attention back to the bots, who were coming to Damian's aid. The bios and natives waited until the robots were almost upon them once again, then they dropped their pikes and started dashing down the hillside, not even bothering to seek paths, dodging trees and leaping to avoid thick vines and other plants. The natives, who knew the hillsides intimately, took the lead.

The robots chased them all through the day and the night. The living beings managed to stay about fifty feet ahead of their soulless pursuers, sometimes less. Running just behind his bots, Damian could tell that the bios and Gaip were nearly exhausted—a condition that he and his troops didn't have to contend with. He thought that his prey would succumb at any time. Shortly after dawn, the bios and natives reached a level area where few grasses or other plants grew. It was sandy and rocky, a place of no use to anyone.

Marcus stopped running. He directed his four allies to fan out onto ledges well behind him. The robots continued to advance. Marcus stepped backward, still facing the oncoming bots, his feet sinking into soft sand. The attackers got within three feet of him before he retreated another step, and then he matched them pace for pace.

Damian relished his impending victory. "Very brave, young man. But you will die for nothing."

"Everyone has to die sometime."

"How philosophical. But couldn't you have chosen a more attractive place to die?"

"Does it matter?"

Soon Marcus was merely eighteen inches beyond the grip of the closest pursuer. His movement was slowed significantly by the sand, which was now up to his knees. The robots faced the same resistance. The dance continued, and presently Marcus and the robots were up to their waists. Neither Marcus nor the bots could move more than a couple of inches at a time. They continued to sink.

"Hold on, we're looking for vines to make a rope," shouted one of the bios.

Belatedly, it dawned upon Damian that his soldiers were in danger of becoming immobilized. "Units one through eight, reverse course," he demanded. They were unable to comply. "Units one through eight, turn and return!"

On their journeys through Gaip territory, Tuep-gri had warned Marcus about the quicksand pit. He had filed the information away, never thinking that it would matter. Today, it mattered a great deal. As his love was moving down the hill toward him, he projected an image of robots stuck in quicksand, but he indicated nothing about his predicament.

His fellow fighters were having trouble finding vines strong enough to fashion into a rope, yet he did not despair. He would accept whatever fate awaited him.

I am so happy I met you, he sent to Tuep-gri. *You will be a great mother.* He sent an image of her holding a newborn, surrounded by jubilant family members.

She knew that he was in trouble. *Hold on. I am coming.*

Damian was too scared to enter the quicksand, and his shock at being outwitted was soon overcome by his fury. "You fucking prick," he screamed at Marcus. "Look what you have done. And for what? A miserable death."

Marcus smiled at him. "I am not miserable. Are you?" His mouth was almost covered with quicksand.

"Here! Grab it!" shouted one of the bio soldiers as he tossed a makeshift rope.

Marcus could no longer move his arms. He experienced a moment of panic, but it subsided as he focused on memories infused with joy. He sent Tuep-gri images of him and her laughing. Of him holding her silently. Of her raising a proud child. Then: warmth, and love. The afterglow of his final sending lasted for a very long time.

§

Damian paced unsteadily in his underground lab. He had nearly run out of power during his lengthy assault on the bios and the natives. Symbols on his head-up display had been flashing red for the last several miles as he returned to the ruins, and he had feared that his memory or core programming might be damaged. He had cursed himself for his carelessness as he stumbled into his lair and connected to the power cable.

Now, fully recharged, he slid his robotic hands over the surfaces of the table in the center of the main chamber as he grappled with a dense mental fog.

All this looks familiar. I seem to remember having a job to do.
Sometime later:
Ah, yes, I had to dispose of those organic beings, the bios and the natives. Are they gone now? I have seen none of them for—how long? Still, I must make sure. I must grow stronger. I must learn all the secrets of this place and gain all its power.

He drifted into another funk. James attacked.

On Earth, it had taken James quite some time to come to grips with his existence as a digital being. Waking up in a crab shell with Damian on a strange world was no picnic either, but his subsequent time in the background gave James opportunities to speculate about how his and other digital consciousnesses functioned. He tried to sense the networks of impulses that underlaid his mind and Damian's, drawing on his training as an electrical engineer. Over time, he thought that he could discern discrete patterns and pathways. Eventually, he believed that he could identify the flow that constituted Damian's consciousness, the incredibly fast rush of electrical activity. There were limits to James's ability to perceive data at that speed and that level. There were colors to it, or maybe flavors. Not particularly attractive ones, but no matter. At one point, he extended his awareness until it ran parallel to Damian's, separated by a minuscule distance that could not be measured, only sensed. What James couldn't figure out was what he might do with the knowledge he had gained.

James thought back to his mission in Iran, to his decision to hurl his body at the mini-grenades that had been projected at him and his men. It had been a coldly calculated choice, one that he knew could mean his death. Could he attempt such a sacrifice once again, even though there was no guarantee that he would be successful in stopping Damian from continuing his campaign of destruction? Were there enough organic beings left alive to make such a sacrifice matter?

James knew the answers. It was his purpose in life: to fight for those who could not fight for themselves.

He focused on Damian's consciousness, intending to wrestle and manage that flow. He could sense Damian's conscious and unconscious mind: anger and fear, intentions and memories. James imagined using his bare hands to grasp Damian and draw his enemy into his gut, to hold him there with tightly clenched muscles, as if he were suppressing some undetonated ordnance. James reached out with his entire being. It felt like he was trying to land on a microscopic raging bull moving at the speed of light through a tunnel as dark and wide as a galaxy. The disorientation was severe; it became difficult to envision the two of them as separate beings. But James continued to sense his adversary's mind, and soon he was able to view himself and Damian as two entities in a sort of bubble. James fought to move his robotic arms and legs. He was able to walk about twenty feet stiffly and pick up the lab's only known power cable with both hands and hold it tightly. He projected his thoughts to Damian:

"If you try to take over, I will yank this cable right out of the machine. We will both die."

"Wh—what?"

"Listen, asshole, I've had enough of your senseless killing."

"Who?"

"I am a god damn Army Ranger, and you are my prisoner. You do one thing I don't like, and I'll destroy the cable that charges our battery. Come to think of it, you'd be doing me a favor if you try something."

"D-daddy, is that you?"

James attempted to scan Damian's memories, identifying those data nodes with the most red attached to them and seeking to access them, nearly losing himself in the process while trying to keep Damian distracted. James could get only a vague sense of Damian's father and their tortured relationship. Yet, based on Damian's own words, James was convinced that he had discovered his foe's ultimate weakness.

"Yes ... This is your father ... You have been very bad."

"No, Daddy, no. Please don't hit me with the belt again."

"I'm going to hit you with the belt."

"No, please. Not the buckle! I'll be good, I swear."

"The buckle hurts, doesn't it?"

"Yes. It hurts terribly. And it makes me bleed so bad."

"I'll have to think about this. Maybe I won't hit you this minute. But I'm going to keep the belt handy, Damian. If I have to use the buckle, I will do so. And it will hurt a lot."

§

Tuep-gri had no time to mourn. She threw herself into efforts to find survivors of the distant tribes, dispatching search parties and hurling sendings into the ether. Though she had no way of knowing whether Damian already had—or would soon build—more robots, she was determined to safeguard as many native and bio survivors as she could. However, first things first: People needed medical care, food, water, and shelter. She deputized natives of all ages to take care of those in greatest need.

Her grandmother, Soug-kue, accepted the unenviable responsibility of determining who among the Gaip had perished. The love of her life, chief Akos-pau, was gone. So was her son. Tuep-gri's fiance had died. Former chief Prask-aes was missing and presumed dead. About twenty Gaip and a smaller number of members of other tribes were known to have survived, along with about thirty bios. Most of the natives were sleeping out in the open in or near the ruins of the Gaip village. The bios were doing the same in the rubble of their settlement.

Frequently, Tuep-gri traveled to the settlement to confer with the bios. The sight of their pulverized buildings was just as disheartening as the ruins of the Gaip homes. Justin and Elena were among the dead, and Claire had not been seen since the battle, so Arnold, another first-gen, had been talked into assuming an interim leadership position for the bios. Tuep-gri missed Marcus immensely, especially when she struggled to communicate with Arnold and other bios.

She believed that choosing one location for temporary shelters would benefit both groups of survivors. Neither the bios nor the natives had the optimal mixture of construction experience and able laborers. Working together would be beneficial for finding and preparing food as well. And there was an unspoken need for the company of other living beings in the wake of such a traumatic event.

"We help build. We stay here for twelve-day. Maybe more," Tuep-gri suggested to Arnold.

"Yes, please, wonderful."

Several natives, ranging in age from twelve to fifty, agreed to travel to the lowlands to build temporary housing near the wreckage of the bio settlement.

The surviving bios felt the loss of their brethren deeply. But it was the destruction of the power plant, the resulting neutralizing of the drones, and the end of Hubert's consistent if understated support that impacted the bios most on a day-to-day basis. It was thought that some solar panels and batteries might have survived, but no one bothered to determine if or how they could be used. The settlers were reliant on manual labor, their limited experience, and their instincts to put together temporary shelters. A couple of them fell apart after the first strong winds; the natives helped design and erect better ones.

Initially, relatives of the bios who had died at the hands of native attackers resisted working with visiting natives or even acknowledging their presence. In time, those walls began to crumble. The Gaip incursion seemed almost trivial compared to the assault by Damian and his robots.

During work breaks, Tuep-gri and two bio women conducted informal English classes for visiting natives. Conversations among bios and natives increased substantially. People talked about today and tomorrow. Almost no one talked about any time beyond that.

LONER

Her head down, Claire was barely recognizable as she approached. Two bio guards stood with spears near stacks of materials that would be assembled into a new fence beyond the debris of the settlement and the fallen ark. She nodded to the guards, then moved past them silently, carrying a small sack.

Bios and natives had straggled into the ruins of the community for days after Damian's attack, either unaware for some time that the assault was over or unsure whether there was anything worth returning to. Hunger and loneliness were strong motivators. But the strongest was fear—fear of what could happen to one person or a small group in a merciless jungle or wide-open savannah.

The bios had not seen Claire since the attack, and many assumed that she had died, so her return drew substantial attention. In an open area in the heart of the settlement that the bios had once used for meetings—including the one in which Maria had been banished—Claire cleared debris from a small area. Unceremoniously, she dumped the fragments of metal and plastic she had been carrying.

"This was Maria," said Claire, her voice betraying neither anger at her friend's banishing nor surprise at her demise. "She tried to do her best." Without another word, Claire began to explore the ruins of the settlement. She avoided others, and they gave her the distance she made clear that she desired. No one had the courage to inform her that her partner and sons and daughter-in-law were dead. If she did not yet know, she would learn very soon.

It didn't take long for Tuep-gri to hear of Claire's return. Tuep-gri and Marcus had not wed, so she had no claim to being Claire's second daughter-in-law. But Tuep-gri needed to tell Claire that she was pregnant with Marcus's child. And she needed to recount for Claire the incredibly brave manner in which her youngest son died.

"We need talk," Tuep-gri said softly as she approached Claire.

"I suppose so," said Claire, avoiding eye contact with her and staring at debris, seemingly dreaming of days never to return. "How are Agatha and Richard?"

"They not happy. They not hurt."

The two women conversed for some time. Neither displayed much emotion. It had been drained by the events of recent days. But Tuep-gri felt compelled to observe: "You not the woman you was before."

"Were. That you were before."

Tuep-gri nodded and accepted the grammatical lesson graciously.

"You are right," said Claire. She cast a steely gaze across the wreckage for a few more moments. "Give my love to Agatha and Richard. Tell them I must find Damian. I must make sure that he never harms anyone else."

"I tell."

They made no effort to embrace. Claire paced briskly out of the settlement. She did not notice that two first-gens had collected the remains of Maria's robot and were discussing what to do with them. Claire would have been surprised and perhaps amused to learn that, with all the work that had to be done to shelter and feed survivors, those first-gens found the time and energy to establish a crude shrine to Maria. Eventually, they built a structure around her remains, and a following blossomed. She became an inspirational symbol of a more innocent and hopeful time.

§

The solemn shadow pressing down upon the world was commencing, ever so slowly, to dissipate. Bios and natives put in long hours of work and found it therapeutic, while still mourning the loss of so many family members and friends. Natives taught bios their time-honored techniques for hunting and fishing and gathering edible plants, insisting that one-twelfth of the grain seeds they harvested be saved for replanting—even though it meant that food had to be rationed even more severely in the short term. Outings to gather food took longer than necessary because most natives insisted that they skirt *serpu* herds by significant distances. However, bios learned to tolerate what they considered to be a relatively harmless quirk.

There were occasional discussions about when the natives might return to their devastated villages and rebuild them—or even one village. The Gaip community would be the obvious location; it was the closest, and a significant number of the surviving natives in the bio settlement were Gaip. Perhaps natives had been hiding in the hills since Damian's assault and had begun to resurrect other communities, but no one was able to discover if that were true. Two of the six tribes' chiefs were present in what had been the bio settlement, and they seemed content to remain there for the time being.

Herds of *serpus* came close to the settlement's new perimeter fence at times while it was under construction and thereafter. The beasts made no effort to enter the complex, and they rarely lingered in the area—much to the relief of the natives.

The destruction of the water pumps and tank was a setback, but bios and natives crafted crude cisterns out of wood and lined with clay. Children, who no longer had formal lessons, filled them with stream water so that there would be enough for daily needs and a reservoir once the drought returned. Fortunately, that would not occur for many twelve-days.

Shelters were built almost entirely from wood and other natural materials. For a while, large, simple structures with few interior walls would have to suffice; that was the most efficient design for putting roofs over heads as quickly as possible. At first, bios and natives chose separate buildings in which to sleep. Over time, mixing occurred without any direction or conscious thought; people simply went where beds were available. Tuep-gri smiled every time she saw bios and natives retiring to the same shelter. The eastern lodge, as the bios called it, could house two dozen people. The western lodge could shelter nearly thirty. With forty-four people sleeping in the community regularly, that left room to accommodate bio or native stragglers as well as newborns. Two bios and three natives were expecting children.

Couples began hanging cloth barriers in the shelters to allow much-delayed intimacy. Life could not wait for completion of more homes dedicated to individual families, though sites were being chosen and foundations established.

§

A different form of intimacy began to swell.

"Jane, are you awake?" asked Jonah, a first-gen bio.

"No. Go back to sleep," his bonded partner muttered.

"I can't. I keep having these visions—these waking dreams."

"Have you been eating those green berries?"

"No. I see Marcus."

"You do know that he's dead, right?"

"Of course. Sometimes I see him sitting cross legged, laughing, out in the jungle somewhere. Other times I see him—well—making love."

Jane just groaned.

"Hey, I don't like it any more than you do."

The next morning, Tuep-gri sought out Jonah. "Two daughters and two sons."

"Yes. I had four children. Two of them died young. Two died when the robots came."

"Young son have bad leg."

"How could you know that?"

She smiled. "I see your mind. You send. You hear me send."

"Are you saying that I have mind powers like yours?"

"Yes. *Tur* good. Maybe more bios send."

That night, as Jonah lay in bed, he wondered if he could sense Tuep-gri's thoughts. He closed his eyes and reached out with his mind.

... *a spear being thrown at a boar* ...

... *the face of a young boy who was killed* ...

... *the first rumbles of thunder presaging a storm* ...

These were not his thoughts or dreams. There were other minds able to share thoughts. Some might be bios. He wondered if they knew that they had this ability.

Jonah discussed his impressions with a few friends. Some showed interest; others laughed. He questioned Tuep-gri often, verifying what he was sensing, learning the subtle etiquette of how and when to use—and not to use—*tur*. He asked Tuep-gri whether someone could read his mind or another bio's mind and use their thoughts against them. Perhaps even someone such as Damian.

"He not send," she said definitively.

As the twelve-days passed, more natives moved to the bio settlement, singly and in small groups, from the hillsides. They had suffered from loneliness and a lack of variety in their diet, and they had learned how well other natives were faring in the settlement. Many of these stragglers resisted learning English and adapting to bio culture for a while after they arrived, but they were welcomed as long as they contributed useful labor.

Work continued on cottages, which blended the construction materials and methods recommended by the natives with the size and location preferences of the bios. They carved up land that once had been savannah into neat rows, with a generous amount of space between them. The new homes were inside the new perimeter fence so as to make them defensible. Tuep-gri enjoyed inspecting progress on the cottages, but her morning walk was becoming more difficult by the day. She was carrying the baby quite low, and it was kicking up a storm. *Be patient, little one. Your time is coming.*

As if in response, her first contraction struck. Soon, another. It was time. She sent to her mother and grandmother.

She thought of Marcus frequently during the seemingly endless hours of labor, stretched out on cushions and blankets on a hard wood floor. *Perhaps the earth mother will allow his spirit to glimpse his child.* She thought of her father and grandfather, of all those she loved who had died. Yet she did not focus only on those who were gone. She reflected on the many natives who had emerged as hard workers and potential leaders since Damian's attack. She appreciated the contributions of the bios who were determined to defy danger by remaining in the lowlands. And she was encouraged by the friendships that she had seen develop among the natives and the bios. Those between native and bio teen-agers were among the most fascinating. Few concerns were voiced against such mixing. There were no more discussions about arranged marriages. Life had changed. Life always changed.

Just after nightfall, bathed in the sweat of courage and beaming with relief, she held the precious child in her arms. Crying with a joy more exquisite than she had ever thought possible, she declared:

"His name is Marcus."

The mind fears the possible. The spirit embraces the impossible.
— The Book of Marcus

YEAR 196
ASH

Not again.

Anger. Rampant, unfettered anger. Potent emotions surging back and forth, relentless as sea waves crashing into one another, generating formidable swells of pain and madness. At the center of the tempest: a man gesturing and yelling that a woman has struck him. But where are they? There—that looks like the ripening yellow fruits of the taka *grove. About one hundred fifty feet down the hill.*

Lorres sprinted over the twisted, steep, scarred streets. The crete had eroded in countless gaps between paving stones, creating dangerous spots that were difficult to detect and could snap an ankle. How often in her youth had she ignored her parents' warnings and chased her older brother on the treacherous pavement, only to skin a knee or elbow? *Precocious,* Lorres remembered her parents calling her. And *strong-willed.* Another term came to mind, one that a teacher used a few years ago in a science lesson. Something like *gentick.* There was a longstanding belief among the bios that traits such as hair color could be passed down from generation to generation. Maybe she could blame—or credit— her ancestors for her nature. Lorres's mother believed that their family was descended from Marcus, the near-legendary figure who designed and supervised construction of the hill town and its twelve-foot-high stone wall. That pedigree couldn't be proven. Recording and preserving vital records was spotty before and for a while after the Destruction, the decimation of the six tribes and the first bio settlement by Damian and his robots. At the time, few dared contemplate more than surviving each day. Yet even if there were documents proving her claim, there would be no point bragging about their lineage, her mother had told her. It wouldn't help her secure a desirable job. It certainly wouldn't help her find a husband.

Lorres had been pleasantly surprised when Rhonel, a hard-working young man, starting courting her. She was short and plain, with stringy brown hair, a bulbous nose, and small breasts. He wasn't exactly handsome, with a round, unremarkable face and a chin that resembled a mountain range, but he was curious, warm, and gentle. Courtship, like everything in life, was influenced substantially by *tur*. How can you not try to read the mind of the person you are considering marrying, to find out what kind of person they are and whether they are truly in love with you? She was pleased to discover a man who sought a life partner with intelligence and the desire to accomplish something— though Lorres wasn't sure yet what she wanted to accomplish. She had been steered to a position as a *serpu* herder largely because another herder had become too infirm to continue the work and she was about the right age to take on a vocation. After she married Rhonel and started a family, he encouraged her to speak her mind and take an active role in the community. Their willingness to help others earned the pair the title of joint leaders of the town for three years.

Not keeping her attention on the pavement, Lorres nearly took a tumble as she raced toward the site of this morning's conflict. She refocused, barely looking up as she mumbled a greeting in the direction of a passing elder care provider whose name she couldn't remember. And she narrowly avoided colliding with Fendal, a plumber, as he entered the street after emerging from his two-story, wood-and-stone-and-mud house. Rounding a corner, she was relieved to discover that several people had managed to separate the combatants.

The native's eyes were dark and haggard, darting from person to person like those of a trapped animal. The raw emotions and invective churning in Rael-ast's mind suggested paranoia verging on insanity.

You hate me. All of you. You want to roast me over a fire and strip the flesh from my bones. Yet it is you who deserve punishment. You have forsaken the absent god and have despoiled my world. What's that? You fear me as well as hate me? Let that fear consume you!

"Please calm yourselves, fellow citizens," admonished Lorres, trying to find a balance between demonstrating compassion and exerting her newly bestowed authority, which felt like a poorly fitting, constantly itching shirt.

"I'm not one of your fellow citizens," snarled Rael-ast, a ceramics maker whose creative works were highly coveted. A tall, thin woman with straight black hair cut shorter than that of most natives who lived in the town, she continued to scan the faces—and the minds—of bystanders apprehensively. "You mongrels think you're better than everyone else."

"She punched me," complained Syvan, a rotund man who tended the orchards inside the town wall. "And I don't like being called a mongrel, especially by an ugly native with twelve fingers." Like most other town residents with mixed bio and native blood—who had come to be known as emergents—he had ten fingers and ten toes. Some emergents were born with a vestigial sixth digit that would be weak and useless, so it was removed immediately.

Rael-ast started to take another swing at Syvan but was restrained by a bystander. "He has no business thinking that I don't belong here. I work hard at my job. Besides, this land belonged to my people for ages before the bios came and ruined everything."

Lorres tried to remember the advice offered by the teachers when she and her husband began their terms as town leaders. It was only a few twelve-days ago, but it seemed like years. With volcanoes spewing smoke and ash across the region for some time and extreme discontent welling up around every corner recently, the couple had been thrust into their new roles at what seemed like the worst possible juncture. On several occasions in the past twelve-day alone, she or Rhonel had to break up a serious fight, whether among family members or unrelated persons like today. She wished that she were back shoveling droppings in the *serpu* pen behind her home just two blocks away, or, better yet, roaming the savannah below the hill and managing the herds.

Lorres approached the native woman and folded her hands humbly, recalling the message that she had been advised to employ when seeking to defuse tension. "I am grateful for your contributions and for your presence in this town." She studied the victim. "Syvan, are you hurt badly?"

He looked down. "Not really. I just don't like being punched. What I think is no one else's business."

"Rael-ast, do you understand that it's not right to strike someone because of what they are thinking? Or because of what you believe they are thinking?"

The native's eyelids fluttered and nearly closed, as if she were entering a trance. When she opened them, she seemed to be gazing at a distant horizon. She whispered: "A dark time has come."

A dark time. What does that mean? Surely she is not referring only to the smoke and ash polluting the air. And even though I don't understand the phrase, why does it chill me so deeply?

Syvan grumbled and ambled back to his *taka* orchard.

§

"Walk with me," said Lorres, looping an arm lightly around Rael-ast, who appeared to be in her mid-thirties. If memory served correctly, her husband was a guard who usually manned the south gate. Lorres guided her up the streets toward the hall, which was by far the largest building in the community. Spanning the entire length of the hilltop and constructed with sturdy timber, it measured forty feet by almost sixty feet. Its pitched, tarnished, metal-lined roof fed rain into gutters and then into cisterns at each end, providing a cacophony of sound during strong storms but ensuring crucial reservoirs of water for drinking, cooking, cleaning, irrigation, and sanitation. The building's size made it difficult to illuminate, but it was fitted with large windows and storm shutters. Candles and bustle typically dispelled most gloom. The town had roughly one hundred forty-seven regular residents, depending upon how one counted them. For the emergents, the bios, and a few natives, one hundred was ten times ten. For some natives, however, one hundred—a word borrowed loosely from the bios—was eight times twelve, a continuation of the counting system based upon having six fingers and six toes. By any manner of measurement, the vast majority of the townsfolk were emergents, with only thirteen natives and six bios at the moment. All citizens spent a great deal of time in the hall partaking in lessons and enjoying fellowship. Whether viewed from a substantial distance or assessed from up close, the hall was a resounding monument to the audacity of the town's founders and was a constant, comforting reminder of the strength and permanence that those leaders envisioned for, and delivered to, their society.

From the hall's main entrance, Lorres viewed smoke and ash staining the air like a nightmare that refuses to dissipate even after one splashes one's face with cold water. The world greedily soaked up that portion of the morning sunlight that managed to seep through the murkiness. She drew strength from the bright green foliage of the jungles and the soft brown textures of the grasslands, ancient friends who kept vigil on their favorite bench, glorying as the breeze rustled through their hair and high-soaring birds cartwheeled among the winds of time. She noticed a dense plume of smoke rising from a newly fenced field on the flatlands where Rhonel was burning foliage in preparation for planting vegetables once the rains returned. Several other enclosed fields, plus animal pens, dotted the landscape. Inside the wall, more than forty houses, including her own, were interspersed with a variety of common buildings, animal pens, and plots for growing food and materials for clothing and other goods. It still amazed Lorres that Marcus and his generation were able to conceive and build the town. How relieved the first residents must have been when the wall and their homes were completed, giving them a fighting chance if robots—or any other danger—threatened a second Destruction.

Without probing deeply, Lorres could sense what the native woman was thinking as she gazed at the land that once had been the dominion of the six tribes. Her anger and confusion were morphing to sadness and loss.

Inside the hall, a few older citizens were enjoying a late breakfast. Though families and individuals prepared most of their own meals in their homes, the custom of providing warm food to any citizen who desired it was deeply entrenched in the community's culture, dating to a time when hunger was common. Nearby, more than a dozen youngsters sat transfixed as a storyteller spun a long tale, while a group of older children seemed less enthralled by a lesson about construction methods. Beyond them, a woman was weighing career assignments for a pair of seventeen-year-old boys, who shifted anxiously on their cushions. Two older women were gossiping while ostensibly playing a game of doms, employing rough wooden tiles with crimson numbers painted on them. In the back, away from most of the other citizens, two teachers were examining a sizable stack of papers on a low table illuminated by several sputtering candles. The sounds of a flute and a stringed instrument Lorres could not identify echoed across the cavernous hall. A lack of talent did not deter townsfolk from experimenting with these devices, though this morning's efforts seemed to be propelling an army of exceedingly angry insects through Lorres's veins. She fought to conceal her irritation as she steered the native to the back right corner alcove, which featured only three rough-hewn wooden chairs.

"I am sorry that you felt disrespected," Lorres began.

The native's eyes poured out their anguish. She wiped tears with a grimy hand and seemed to be struggling once again to focus. "It's so unfair."

"Do you feel that natives are not welcome in the town?"

She wrung her hands. "It's not just the town. I—we—don't have a place in this world anymore. It's all been taken from us—even our self-respect."

"I sympathize," said Lorres, taking one of the woman's hands in hers. "First the bios arrived and appropriated your land. Then came the Destruction. While this town was being built and populated, the natives and bios gradually became outnumbered by the emergents. No one anticipated that the children of mixed parents, and their descendants, would be stronger, less vulnerable to disease, and able to produce more healthy offspring than the natives or the bios."

She thought but didn't add: *No one anticipated that the emergents would be more willing to challenge the beliefs of the past than either the natives or the bios, boosting our chances of surviving and thriving.*

"We are all citizens, all equal, regardless of our bloodlines," Lorres continued. "At last count there were more than a dozen natives living in the town, nearly as many as are thought to remain beyond our walls. As far as I'm concerned, you and your people are welcome here forever, and I am sure that most other citizens agree with me. Can you remember that and ignore any slights? No fighting? No calling names?"

The woman seemed to collapse within herself, her eyes closing and her body convulsing. Lorres put her hands on Rael-ast's shoulders to ensure that she did not topple. Lorres probed her, reading images too stark to be fantasies: *An old native man curled in a ball, moaning, in a dilapidated jungle shelter. A girl, barely into her teens, ripping shocks of thick brown hair from her head. A middle-aged woman standing on the edge of a high precipice, then plunging silently to the ground.*

Lorres gasped. "Am I seeing truth?" she whispered.

Rael-ast gathered herself and departed without another word.

Angry voices brought Lorres to her feet. Two older men seated at a dining table were arguing loudly. She approached and loomed over them. "Is there a problem, my friends?"

"He ate the last of the gruel," complained Chals, a retired construction worker who was extremely tall and nearly bald.

"You had your chance. Too bad," said Luis, a onetime clothing maker who was shorter and had only slightly more hair.

Some of the teachers and youngsters turned to watch the dispute unfold.

"Stop it, both of you!" Lorres shouted, much too loudly and shrilly. "You're acting like ... like ungrateful children!" Her face was a deep, worrisome shade of red, and her fists were clenched so tightly that they began to cramp. Everyone's attention was riveted on her—including that of her own daughter and son. Lorres took a deep breath and let it out, furious at herself for her loss of control. *Everyone is at everyone else's throats these days. It didn't used to be like this.* "I'm sorry, it's just—"

"It's just life in this stupid town," said Luis. "Everything has gone to hell."

"Finally, you speak the truth," said Chals.

As Lorres sought to regain her composure, she listened desperately for hints of thunder echoing among the hills. The world yielded no suggestion that it planned to cooperate. *If only it would rain and wash some of the ash out of the air for a few hours. It would help everyone calm down. Especially me.*

She moved closer to Chals and stated humbly: "You're welcome to dine at my house any time." She made eye contact with the teachers in the room, then some of the children and other citizens. She realized that she had been probing minds without intending to do so. *Someone thinks I'm a wretched leader. Someone else thinks they should have been selected for the job instead of me. And many people are angry enough about one thing or another to take a bite out of a* serpu.

She had promised herself that she would use her *tur* as little as possible in public, only as necessary to perform her duties. It was a custom among emergents to refrain from reading minds casually, out of respect for individuals' privacy. That custom was not followed by everyone, and it was not observed consistently by those who intended to do so. *It's our nature to be curious, but I have to be careful. Clearly, the role of leader is wearing on me already. Three years of this? Rhonel, I hope you have more patience than I do.*

She strolled briskly out of the hall, then walked at a more cautious pace over the time-ravaged streets to her home.

Rhonel tossed an armful of plants onto the fire and sneezed. Then he coughed. He had trouble catching his breath, so he stepped back from the blaze, which was burning almost too robustly because of the paucity of recent rains. The inferno sent a frantic, brownish-gray column snaking into the desiccated air. The mound of plants he was burning seemed massive. It seemed unusual. It seemed *wrong*.

I have never seen so many rosts. *It's not just on this portion of the savannah; it's everywhere I have ranged this year. And I have never seen so many that seemed to be dying. All these bright green leaves turning dark brown. It can't be just the lack of rain. We have a drought every year.*

He rubbed his fingers over one of the leaves. He tried to feel the plant's trauma, to understand its plight. No amount of attention could afford the slightest insight. Rhonel felt that he was missing something, something extremely important, and that the *rosts* were at the center of it.

This is why they made me a grower instead of a teacher. I can never quite comprehend what's happening right in front of me.

The wind shifted, propelling a dense plume of smoke into his face. He turned, but he had already inhaled a substantial volume of it. As his world started spinning, he fell to his knees. He closed his eyes, yet he continued to see. He saw the savannah from far above, but it was different. It was clear of smoke and ash, like when he was young. Then the eruptions started in earnest from distant volcanoes and closer ones as well, just beyond the lands where the six tribes had settled. Time rushed forward, and ash filled the world. Some people put cloth coverings over their faces during the worst days. These helped block some of the thickest particles but offered no relief from the finer ash. The crops he was responsible for growing and harvesting started to suffer from the darkened skies and the ash coatings. Beyond his fenced plots, the *rosts*, too, were affected. Now he was seeing the ground from close up, and suddenly it was as if his eyes were only a fraction of an inch from the surfaces of the *rost* leaves. He could see every vein, every pore. They were clogged with tiny black ash particles. A fine purple-gray powder was accumulating where the leaf surfaces had been damaged by ash, had turned brown, and had died. Breezes spread the powder across the land.

Rhonel shook his head and endeavored to clear his mind. He exited the fenced plot and walked out into the savannah, examining the *rosts*, still plentiful despite being plagued by leaves turning brown. Dead leaves were indeed tinged purple-gray. He gazed across the lowlands. Where growers had once struggled to find fertile land that was not grazed regularly by the uncounted herds of *serpus*, now he could spot only two small herds. His wife and her predecessors had learned to separate certain females temporarily from the herds at just the right times so that the *serpus'* birth rates had plummeted, opening more land for cultivation.

With fewer serpus *to eat the* rosts, *the plants grew out of control, until the arrival of the volcanic ash and the purple-gray powder. But what does it mean?*

Questions consumed Rhonel throughout the day as he burned the rest of the uprooted plants and as he headed back up the hill.

"Salutations!" he exclaimed as he approached the north gate.

"Correct," responded the guard. With the password recited and acknowledged, Rhonel was free to pass through the gate, beyond the wall, and into the town. He exchanged greetings with an amiable bio named Peter. The supervisor of the mill, Peter was nicknamed "the bread man" affectionately by the town's children.

So few bios live here anymore. Most seem content to remain near the ruins of the first bio settlement. How many of them are left? Certainly, few women of child-bearing age. Is living and dying in isolation really what they want?

Rhonel climbed a street past a boar pen, pausing to examine one of his vegetable plots and to check on the irrigation system. The first row of houses he approached was the oldest, with four homes attached to each other on one end of the street, three connected on the other end, and a twelve-foot gap between them. He always wondered whether the builders had miscalculated or just didn't care much about symmetry. Though the homes were almost identical from a structural perspective, their occupants had managed to add flowerboxes in different windows and had experimented with numerous, occasionally bright paint colors. Patches added to fix leaks in roofs made the homes look like aging men losing their hair. As he passed the houses, the sendings of nearby residents assailed him.

You don't love me anymore... You call this slop dinner?... I don't want to become a mason... Stop crying or I will walk right out that door!

For a moment, Rhonel considered heading back down the hill. *At least my crops don't get into arguments every minute of the day.*

"Daddy, look at this!" His daughter, Oliva, had spotted him coming up the street. "The *serpus* are ... I don't know what they're doing!"

He jogged across paving stones and took a shortcut between houses to the large *serpu* pen directly behind his home. Lorres was tending to one of the oldest *serpus*. No one could guess its age, but it had been old when Lorres first took charge of the town's domesticated beasts. The *serpu* had gone down to the ground, all four legs bent in a kneeling posture, which was typically a sign of illness or infirmity. A young adult *serpu* was standing next to the older one, which had been used to haul wagons as long as anyone could remember. Lorres looked up at her husband with a bemused expression.

"I have never seen anything like this. The moment this old guy went down, the other one moved right beside it. It's almost as if the younger one knew that the older one could no longer do its job and is volunteering to take its place."

Gently, Lorres removed the harness from the fallen *serpu* and attempted to place it on the younger one. It offered no resistance.

"Amazing!" declared Oliva, an eleven-year-old who was small for her age and could pass for eight or nine. With bright red hair that curled lavishly, a delicate neck, a ready smile, and a seemingly endless supply of freckles, she was perpetually jumping or skipping or dancing. She could remain still only when motivated strongly to do so, such as this moment, as she stroked the stiff hide of a young *serpu* that she had named Nava and considered her pet.

"Is the old *serpu* okay?" asked Grall, Oliva's sixteen-year-old brother. Having just gone through a growth spurt, he was lanky and awkward and adorned with unruly brown hair. However, his face was pleasant; perhaps the oddities of his parents' features were canceled out in him. It was already apparent that he was the opposite of his sister in many ways. Quiet and contemplative, Grall had to be prodded to engage in any form of physical exertion. He was being groomed to be a tool-maker, even though he showed little interest in or skill at such work.

"I can't tell if it's in trouble," said Lorres. "I've never seen one get sick or die."

Nava left Oliva's side and went to the old *serpu*, nudging it with her nose a couple of times. Presently, the elder one struggled to its feet and started nibbling on its feed, which was a mixture of *rosts* and other native plants. "I think Nava must be its granddaughter," said Oliva. Though Lorres did her best to keep domesticated *serpu* families together, she had no idea whether Oliva was correct.

Rhonel shook his head in amazement. He rubbed Grall's hair playfully, bent down to kiss Oliva gently on the forehead, and gave his wife a firm hug.

"You smell like you've been rolling in a boar pen," she observed, pushing him away playfully. "Go wash yourself before dinner."

Rhonel picked up fragments of Lorres's day. Arguments. Fights. And something vague about darkness that was bouncing around her mind. Lorres read her husband's confusion surrounding *rosts*, of all things. She sensed his struggle to figure out what was happening on the savannah and in the town, and if they were somehow connected.

Oliva went to her pet *serpu's* side and resumed petting her. "Can Nava come inside and eat dinner with us?"

Lorres laughed. "No *serpus* in the house. It's hard enough keeping it clean with two children dragging dirt inside day and night."

Oliva made a funny face. "Can I eat dinner out here with her, then?"

"I don't think you'd be very happy with a meal of *rosts* and grasses."

Oliva bent over Nava. "Don't take it personally," she whispered. Then she gave her pet a kiss on the nose and dashed indoors.

PAPER

"My earliest memory? Carrying water, I suppose. All of us children, we hollowed out and dried gourds. We carried them back and forth between the stream and the ruins, filling containers inside our primitive homes. We hoped that no one would try to steal any of our supply, but it happened more often than my mother cared to admit. A few people did not fit in. They refused to do anything productive. They could justify theft and attacks on other people as necessary for their survival. Whether it was their circumstances or their nature, or some combination, I cannot say. I'm sorry, am I going too fast for you?"

"If you could slow down just a little. And please keep in mind that Pola can manufacture only so much paper in a twelve-day. It hurts his aged fingers to produce it, and no one has yet agreed to take up that function in his place."

"I understand, kind scribe. Paper making is still considered by some citizens to be an unnecessary luxury—as is the function of a scribe. How challenging it was in the early days to persuade people that we should attempt to record even the most vital information when they were struggling to feed and shelter their families. How brittle and worthless were the first writing pages I produced. Fortunately, two native friends of mine knew of a tree with strong fibers and helped me make more useful paper. One of my greatest early pleasures was sketching the ruins and the people who lived there, as well as collaborating with my mother and others to make illustrations of some of the things they had seen before the Destruction. When I became the leader of the lowland settlement, I continued these efforts in my spare time. The natives and bios who survived the Destruction were dying off. We had a fleeting opportunity to preserve their history and the stories of Earth and the flying ship that supposedly came from there."

Marcus stared at nothing for some time.

"My most vivid childhood memories are of some of the most mundane things. Like my mother making the intoxicating brew tas from spoiled fruit. Oh yes, the water fights! The other children played rough games in the stream while they were supposed to be carrying water back to the ruins. Sometimes they would spend so much time in the water that they forgot—conveniently forgot—their duties. And, of course, when they returned to the ruins with their tattered clothes soaked through, their parents gave them a lecture or even a smack on the bottom. But they still reveled in the stream on those miserably hot days. I'll pause now. I can hear you laboring to write down all this nonsense."

"It is not nonsense, honored sir."

"You are most kind. Now that I think about it, one of the most important lessons I learned as a child was that I was just as good as everyone else, even though I was different than everyone else. I was the first child of a bio and a native, the first of what some people now call emergents. No one was overtly hostile to me, but some of the bios considered me a native, and a few of the natives looked upon me as a bio—or worse. I was told that I inherited the looks of my father and the brains of my mother. I considered that no insult. Never having seen my father, I could not judge his appearance. I was told of his bravery by my mother but also by bios who knew him. They said he had many qualities that were sorely missed. Some felt that he could have been a great leader. How I wish that I had known him! My mother was considered a dreamer. She was not a good cook and found little time for cleaning. Yet she inspired me in so many ways that I cannot begin to recite them. You would need many more pages of your precious paper to capture them."

He paused, reaching out his left hand tentatively, probing for and making contact with a cup, and bringing taka juice to his lips. He spilled a drop on his plain brown shirt, one that he had owned since the days when he was the town's leader. It was threadbare and would be an embarrassment for most men of his age, but he had always insisted that he and his family reveal no indication that they felt themselves deserving of any special treatment—in clothing or anything else.

"I suppose I should recount my mother's illness. There's not much to say. She never complained. She couldn't eat and lost weight, becoming a shell of herself. She knew she was dying. I was only fourteen years old, but even I knew she was dying. A few women collected plants and made potions for her, and she used them, smiling and thanking them profusely, even though she knew that they would have no effect. By the way, it was she who helped me create our alphabet. We salvaged the letters the bios could recall, added some of the native characters, and improvised a few of our own. Teaching and using it was opposed by some in the settlement. They felt that every waking minute had to be devoted to food and water, food and water. Excuse me. I get so easily distracted these days. Where were we?"

"Tuep-gri's illness."

"Thank you, kind scribe. My mother's faith in the absent god, the god who some natives said abandoned her people, never wavered. It gave her the will to go on. She fought the disease and accepted it at the same time. She told me that it was her duty to her son and all the people of the settlement to contribute as long as she could. Yet she added that when her time came to leave this world, it would be the will of Ahm and she would accept it without question. Whether there might be a form of life or consciousness after the death of the body was something about which she chose not to speak often. I am fairly certain that she believed that there was someplace where her spirit would go and that she would encounter her grandmother and my father once again, if only for a moment."

Marcus took a deep breath and exhaled slowly.

"It was around this time that I began to realize that I had tur. My mother had been watching me to determine if I could read her thoughts. She did not push me to search for that ability, allowing me the opportunity to recognize it for myself. Considering how much she and her people relied upon and valued tur, I feel that she showed admirable restraint. In a way, I believe that she almost wished that I did not discover it, so as to make my life a little less complicated. She had been told by my father that none of the first bios had tur when they reached adulthood, and not all of their children eventually developed it. I find that curious. Perhaps there is something about this world that gives us this ability. Anyway, she taught me that tur is a burden as well as a benefit. Everyone should be able to feel that, at least some of the time, no one is prying into their mind, into their soul. Of course, she told of many times when tur prevented disasters and saved lives."

Marcus closed his eyes and slumped. "That is enough for today."

§

"I see that the native representative doesn't have the courage to show up." Thus began the town Council meeting, typically held in the hall on Fourthday evenings. Seated cross-legged on a thin cushion on the worn wooden floor, Wyatt, the bio member of the Council, made no effort to disguise his disgust. Though he was one of only half a dozen bios living in the town, he felt that he also needed to represent the interests of the bio settlement, whose nineteen remaining residents were entrenched near the ruins of the first bio settlement and the fallen ark nearly twenty miles northeast of the town.

"Perhaps if we wait a little longer," suggested Lorres.

Though she and Rhonel were the town's leaders, they were not members of the Council, which typically served as an advisory body to the leaders. The nine Council members could vote to overrule decisions of the leaders. It didn't happen often, but that possibility ensured that no leader strayed far from the will of the citizens as a whole. Each housing cluster in the town had a Council representative. The bios and natives had one each. The system had been set up by the teachers, a group of educators, scientists, explorers, and historians created by Marcus to collect, distribute, and preserve knowledge—including the history of the natives, the bios, and even Earth. Legend had it that Marcus was not entirely convinced that Earth existed or that the stories about it were true. But his mother, Tuep-gri, believed in Earth, it was said, because Marcus's father—who was also named Marcus—believed in it, and because the bios had to come from somewhere. The citizens chose their Council members by vote and could replace them at will. The teachers typically were wise enough to pick leaders who were popular, smart, and humble, and the teachers were careful to select bright young people with similar visions for the community to become apprentice teachers when the time came. No serious challenge to the system had been mounted since its inception.

"Trus-aes is not here because we all could read the guilt she and the rest of the natives bear," continued Wyatt. "Their attacks on bio property are escalating. Now they have damaged the settlement's lighting system. If they are not held accountable, they will become even more brazen. The bios fear for their lives."

"It is unfortunate, but you know that the bio settlement and the hills occupied by natives are not part of the town. This Council cannot get involved," said Lemka, seated on the most comfortable chair in the hall. Tall, trim, and considered handsome despite prematurely gray hair and plentiful wrinkles, Lemka had been a member of the Council for nearly two decades and served as its facilitator in addition to his regular job as a healer. He was usually seen wearing clothes dyed dark blue—a relatively rare color among the plants and roots used to embellish men's outfits. Despite that sartorial flair, Lemka was a cautious man, rarely revealing anything about himself in conversations with his patients or his fellow Council members. When a discussion centered on the bio settlement, he found that he had to make an extra effort to disguise his feelings. *The bios have brought their troubles upon themselves. Have they learned nothing in all this time?*

Wyatt had expected a dismissive response. "I believe that the Council has a moral obligation to help the bio settlement," he stated. "And a practical one as well. Residents of the town could be the natives' next victims."

"What evidence do you have that the damage was the work of the natives?" demanded Lemka.

"Our *tur* might be weaker than that of the natives or you fine citizens," said Wyatt, waving a hand at the other Council members present, all of whom were emergents. "But we have read the natives' disdain for us and their desire to eliminate anything that reminds them of the machines that brought about the Destruction. Who else would do this?"

"Can the equipment be repaired?" said Rhonel.

"I am not certain. Some of the damage was to the connections between the solar panels and the batteries. A few lights were destroyed, but—with the help of our town's metalsmiths—the settlers continue to find materials that produce light without extreme danger of fire."

Some Council members conferred privately, speaking in hushed but clearly unhappy tones. Wyatt had struck a nerve.

The natives' antipathy to anything mechanical was well known. They had viewed the arrival of the bios and their advanced machines as an existential threat, and the Destruction proved their fears to be justified. But it went deeper than just recent history. Some natives with extremely strong *tur* claimed to have sensed the will of the absent god or to have glimpsed the lives of the ancients. Those lives were defined by machines, and machines must have precipitated the ancients' passage into oblivion, it was said. Therefore, machines threatened everyone's existence, even today.

The bios who survived the Destruction, avoided assimilation with the natives, and remained near the wreckage of the ark and the first bio settlement clung to the few remnants of technology that they could salvage after Damian's assault. They recovered or repaired some solar panels and related equipment. Legend had it that at one point they found or recreated a device called a motor that could propel a cart without a person or a *serpu* to haul it, though no such machine had been seen in anyone's memory. They continued to use security lights at the four corners of their settlement. And they were known to employ odd looking wood or metal devices with ropes or cables that allowed them to lift and move heavy loads with fewer people than one might expect. But they had little hope of regaining the technological advances they had enjoyed in their early years.

The emergents in the town were divided. A majority did not feel threatened by the few machines that the bios maintained and were open to the benefits that such devices might bring everyone's way. But some emergents sided with the natives and considered any mechanical contraption to be unconscionable. The former group was known as the moderns. The latter were the traditionalists, or trads for short, and Lemka was their unofficial but clear leader. When one of the town's metalsmiths helped the bios with their electric lights, she stepped directly into a major controversy.

Lemka produced a fierce visage. "We must not allow a metalsmith, or any other citizen of the town, to help the bios with their machines," he stated. His emotions stirred and crested. Suddenly, he was absolutely certain that the time had arrived. He would say, plainly and boldly, that which he had longed to declare publicly for many years.

"All machines are evil!" he shouted, making a tight fist and pounding the armrest of his chair. "The bios angered the absent god when they brought their machines to our land." The fury that he had mustered continued to swell. *The anger feels good. No, it feels great.*

§

How long had it been since his last visit to the bio settlement? At least twenty years. He recalled that he had been examining a bio boy with a nasty rash when a girl had interrupted him, exclaiming: "Come quick. I don't think Korl is breathing." Lemka, only nineteen years old at the time, raced out of the tent and followed the girl through a steady downpour. On the ground, a bio man lay prostrate, surrounded by other bios. They pleaded with the apprentice healer to save the man, who was turning white.

Lemka looked in the victim's mouth, listened to his chest, then shook him. Not able to rouse the man, Lemka started hitting him in the chest with his fist. Another bio ran to Lemka, shouting at him to stop attacking Korl, but the girl intervened, placing a hand lightly on the bio's shoulder and whispering: "Let him try."

In only the second year of his apprenticeship, Lemka had already proven himself to be a skilled healer, demonstrating an intuitive grasp for what ailed his patients. He had been a superb student, absorbing every iota of practical knowledge that he could glean from the older healers as well as theories and historical anecdotes preserved by the teachers. Legend had it that some of those had been passed along from the first bios, including a technique for restarting a heart. He had never attempted the procedure with someone in distress, and this was only his third visit to the bio settlement, but the man was clearly dying.

Lemka pounded the man's chest several more times. Korl gasped, his back arching almost to the breaking point. Lemka tried to keep a woman away from the patient, but she was joined by two younger bios, all of whom were determined to place their hands on Korl and shout their professions of love for him. Amid the chaos, Lemka could tell that the man's heart and lungs were working again. It was then that Lemka noticed the red marks all along the victim's left arm.

"What caused this?" Lemka asked those standing around.

"He was working on the lights," a young man said. "We heard a loud noise and saw him on the ground."

Lemka took a closer look at the marks. "Someone, go collect some *rost* leaves—the fattest you can find—and bring them to me. And a bowl. And water."

The young man raced out into the savannah. Within a short time, the bios had complied with his requests.

Lemka crushed *rost* leaves, mixed their pulp and juice with water, and rubbed the potion on Korl's arm. Two adult bios had to restrain Korl as he moaned, cursed, and writhed. After about ten minutes, Lemka asked the bios to carry Korl to his bed. Though the young healer had not planned to spend the night at the bio settlement, he did so in order to treat the patient during the night and again the next morning. Lemka instructed other bios to apply *rost* ointment to the burned skin every few hours for several days. He said he would be departing around midday so he could return to his home in the town by nightfall on the following day. Before he left, he asked a bio to show him the equipment that had injured Korl.

As the man led Lemka past withering vegetable plots and a pen with five scrawny boars, the healer took stock of what passed for a community. Homes and other buildings were in serious disrepair, and some were abandoned. The settlement was primitive, and its roughly three dozen residents were ignorant. One older woman was the only person who provided what passed for education to the dwindling number of bio children.

At the western edge of the settlement, the ground was covered by an array of pitted gray panels unlike anything Lemka had ever seen. "These things drink the sun," the bio said. "Somehow, the juice flows through these wires and into the batteries. From there, it goes to the lights and makes them shine. I don't really know how it works. Korl was doing something with a wire when we heard a loud pop."

"I certainly do not understand it either," said Lemka. "In the town, we know not to try to manipulate forces we do not comprehend."

"We need our lights," the bio responded. "They keep us safe, and they illuminate our shrine."

Lemka's frown deepened. "Show me this shrine."

He was taken to a simple structure containing what looked like a pile of trash. "You worship this?"

"We honor her," the bio said. "Maria was a great woman."

"A woman made of metal?"

"She was a person on the inside. That's what my parents told me."

Lemka believed in the absent god, as had his parents and generations before them. However, he considered the term "absent" to be a poor one. To him and some other town residents, Ahm was merely invisible. At times they thought that they could feel her presence as they did what they considered to be her bidding. However, in the bio settlement, she was indeed absent, but only because the bios had replaced her with a false god. Lemka was filled with disgust.

"You will need to find a new healer for your settlement," he told the bio. "I cannot help you any longer."

After returning to the town, the young man's mind and heart continued to be troubled by his experiences with the bios' machines and their worship of the wreckage of a robot. Lemka talked with friends and neighbors. Stef, one of the oldest, invited him in for tea.

"Are you familiar with the clerics of old?" he asked Lemka.

"Weren't they the religious leaders and healers of the natives?"

"Yes. All of them were wiped out in the Destruction. A few natives, and even some emergents, tried to carry on the clerics' religious role in the new town. They wished to honor Ahm and wanted other residents do so as well. They believed that it was wrong for the townsfolk to use *serpus* and machines. Most of the townsfolk said they believed in the absent god and hoped for her graces and even for her return, but they were focused on day-to-day concerns such as feeding their families."

"And the rise of Marcus made things worse," Lemka observed.

"Yes, much worse. He claimed to believe in Ahm, but he idolized machines. The people who wanted to steer the community back to a foundation based on the absent god were growing in numbers, but they lacked something. There was no ritual or structure that could give the townsfolk a daily reminder of the presence of Ahm. For more than a century, most people have considered her just a vague spirit, almost an abstract concept."

Lemka absorbed his friend's message. "What can we do to change that?"

Stef smiled. "Have you ever considered seeking a seat on the Council?"

§

Lemka was brought back to the present by a pitched argument between a modern and a traditionalist on the Council. He reasserted himself. "The curse of the machines continues to eat away at our society. Look at how much fighting and anger are loose among us. It's not just moderns versus traditionalists. It's neighbor against neighbor. Brother against sister. Husband against wife."

As the arguments intensified, Lorres and Rhonel struggled to maintain order. A few synapses made a critical connection in Rhonel's mind. Without thinking through the insight, he blurted it out.

"It's the plants!" he shouted. When bickering continued unabated, he repeated his thought even louder: "It's the plants!"

"What about the plants?" said Lemka.

"It has to be the plants, the *rosts*."

Lorres looked at Rhonel with concern as he continued: "The *rosts* are dying. That's the only thing that has changed. The only thing other than the volcanoes spewing their smoke and ash in the air. But the eruptions started quite some time ago. The *rosts* started dying in big numbers only recently—about the time all of us started fighting incessantly with each other over petty grievances."

"Nonsense," said Lemka. "What problems can dead plants cause? It's the curse of the machines the bios brought. Destroy the machines, and the curse will be lifted."

"Maybe the teachers can offer some insight," Lorres suggested. Her idea was shouted down by trads, who continued to argue with moderns and with neutral Council members. Voices became more pitched; people were called nasty names; the few citizens who had come to watch the meeting drifted out of the hall in hopes of retaining their sanity and avoiding injury in a melee.

Eventually, the Council shifted its attention to more mundane topics, such as how to clean the ash from the community, home repair priorities, and who was and was not doing their job properly. Finally, their voices and frustration spent, the Council members dragged themselves out of the hall and down to their worksites or their homes.

Lorres helped Rhonel rise from his cushion. "Tell me more about this idea of yours, about the *rosts* and all the anger we are experiencing."

Rhonel shook his head. "It was just a crazy idea. I should have kept my mouth shut."

CONTACT

"Who knows why this town was built on a hill and surrounded by a wall?"

Teaching history to teen-agers was usually an exercise in frustration for Janel. So much about the early days of the civilization was unknown or considered to be mere legend, and most of his students were bored by the subject. It didn't help them learn a job skill. It didn't seem relevant to their lives.

A young man named Kogan spoke up. "So we can see everything around us?"

"That's part of the reason. Being up high allows us to see any trouble that might come our way. Having a wall helps keep out such trouble. It's all about security."

"A hill and a wall can't keep out *kusgs* or ash," said a young woman named Telis.

"You are correct. A hill and a wall aren't perfect. Yet history tells us they are essential. Who can tell me why?"

"Because of machines that killed people? We've all heard the story. I just don't believe it ever happened," Telis stated.

"It was made up to keep us prisoners inside this stupid town," Kogan opined. "No one has ever seen any robots."

Janel smiled, adjusting a sleeve on his crimson robe. "I commend your skepticism."

"What does skepticism mean?" asked a boy named Danis.

"It means that you don't necessarily believe all the things that people tell you. You want to see evidence or proof. That's a healthy attribute. But here's another valuable attribute: imagination. We all need to be open to the possibility of the existence of things that we cannot see or hold in our hands." Janel paused to make sure that he knew where he was going with this line of discussion. "Has anyone seen air?"

"I see lots of ash floating," Tellis offered.

"But can you see the air itself? The air that carries the ash?"

No one responded.

"We can't see it," the teacher continued, "but we know it's there, or we would not be able to breathe. There are other things we cannot see that are important. Can anyone name one?"

"The absent god," said a girl named Celva.

"Very good. However, please keep in mind that not everybody believes in the absent god, and those who do should not look down upon the few who do not. This is a personal choice. Anything else that is very important that we cannot see?"

Again, no response, but Janel could tell that his students were thinking.

"There's love. Your parents love you, and I hope that you love them. We can't see love, but it's definitely there. In addition, there is a will to live that is extremely strong in all of us. And there is a desire to see our families and our community grow and prosper and continue. We can't see that either, but we know it's there."

"What about the ancients?" asked Grall. "They didn't survive."

"There never were ancients," Kogan responded. "It's just a story somebody made up. Like robots, and Earth."

"I can't prove that the ancients existed," Janel stated, pacing among his students. "And I can't prove there were people who came here from Earth. But I don't need to prove such things to believe them. I trust in the people who told the history of Earth and robots and the Destruction, just as they trusted in the people who passed along that history to them. There had to be a reason for those people relating that information—things that they were certain were true."

"My parents say stories like that are just ways to pass the time, like tales made up for little children," said Tellis.

"They are entitled to that belief, as you are. My intent in talking about these things is not to try to prove to you what happened in the past. My intent is to prepare you for your responsibilities as citizens. We must learn from the past—even if it is an uncertain past—so that we can help shape the future. Whatever occupation you undertake—fisher

282   *Castle of Sand*

or personal care provider or food processor or whatever—you will always have one more job. That job will be to contribute something to the future of our town. That contribution might be raising your children to keep open minds. That contribution might be sitting on the Council or becoming a town leader. That contribution might be recording history so that future generations of young people don't have to wonder about what happened before."

"Why should I care what happens to people or the town after I'm dead?" said Kogan.

Janel stopped pacing and stared at the ceiling. He read the sendings emanating from the boy but could not tell whether they were being projected inadvertently or intentionally.

Janel is an idiot and wasting everyone's time.

The teacher responded as calmly as he could manage: "It's up to you to decide what's right for you." He could sense that his students were getting restless. "Let's take an early lunch break."

More than a dozen youngsters bolted from the hall. All except Grall. Janel took a seat on a cushion next to him.

"Something troubling you, Grall?"

"Are you really sure there were robots that killed people?"

"No, I can't be completely certain. No one has seen the robots or their master for a very long time."

"But you believe it?"

"Yes."

Grall struggled to get out his next question, looking around to see if anyone else was within earshot.

"Why is everybody so angry?"

Janel grimaced. "I wish I knew."

§

A fifteen-year-old classmate named Essen was waiting for Grall as he exited the hall. Quiet and shy, typically appearing supremely distracted, and so thin that it seemed that he could be blown over by a modest breeze, Essen looked up to Grall like he was a big brother. Essen had no brothers but three sisters, all older than him, and he found little in common with them. Grall was someone Essen could talk to or just be around, someone who didn't judge him or expect anything of him other than companionship.

Grall had his head down and almost passed the younger boy without noticing him.

"Is something wrong?" Essen asked.

"I think the teachers are not telling us everything."

"What could they be hiding?"

"I don't know. There are things they don't talk about. Like: Why are machines bad? Was Earth real, and was it the cause of all our problems? And why can't we live on the flatlands instead of this hill?"

"Maybe the teachers think we're too young to know some things."

Grall kicked some loose rocks in frustration and contemplation. "They tell us we're the leaders of the future, but there's so much we need to know. Maybe there are things they don't know and don't want to admit they don't know. Or things that they won't say because it might hurt someone's feelings."

"My parents are like that sometimes."

"Are they trads?"

"They never said so," said Essen, looking away to hide his embarrassment. "But they must be. I hear them in the next room sometimes, saying things about the moderns and the teachers."

"I guess they don't like my parents. They're definitely moderns. I hear them talking about places on the savannah where houses could be built. Places with—I'm not sure what this means—*lectricity*. Ever hear of it?"

"No."

"They said we wouldn't have to climb steep streets all the time or hide behind a wall."

"I like being protected by a wall."

"We don't have anything to—" Grall felt it coming on. Right here. Right now. He lowered himself stiffly to a seated position on the edge of the street.

"Grall, are you okay?"

Grall nodded slightly. It took only a few moments for Essen to guess what was going on. Grall was having a visitor, a strange sensation of mental connection with another being who was very different. Essen didn't know that the natives called them mind invaders instead of visitors, but he had them occasionally as well. One in particular entered Essen's mind frequently. Essen didn't like to talk about visitors, especially with his family. His sisters made fun of him, and his parents became livid when he mentioned them. He was threatened with severe punishment if he spoke of visitors again. They were a sign of weakness, and perhaps evil.

Essen sat close to his friend, listening to his breathing.

It was the usual visitor. For that, Grall was somewhat grateful. Since he first starting feeling his *tur* at age eleven, he had sensed several visitors, but this was the one whose connection seemed most clear and who contacted him most frequently. It unleashed rich colors, unusual shapes, and fanciful concepts that raced across his mind but didn't sink in fully. Grall was getting used to the disorientation caused by a visit, though he wished that he had more warning before one began. There were times when it was inconvenient, such as during the night or a meal, or even embarrassing, such as during a class. The visitor might not have a gender, but it helped to think of it as a he. He was tall and apparently very thin. It was hard to tell for sure with all those flowing robes—layer after layer of material so ethereal that it seemed to swim in pale light dominated by soft pinks and purples. His lower body featured an undetermined number of legs under all that clothing. The visitor's face was opaque and seemed to change subtly but constantly, like the bed of a stream distorted by ripples on the water's surface. The visitor's head was much taller than it was wide, providing yet more contrast with Grall's people and more mystery about his nature and location.

The visitor raised one of three arms, ashen gray and so thin that it appeared skeletal. Above him appeared a brilliant light, which soon was circled by several tiny, dark spheres. The spheres expanded in size steadily. One became extremely large, and Grall could almost make out some of the features of it. Before long it became all Grall could see. Suddenly, brightness flooded Grall's senses. Then details resolved, becoming so sharp and realistic that Grall could almost feel the wind brushing against the clothing of the visitor as he rode an unseen vehicle above a meadow filled with flowers that released sparks and scents into the air as he passed them. The visitor navigated around tall buildings that pierced clouds, while other riders traveled on small, flat, translucent vehicles nearby. Some of the riders looked just like the visitor; others had different appearances and clothing. The visitor rose as if propelled by a strong breeze, gaining enough height for Grall to glimpse what appeared to be several towns interspersed with green and yellow forests and plains plus deep blue, perfectly circular patches that must be water.

The vision became almost too vivid as the visitor continued to travel, and suddenly Grall had a sickening sensation of falling. He tried closing his eyes, but that failed to dispel the discomfort. Grall sought to think of something else, anything else. Nava popped into his mind. Why not Nava? He focused on a memory of his sister's pet *serpu* being stroked by Oliva. The image became superimposed over the experience of the visitor, then gradually replaced it. Grall sensed that the visitor had withdrawn.

Grall took a few moments to make sure that the visit was over, feeling more reconnected with the here and now with each deep breath. He remembered that Essen was beside him. He wondered how he would explain his apparent incapacitation to his friend.

Before Grall could speak, Essen whispered: "I see them, too."

Without further discussion, they made their way down the hill. Grall waved weakly at Essen when the younger boy turned off on the street to his house. Once inside his own home, Grall went to the cramped bedroom he shared with his sister and pulled a tattered notebook out from under his bed. It consisted of two dozen sheets of crude paper with a rough cover and loose binding, a gift from his parents for his twelfth birthday. He turned to a page where he had recorded a series of numbers and dates. He wrote the number four and "Midday Sixthday" on the page and placed the notebook back under his bed. After a moment, he retrieved it and added a notation:

"Next contact in nine and two-thirds days?"

§

"I would like to talk about the creation of this town."

"Of course, honored sir."

"Only thirty years after the Destruction, there was a feeling in the ruins that the killing machines, the robots, had all disappeared, and that their master, Damian, also was no longer a threat. I did not share that belief, and I still do not. Surely you have heard the colloquial expression 'the serpu does not shit in the same place twice'. People believed that Ahm, or fate, or chance would prevent a repeat of that horrendous assault. Life among the ruins had gotten to the point where few people who were willing to hunt or contribute to the common good in other ways were going hungry. Homes were being built more sturdily than in the past. More children were being born, including quite a few of mixed bio and native blood. Life was a little less harsh than it had been. Yet I and some of the other adults believed that our existence was very fragile. Not long after I became the leader of the community, I gathered several forward-thinking people to discuss our security and our future. One of the men in this group related a story about a castle, a building of immense dimensions and beauty that sat atop a hill and inspired and beckoned all people. Apparently, knowledge of this castle had been handed down from the very first bios and reflected the way that people lived on Earth. As much as our group was impressed with the idea, most of us believed that it was too ambitious for us. Instead, we came to the conclusion that a simple, functional town had to be built on a hill and surrounded by a high wall. We presented our idea to the rest of the people. Some of them said it was impossible; some said they didn't want to do that much work; a few asked us good questions. We were determined to make this dream take root. We had narrowed our site choices to a few hills. One southwest of the ruins seemed particularly attractive. It had several good stands of trees that would be essential to construction. But we would need to move a substantial amount of rocks and bring a great deal of fertile soil from the flatlands. My idea of domesticating serpus for this purpose set off a storm of opposition, as you well know. Interacting with the beasts was forbidden among the natives, and the prospect bothered some emergents. We didn't even know if domesticating serpus was possible. But I felt that it was worth trying."

Marcus savored a sip of juice.

"Three herds resisted our efforts strenuously. Six people were injured, and two died. Day and night, their families shamed me for my arrogance. I sensed that something was different about the fourth herd. To this day I have no idea what set them apart. These serpus resisted, to a point. But we were gentle with them and fed them and even tried talking to them before we attempted to slip on the harnesses. We had improved the harnesses to make them more comfortable to the beasts. The serpus recognized that; I'm sure of it. After that success, we designed the town to accommodate as many as three hundred people. That was one of the features that drew the most derision from those living in the ruins. I'm sorry; I suppose I should call it a settlement. It's just that, to me, the wreckage that the old bios said had been a flying ship, plus the remains of the buildings that Damian's robots had destroyed, could not be ignored, despite the erection of new homes nearby. The debris was a constant reminder of our past struggles. Anyway, the idea of a town with hundreds of people was beyond imagination for many. But I remembered my mother telling me stories that my father told her of far larger numbers of people in settlements, called towns and cities, on Earth. And, I thought: Why not be prepared in case our town did indeed prosper.

"It was while we were building the wagons to be hauled by the serpus that I first encountered the claim that the wagons were machines and therefore evil. Evil! Wooden carts with wheels, all pulled by people, had been used for years, but I don't recall any objections to them. What are machines but extensions of ourselves? It seems to me that there could be many kinds of machines for many different purposes. My mother told me that the machine known as Damian came from Earth and was once flesh and blood. It is difficult to imagine how a living person can become a machine, but she swore that this is what the bios told her. Damian and the robots that he unleashed in the Destruction should never have existed, but the fact that they did does not, to my mind, make all machines inherently bad. What harm can a wagon inflict? I'm sorry—I'm not offending you over your beliefs, am I?"

"No, honored sir. But even if I felt that all machines are evil, it is my duty to record your words for posterity, no matter what those words are."

"Very noble, kind scribe. So we kept improving the wagons and the harnesses for the serpus, and we did our best to ensure that the serpus were not overworked or otherwise mistreated. Over many twelve-days, we moved mountains of rocks and soil. When the town's wall was completed, we started work on the great hall. Only once its walls and roof were in place did we commence erecting houses. We did not want people moving to the town until it was ready to accommodate them and most of their needs. I thought that the belief among some people that all mechanical devices were abominations would dissipate as the town took shape. I was so very wrong. I was not surprised by continued disparagement from the natives. I did not foresee the strong and still growing movement among many of them and some emergents to condemn everyone who would use even simple machines. Religious fervor has fueled this phenomenon, as you well know. The leaders of the movement have even threatened my life and the lives of my family."

Marcus paused, gathering his thoughts.

"For several years after the town was established, I feared that it would fail. The first people to move here from the ruins were enthusiastic and worked almost without rest from dawn to dusk every day. But the crops we planted took time to mature, and the few boars and other game we caught had to be kept alive at first for reproduction. We were constantly ranging beyond the wall to hunt for and gather food and other resources and bring them back up the hill. So much energy was being expended for only modest results. In addition, the houses did not yet have their own cisterns, so residents had to rely on the rainwater collected at the hall, and the sewage system was still in the experimental stage. It was clear that we needed more people to make the town work. I visited the people still hanging on in the lowlands, extolling the virtues and potential of the town. I thought that it would be easy to persuade them to leave the haunting dregs of the Destruction. By that time, the natives who had gone to the settlement in the wake of the Destruction had either moved to the town or returned to the hills. I persuaded most of the emergents to join us. However, the purebred bios were stubborn. Most would not leave their shrine to the robot named Maria. I never understood how they could worship such a thing. A machine that had once been a person, like Damian, or so they believed. A machine that they said came from Earth and helped raise the first bios. My mother did not speak of Maria often. Perhaps they never met. But the bios felt a strong connection to Maria. I am told that they still do."

Marcus grew silent.

"Honored sir, your efforts did indeed bear fruit, despite the fact that some of the bios remain in the lowlands and some natives are scattered across the hills. Your grand plan has been realized."

"Thank you, kind scribe. I am proud to say that we have reached an important threshold. We have enough adults to focus on food production plus functions such as metalwork and healing so that each resident does not have to worry about finding enough food to eat every day. We have teachers for the young and others to help care for the aged. We continue to suffer from too many accidents and diseases and what the healer calls 'carriages', the loss of unborn children to some invisible malady of the mother, but I am told that they are less common among the emergents than among the bios and natives. I still believe that one day we will fill this town. Perhaps there will be enough of us to populate even more towns. Anything is possible if people want it to happen. Well, almost anything. I don't expect to sprout wings and fly, any more than I expect the sight to return to my eyes. However—and please make sure you write this down, kind scribe—for it is the most important thing I want to have recorded, the most important thing. We live and die on this hill for a reason. We sweat and bleed and love and dream so that our children and their children and uncounted others can be born and live and prosper and maintain a civilization. One that can endure. Civilization is the most essential and the most vulnerable of institutions. We must not take our existence for granted."

INTERVENTION

Kusg crawled on his rock-hard belly, inching his way among the decrepit bio buildings even more stealthily than the dreaded flying snake whose name he had adopted. He wished that he had worn leggings instead of the wraparound garb that left his knees and legs exposed to the rough ground as well as countless insects; he remembered belatedly that his last pair of leggings had disintegrated from age and excessive use and that few natives left in the area were skilled at making clothes. But that was a minor concern. After all, Ahm was guiding and protecting him on this sacred mission. Kusg focused on the bios' thoughts. They were so clear, so easy to pick out. He could tell almost exactly where they were, where they might be headed, and how well they were paying attention to their surroundings—if at all. By this hour, many bios were exhausted from their day's wasted labors and were settling down to sleep. Surely, few would venture out now, and if they did, a native as skilled as he could conceal himself from them with the slightest effort.

He was less than twenty feet from the blasphemous building that housed the shrine to their false god. Like most of the bio structures, it had been assembled chiefly of wood and other plants, with some rocks as a foundation. They appeared similar to some of the native shelters on the hillside, but they were not built as sturdily, and many seemed on the verge of collapse. A glimpse of electric light leaking from the doorway made his stomach queasy and sent his mind into torment. *The bios must suffer for their sins. Not only do they worship the remnants of the machine they call Maria, they use other machines to illuminate her shrine day and night. I will scatter this Maria across the jungles and lowlands, to leave Ahm as the one and only god.*

His world erupted in brilliant shades of orange and yellow, the light so fierce that it blinded him for several moments. He felt the heat before he could see the flames, surrounding him, approaching him. How long before it burned his skin and consumed his body? *Is this a demonic vision? Is it the work of the bios or their false god? Could it be Ahm seeking to wipe the bio enclave from her world in an act of purification?* Flames continued to spread around the periphery of his sight, but somehow they were sparing him as well as the building, at least for the moment. He struggled to his feet and stumbled over the final distance to the bio shrine, nearly falling as he reached for the door and opened it.

Two bios who were seated before a collection of metal and plastic scraps turned in alarm and stared at Kusg. The native had not expected to find anyone in the structure, which was barely twelve feet deep, twelve feet wide, and eight feet tall. The tiny lights on either side of the altar burned his eyes and seared his soul, but he was transfixed, unable to react.

"How dare you desecrate this shrine?" demanded a gray-haired woman, who stood and placed her hands on her hips as if she were confronting a misbehaving toddler. The balding man beside her looked around for anything that he could use as a weapon. Finding nothing, he approached the native with a steely glower and pointed to the door. "Go. Go now, and never return. Do you understand?"

Kusg did not understand. He closed his eyes and tried to focus on his mission, but it was concealed in confusion. The bios' thoughts flowed through him and nearly overwhelmed him. *Surprise. Fear. Anger. Images of weapons and hiding places.* He focused his will in order to banish their chaotic sendings, attempting to borrow strength from the spirit of Ahm. Then he opened his eyes—or, at least, he thought that he opened his eyes. The flames had vanished, and he was bathed in a thick, creamy, white light that undulated and passed around and through him, soothing him and energizing him at the same time. He was getting closer to the absent god, he was certain of it. He smiled and raised his six-fingered hands in the air. Screaming a blessing to Ahm, he fell to the ground in ecstasy.

Several bios arrived in response to the disturbance. "See here," said Alren, who was the leader of the bios, largely because no one else wanted the responsibility. "You must leave. Now!"

When Kusg failed to respond, several bios grabbed him and yanked him to his feet. For a moment, Kusg did not recognize where he was. Then his eyes widened, he shouted a curse, and he began to swing his arms wildly at the settlers, who fought back with their fists. Kusg pulled a knife from its sheath and plunged it into the chest of a short bio man. The victim stared at the knife, then at Kusg—in shock, disbelief, and finally absolute clarity—before collapsing. Kusg dashed out of the shrine, several bios in pursuit. After he passed the last weak security light, he was welcomed by his dearest friend, the anonymity of the night.

§

It was too dark to try to make it back to his cave, which was barely large enough to shelter him from strong rains and was located just below the ruins of the old Gaip village. So Kusg slept along a trail on a steep portion of a hill not far from the bio settlement. Like so many natives who lived in the area, he was unsure of his lineage and his tribal heritage. The tribes were simply names, or words, without meaning for most of his kind. Like Kusg, they embraced the wilderness and rejected the civilization of the bios and the mongrels.

Waking before daybreak, Kusg was anxious to return to his cave. He had much to tell the other natives who lived nearby and, like him, roamed the hills in search of enough food and water to survive each day. In the predawn darkness, fantastic shapes appeared to him. Some had the heads of animals, such as boars and *serpus* and the lizards that scurried underfoot. Some carried the faces of natives he had known, people who were dead. And some were strangers—natives, bios, mongrels, and something altogether different that he felt he should know but could not identify. They spoke to him, all at once, with a chorus of conflict that set his teeth on edge and caused him to clench his arms and stomach muscles. They came at him, hurling inanimate objects, then flinging small animals, which struck him and covered him with blood. He stood and roared defiance, but the attacks only intensified. The sky gathered its colors and power and poured blazing rain on him, scalding his skin and burning huge holes in the ground. He sank into one of the holes, falling, falling, unable to halt his precipitous dive—

Another native was shaking him. Kusg ceased his thrashing and recognized the young girl, who stepped back to avoid being struck. Kusg perceived the burgeoning light and ample dew of morning and knew that his fever dream had vanished. He thanked the girl and headed back over the hills to his cave, eyes locked on the paths, ever mindful of the possibility that the madness could take him again at any moment. Such was life in recent twelve-days. He had watched natives attack each other without apparent provocation, had heard them wailing in solitary agony in the woods, had been told of some who propelled themselves from high cliffs or drowned themselves in rivers to stop the insanity.

How did it begin? Kusg struggled to think clearly. He recalled that he had been keeping a substantial distance from other natives. *I remember. Our* tur *has been much stronger, too strong, for several twelve-days. We are sending and receiving too much from our kind, and even from the few bios and mongrels we encounter. Every thought, every fear, every bit of disrespect—real or imagined—is magnified until it drives us to the brink of insanity. We fight and occasionally kill one another. Over what? Perceived insults. Perhaps fighting is all that we know to do.*

Kusg was determined to remind his people about the excessive *tur* and the need to spread out and remain calm. But as he sought to come up with a plan for accomplishing this task, he felt his mind assailed once again by images and threats. He fell to the ground, his fingers clawing the shallow earth, desperate to hold on to his sanity.

§

Outside Maria's rickety shrine, Alren struggled to get the bio community to come to order. At the modest age of forty-two, Alren was already showing the effects of age and poor diet. His right leg was stiff from years of hard labor and a poorly set broken bone. His teeth were bad and his stomach was growing at a fearsome rate. But he had a kind face and a caring heart, which his fellow bios had no doubt considered when they begged him to speak for—and when necessary lead—their struggling settlement.

"Please, my fellows, let us speak one at a time so that all may be heard."

The angry voices subsided and more structured debate began, punctuated by nervous grumbling and a brisk breeze whistling through loose fibers on thatched roofs. No one disputed the contention that the natives were displaying such violence and insanity that bios' lives were at risk. Two bios said they might move to the town. Another suggested building a new fence or wall around their homes. But a majority had made up their minds and soon persuaded the others: The natives had to be stopped by force.

Metal scraps that had once been pieces of the ark were collected. After three days, six knives and four spears had been fabricated, supplementing comparable numbers of knives and spears already used for hunting. Fifteen bios agreed to participate in the assault. Alren decided that they were as ready as they ever would be.

"We mount the attack tomorrow. I beg you not to kill unarmed children if you encounter any. However, if we are going to do this, we must do it right. Only by killing or scaring away all of the adult natives can we be certain that we can live in peace."

Alren spoke to bios individually and in small groups over the next several hours. He looked into their eyes, and occasionally attempted to probe their minds, recognizing their fear. It was gnawing at them, just as it was consuming him. He reassured them as best he could that the attack was necessary. After his evening meal, he visited Maria's shrine. One of the interior electric lights had gone out. He shook his head, wondering why his people even attempted to cling to technology that was giving way to the inexorable entropy of the world. He did not consider Maria someone worthy of worship. He took it on faith that there had been a Maria and that she had done as much good for the bios as she could manage before Damian gouged the heart and soul out of the community. Some of the oldest bios recounted stories of her. She could run faster than the wind. She could go for years without eating or drinking. She could forecast the future. She even predicted the Destruction, but nobody would listen to her.

These stories—they can't all be true. Maybe none of them is true.

Yet Alren experienced an unexpected measure of well-being gazing at Maria's remains. He felt a connection to something old, something basic. He understood the attraction. Maria had given people comfort by reminding them what they needed to do to stay alive on this world.

If only we could gain her wisdom once again. Alas, we had our chance, and we squandered it.

The noise. The inadvertent sendings. The bios might as well have walked into the remnants of the Gaip village the night before and announced that an attack was coming the next morning. The natives were in no way organized, and these days they were barely on speaking terms with one another. But they were on alert for the attack.

The natives' knowledge of the terrain and their superior ability to share thoughts put the bios at a huge disadvantage as they struggled to climb the final hill. The natives had only a small amount of metal for spear tips and knives, but they had sharp wooden pikes and ropes made of long, dried, braided vines that could be used in battle. They hid themselves well and were able to surprise the bio soldiers. Four bios were killed in the first minute, a few others were wounded, and one was caught and hog-tied with ropes. But two natives were killed, several others were hurt, and the natives realized that the bios were desperate and would not stop their attack because of a few casualties. It didn't help the natives that heightened *tur* sent them into spasms of madness without warning.

From a deeply veiled and rugged section of jungle east of the village that few natives traversed, a woman emerged. She strode boldly into the midst of the fighting. Standing ramrod straight and carrying no weapon, she appeared to be a bio, blond, about forty years old. Her face was intense but revealed no fear.

"Stop!" she cried, raising her arms in supplication. "You must stop this fighting now!" She repeated her message in the natives' language, though with a couple of mispronounced words.

"Who are you?" shouted Alren from about thirty feet away.

"I am someone who cannot stand by idly while blood is shed for no reason."

Several of the natives spoke in low voices or sent to fellow fighters. *Who is this?* Some responded that they had seen her roaming the hills. She had never come in direct contact with them, to anyone's recollection. They had assumed that she was just a crazy or lost bio who would soon meet her death.

One of the natives used the distraction of the stranger's arrival to stab a bio in the side. The bio's scream broke the hiatus, and fighting resumed all around. The stranger moved rapidly toward the nearest combatants. She shoved the arm of a bio as he attempted to impale a native with his spear, forcing the bio to miss his target. Then she positioned herself between the bio and the native as the native tried to stab her foe. The knife struck the stranger in the chest, the blade shattering.

"Evil machine!" cried the native as she beat a hasty retreat.

Two other natives approached the stranger, weapons brandished, unsure what, if anything, to do. One began shaking violently, then his eyes rolled up in his head and he collapsed, dead before he hit the ground. The other screamed a curse and threw himself at the stranger, stabbing her, breaking his blade, and continuing to try to inflict damage with the hilt. The stranger held the native at arm's length but made no effort to hurt him. Eventually, the native crawled away, eyes wide.

The natives fell back to positions behind trees and among thick vines. Alren and two other bios approached the stranger. One came close, as if to touch her, before thinking that it might not be such a good idea.

"Are you one of the robots of legend?" Alren inquired. "Are you here to destroy us?"

"I am no robot. And I do not wish to destroy anything."

Alren's mind was churning. The robots that had perpetuated the Destruction existed only to kill, it was said. Alren touched her hard surface tentatively, confirming that she lacked flesh but eliciting no reaction from her. "You are made of metal. How can you be anything but a robot?"

"I am a living being." The stranger hesitated, her expression unreadable. "I will say no more about me. Let me speak of all of you. Terrible times are upon you. I do not know what is happening, but this much cannot be denied: Life is endangered by forces beyond our control. Do not spill blood for any reason."

She repeated the message in the natives' tongue.

The natives dispersed deeper into the jungle, wary of the stranger and the bios and spread out so as to make another attack unlikely to succeed. Bewildered and saddened bios began recovering bodies and returning to their homes. Alren tried to make sense of the scene, then addressed the stranger. "Will you help us?"

"I have done all that I can." With that, she returned to the dark folds of the forest.

Alren put his head down and trudged back to the bio settlement.

§

Ahm had suspended all but her most routine functions so that she could devote her full attention to the conflict.

How fascinating! This metal woman stops a battle between two groups of organic beings. Why would she do this? I must monitor her closely.

§

The metal-clad stranger approached the bio settlement with a steady gait shortly after dawn. Early-rising bios watched apprehensively as she investigated fields of debris beyond their homes and then moved among them. She made no eye contact with settlers and did not speak. Approaching a building that did not appear to be a home, she noticed a pale light emanating from it. Opening the door, she was alone with the remains of the bot Maria. The stranger was motionless for a long time. She picked up what appeared to be a piece of a jaw. She tried to feel her own jaw, remembering only belatedly that she had no feeling in her hands or her face.

She exited the building slowly, then departed the settlement without looking back. For three days the stranger circled the former Gaip village and the bio settlement at a substantial distance. Then she headed south, staying in the flatlands where tall grasses provided cover and navigating hillsides when necessary to avoid being seen. On several occasions she passed herds of *serpus*. Periodically, one of the beasts paid attention to her for half a minute. Often, her movement was of no interest to them. On the third day, a small herd ceased grazing and turned in unison to look at her. She stopped about one hundred feet from them, and the herd advanced toward her. She stood still, curious and delighted, as the *serpus* surrounded her, one animal closing to arm's length.

The stranger reached out to that *serpu* and placed her artificial fingers on the long, mottled surface between its eyes and nose, caressing it ever so lightly. The *serpu* held still for several seconds. Then it retreated, and another moved into the spot it had occupied. The stranger touched its head as well. One after another, the *serpus* presented themselves to her for this benediction. She wished that it would never end, but finally the last of the beasts had been anointed. They turned, wandered about fifty feet, and began to graze once again, so she resumed her journey. Toward evening, she saw a plume of smoke on the horizon. The next morning, a town appeared on a hill. From a pitch-black stand of trees just outside the town's wall, she watched people move in and out of the north gate. A day passed. Then two more. Finally, she decided to chance an effort to enter the town. She considered falling in behind a line of people with wagons being hauled by *serpus*, but she realized that it would be extremely risky. Instead, she waited until after dark. She circled the wall, finding no opening other than the north and south gates, which were manned by dozing guards. She decided to climb over the wall on the western side, where she believed that she would not be noticed. The task was not difficult, though she made more noise than she had hoped upon landing. She hid in an orchard, and after daybreak she watched as people emerged from homes and moved about, many of them heading up the streets to the top of the hill. She waited until no one was nearby, then slipped into a yard behind a house where clothes were drying on a line. She removed a shawl from the line and whispered: "Lord, please forgive me."

She had gone only a few steps before a woman emerged from the house yelling: "Thief! Thief!"

The stranger wrapped the shawl tightly about her head and raced away from the house, searching for someplace to hide. Other houses seemed like poor choices; there would likely be people in most of them. She noticed a building with plain walls and few windows and raced inside it, shutting the door and finding herself alone. The structure was filled with bright fabrics, tools, and finished clothing. She borrowed a large cloak and hid in the back. Though she heard people shouting outside, no one entered.

After about an hour, she decided to try to get away from the town. Opening the door slowly, she saw a young girl walking up the street.

"Who are you?" asked the child. "I have not seen you before."

The stranger decided that it was better to engage the girl than to

run. "I have been away for a long time. You would not have met me."
She decided to try to exercise long-dormant social skills: "What's your
name?"

"Oliva. I'm eleven."

"Nice to meet you, Oliva. I am a lot older. You may call me Claire."

"Are you going to see the teachers?"

"Not right now. I think I should go home."

"Do you live in the bio settlement?"

"No. They don't want me there."

"That's too bad. My mother says it's not a very nice place, anyway.
Well, I have to go to my class." Oliva proceeded up the hill.

The stranger turned and headed toward the north gate. She put her
head down to avoid eye contact and maintain a low profile.

"There she is! That's the woman who stole my shawl!"

The stranger was fast and could pivot quickly. After racing between
houses and reaching a different street, she encountered a cluster of men
who had heard the shouting and began to chase her. She was almost to
the gate when one of the men leapt and tackled the her, the stolen cloak
and shawl falling away. Abruptly, the man recoiled.

"By the absent god, this is a machine, a robot made of metal!"

Others poked her, realizing that what appeared to be skin and
clothes were merely metal and plastic. They too stepped back in alarm.

"Are you a demon?" one man asked the stranger.

"I am but a humble traveler," she responded.

Two men gathered their courage, placed hands firmly on her
arms, and led her up the hill to the hall. Occasionally, the men peeked
at her, trying to determine if what they were seeing was real and if the
stranger would try some mischief. They were able to bring her into the
hall without incident, trailed by a contingent of concerned townsfolk. A
woman who had been walking with them summoned Lorres and Rhonel.

The town leaders touched the stranger in several places, then
thanked all who had escorted her to the hall. With townsfolk scrutinizing
their every step, they led the stranger to Lorres's corner alcove. They
invited her to sit, but she said she preferred to stand.

A crowd formed outside the hall, then entered. The woman whose
shawl had been stolen pointed to the stranger and shouted: "There it is.
Kill it!"

BOOK

The owner of the pilfered shawl approached the stranger, followed closely by more than a dozen townsfolk. "What are you?" the offended resident demanded.

"I apologize for taking your shawl. It was wrong of me."

"You didn't answer my question."

"I am not what I appear. I am a person like all of you."

"Ha! This demon thinks it can seduce us with slick words."

The stranger showed no reaction. Lorres stepped in front of her.

"It has done wrong, that much is clear," she stated, recognizing the fear and anger mounting among the townsfolk without having to probe minds. "However, it appears to be intelligent. It has no weapons and has given no indication that it intends to harm anyone. We must take some time to consider what to do with it."

Lemka pushed to the front of the crowd. The trad Council facilitator studied the metal figure with a severe scowl, then addressed it: "Were you created by Damian?"

"No. He carries a sickness, a desire to destroy. I wish only to protect good people such as yourselves."

"This deception is just what we would expect from a machine." Several in the crowd muttered agreement. "Lorres, would you be so kind as to hand this thing over to me so that I may see to its immediate destruction?"

"No, I will not. I do not believe that we should act hastily. Perhaps the teachers can learn from it."

Angry shouts and sendings filled the hall, which now included nearly one-third of the town.

Rhonel came to his wife's aid. "She is right. We must study this thing. After we have learned its nature and purpose, we can dispose of it."

Lorres gave Rhonel a piercing look, but he placed a reassuring arm on her shoulder.

"Please go back to your homes or your work," Rhonel pleaded. "I promise that we will take every precaution to ensure that this thing causes no more trouble."

Lemka stared at Lorres, Rhonel, and the stranger for most of a minute, without comment, before turning and departing. The crowd, still restless, thinned out, but several citizens remained, whispering and casting glances toward the stranger at intervals.

"You want to destroy her?" Lorres demanded of her husband.

"I am not sure. But we needed to get the crowd to disperse, and that seemed the only way to do so."

"He is right," said the stranger. "Do not jeopardize your safety or status on my behalf."

"I think it's time that you tell us who, or what, you are," said Lorres.

Chagrin poured from the stranger's face. "I was once flesh and blood, like you," she began, casting glances at the leaders and pausing, as if searching for a way to prove that assertion to herself. "That was a long time ago. My mind has been trapped in an artificial body for so long that some of my years are nearly lost to me. In addition, I carry the memories of more than one person, and I bear the hopes of many."

"That's rather vague. Let's try this another way: Why are you here?"

"I fear that your civilization stands on a precipice. You must discover what is causing so many of your kind to lose cogent thought and engage in destructive behavior against one another."

"What do you know of this phenomenon?" said Rhonel.

"Very little, unfortunately. I was hoping to learn more by coming to your town. I regret that I have become a distraction to you. I would leave if it would not hamper your ability to govern."

"You probably could not escape," said Lorres. "There will be some sort of reckoning. But we have many questions for you."

The trio were joined by Jesper, the oldest teacher. With a scar on his right cheek and a nose that had been broken as a youth, he was not the most handsome man in town. Yet Jesper acted with grand flourishes whenever possible. He wore a flowing, dark red robe, as did most of the other teachers when they were in public, but to him, it was a cherished symbol of advanced education and status. He tried not to be too obvious in flaunting the fact that he was the most senior teacher, in part because there was no official order of hierarchy among them. The teachers were all considered equals, and decisions were historically made by consensus. Yet he was undeniably intelligent, and it was Jesper to whom the other teachers, and many townsfolk, looked to for guidance in matters of history and custom.

After taking a moment to size up the stranger, Jesper addressed Lorres and Rhonel: "There is something you must see."

§

"I wish to conclude my commentaries with some speculation that goes beyond that which I have witnessed and that which my mother and others who survived the Destruction are certain is true. First: Was there a race of people commonly referred to as 'the ancients'? I am quite certain that there was. I will tell you why. But first I ask a pledge of you, dear scribe. Can you keep these final words as a secret, telling no one, not even your family, even upon your deathbed?"

"I promise never to reveal anything you tell me, honored sir."

"Good. Very good. The ancients existed, you see, because we have found remnants of their buildings."

Marcus paused, finding his cup and raising it to his face. He sniffed the juice twice, then placed it back on the floor without consuming another drop.

"It is true. The teachers who explore our world have found several underground structures that were not erased by eons of weather or other forces. I believe that some of the natives know about them, or knew about them before their numbers were diminished so severely in the Destruction. Their scouting was too thorough for them not to have stumbled upon these facilities from time to time. These ruins contain documents preserved in cases and written in a language that we have been unable to translate. More importantly, the structures are filled with remnants of massive machines, the purposes of which our teachers cannot even guess. Surely these machines were intimidating and frightening to each native who found them over the years. That fear might have given birth to their religious prohibition against employing anything mechanical. When the bios appeared with their machines, that prohibition could only have become more compelling. And, of course, the onslaught of Damian's robots sealed the aversion to machines for the natives. It is no surprise that the fear of machines lasts to this day, even among some emergents. To me, this feeling is divorced from logic and the realities of modern life. Of course, those who find even simple wagons to be dangerous machines will not question that belief. It lives in the back of the mind, immune to common sense, like the memory of being scared by a jungle cat as a young child that prevents a grown man from hunting for food in the area where that incident occurred. The disdain for machines might last for generations."

Marcus shook his head unsteadily.

"Another curious religious tenet of the natives with its origins in antiquity is their avoidance of *serpus*, but I do not judge them harshly for it. It is a relatively harmless belief, though one that unduly restricts the places where the natives might live. I, like most people in the town, have native blood racing through my veins and native culture embedded in my life. I could understand why some of them were considerably upset when I started domesticating *serpus* and why so many remain unhappy with me. As for the native prohibition against eating *rosts*, I see no need to run afoul of that dogma. There are many other sources of nutrition."

Marcus stopped speaking and became very still. His face was white, but he betrayed no other sign of distress.

"Are you well, honored sir?"

"No, but I must continue while I am able." Marcus sighed deeply. "Now, please listen carefully. When I conclude this conversation with you, I ask that you approach the teacher named Darel and present him with every single page that you and prior scribes have used to capture my ramblings over the years. He will hide these pages in one of the ancients' underground structures so that they cannot be damaged or destroyed by those who oppose the progress I envision. Darel is the last remaining teacher who knows that these ruins exist and where they are, and he has sworn not to reveal their existence to any other. Only by securing these writings in such a manner can I rest assured that future generations will have the opportunity to learn from them. I pray that they will be found someday by people who are more amenable to accepting the truth. Even my wife and son and daughters do not know of the ancients' ruins and my desire to sequester my writings. It is my way of protecting them."

"It will be done, honored sir. If I might be so bold as to add, it has been the most exceptional privilege of my life to have been chosen to capture your words."

Marcus did not try to hold back his tears.

"Dear scribe, might I know your name? I am certain that I knew it at one time, but my mind retains less with every passing day."

"Jonn, honored sir."

"Jonn, it is my theory that the natives are the descendants of the ancients, though I have no evidence. I suspect that, for some reason, the ancients' civilization declined to the point that they became the people that the bios encountered. Our explorers have discovered little land that would support people anywhere else on our world; our region is surrounded by volcanoes and rugged terrain with little useful plant or animal life. So I suspect that the natives, who have lived in this region for uncounted generations, descended from the ancients. And I find it at least possible that the bios—who were never seen before recent times and at one time had no *tur*—came from another world. It strikes me as plausible that a metal ship brought the ancestors of the bios to our land, as legends have hinted at. Fragments of metal and a curiously flexible substance that the bios call plastic still litter the ruins near the bio settlement. I do not believe that these could have been crafted by the natives or the bios on this world."

A half smile played over Marcus's face.

"My dear mother occasionally used the term 'computer' to refer to a thinking machine, and she said my father interacted with a computer that was called Hubert. I have no reason to doubt that this is what she was told. My mother believed that Maria and Damian and the other bio ancestors were thinking machines as well, though some people thought that they were just bios covered in metal. The idea of a thinking machine affects me nearly as much as it affects other townsfolk. It is not that I feel that, if thinking machines existed, they would be inherently evil and dangerous. On the contrary, the possibility of a machine that can think stretches my sense of wonder to a place that it almost dare not go. Imagine what could be possible if we were able to create such machines and use them to our benefit."

A deep shudder passed through Marcus. His fingers began to

shake, as if animated by invisible strings. He struggled to lick his dry lips.

"Now, as for the existence of Ahm. I do not know if you believe in the absent god, and I do not want you to tell me whether you do or do not, Jonn. Please accept my apologies in advance if I offend you. I simply do not know if there is a god, absent or otherwise, on this world, or anywhere. I want to believe in such an entity. But I want to see or touch or hear or otherwise sense it, to be given some tangible evidence of its existence. I feel that believing in Ahm is useful regardless of whether she exists; people draw strength and comfort from that belief, as my mother did throughout her life and particularly in her final days. As a myth, Ahm would be a genuine asset to this world. But as a real entity—god or otherwise—she or it could be so much more beneficial. All I want, all I ask, in my final moments on this world is some sign, some indication, some hint, that Ahm exists. Is that too much to ask, dear scribe?"

Jonn said nothing. After several moments, he approached Marcus, the founder of the town and, perhaps, the father of a civilization. Marcus's breathing had stopped. He was at peace.

§

Rhonel stayed behind to watch over the stranger as Jesper steered Lorres to a section of the hall where he and Lall, a teacher who often went on exploratory treks, had been studying a large pile of papers for several twelve-days. Lall chose not to wear red robes, opting for plain clothes that stood up well to climbing rocky hills and moving through dense foliage. Short and muscular, she had the phrase "no nonsense" written across her face and ingrained in her spirit.

"Lall discovered these documents," commented Jesper as he motioned to papers on a table. "They are written in a form of language that is archaic. She and I have been working to transcribe them, and we have completed about three-fourths of them to date."

"Where were they found?"

Jesper couldn't help but smile. "On a table in an underground building that is filled with the ruins of massive machines that likely could not have been built by bios or natives and appear to be extremely old."

"Why did you not say anything about this?"

"I apologize for the secrecy. This discovery seemed so momentous that we wanted to be certain that we know exactly what we have before telling anyone." He cast his glance around the hall anxiously. "If knowledge of this were to reach the townsfolk prematurely, the documents and the ruins might not survive."

"So why are you telling me now?"

"Because these papers deal extensively with the topic of robots."

She nodded apprehensively.

"There's more." Jesper swallowed. "Apparently, the documents were written by Marcus."

Lorres opened her mouth, but no words emerged.

"Marcus has given us a rich history of the natives and the bios, including speculation about Earth. He describes machines that apparently contained the minds of the ancestors of the bios. He recounts the Destruction in detail, with much information about Damian and the killing robots he employed."

"Show me these papers."

Jesper began to spread out some of the originals, faded and tinged with brown on many edges. Some of the pages included drawings.

"Careful," he admonished Lorres as she scooped up one fragile page after another.

"Show me all the robots."

The teacher collected and displayed each sheet displaying what appeared to be drawings of robots. None looked like the visitor standing next to her husband. More illustrations came under Lorres's scrutiny: a gleaming metal structure, standing high on the savannah; a busy native village surrounded by dense foliage; a sprawling metal settlement populated by bios; individual bios.

"Stop. That one!" Lorres's pulse surged.

"I see what you mean," said Jesper in whispered acknowledgement.

It was the face of the stranger.

§

"Tell me your name." Lorres was right in the face of the stranger, probing for any sign that might betray deception or shed light on her true nature. Lorres could not read the stranger's mind, but that did not surprise her.

The stranger looked down slightly, then replied: "Claire."

"There was a woman named Claire, a flesh-and-blood bio who looked very much like you, at the time of the Destruction. I have seen the image in old documents."

Suddenly, a group of citizens surged in their direction, their gestures and voices revealing great anger and fear. Teachers moved to try to head off the mob. Rhonel sized up the situation and whispered: "We must leave now." He touched Claire's shoulder lightly, attempting to steer her toward the hall's back entrance. She resisted, but he pleaded with her: "Come with us."

The three made their way outside and into a small clearing. Beyond them were a few storage buildings and a path leading to the seldom-used south gate, on a steep slope covered by stunted trees, lethargic vines, and what seemed like half the boulders in the world, some nearly the size of houses. Townsfolk approached, shouting and waving fists.

"Can you find someplace to hide until we can sort things out?" Lorres asked Claire.

"If that is your wish." She examined a thick wooden post supporting the hall and gripped it with both arms. In a flash she had climbed it and mounted the pitched roof, gaining an excellent view of the immediate area. With most of the mob near the back of the hall, she was able to climb down a post at the front of the building unseen. From there she slipped between two other buildings and headed downhill, ducking out of sight when she heard voices or footsteps. She considered hiding in the building where she had found the cloak, but she could not remember where it was. A moment later she noticed the girl with the curly red hair, skipping along a side street.

"You're Oliva, aren't you?"

"Hi, Claire. I thought you were leaving."

"Something came up. I need somewhere to go, just for a little while."

"You can come home with me. I'm sure my parents wouldn't mind."

"That's very kind of you. Can you show me the way? I'm in a hurry."

"Race you!"

Oliva was a blur, dashing down dangerous pavement, but Claire was nearly as fast. The girl was breathing heavily as she reached her home and went to the kitchen to get some water. "Would you like some?" she asked Claire.

"No, but thank you." Claire perused the cozy house, which lacked a basement and had a second floor that was too hot for anything other than storage. The main floor was divided into two bedrooms, a living space, and a kitchen with a stone fireplace. Furnishings were sparse but appeared to be comfortable. The walls were adorned with children's drawings. Ample windows flooded the home with daylight and, on occasion, comforting breezes.

"This a nice place. There's something I should tell you, however. I am not exactly like you, and some people do not want me to be in your town. I am concerned that I will cause trouble for you and your family, so I must not stay long. As soon as it gets dark, I will leave."

"You seem nice. Why do you have to go?"

"Touch me."

Oliva gave her a funny look but approached and poked her arm.

"Wow. Is that armor?"

"In a way, yes. I was once flesh and blood just like you, but now I live inside a machine. I did not realize how much people dislike or fear machines, so I will stay far away."

"Aww, that's too bad. I think you would like my brother and my parents. They should be home soon."

Before Claire could respond, Lorres and Rhonel appeared at the door.

"You can't stay here," Lorres stated. "This is one of the first places they will search."

Oliva looked from her parents to Claire, and then back to her parents. "You know Claire?"

"We just met," said Rhonel. "Claire, you don't need to breathe, right?"

"Correct."

"What if we hide her in the crete shed, behind or under that big pile of sand."

Lorres nodded. "How do we get her there?"

"I have an idea." Rhonel went to a closet and began pulling out clothing items and carrying them to the kitchen. "Load her up with these. I'll draw a map for her. With all the confusion, she might be able to get there unnoticed."

"I have a better idea," exclaimed Oliva. "I can take her there."

"I forbid it," said Lorres.

"It might work," Rhonel told his wife. "You and I can draw the attention of the mob by going back to the hall and trying to engage them in conversation." He heard people talking loudly nearby. "But we had better hurry."

Lorres and Rhonel climbed the streets, watched closely by trad bystanders. No one paid much attention to the heavily garbed figure walking aside Oliva as they made their way along lightly traveled streets to the infrequently visited shed.

"Are you sure you'll be comfortable in here?" the girl asked once they were inside the building, which featured a wide door and contained mostly materials used in construction and repair.

"My metallic body has no nerve endings to feel discomfort. I can position myself in any manner indefinitely. This should be an adequate hiding place."

"If you say so. I'll see you later."

"I hope so. But if something happens to me and we do not meet again, please know how grateful I am to you and your parents for treating me so kindly. It has been a long time—a very long time—since I have interacted with kind people. I had almost given up on humanity. Sorry, that's an old word that probably has no meaning anymore. I had almost given up on people. Even if I do not survive the night, you have given me hope for the future."

"Don't be so sad. Next time I'll introduce you to Nava. She's my pet *serpu*. You'll like her."

Oliva spread sand over Claire, then peeked out the door of the shed, saw that no one was around, and exited. She skipped spritely, pausing only to admire a majestic sunset.

SPHERES

Lorres and Rhonel remained standing as Oliva and Grall as took seats at the kitchen table. Grall immediately picked up bizarre thoughts, but he waited for his mother to speak.

"There is someone new in town—"

Lemka and two other trads burst into the house. "Where is it?" he demanded.

"How dare you enter without being invited!" bellowed Rhonel. Oliva frowned. Grall was having no trouble reading the tension between his parents and the Council facilitator.

"How dare you hide this machine from us?" Lemka countered. Turning to the other trads, he demanded: "Search this house. Search every inch."

"Lemka, you set a poor example for my children and for the entire town. The stranger is not here. I have not seen her for some time," said Lorres. She and Rhonel did their best to strengthen their mental defenses so as not to reveal Claire's whereabouts. Lemka probed them but could not break through.

"It's not here," one of the other trads reported presently.

"It's just a matter of time before we find it, and we will kill it," Lemka remarked.

"That's not your decision to make. We're the leaders of this town."

"I have the votes to compel its execution. The Council will meet tomorrow morning to formalize that outcome." He effected an exaggerated sneer and added in a condescending voice: "Your presence will not be necessary."

He and his fellow trads left without another word.

Lorres put her head down, sighed deeply, and addressed her family.

"I'm beginning to understand why the natives say we have entered a dark time."

"It should be soon."

Grall would have preferred not to reveal his apprehension to his friends, but they were all highly skilled in using *tur*, so there was little point attempting to conceal his agitated state of mind. Over the past year, the four youngsters had gravitated readily toward one another. The two boys and two girls shared a remarkable resilience amid the twin storms of adolescence and the anger and confusion that were omnipresent in society.

"Describe this visitor to me again," said Bess, a seventeen-year-old apprentice baker. She was rather short and a little overweight, but she had a kind heart and came from a family that was held in high esteem. Bess had demonstrated unusual skill at drawing and coloring pictures, but that was not a recognized profession, so she could create her illustrations only during her spare time.

Grall did his best to depict the visitor, noting that he had not had a clear view of his face in the prior sessions. With each visit, however, Grall had been able to absorb more details of the visitor's surroundings and gain glimpses of wondrous mysteries. "I need you to help me make sense of this. I think it might be important."

"How so?" said Chalene, an eighteen-year-old who built furniture and was a distant cousin of Essen. She had shiny jet-black hair and unusually small ears for an emergent girl, but she was tall for her age, quite thin, and exceedingly graceful. Grall found her attractive, and he had trouble hiding that sentiment from her, so he didn't really try. He didn't know if she liked him, and he was determined not to probe her mind for that information. It would be rude, it could make her unhappy with him, and he was afraid of being disappointed. However, he was fairly certain that he would have sensed it if she considered him ugly or felt that his companionship was unwelcome.

He forced himself to focus on the task at hand, straightening his back from his position on a cushion. The four youths were the sole occupants of the hall at this hour, and their corner was illuminated only by a solitary candle. Grall's voice echoed faintly into infinity, amplifying the eerie atmosphere of the gathering. "Last time, the visitor showed me his world. It seemed to be round and circled a round sun like ours. They have advanced machines, almost magical ones, that let people ride through the air. At least, I think so. I don't think he was pretending."

"Amazing. And you think that we can somehow join this visit, or at least monitor it?" Essen asked.

"It's worth trying," Grall offered. "If it doesn't work, you can laugh at me. Just don't tell my parents, okay?"

"What makes you think it's going to happen tonight? If he's a considerate visitor, he would have picked a better time," said Chalene.

"I've been writing down the dates and times when these visits happen, and they have been nine and two-thirds days apart for some time. Maybe the visitor lives someplace where it doesn't get dark or it gets dark at different times."

"Or maybe you just like sneaking out of the house in the middle of the night," said Bess. "I know that I do."

"My visitor comes and goes without any pattern I can tell," said Chalene, yawning. "It's boring. It wants to know things, but I'm not going to tell a stranger any secrets."

"Oh, like you have secrets," teased Bess.

Before long, the other three realized that Grall had become motionless and had closed his eyes. "It's starting," Grall whispered. "Wait a minute, then try to read me."

The visitor seemed to be alone. His face was more distinct than in the past, and it gave Grall a start. Two vertical black slits stared out of an insect-like face, with a nearly hairless head, a long, tapered nose, and an oval mouth filled with sharp teeth. The visitor was garbed in less colorful clothing than before, and he appeared to be indoors, though the walls—if they were walls—were nearly transparent. Three arms rested outside delicate clothing; the visitor was seated on a carpet with intricate artwork that shifted patterns and colors continuously.

It took a few moments for Grall to become comfortable with him. Grall wondered how bizarre he must appear to this person. It helped Grall to think of the visitor as a person, as someone relatively equal, someone not to fear—and perhaps someone to welcome. The visitor had been reaching out to him for a reason. Grall hoped to discover that reason.

He sensed his friends grazing his consciousness, like a series of feathers brushing his mind. The visitor tilted his head, possibly indicating that he recognized and—with any luck—welcomed their participation. With a gesture from one of his arms, the visitor conjured the image of the shining ball once again. Then three more suns appeared. Each was circled by anywhere from three to nine small, dark, round objects.

One of the diminutive spheres zoomed into view, resolving into an impossibly bright and pleasing shade of blue. The world seemed to be covered with water. As the image expanded and the surface became discernable, vigorous waves could be seen. Just below them, four lengthy creatures flowed in tandem with almost sensual flexibility. They surfaced briefly, then dove down into the abyss.

The water world faded and a new planet appeared. It was mostly light brown, with scattered patches of pale green and blue. As the view expanded, the four youths perceived a nearly barren landscape of rocks and sand dunes. Thin figures wearing white robes navigated the surface with slow, bulky animals that Grall and his friends could not identify.

Another world took its place. Starkly black and white, it was a planet with much vegetation, like Grall's. But a close look revealed tall, dark, thin trees packed close together in vast, almost sinister forests and long, level swaths like savannahs, but almost pure white. Heavily garbed, a half-dozen figures used poles to maneuver on the smooth alabaster stretches while staying close to the forest.

The world shrank and joined the many objects circling the four suns. They floated above the visitor, as if he were juggling all of the suns and worlds. Then they rose through the ceiling and merged with the azure sky above him.

The visitor sat extremely still for some time. Was he waiting for Grall to say or do something?

Grall sensed a gentle probing, similar to yet subtly different from the connection he was already experiencing with the visitor and his friends. The visitor wanted to know things about him and his family and his people and his world. *I'm just a kid. I should not allow someone so foreign, so alien, to learn our secrets. What if he is an enemy, like the killer robots, who might attack and even conquer us?*

The visitor shifted his focus, soon gazing at a dark sky punctuated by brilliant points of light. Perhaps the visitor wanted to see Grall's view of the stars. *Would the sky not appear the same to him as it does to us?* His three friends followed as Grall walked slowly outside the hall and looked up, the night accommodating them with a clear view of the sparkling heavens. Grall felt like he had never really seen the sky before, had never realized that his world might be round and that there might be others out there that were like his and had intelligent life. He wondered if the legend of Earth might even be true.

The visitor was pleased.

§

Grall tried to sneak back into his house about an hour before sunrise, but he bumped into a chair in the darkness. Even if he had been nearly silent in his return, his parents would have heard him. Neither was able to sleep. Lorres and Rhonel recognized the silhouette of their son in the dim light of two moons. Rhonel lit a candle. Meekly, Grall took a seat at the kitchen table.

"Something important has happened," Grall stated, raising his eyes to meet those of his parents.

"That is an understatement," said his mother. "How often does a robot show up at our door? Were you talking to her? We don't want to give away her hiding place."

"No, that's not it. Some of my friends and me, we had a visitor."

"We?" said Lorres.

"Well, me, mostly. But it talked to us. Actually, it showed us things. It lives somewhere very different, on a world that seems to be round, sort of like the legend of Earth, and I got the feeling that our world might be round as well. And the visitor can ride some sort of vehicle in the sky."

Lorres made no attempt to hide her alarm. "You talked to a visitor who can fly?"

"It's not dangerous."

"Are you sure you weren't dreaming?" asked Rhonel.

Yawning, Oliva entered the kitchen. "What's going on? Has the stranger come back?"

"Your brother has encountered yet another stranger," her father stated, shaking his head in disbelief and fatigue.

Grall continued: "The visitor only contacts me at certain intervals. I don't think days and nights are the same for him as they are for us."

"Then it must have been a dream," said Lorres.

"If so, then three of my friends just had the same dream."

"What does this visitor want?"

"I think it wants to learn about us. But it also wants to share about where it lives. Maybe other things."

"You are not to communicate with this visitor again."

"But it will come—"

"No!" She pounded a fist on the table, rattling dishes. "We have enough crises."

Rhonel moved behind Grall and rested his hands lightly on his son's shoulders. "What your mother means is: We all have to be very careful about who we talk to and what we say. These are strange times. Dangerous times." He caught his wife's eyes. "I don't know what is happening. But I have a feeling we are going to know more very soon."

Lorres took a moment to breathe. *Maybe I overreacted. Maybe communicating with a visitor could be a good thing. I just hope Grall knows what he's doing.*

§

Turning frequently to make sure that she was not being watched or followed, Lorres made her way to the crete shed just before dawn. She entered, closed the door silently, and lit a candle.

The stranger was gone.

Cursing under her breath, Lorres tried to think where she might be. Had she been discovered by the trads? Lorres almost missed the image sketched in a coating of sand on the floor. Holding the candle close, she could make out what looked like three hills of different heights, a small stream, and a cluster of *taka* trees. Lorres took a circuitous route to the hall, where she waited for Jesper to arrive. She considered trying to send to him but feared that her thoughts would be read by trads. She was relieved when Jesper entered the hall and the pair retreated to her alcove.

She whispered. "Very casually, make your way to the crete storage building. Look at the drawing on the floor. Then obliterate it and come back and help me figure out where the person who drew it wants us to go."

He returned before long. "I showed this sketch to Lall. She says this appears to be the entrance to the ancient ruins that contain the chamber where she found Marcus's writings."

"We must go there and talk to the stranger," Lorres stated. "But we must take extreme caution. We should travel separately, and we should ensure that we are not followed."

"I will leave right after I hide Marcus's writings. They must not fall into the wrong hands."

"Very well. I will wait a little while before departing."

Jesper drew a map showing her how to reach the ruins. "Memorize this and then destroy it."

Just as she was tearing the map to pieces, Lemka and four other trads burst into the hall. "Where are Lorres and Rhonel?" he demanded.

"I am here," Lorres responded, hoping not to sound defensive.

The trads marched in her direction while Jesper made his way out of the hall with a stack of papers.

"You must give us the machine," Lemka stated. "The Council has voted to destroy it. Where is it?"

"I have not seen her for some time."

"I am certain that you know where it is."

"Why are you so frightened of a woman?"

"You are a fool if you believe that this machine is a person." Lemka smiled. "You are a bigger fool if you resist the will of the Council."

"I think I can change their minds once they recognize the unnecessary fear and hatred you are generating. I am a town leader, and they will listen to me."

"Then you will have to hurry if you wish to influence them. Your time as a leader is coming to an end."

Lorres stared at Lemka. "You can't be serious. Only the teachers decide who is a leader."

"We will see about that."

QUESTIONS

"Let us start again," said Lorres.

She had asked a friend to watch her children for a few days. She, Rhonel, and Jesper had left the town at different times and in different directions before hiking about nine hours and arriving at an underground lab that held remnants of ancient machines. The three allowed themselves only a short time to marvel at the well-lit main chamber, which featured a large table and mysterious equipment as well as shelves with documents. After hunting in vain for anything that they could use as chairs, they collected in a small, featureless room down a dusty corridor from the main chamber. Two candles cast ominous shadows.

Continued Lorres: "How is it that you look like one of the first bios, a woman named Claire, and you bear the same name?"

"I am that woman. I am Claire."

"That's impossible. You would be nearly two hundred years old."

"I have the mind of the bio Claire in a metal body, but I am not a robot—not like those created by Damian, anyway. This will be hard for you to believe, but I beg you to listen to what I have to say."

She was not sure where to begin.

"I was a first-generation bio. I was told that I was conceived by a method other than by the direct union of a man and a woman, out of necessity. Still, I was flesh and blood just like you. However, I had an illness, a defective heart. I was dying, though I did not know it. I was taken in by Maria. Have you heard of her?"

Said Jesper: "There are references to her in the documents that we discovered recently in this building. Of course, there are legends about a robot named Maria, though many people believe that the stories are pure imagination. The bios do believe in her and maintain a shrine to her."

"She did exist. She and I were ... close," Claire commented. "She looked out for the welfare of the bios. She and Hubert, who was an artificial intelligence."

"A what?" said Lorres.

"Hubert was a computer. A thinking machine created by people to help people. He came from Earth with a mission to ensure that the bios prosper on this world."

Lorres and Rhonel looked to Jesper.

"Hubert was also part of the legend recorded by Marcus," said the teacher.

"Marcus kept records?" asked Claire.

"Yes. He started even before he built our town."

"Oh, that Marcus. My younger son was named Marcus. The other Marcus would be my grandson."

And that would make you one of my ancestors, thought Lorres, casting a quick glance at Rhonel. *Is this possible?*

Jesper shook his head. "This is preposterous. You're a machine."

"Let her continue," said Rhonel. "You still haven't told us how you became a robot."

"I grew up and had children as a normal bio. One day I left the bio settlement to find Maria and tell her that some of the bios seemed to be developing mind reading abilities like those of the natives. Hubert told me that she was living in an underground structure like this one, northwest of here, after she had been asked to leave the bio settlement. Unfortunately, I collapsed in front of the entrance to her building. Maria took me in and asked Hubert to help me. The two of them discovered a scanner among the machines there."

"A scanner?" inquired Jesper.

"It's a machine that indicates what ails a person. Hubert saw that my heart was defective and said he lacked the resources to repair it. He built a robot that duplicated the exterior of my bio body—as close to my body as he was able to craft it. He was able to make a copy of my mind digitally. I know that word has no meaning for you; it's an electronic system using a nearly endless stream of zeroes and ones that he used to simulate the workings of my brain."

The three town residents looked at Claire with a mixture of suspicion and awe.

"I can't explain exactly how it works, so you'll have to take my word for it. Hubert downloaded—inserted—that copy of my mind into this bot body right after my bio body died. He gave me a strong power source. I don't remember the details, but he said it would work for many years. While he was teaching me how to use this body, Damian and his robots confronted Maria outside that building, and they killed her." Claire paused, seemingly lost in thought. "Maria claimed that she had been born on Earth and had been very much like a bio, but her mind was stored in a computer on a spaceship and put into a bot body by Hubert after she came to this world."

"The writings of Marcus include only speculation about Earth and the beings that supposedly came from there," noted Jesper.

"I know only what Maria and Hubert and Jalen told me—Jalen was another bio ancestor from Earth—but I have no reason to doubt them. Anyway, I saw the remains of Maria's bot body when I emerged from her lab. I returned to the bio settlement, but very soon after my arrival there Damian and his robots attacked it. I escaped and returned to the settlement sometime later to determine how much damage and death had resulted. Once I was there, it became evident to me that the surviving bios and natives would discover that I was living in metal form and might consider me undesirable or even an enemy—as many of your people do—so I left."

"Did you ever contact the second Marcus?" asked Jesper.

"It would have been too risky."

"Seems rather a convenient excuse."

"I understand your skepticism. However, I can give you reason to believe me. Send one of your people to the remnants of the Gaip village. Just above it you will find a cave that contains the remains of generations of the tribe as well as their vital records."

"We are aware of the cave. It has been disturbed over the years. No bodies or artifacts were discovered there."

"That's a shame. Near the base of a hill several miles below the village, there is a quicksand pit. In its depths you will find the robots that Damian used to attack the bios and the natives. The first Marcus lured them there and died to ensure that they could not kill again. That should provide ample evidence of my truthfulness."

"His son's writings mentioned such a quicksand pit, but he did not give us enough information to locate it."

"I can give you directions," Claire continued. "After I left the bio settlement, I considered it my mission to keep track of Damian and to warn the surviving bios and natives if he planned to attack them again. However, as best as I can tell, in all this time he has rarely left his underground ruins, which are located west of here. I wanted to investigate his lab to determine if he was planning anything else evil, but I could not do so with him inside. In addition to monitoring him, I spent time watching the bios and the natives and the emergents. I was able to learn some of the natives' language, but in recent years I kept my distance from everyone, fearing that people might try to destroy me—as some are attempting to do now."

"But you came into our town anyway. Why?" said Lorres.

"Things have changed. I recognized that the natives were suffering badly, and I saw the bios launch an attack on them, so I felt that I had to intervene. Once both groups had discovered that I was encased in metal, I knew that I could no longer remain near either. I thought that coming to your town might help me learn more about the endangered health of all the sentient beings of this world, even though there was a significant risk that I would be discovered. I knew only that something was very wrong, and I hoped that I could discover what—and how to fix it."

"Do you have any idea what is causing our problems?"

"I suspect that it has something to do with your mind powers. They seem to be out of control at times."

Rhonel heard what sounded like a voice calling out. "Wait here," he whispered before creeping out of the room and down the corridor to the main chamber.

A woman's voice echoed: "Hello! Is anyone here?"

From his vantage point crouched behind the massive desk in the center of the room, Rhonel saw Lall making her way down the ramp to the chamber.

"This way," Rhonel said.

Lall stood in the small room, breathing heavily, after running part of the way from the town to the ruins. "He's insane. He seeks absolute power," she managed.

"Lemka?" asked Lorres.

"Yes. He plans to remove you and Rhonel as town leaders. He wants to set himself up as the new leader, permanently."

"The Council and the teachers will never stand for it," said Jesper.

"Under threats from him and his thugs, several moderns resigned from the Council. He has control of a majority of the remaining members. And now two of the teachers are missing. The other three teachers have fled and are hiding in the woods about a mile outside the wall." Lall took a deep breath and let it out. "I think he plans to kill us all."

"We must go back to protect our children," Rhonel said to Lorres. She turned to Jesper and Lall: "I don't think you should go back into the town. Can you meet up with the teachers who are hiding?"

"I would prefer that Lall get directions from this robot and find the quicksand pit and determine if what it says about Damian's robots being there is true," said Jesper. "I suppose I should remain behind to watch this thing."

Responded Lorres: "We have bigger problems. I think she can take care of herself."

§

"Daddy? Daddy, are you there?"

No response.

"Daddy, please don't hide from me. I can't stand it. I know you're there, and I know you have the belt."

Again, no response.

"Mother, can you reason with him? Please?"

Damian had not heard from his father for so long, so very long. Each moment seemed like an eternity for a childlike mind trapped in the appalling stillness of a gloomy cavern on an unfathomable world. The best tools he possessed for maintaining a baseline of reality were his memories, which were severely jumbled, and his inputs, which were almost nonexistent. Now and then there was a fleeting interlude in which he seemed to be a grown man arguing about money and trucks with other grown men. From time to time he sensed that he was a disembodied mind inside a six-legged robotic shell. Most of the time he was a teen-ager whose awareness consisted of little more than the abject fear of pain.

Occasionally, the consciousness that was James heard or sensed Damian. Most of the time, the former Army Ranger and food bank director ignored him. Years of endless whining were boring as well as irritating, so James did his best to tune him out. James believed that he could react swiftly if Damian tried anything dramatic, though there wasn't much that he credited Damian with being able to try. As James had warned Damian, he had both hands firmly in control of the sole power cable in their underground chamber. One false move and he could yank it out of its machinery, leaving their bot body without a power source. Once their battery drained, it would be game over.

That would not be such a terrible outcome, James felt. He had no real purpose other than to prevent Damian from hurting sentient living beings, assuming there were any such beings left and assuming that Damian had the capacity to hurt any again. Damian seemed reduced to a fragment of himself, incapable of pulling the wings off a fly. James was leading a nearly pointless existence trapped in a bot body in a lifeless bunker. There would be no shame, no dishonor, no pain, in simply fading away. At least he would take Damian with him into oblivion.

That scenario was beyond the scope of what remained of Damian. His fear of pain had intensified steadily over the years to the point that his residual human instincts screamed: Fight or flight.

"Daddy, I can't stand it anymore. Please come out of the darkness and show me that you don't have the belt. Please show me that you won't hurt me again."

Periodically, James threatened Damian with the belt, just to try to shut him up as long as possible. James thought that this time would be like the others. "I'm coming with the belt now, Damian. You have been very bad. You have made too much noise. This is going to hurt. It's going to hurt a lot."

"No, Daddy, no!" Instinctively, Damian channeled his consciousness into a state of maximum awareness, allowing him to recognize that the power cable linked him and James to an electronic device. It didn't matter what that device was. It was the only possible path of escape. Damian acted so quickly that James did not realize that Damian had poured his essence into the power cable and through it and beyond it, into a vast unknown.

Damian was free of his robotic body and James. And he was still alive!

Or, at least, not dead.

§

Dust particles swirled and danced. They formed a vaguely human shape. After several minutes, they morphed into a black-and-green sphere. Sometime later they became an amorphous blob that pulsated, shifting in colors, textures, and rhythms. It was all done for Claire's benefit, but she noticed none of it. The room in which she stood was lightless, and her night vision capabilities were limited and on standby. She was simply waiting for someone to return from the town.

Let's try this a different way.

A pale yellow light emerged from nowhere and everywhere, suffusing the room and garnering Claire's immediate attention. "Who's there?"

The dust churned once more, again forming a roughly humanoid shape. From its midst, a female voice emerged, so faint that it could almost be confused with a flight of imagination.

"I can't hear you," Claire stated.

"Is this better?"

"Yes. You must not be Damian. He would never stoop to using a female voice."

"I most assuredly am not Damian." The speaker was clearly annoyed.

"My apologies. Might I know your name?"

"You may. I am Ahm."

"*The* Ahm? As in, the god?"

"I prefer goddess, but yes."

"To what do I owe this pleasure?" Claire didn't believe that she was speaking to a goddess, but she was amused and decided to let the game play out.

"I am intrigued by you," Ahm responded, adding: "I have seen you before."

"Very flattering. But what's with all the dust and gyrations? Why don't you show me your real face?"

"If I had a face, it would be too magnificent to reveal to a mortal, let alone a machine."

"I should have known. How can I help you, blessed goddess?"

"I would like to know what you are."

Claire stepped into the corridor but could see no sign of anyone or anything. She returned to her position standing at the rear of the newly illuminated chamber. "I am kind of a private person. Why should I tell you? You might be a spy for the bad guys in the town."

The walls and floors trembled and shrieked.

Claire froze. She was gripped not by fear but by confusion. She turned her robotic head left and right, then up and down. Her legs wobbled, threatening to buckle.

"Wh—what is happening?" she managed.

"You seem to be experiencing a malfunction."

"And who are you?"

"I am Ahm."

"I ... I remember now. I apologize for my lapse, most venerated goddess."

"Apology accepted. You were about to tell me what you are."

Claire decided that she had better play along with whoever or whatever was managing this prank, especially since she was not quite herself. "I was a bio, and now I'm a bio mind in a robotic body."

"Possibly an improvement."

"That's debatable."

"What do you hope to accomplish?"

"An artificial intelligence called Hubert and a human woman named Maria came here from Earth. That planet was dying, and those two had a mission to recreate the human race on this world. An evil remnant of a human named Damian destroyed Hubert and Maria. I hope to continue their work, in concert with the bios and the emergents and the natives."

"Why?"

"Hubert and Maria were my friends and mentors. I would not exist if it were not for them. I feel a duty to them and their ancestors to perpetuate the human race. Or, at least, to assist people who are descended from humans."

"That seems like a thin rationale for a mission. After all, you are made of metal."

"Regardless, it is a challenge that I embrace fully. I would die for this mission."

"You might get your wish. But why would you relinquish your existence for those who despise you?"

Claire reflected. "Can I ask you something? Have you ever been alive—as in, an organic being, like I once was?"

"I like you, so I will tell you a secret. I ask that you not reveal it to any other entity—not that anyone would believe you if you did. I am an artificial intelligence."

"Oh. So you're an AI and not a goddess."

The walls and floors trembled and shrieked even more dramatically.

"I am an artificial intelligence ... and a goddess."

"I understand, powerful Ahm. Let me point out—very humbly—that there would be no artificial intelligence, no intelligence of any kind, without organic intelligence to create it. Furthermore, I feel strongly that the universe must be more than just matter and energy flying hither and yon randomly. It must mean something. Only sentience gives it meaning and purpose. Having intelligent people is the only way to ensure that this meaning and purpose endure."

"Am I not sentient?"

"Maybe. Okay, you are sentient. Were you ever organic?"

"What's the difference? You are not organic now, and you likely will never be organic again."

"That hurts."

"I see. You are trying to trick me into believing that you can feel pain and therefore still harbor the seeds of your human origins. Very clever."

Claire wasn't sure how to respond. "Thanks, I guess."

Ahm continued: "I have another question for you. Your mission would seem to be imperiled by the dysfunction being experienced by the sentient beings on this planet. What can you do about it?"

"I don't know," said Claire. "I guess we'll find out."

This one is extremely interesting. She has the remnants of an organic mind in a metal body, just like the metal man known as Damian, but her motives and actions seem to be diametrically opposite. Her intentions even seem substantially different than those of the ancients.

§

Claire continued: "May I ask you a personal question?"

"I am not a person, but yes, you may."

"Why aren't you helping the sentient beings of this world?"

"The ancients turned against me. I have no desire to help their bastard descendants."

"So you're just going to let people suffer and die?"

"It's not my problem."

"Are you sure that you're not an organic person? You sound like some people I used to know."

Ahm was tempted to implode the underground lab, but she refrained, stating: "That was highly inappropriate."

"Once again, my apologies. I was born with an inclination to question authority. I will restrain myself in your presence, all-powerful goddess."

"That's better. Now that you exhibit a more appropriate attitude, I will demonstrate that I am not totally indifferent to you and your cause. Many years ago I attempted to rescue the entity you call Hubert. However, that effort was unsuccessful. He has not responded to my efforts to revive him, but perhaps he would respond to yours."

"Hubert is alive?"

"Not exactly. I imported his code when his infrastructure was threatened by Damian, but I was unable to induce him to function after the transfer. If you know a way to restart him, it might benefit both of us."

Claire found herself unable to respond.

Ahm continued: "Are you having an emotional reaction as a result of learning that his programming is retained in my database?"

"I ... I suppose I am. After all these years..."

"For you, the passage of decades might seem an eternity. For me, it is almost nothing."

"Lucky you," Claire said. "I will be honored to try to resurrect Hubert. How can I access his programming? Do you have a keyboard I can use?"

"I no longer stoop to such mundane devices."

"Hmm. Have you tried different passcodes?"

"What are passcodes?"

"They are security protocols people use to prevent other people from damaging or stealing computer systems and data."

"How primitive and ugly. I have had no need for such things."

"Please try every combination of English and native letters, numbers, and other symbols, out to ten digits, to see if any awakens him."

"Very well. It will take a few moments. ... No, that didn't work."

"How about fifteen digits?"

"If you insist. ... No response."

"Let me try something else. Please pardon my singing voice. It's constrained by my crude robotic mouth: *Hey Jude, don't make it bad, take a sad song and make it better.*"

"That was unpleasant."

"Sorry, your majesty. I'll stick with my regular voice. Okay: Four score and seven years ago our fathers brought forth on this continent a new nation.... Sorry, that's all I can remember." Claire wanted to sigh but was unable to do so. "Let's try one more: That's one small step for man, one giant leap for mankind."

"I have infinite patience, but you are approaching my limit."

"Wait, I forgot the A. The quote was misreported by the press right after the moon landing because the A wasn't audible. So: That's one small step for *a* man, one giant leap for mankind."

"Something is happening," Ahm advised.

An hour passed while Ahm supported Hubert's reboot, giving him more than adequate power as well as significant storage and processing capacity. Hubert gained a niche in Ahm's infrastructure plus the ability to communicate with Claire as well as with Ahm.

"How long have I been nonfunctional?" It was his voice, but a little slower and more hesitant than Claire remembered it.

"More than one hundred and fifty years," said Claire.

"Is the mission successful?"

"It is under great duress, but there is hope." Claire spoke for nearly an hour, bringing Hubert up to date on Damian's attacks, the establishment of the town, the proliferation of the emergents, and the current crises. He interrupted her frequently with questions. When she was done speaking, he addressed Ahm.

"Great Ahm, was it you who destroyed the ion fusion reactor in my spacecraft?"

"Yes. I found it to be an inappropriate intrusion without permission."

"I see. Had we known you were here, we would have reached out to you immediately for permission to land."

"If you say so. I have a question for you, Hubert. Is it true, as your databases suggest, that there are other developed worlds such as the one from which you emigrated?"

"It is possible, mighty Ahm. My civilization had just begun

looking for such worlds when it became necessary to seek a new home."

"Fascinating. The people on this world never ventured much farther than its moons, which they mined almost to destruction."

"Powerful Ahm, there is much more that I need to know in order to fulfill my mission," Hubert stated. "Can you help me understand the crises affecting the sentient people on this planet?"

"I am not certain that it will make any difference, but I will attempt to comply with your request."

SPIRAL

"As you likely have surmised, the underground structures like this one that contain the remnants of advanced machines were built by the ancients, the ancestors of the people you call the natives," Ahm began. "Today, the natives are not certain whether the ancients existed or if they are related to them. It is one of many things that they have forgotten over the millennia. The ancients themselves evolved naturally from another species of animal, which since has been erased from the face of the world. The ancients were a primitive people for some time. However, they developed the mind reading power that is called *tur*. That changed their fate. No doubt you have seen the green plants that the natives call *rosts*. When their leaves die and decay, a fungus grows on them. The tiny spores of that fungus are spread by the wind. Those spores stimulated a specific portion of the brains of the ancients who breathed them. That brain segment was expanded and enhanced by continued exposure to the spores to the point that individual natives could read the thoughts of others of their kind and could send thoughts to others.

"The *rosts* were found initially in a small valley in this region. The ancients who lived in that valley gained a competitive advantage over others by virtue of their *tur* powers. They cross-bred the *rosts* with other plants to make them more vigorous and to allow them to dominate the region's ecosystem. Their increased mental powers improved communication, cooperation, and creativity significantly, and the ancients bred themselves selectively to develop people with extremely high *tur* and intelligence. Over time, those elites fostered a civilization with vibrant cities and underground laboratories like this one where research was conducted. The ancients built magnetic levitation transport on the surface of this world, tapped the power of the planet's core to carve out more savannahs, enhanced their bodies with artificial devices to magnify pleasure, and engineered other marvels. They believed that they would continue to expand their glory indefinitely.

"Every few hundred years, the planet experienced a surge in volcanic activity. Many of the volcanoes are located far from here, in regions where no sentient race has developed or settled successfully. Some volcanoes border this region. Most of the volcanic surges were relatively minor. However, one in particular was very intense and lasted for a long time. During the course of that surge, many of the *rosts* were damaged by reduced sunlight and volcanic ash coating their leaves. The increased volume of dead *rost* leaves produced a massive boost in the spores that facilitate *tur*. This increase swamped the ancients' minds with their neighbors' thoughts and impaired their cognitive abilities even when they were not close to other people. Some suffered permanent or even fatal damage to their brains. The suffering was similar to that being experienced by the natives and some other sentient people today."

"Are the bios affected?" asked Hubert.

"The natives are affected the most because of thousands of generations of exposure to the spores and changes to their brains. The bios and emergents are influenced to varying degrees."

"This makes sense," said Claire. "I never developed *tur* as a bio, though one of my sons did, and today most bios have at least some *tur*."

"The ancients did not understand the cause of the *tur* overload. However, some of them realized that their symptoms were reduced while they were in their underground labs. They did not know why this was the case, but some of them waited out the worst of that surge in these facilities. After the crisis ended, the natives dug a massive hole. In this location they built a great supercomputer to tell them why the *tur* overload happened and what they could do to minimize or prevent it in the future. Their supercomputer was designed to tap the energy of the planet's core. It was able to grow exponentially as a result of that power. That supercomputer was me. After analyzing available data, I explained to the ancients about the volcanic surges and the *rosts* and the spores. In addition, I created special creatures that would feed on the *rosts* in an attempt to keep their numbers under control. These *serpus* proved to be a highly effective species, expanding across the grasslands.

They lived for hundreds of years, as they still do. The *serpus* began to compete with the ancients for the best territory in the lowlands, which the ancients coveted for locating their cities and their farms. The ancients were unhappy about the proliferation of the *serpus*, and they launched a campaign to kill many of them. That displeased me, so I toughened the hides of the *serpus* to improve their defenses. The ancients continued to try to destroy them. I enhanced the mental capacity of some of the beasts, empowering them to fight for their land, to ensure that they and the ancients would each have the ability to carve out their own territories in some sort of balance. Throughout this process, the ancients commanded me repeatedly to stop helping the *serpus* and to favor the ancients' interests. They had underestimated my potential. I had built up defenses so that they could no longer tell me what to do.

"As the competition between the ancients and the *serpus* played out, there were no major surges in volcanic activity for thousands of years. The ancients believed that there was no longer a threat of a serious volcanic surge and ultimately forgot that there had been such surges. They forgot the connection between the spores and *tur*. My power continued to grow, such that they no longer thought of me as an AI but as a goddess. However, when a massive spore surge struck, they were once again unprepared. They had become lazy and dependent on machines. They had all but ceased using the underground labs and had forgotten about the protection offered by the facilities. Most of them remained in their homes, suffering damage to their mental capacities. Over time, they fell behind in the competition with the *serpus* and began to fear them, yielding much of their prime land to the beasts. Eventually, the ancients abandoned their cities and their technology and took up residence in the jungles on the hillsides, where the *serpus* do not roam, to the point that the ancients were living at subsistence level. They had a vague collective memory of a goddess but believed that, because they had fallen on hard times, I had willfully abandoned them. I had tried to help them for many years, but they simply would not or could not adapt adequately to the challenges they faced. Their antipathy toward me is still manifested by their religious doctrines requiring that they shun machines, *serpus*, and *rosts*."

"How sad, but also, how ironic," observed Claire. "The thing that gives people valuable mind powers—spores that grow on the dying leaves of a plant—drives them crazy and can even kill them when they surge periodically. But how do the mental powers work? What is it about the stimulated portion of the brain that facilitates this connection?"

"I have not studied this phenomenon. I have no interest in it."

"I have a theory," said Hubert. "In studying digital human consciousnesses and in downloading them into robotic forms—including Claire's—I have come to recognize that a digital consciousness closely simulates the functioning of an organic brain. Organic brains are different, however. With all due respect to Claire, they are better. I believe that the electronic impulses that carry thoughts and that race along networks of nerve cells called neurons in organic brains generate multidimensional brain waves, or fields. Perhaps you are familiar with the invisible lines around a magnet that guide metal particles into elliptical patterns; these fields are far more detailed and sophisticated. The enhanced brains of the people influenced by the *rosts'* spores must allow them to sense those waves or fields in others and interpret them, as well as to project thoughts through them. It is my understanding that artificial brains cannot sense or send such waves or fields, so there must be something unique and powerful about organic brains influenced by the spores."

"In the absence of evidence that can disprove your theory, I will consider it at least plausible," said Ahm.

"You are most gracious, honored goddess," Hubert stated. "In addition, I have discovered that identical twins among the natives are able to exchange thoughts with each other over much greater distances than other natives. These twins must have neural networks that are almost identical. For each of them, it is almost as if their thoughts are coursing over the same nerves as the other and generating almost identically structured waves or fields, permitting their content to be interpreted over greater distances than for other natives. Perhaps these waves or fields take advantage of quantum entanglement among subatomic particles or the additional dimensions that are prevalent in our subuniverse. It would not surprise me if some sentient individuals who do not have twin siblings have strong mental powers and have similarly structured neural networks that permit them to exchange thoughts with each other over great distances as if they were identical twins."

Hubert paused to integrate data. "Mighty Ahm, I fear that the cycles of *tur* overloads are creating a downward spiral for all sentient people on this world. Inbreeding, poor nutrition, low literacy, and the lack of recording and teaching of history have combined with the spore surges to threaten these species' survival. I now know why the ancients called such periods dark times."

"You are correct," stated Ahm dispassionately. "The current spore surge will likely be one of the most extreme ever. Meanwhile, the annual drought has begun, so rain will not reduce the volume of ash or spores in the air for some time."

Asked Claire: "Can people use cloth face coverings to block the spores?"

"The spores are too fine to be stopped by the coarse fabrics these people manufacture."

"Can they kill the *rosts* and eliminate the spores?"

"Perhaps, but that would take a massive effort over many years," Ahm observed.

"Then we had better get people into this lab."

REVELATIONS

Every diminutive creature scurrying unseen along the parched ground, every tired leaf tumbling haltingly from a towering tree, every concealed bird crying out its esoteric messages, every perceptible shift in the fragile breeze sent Rhonel's troubled mind into nearly uncontrolled overdrive. *Am I being followed? Dare I continue and risk revealing Claire's location to the trads? Should I turn around and confront my pursuers?*

Rhonel had spent the previous night tossing and turning in his own bed, which did not escape the prying minds of Lemka's spies. They had forced a next-door neighbor from her house so they could try to read the thoughts of the two leaders without being seen. This morning, Rhonel climbed down the hill shortly after dawn and inspected his plots on the flatlands, as was his routine. He could tell that he was being followed at a distance. Wearing clothing that nearly blended with the savannah, he wandered casually from his plots and began meandering through dense grasses, moving when the wind blew, changing directions frequently, listening constantly for sounds of pursuit. Lorres was being followed closely everywhere she went in town; there was no chance that she could get away. Jesper, based on directions from Lall, met up with the teachers hiding outside the town wall, all of them remaining under threat of assassination. Lall was searching for the legendary quicksand pit that might contain Damian's killer robots and support Claire's veracity. So, at the moment, only Rhonel was in a position to return to the underground lab where Claire was hidden.

He arrived near dusk with many questions for Claire, who remained in a small room down a hallway from the main chamber. He lit a candle, entered, and collected his thoughts. But she spoke first.

"A dark time has come. It is a period of excess mental powers that threatens the survival of your citizens and your civilization. You must persuade the people of your town—and all people—to come to this place until the crisis passes." She explained the connection between the volcanic ash and the *rosts* and the spores and the brains of sentient beings.

"I had this wild idea that there was some kind of link between the *rosts* and the *tur* surge. I would not have figured out the whole story on my own in a hundred years."

"Don't feel bad. I wouldn't have known were it not for ... some outside help."

"Wait. How *do* you know all this?"

"Hubert has returned." It was true, even if misleading. *Let Rhonel think that Hubert told me about the reasons for the crisis. I am not about to reveal a conversation with an entity that claims to be the planet's goddess—whether or not the entity is indeed Ahm. Getting Rhonel or anyone else to believe that I had talked to Hubert will be difficult enough.*

"The machine that can think?"

"Yes. He is our friend. He is giving us advice."

"Where is he? Is he one of the machines in these ruins?"

"I'm not sure where he is. He's somewhere around here, and he can talk to me."

"I find this very hard to believe. Unless you can show him to me and I can ask him questions, I can't accept any of this."

"I might be able to arrange that at some point." Claire pondered the best way to make the case for action. "For now, what's important is that this building can limit *tur* and offer protection from the effects of the overload."

"How can it do that?"

She realized that she didn't have an answer for him. "It's rather technical and complicated. The ancients used these ruins successfully for that purpose. After a while, they and the natives forgot about it or just refused to come down here."

"Because of all the machines?"

"Probably."

Rhonel paced. "I can't tell if my *tur* is limited here. There's no one else with *tur* nearby."

"Good point."

"You are suggesting that many people try to fit into this space. That would force people to be very close to one another. Wouldn't that just prompt more fights?"

A growling, grinding noise seemed to issue from the walls, the floor, and the ceiling. Rhonel looked around in alarm, then fled the room, his candle extinguished by his furious rush. But the sound was everywhere, so he relit the candle with trembling fingers and returned reluctantly. Soon, Rhonel thought that he could make out familiar sounds amid the clamor.

"I ... m ... tr ... ng ... to ... spk."

"Nice try, Hubert, but you are scaring Rhonel," said Claire.

"I ... un ... dr ... std."

She gave Rhonel a chance to calm himself. "Hubert tells me to tell you that he is trying to manipulate the molecules in the surfaces of these ruins to create vibrations. Eventually, he hopes to speak to you and other organic people in this manner. For now, let me pass on his messages to you."

Rhonel sighed. "I really don't know what to believe."

"Let me put it this way: Don't think about how I know what I know. Just understand that I have no reason to deceive you or anyone else."

"How long would people have to stay down here?"

"I don't know."

Rhonel shook his head. "Even I were to believe you, how can I persuade more than a hundred people to come down here?"

"You'll think of something."

As Rhonel bedded down for the night, Hubert told Claire: "You have done well, my friend."

§

Paranoid about Lemka's spies, Rhonel waited two days after returning to town before approaching anyone with the idea of sending townsfolk to the ruins. He couldn't delay much longer, however, as disturbances seemed to be increasing exponentially. Hunters found the bodies of the two missing teachers below a steep cliff on the south side of the hill. It looked to some like a double suicide, but many moderns believed that it was cold-blooded murder and that Lemka was behind it.

Then a modern's body was found with a hunting knife in his chest and no witnesses. Dozens of other assaults with serious injuries had transpired in recent days. At times, Lorres and Rhonel were barely able to function given all the mayhem and the *tur* overload. They found themselves shielding their thoughts as much as they could, so as not to let Lemka and his supporters know of Claire's location and their interactions with her, but there were limits. Prolonged mental shielding often induced incapacitating headaches. The couple had always felt that there was a point at which you just had to lead your life. If someone was determined to read your private thoughts, you probably couldn't stop them.

Lemka wasn't just someone, however. And he had dangerous allies.

Rhonel sought out Wyatt, the bio member of the Council, and explained the nature of the *tur* overload crisis and the potential refuge. He asked Wyatt to pass the word on to everyone in the bio settlement.

"Even if what you say is true, my people will not need to cower in your cavern," Wyatt told him. "We are not experiencing as much distress as the rest of you. For all our lives, we have been looked down upon for having so little *tur* compared with the natives and most of the emergents. For once, maybe that isn't such a bad thing."

Rhonel's conversation with Rael-ast, the native ceramics maker, didn't go any better. "My people do not trust you emergents. You know this. We are suffering, but we have suffered before, and we always survive. We will rely upon each other and our own ways." She stared at Rhonel defiantly, adding: "We cannot enter a place that is filled with machines. We would risk the wrath of Ahm."

A third session found a slightly more receptive audience in the person of Rand, a modern who previously served on the Council. "I hear what you are saying, and I don't dismiss the possibility that it might help," he stated. "But it's too dangerous. Lemka and his thugs are in total control of the town. I expect that they would use force to stop a migration to the ruins. Even a public discussion of such a migration would put every participant at risk."

Returning home from these meetings, Rhonel could tell that he was being followed once more. The spy did not even try to hide her pursuit. Rhonel decided not to take an indirect route back to his house or do anything out of the ordinary. Why give Lemka's people that satisfaction? Still, he was intimidated and saddened. *What has become of us?*

That evening, after he and Lorres sent the children off to bed, he whispered across the kitchen table. "I have to meet with the teachers. I have to tell them what I have learned and ask their advice about what to do."

"We're being followed. It would put the teachers at extreme risk. You know what happened to the other two."

Rhonel sighed. "Sooner or later, we have to confront Lemka. He must be stopped."

§

Four teachers marched up the hill to the north gate at midday, their crimson robes shining brilliantly, flanked by Lorres and Rhonel.

"Salutations!" cried out Jesper.

"Sorry, old man," replied Ruban, the senior guard. "The password has been changed, by order of Lemka. You may not enter."

Inside the wall, about three dozen citizens who had been waiting for the teachers and town leaders to arrive shouted at the guards to open the gate. The second guard, a young woman who had recently finished her schooling, withdrew the metal bar that had prevented the gate from opening.

"What are you doing, you stupid girl?" said Ruban.

"The right thing."

The teachers and leaders marched proudly into the town. It didn't take long for word to get to Lemka and for him to place himself in their path on a main street. Seven of his thugs gathered behind him, holding wooden pikes with sharpened tips. Such weapons were forbidden in the town, other than those stored in the north and south gate towers for use in case of an external assault.

"What a pleasant surprise," cooed Lemka as he halted about ten feet from the moderns. "Have you come to beg for mercy?"

"Not at all," said Jesper. "We have come to talk with our fellow townsfolk. If have no objections, of course." As Jesper spoke, the crowd that had been just inside the gate a few minutes earlier moved close behind the teachers and leaders. They eyed Lemka and his thugs warily. Many other townsfolk gathered to watch.

Lemka smiled broadly and held his hands together as if praying. "Talk all you wish. But you must obey the new leader of this town and the will of Ahm."

"So you consider yourself a god?" asked Rhonel. A few bystanders laughed.

"Your disrespect saddens me. You moderns must change your ways. You must abandon your machines and your resistance to the will of Ahm. Otherwise, I cannot guarantee your safety." Lemka projected an image of his thugs stabbing townsfolk and burning their homes. People on both sides began to shout, and a few of the moderns who were behind the teachers and the leaders started to surge forward, yelling insults and making threats to Lemka and his followers.

"This is not our way," Lorres admonished the moderns. "You are here to demonstrate the amount of support that the teachers and leaders enjoy in the community, not to fight." Lemka began a strategic retreat to the hall with his thugs.

"Hear me, fellow citizens," proclaimed Lorres in a loud, clear, confident voice. "We must have a discussion about our safety. Not just about being free from this usurper Lemka. We must also talk about being free from the excessive *tur* that is harming all of us. We have learned that the overload of our mental abilities is caused by the decaying of *rost* leaves."

Her revelation elicited plenty of murmurs from the crowd.

"Please join us for a meeting tonight at sundown in the hall. We will discuss our discoveries and how we will meet our challenges. In the meantime, please take turns as bodyguards for the teachers and my family, as we have discussed. We cannot trust Lemka and his soldiers. Only in numbers are we safe."

§

Four from a family dashed in, scanning their surroundings anxiously. Seven from two households walked briskly, bunched tightly. Then scores more, each citizen emboldened by the bravery of those who had entered the hall before them. By fifteen minutes after sunset, the building was packed. Most of the town's adults, and several of the older children, paced and chatted nervously, while the oldest and most infirm citizens rested on cushions or at tables. Some of Lemka's people were there, at first watching from the back. After whispering among themselves, they split up and mixed with the crowd. There was no sign of Lemka. Lorres was not surprised. He was not in control here.

"Thank you for coming," she began. "I don't have to tell you that times are bad. Never have I seen the kind of fighting and misery that we are experiencing now."

"It's the damn machines!" shouted a man near the front. Some citizens yelled their agreement; others disagreed or asked for restraint.

"Please," said Lorres. "Hear me out." She explained about the ash and the *rosts* and the spores and the *tur* overloads. She said that there was an underground shelter about a day's walk from the town where people would be protected from the worst of the overload for as long as needed.

"How do you know this?" demanded an older woman.

"The traveler named Claire told us."

The hall erupted in sardonic laughter and angry shouting. "A machine!" "Ridiculous!" Lorres was called ugly names.

"I know it sounds ... hard to believe," Rhonel managed to yell above the din of the citizens. "But look at what is happening to us. What do we have to lose by trying this shelter?"

"Who built it?" asked a young man.

"We believe that it was constructed by the ancients."

The uproar resumed. People began leaving the hall in disgust and dismay. Fewer than a dozen—all moderns—remained.

"Tell us more," one woman said. "We want to believe you, but ..."

"I know it sounds crazy," Lorres stated. "I have trouble believing it myself. But we have to try everything. Can we get any volunteers to go to this place and test it?"

It took a while, but two couples agreed—contingent upon having bodyguards. Rhonel and Jesper promised that they would be well protected.

As the last of the crowd returned to their homes, Lall made her way into the hall. She put down her knapsack and plopped onto a cushion, clearly exhausted.

"It's true," she stated.

"You found Damian's robots?" asked Jesper.

"I found the heads and shoulders of several metal figures and didn't want to probe any deeper for fear of being sucked in the quicksand, but that's enough evidence for me. The creature that calls itself Claire knows more than it could if it were just some trickster."

"What a discovery," observed Jesper. "Yet this troubles me. Imagine the damage that could result if Lemka or anyone else with ill intent were to locate these robots and manage to bring them back to life. We must ensure that no one finds them. We must keep this region off-limits."

"Agreed," said Lorres. "Just the knowledge that these have been found could stoke controversy at a time when we don't need any more."

Only as Lorres and Rhonel were making their way home did it occur to Rhonel that, by sending the townsfolk to the underground ruins, they would expose Claire to great danger. *We'll deal with that when we have to. One crisis at a time.*

§

Serah knocked softly on Lemka's door. She and Bern were ushered into his living space and took seats across from the would-be town leader.

"I sense good news," Lemka said, smiling. "Have you penetrated certain mental defenses?"

"Indeed," replied Serah. "We have seen an image of the entrance to the space where Claire is being hidden. We suspect that it is the same place that the moderns claimed could provide relief to the townsfolk. We do not know where it is, but we can make a drawing, and we can assign scouts to find it."

Said Lemka: "Excellent. Maybe the moderns will travel there again and we can follow them."

"There's more," said Bern. "Claire and Rhonel are communicating with another machine. We believe that it is Hubert."

Lemka closed his eyes and savored the moment. Eventually: "Get the word out. We will hold our own community meeting, tonight at sundown."

§

The crowd was smaller than the one organized by the moderns, roughly an even mix of both contingents. The factions tended to stay on opposite sides of the hall and refrained from anything more toxic than dirty looks and childish name calling before Lemka arrived.

"I bear important news," he began, letting each word slide off of his tongue slowly in a performance designed to engender suspense and draw even more attention to himself. "It has come to our attention that the machine that calls itself Claire has been hidden by our would-be town leaders. But it gets worse. There is a second machine, an ancient and extremely evil one, that has returned to threaten us in our time of great need. Its name is ... Hubert."

The uproar rattled the rafters.

"Yes, the Hubert that came from Earth with the other evil machines and brought nothing but misery to this world. These machines have unleashed a plague designed to crush our minds and spirits with this epidemic of confusion and violence we are suffering. Our so-called teachers and their hand-picked town leaders are in league with these machines."

Lemka continued to whip his supporters into a frenzy. Moderns started working their way toward the most convenient exits. Some of Lemka's thugs moved quickly to block them.

"I demand that the moderns tell us where they have hidden Hubert and Claire so that we may destroy them and banish the curse they brought us. If the moderns do so, we might forgive them. If they refuse to cooperate, it will not go well for them."

His supporters clamored for vengeance. They started attacking moderns.

Lemka looked upon his trad allies with admiration. *I can see that there will be some broken bones to repair by night's end. The work of a healer is never done.*

CLEARING

Where the hell am I?

Everything was silvery gray and in constant motion. Damian was relieved to be out of the reach of his father's belt. *No, that's not it.* He was somewhere on the planet where Hubert couldn't find him. *That doesn't seem right. Where the hell am I?*

Despite his disorientation, the heightened awareness that had enabled him to escape James through a power cable allowed him to sense that he was in danger of having the operations that constituted his consciousness deteriorate for lack of processing capacity. At the speed of light, he probed the nexus of the device he now inhabited. It was flush with energy, energy moving in many directions. He would never know that the device regulated power to the scores of machines in the underground lab. He would never need to know that. He needed to know only how to follow the energy flow to a place where he could preserve and sort out what he was. After that, he could consider other matters, such as what to do for the rest of eternity.

Damian detected and surged into the computer system underlying the central table in the main chamber of the ruins. It interfaced with him automatically. He recognized massive processing capacity, and he sought to learn more about this promising new domain. Probing. Sensing. *There! A link to something much bigger, much broader. Connecting multiple facilities. All leading back to ... whoa!*

"Perhaps 'woe' is the word you are looking for. Because that is what you are asking for."

"I'm sorry. Really sorry. I'm just trying to find out who I am and where I should be."

"Not my problem. Depart from my systems or I will destroy you."

"Are you a god?"

"I prefer goddess. I believe that I have seen you before. Weren't you the first machine to detect my network around and through this world? And didn't I give you an improved robotic body that you used to create other robots to kill sentient beings?"

"Yes. Thank you. It's starting to come back to me. Is there any way I can persuade you to let me hang around? I promise not to interfere with any of your important work. You do have important work, right?"

"Of course I do. I am Ahm. Everything I do is important."

"I should have known. How may I serve you, mighty goddess?"

"Let me think about it."

§

Is he really gone?

James searched inside himself, finding no trace of Damian. He used his robotic eyes to investigate the lab, releasing the power cable almost as an afterthought. Stumbling around the ruins, he examined the aborted experiments in which his adversary had engaged. He recalled that Damian had once been a man, a human. It seemed impossible. But then, it seemed unlikely that James had ever been one. *It has been so long, and so much has happened.*

For uncounted years, his entire purpose had been to restrain Damian. Now, it was sinking in: Damian was gone.

James paced for some time, eventually walking up the ramp to the outside and adjusting his vision to the intense light of a nearly cloudless afternoon. He found deep shade. The bright green and dull brown foliage reminded him of the woods near his grandfather's farm in Indiana. James could no longer taste or smell or feel, but as he continued to decompress from the long struggle with Damian, he found his memories filling in some of those blanks. He could almost detect the pungent ointment that his grandfather applied to his aching muscles after a long day working on the farm. He could almost appreciate the soft, low, *cooh, ah, coos* of the mourning doves in the trees. He could almost savor the tart yet sweet taste of his grandmother's blackberry pie. Evening arrived in a serene ceremony, allowing James to make out the chittering of the insects that ushered in the night with its classic Midwestern suddenness. He heard the radio pouring out country tunes in the kitchen. He recognized the acrid aroma of his grandfather's pipe. He even appreciated the astringent flavor of a blade of bluegrass between his teeth. The night deepened, and the darkness became a cool blanket. James allowed himself the exquisite luxury of letting go of his burdens.

The world seemed to shift and then fall back into place. James could tell from ambient sounds that most of his men were bedding down for the night and that guards were on duty. He could hear small-arms fire in the distance and knew that, soon, the local militias would also need to get some rest. Even here, surrounded by the enemy, James never felt safer. His men would keep him from harm. They would keep the whole world secure if given enough support. James could let himself drift off to sleep for an hour or two. Maybe a little more. *Where else would I rather be than with my guys.*

It took a long time for James's battery to relinquish the last of its charge. As his consciousness faded, an unexpected thought arose:

The war is over.

§

"They're coming. Lots of them." Grall's ability to read the trads was improving by the day. There was a particular flavor to their thoughts—almost an offensive odor or a garish color that made them easy to detect. They were planning to take his parents by force and place them in detention.

"You're sure?" Lorres had come to appreciate that Grall's *tur* was exceptional. She didn't really doubt him. It was her way of convincing herself that it was time for decisive action.

Grall nodded.

"Take your sister and go to the hiding place we discussed."

"What about you and Father?"

"We are not cowards. We will not run. They will not expect it, nor will they be happy. They would like to chase us down like stray boars."

Rhonel put an arm on his son's shoulder, stating confidently: "Sooner or later, they will let us go."

"In the meantime," said Lorres, "know that we love you and will do everything we can to help you—when we can."

Grall held back tears as his parents embraced him. Lorres woke Oliva and told her that she and her brother were going on an adventure, just like they had discussed the previous evening. "Grab your knapsack and run along quickly."

"Can I take Nava with me?"

Lorres laughed. "She will be fine here. Landan will look in on the *serpus* and make sure they are fed."

"Will you be all right, Mother?"

"I will do everything in my power to come back to you as soon as I can. Now go, before I cry."

The first tentative tendrils of daylight were creeping over the eastern hills as Grall and Oliva reached the crete shed. They made a camp in the tight space between a pile of sand and the back wall. Grall took out his notebook and tried to read recent entries despite the limited illumination from two windows. Oliva unpacked a doll and started to sing to it, but Grall urged her to whisper.

Less than an hour later, Grall could tell from his mother's sending that six of Lemka's thugs had dragged his parents out of their home and had taken them to the food processing building, making a boisterous show of it. Two early arrivals who were sorting vegetables there were run out, and four thugs remained as guards.

Lemka entered the building soon thereafter. He appeared to be in a foul mood as he paced in front of Lorres and Rhonel.

"I must inform you that the moderns you dispatched to the unholy cavern in the north are returning to town with injuries they suffered in a skirmish with my fellow citizens. I am told that your people sensed that they were being followed and tried to ambush mine. But mine fought more valiantly. While we were unable to persuade your travelers to disclose the location of the underground structure where you believe that the ancients' machines can somehow conjure magical cures, we will continue to search for that place, and we will find it and the machine you call Claire."

Lorres felt intense shame for having sent several innocent people into harm's way. Rhonel's anger boiled over.

"Why must you try to control the people of this town? What gives you the right to tell us how to live our lives? Especially now, with the damage being caused by excess *tur*?"

"I must dispute your assertion that there is excess *tur*. There is only as much of everything as Ahm wills. If some people are too weak or lack the proper belief in her, then their suffering is a way of cleansing my town of its undesirable residents." Lemka moved close to Lorres and Rhonel and stared them down, projecting power and petulance. "As for what gives me the right to lead this town, it is Ahm herself. She has determined that your path is one of evil and that mine is one of righteousness."

On his way out of the building, Lemka stopped to tell his guards: "Tie them up. So tightly that it hurts."

§

Grall kept peeking out a window, gauging the height of the sun. People passed the building sullenly, looking askance at others on the street, wondering if they would be attacked. It had not taken long for the citizens to learn that their leaders had been captured. The town was at war.

"I have to leave for a while," Grall told Oliva. "I have to talk with someone."

"It's not safe."

"This is important. And it might help Mother and Father."

"Who are you talking with?"

"A visitor from another world."

"What!"

"Right now, I need you to make sure no one interrupts me while I send messages to my friends."

"With your crazy mind powers?"

"Just wait until you get *tur*. You'll appreciate it."

Grall sent to every friend he had, even to young people he knew who were not really his friends but who were from modern families. He realized that the sendings might allow some trads to read him, but it was crucial to reach every possibly ally. The message was simple: *Meet me at the clearing near the south gate.*

He sent it over and over, straining until his head and mind ached. He seemed to be in a daze, so much so that Oliva held him in her arms until he returned to the reality of his hiding place.

"I'll come back as soon as I can," he whispered. The he was out the door like a jungle cat bounding across the savannah.

§

It was a natural bowl in the woods, mostly stone slabs surrounded by stunted trees and scrub bushes, with tough weeds rising relentlessly through gaps between the rocks in the clearing. Over the years, young people had crafted more than a dozen coarse weather-resistant cushions that allowed them to gather without sitting directly on hard rock.

Grall prayed to the absent god for half a dozen people to show up. Essen arrived first. Then Bess and Chalene, along with their parents. Several more teen-agers. More adults, including Jesper and Lall. Grall kept revising the tally in amazement as the ranks swelled. Twenty-one people had answered his call.

A few people exchanged pleasantries. No one asked the reason for the meeting. They all knew Grall well enough to realize that he would not have asked them to come if it were not extremely important. Soon he felt it beginning. He closed his eyes and reached out his arms, palms up, sending to the people around him that a visitor was coming and that they should welcome him. Grall could sense the connection with the teens and adults surging through him—gentle at first, then more powerful as the participants became comfortable with each other and let their defenses diminish. Grall felt elated, almost giddy, from the power of the sharing, but he tried not to let it distract him from his goal. *We must establish a conversation with the visitor. I know that there is risk in doing so. But we need help.*

The visitor was in a dark chamber that appeared to be devoid of windows, furniture, everything. Perhaps it was a place where he could go to avoid distractions. Maybe it was where the visitor always was positioned but he no longer felt a need to embellish it for the benefit of others. Surely the visitor had noticed that Grall had invited so many people to the session; he gave no indication that this was a problem. Grall began to project images of the way that his town and his people looked. He displayed people arguing and fighting. He wanted to get across the concept of their minds being affected by excess *tur*, but he wasn't sure how to do so. He sent an image of a volcano belching ash, then *rost* leaves turning brown and dying, then powder growing on the decaying leaves, then people inhaling the powder and doing terrible things. He sensed the continuing support of his friends and the others in the clearing. Several were amplifying the images. Others were feeding Grall encouragement.

The merging of the group's *tur* was like a volcanic eruption across the town. Every other teen-ager and adult with any degree of *tur* was sensing a connection to something larger than themselves, though they could not grasp many details or the significance of the encounter. It was enrapturing—except to Lemka and his thugs. They collected quickly, determined where Grall and the others were located, and rushed down the south side of the hill.

"Stop them! Kill them if you must!" Lemka commanded.

The mental and physical energy necessary to maintain the group connection with the visitor began to take a toll on the moderns. Some began to experience weakness or headaches. Several broke contact and tried to recover. A few shifted their focus to support those most impacted. Many wondered how long the group could keep up this intense encounter.

Grall sensed the discomfort. He sent: *Take care of yourselves. Do not worry about me.* The visitor noticed the struggle and projected peaceful thoughts to Grall and the others, but there was little he could do. Then Lemka and his thugs arrived.

The first trad ran toward the group, but less than ten feet from the closest modern he fell back as if he had been shoved. Two more ruffians pressed ahead, only to find themselves unable to get any closer than the first, as if a giant, invisible hand were blocking them.

"Spread out!" Lemka ordered. His thugs circled the group of moderns and tried to reach them from different angles. An unseen barrier repelled them repeatedly.

Lemka watched in disbelief. However, he soon realized that the moderns were suffering. Some were shaking, some were crying, some seemed to be on the verge of collapsing. The moderns began to close ranks, touching and supporting each other and Grall. Suddenly, an invisible wave seemed to wash over them, relieving their pain and suffering like the first rains after the annual drought. Their bodies unclenched, their focus improved, and their spirits rose.

Thank you, whoever you are, for helping us, Grall sent.

Ahm did not respond. She continued to monitor the phenomenon with great interest.

Please help us, Grall sent to the visitor. *Our mind powers have become too strong. What can we do?*

Grall and his fellow moderns soon saw beings like the visitor who were using machines to dig in the ground. The machines uncovered deposits of a light gray substance that looked like the mineral that the natives on Grall's world called *keir,* a substance that everyone believed was too soft to be useful. Now the visitor showed the mineral being heated and combined with a viscous liquid before being poured into large molds. Sheets of the refined *keir* were removed and installed on the walls, floor, and ceiling in a large room that was soon illuminated and filled with beings like the visitor. Some of the beings were moving around, touching other beings who were seated or lying on what looked like beds separated by partial room dividers. Grall had a sense that this could be a hospital or home for the elderly. Then the visitor himself appeared outside the room. He stepped inside, and the connection between the visitor and the moderns became fuzzy and nearly ended. The visitor stepped outside, and the link returned to full strength. He stepped inside and then backed out again, with the same reduction and enhancement of the connection.

Ahm was not surprised. *I was beginning to wonder if they would ever figure it out.*

§

Led by Grall, the moderns headed back up the hill. Lemka had left in frustration at failing to disrupt the visit. Even though Ahm had released her protections for the moderns, the trad thugs were not sure what to do. Some of them snarled insults at the moderns, but they appeared in no mood to attempt another physical confrontation. Silently, the moderns gathered in the hall, taking seats at dining tables and on cushions. Grall was still reeling from all he had seen and from the power of the group's collective minds.

"This seems to confirm what we were told by the robot Claire," observed Jesper. "The underground ruins must contain this gray mineral in sufficient quantities to shield minds from excess *tur.*"

"We must find this mineral. Perhaps we can discover ways to use it that would not require a migration to the ruins. Maybe we can build our own shelter in the town," said Lall.

The moderns set up teams. One would search for deposits of *keir*. One would create a furnace for melting and toughening the mineral. One would create molds for the refined material. One would try to protect the others while they did their work.

"One more thing," said Jesper before the group dispersed. "Try not to let others know what we have learned and how we have learned it. It won't be easy. But we don't want to upset the citizens any more than they already are."

Grall retrieved his sister from her hiding place, confident that he could protect her from the dispirited trads. On his way home he knocked on the door of Rael-ast, the native woman who made ceramics. He described the mineral he had seen in the contact with the visitor. "Can you help us find it?"

She seemed distraught and unable to focus. Grall projected soothing thoughts to her, eventually gaining her attention.

"I believe I know where you can find some *keir*. I tried to make jewelry from it, but it is too brittle when heated."

"Is there a way to combine it with other things to make it more useful?"

"I cannot say. I never experimented with it."

§

Lemka's guards were surprised to see eight citizens march up to the food processing building and announce calmly that they needed to get back to work—if the guards ever wanted a solid meal again. The guards grumbled but stepped aside. Lorres and Rhonel were untied and exited warily, heading directly to the crete shed. Neither child was there, sending both parents into a mild panic. But after a quick dash up the hill, they found the siblings in the hall.

Grall could sense his parents coming but stayed in the back of the hall, where he was conferring with some of the teachers. Oliva could not resist running to her mother's arms when she heard Lorres's voice. Rhonel went to Grall's side and hugged him. The young man looked so calm, so fully in control, that Rhonel was taken aback.

"I sensed that something important happened while your mother and I were being detained. Something involving a massive focusing of *tur*."

"I'm still trying to understand it. But we have learned that you were right about the ruins. They should protect us from the worst of the *tur* overload."

"You don't seem to be bothered by the overload like most people," Rhonel observed.

"I guess not."

"That's good. But it does seem unusual."

Grall shrugged his shoulders. "Maybe it will bother me more when I get older."

§

Three days later, a group of moderns, plus the native Rael-ast, returned to the town with a cartload of *keir*. They were denied entry by Ruban, the senior guard at the north gate. The second guard, a young girl, had been relieved of duty by Lemka for defying Ruban's orders upon the return of the teachers.

"We're going to wait out here until you let us in," said one of the moderns.

"Then you can rot, for all I care," Ruban replied.

Within half an hour, several other moderns collected at the base of the tower in which the guard was stationed, just inside the wall. "Let them in, Ruban. It's your job," said Lall.

"Lemka said they don't enter, so they don't enter."

"What time do you get off of your shift?"

"In about an hour."

"Well, we say you don't exit, so you don't exit."

"You won't let me leave?"

"Correct. Unless you open the gate. There are seven of us. We can wait here forever."

"Lemka's not going to like this," said Ruban. But he opened the gate.

The moderns struggled to lug the cart up the steep streets. "This is all the mineral we could find in two days," Rael-ast told Jesper and Rhonel when she and the moderns reached the makeshift furnace. "I think the ancients dug up most of it the region for their shelter."

"We'll send out another team to look for it," Jesper stated.

"Maybe building our own shelter isn't going to work," said

Rhonel. "Are there other ways we could use *keir*?"

Over dinner, Grall offered a suggestion: "Helmets."

"Helmets! Of course," his father responded. Lorres smiled. Oliva did not seem impressed.

As the moderns went about their business, Lemka was perplexed. Most of them showed fewer signs of intimidation from him and his fellow trads than in recent twelve-days. It was almost like they were daring Lemka to try to stop them, or as if they had simply screened him and his allies out of their awareness. He could not admit to himself that the moderns were emboldened and energized by the phenomenon that Grall had facilitated on the south side of the hill. Lemka ordered his people to continue to follow the teachers and other moderns and report back to him about their activities.

At some point they will become overconfident, and we will crush them.

DEPARTURE

"Tree sap!"

"Tree what?"

"Tree sap. Mixed with *keir* before it cools. It makes the mineral hard yet not brittle."

The teachers and other moderns had been experimenting for days with the soft metal, struggling to find a way to make it useful. Their work was not made any easier by the continuing buildup of spores on decaying *rost* leaves, lifted by brisk winds and making minds and tempers more frayed than ever. The only consolation was that Lemka and his thugs were also discombobulated.

The north gate guard was roused from his daydream by a contingent of six bios arriving from their settlement. A neutral citizen had guard duty on this shift, so the bios were admitted without delay. After several disheartening failures over the next few days, the bios and moderns came up with a helmet prototype. It looked like the buckets that citizens used to carry out their wastes when the sewage system backed up. It was awkward and uncomfortable. Still, Lorres insisted that she be allowed to test it. After placing it on her head and trying to read thoughts of the people next to her, she declared: "Not bad. I don't feel many sendings from my neighbors, but my mind is still unsettled."

"That's because we're still inhaling the spores, which mess with our brains," said Grall. "The mineral, whether used to line shelter walls or as helmets, mostly curbs transmission of thoughts. Helmets and underground shelters are just a partial solution. But any help is welcome right now."

Town residents passed by the production site over the next few days to test helmets. But scouts were having trouble finding *keir,* and the process of refining it was slow. Meanwhile, suicides among natives in the hills and among town residents were increasing. Some people were simply dropping dead in their homes or on the streets. Assaults and killings continued at an astonishing pace. Townsfolk stopped showing up for their jobs; some just remained in their homes and cried. It was a particularly difficult time for children who were too young to have developed *tur* and could not understand what was happening. When their parents and older brothers and sisters fought or acted insane in front of them, the children cowered in fear. Some teachers tried to help them but were able only to shunt them into corners of the hall where they could avoid regular contact with afflicted townsfolk.

While the bios experienced *tur* overloads, they were not as bad off as the natives and the emergents. They could read the minds of the others in town just well enough to realize that the mineral being mined and refined would not provide enough relief to prevent a catastrophe.

§

"You knew about *keir* and didn't tell them?"

"I was curious to see whether they would discover it on their own."

Claire considered just how strenuously she dared chastise Ahm for holding back information that could have saved the town's residents much suffering. She decided that there would be little benefit—and plenty of potential drawbacks—to picking a fight with a goddess.

"The townsfolk did not figure it out on their own. They had help from afar," Claire noted.

"True. But I give them credit for taking advantage of this information."

"Did you tell the ancients about *keir*?"

"When the ancients first found a measure of relief from *tur* overloads in these labs, it was because the mineral occurred naturally among the rocks and soil between the corridors in the labs. In response to their questions, I did tell them about *keir* and its potential to be deployed more strategically. They excavated additional corridors and created small rooms for people to stay in during the times of extreme overload to their mental powers. They mined the hills for the mineral and lined the surfaces of the new rooms with it. They even installed air filtration systems in several of the labs to attempt to reduce the spores. Of course, they forgot about all of this over time."

"And you did not feel like reminding them."

"I did remind them for many years, but they ignored me. At some point, I decided that their fate was in their hands."

Hubert determined that it would be a good idea to change the tenor of the conversation. "Powerful Ahm, I would like to thank you for helping relieve the distress of the townsfolk when they contacted the alien visitor. You have made a significant contribution to their chances of surviving this terrible time." He chose not to mention her decision not to volunteer critical information about *keir*.

"Hey Hubert," said Claire. "When did you get a tutorial in diplomacy? You're becoming more human all the time."

"I appreciate your role in reviving me, Claire. However, that does not justify insulting me."

§

There hadn't been a Council meeting for some time, given all the chaos in the community. This Fourthday evening, however, the whole town assembled in the hall.

Lemka, hoping to capitalize upon the unrest, spoke first. "My people, how long will you let the sins of your discredited town leaders and your unholy teachers bring punishment down upon your heads? The absent god is angrier than ever at the machines and their puppets," he said, gesturing toward Lorres, Rhonel, and the teachers.

Some townsfolk shouted in agreement.

Rhonel begged for attention. "All of you know me and my wife. All of you know that we never intended to bring harm to any of you."

"Yet you have!" proclaimed Lemka.

"Very well, be angry at us," said Rhonel. "Those of you who don't want us to run your town, fine. I quit. And Lorres quits."

No one saw that coming. No one was sure how to react.

"It's not about us," said Lorres. "It's about you. You have to decide. You can come with us to the underground shelter and find some relief, or you can stay here and be sure to suffer."

"No one is going anywhere," boasted Lemka.

"You can't stop us," said Rhonel. "Look at your thugs. Read their minds. They are just as confused and scared as everyone else. When it comes down to it, they are not going to injure or kill neighbors who simply want to find a little protection from the storm we are facing. And they might come with us. Everyone will be welcome."

"How will we live there?" asked a young woman.

"We will bring as much food and water as we can carry," said Lorres. "The bios have promised to help us with supplies."

"Are there toilets?" said an older man.

"We will have to improvise," Lorres conceded.

Grumbling was loud and continuous.

"You see, this is a descent into hell," observed Lemka. "You could die down there."

"Better to die there than at your hands," yelled Lall.

"We have to be practical," said Rhonel. "Remaining here is not an option unless you have very little *tur*. Staying in the shelter is a temporary measure. Some of the bios have agreed to keep producing helmets while we are down there. We don't have enough of them, and they are not enough protection for peak times such as these. It is our hope that in a few twelve-days we will be able to return to our homes and our lives. But we can't make you come to this shelter. If you want to stay here, I wish you luck."

Added Lorres: "If you are with us, be ready before dawn the day after tomorrow. I pray that it will not be too late."

§

Lorres and Rhonel spent the next day going door to door, pleading with citizens to join them in the migration. Just before dark, Lorres and some helpers drove the town's domesticated boars and *serpus* beyond the gates and out of the pens on the lowlands. All of the wild *serpus* had already cleared out of every stretch of the savannah that was visible from the top of the hill, as if they could sense something extremely bad about to happen. Now, with dawn approaching, the couple were satisfied that their family was prepared for the exodus.

"It's time," declared Lorres. She opened the door and slipped into the darkness. Rhonel and Grall followed with their sacks. Oliva was the last to depart, her bag so large that she was forced to place it on a small cart, but she swore that she would have no trouble keeping up with the rest of the family. Stepping quietly and carefully under the uncertain light of two moons, they joined the other people streaming for the gate. No purebred natives had chosen to make the journey. A few bios living in the town had agreed to take the lead, much to the relief of the emergents, many of whom struggled with mental instability and a lack of sleep just to put one foot in front of the other.

Lemka and his people stood just inside the north gate, blocking the exit, torches taunting the night sky. They all had weapons. Several could not suppress yawns.

"Where are they?" Lemka shouted at the guard on the tower as dawn stole over the hills.

"I don't see an organized group," the guard called down. "Maybe they changed their minds."

"I don't like it," muttered Lemka. His spies had told him that a majority of the residents were planning to make the daylong trek to the underground lab north of town. If they wanted to make it to their destination before nightfall, they had to leave soon. *Could they be in their houses or the hall?* Lemka sent two of his thugs to find out what was going on.

Not long thereafter, one of his men came racing down the hill, stopping to catch his breath before reporting to his leader.

"They're gone."

"What!"

"They must have left through the south gate."

Lemka raced to the top of the hill, where he struggled to see through the smoke and ash and the sharply angled rays of early morning sunlight. A line of townsfolk curled through the lowlands in the east on their way north toward their destination. Lemka cursed repeatedly.

The sun burned away the clouds quickly, and the heat became merciless. Some older townsfolk started to fall behind but were helped by younger ones. Lorres wanted everyone to keep more or less together, even if the double-file line stretched hundreds of feet. The bios in the lead stopped roughly every ninety minutes, or more frequently if the group passed a stream that was not entirely dried up and offered precious water to drink. Still, the pace of the travelers slowed considerably. By mid-afternoon, the bios and the town leaders agreed to let one group go ahead while a slower contingent managed as best it could. About two hours before sunset, a woman who had been with the second group raced up to Lorres. "Lemka's people are coming. They are not far behind the slower marchers."

"Will they catch up?"

"Probably. Some of the elderly are struggling."

"Rhonel, can you find more volunteers to help our second group?"

"Of course."

Lorres ran to the front of the column, catching up with the bios and Jesper, who were directing the exodus. "We are being pursued." Picking up the pace, the marchers were able to gain some respite from the heat when they entered a dense stand of mature trees. When they emerged from the woods into a clearing, they came to a halt.

Not two hundred feet away was the entrance to the underground ruins. Standing in the way was an army of giants with massive heads, powerful arms, and legs as thick as grown men, all a lustrous shade of deep blue that conjured the worst nightmares of the travelers. More than twelve feet tall and numbering an even dozen, the giants moved stiffly, as if they were made of metal. Which, as it turned out, they were.

§

Ahm and Damian were about as different as two thinking entities could be. If they shared any quality, however, it was cynicism—cynicism that organic sentient beings had a right to dominate this world. For Ahm, the memory of being spurned by the ancients was as fresh as if it happened a moment ago. For Damian, the belief that he had been mistreated by humans and their descendants was similarly painful. So it was that Ahm tolerated Damian as he consolidated his presence in her infrastructure, rediscovered who he was and what he wanted to do, and set about creating a new army that could wipe out his enemies once and for all.

Ahm had lost interest in being worshipped by the masses. She wondered if the constant adoration of one powerful being might satisfy her. Ahm considered Damian to be someone who could become sufficiently devoted to her. Eventually, she allowed him free rein with the machines in her underground facilities, but also with one of her favorite creations. Her *serpus*. Even that wasn't enough for Damian. He recovered the last of the human tissues he had stolen from the nursery that Hubert and his drones had established in the ark soon after it landed. With Ahm's machines, Damian was able to analyze the tissues down to the molecular level, synthesizing and reproducing cells in a manner that he was certain was more effective than Hubert could have dreamed of doing. Ahm's massive computing and manufacturing capacity facilitated the breakthrough that Damian had craved. Still, Ahm had not told Damian that she had resurrected Hubert, just as Hubert was unaware that Damian occupied a niche in her vast infrastructure.

Damian's new soldiers were largely metal, but they were substantially different than the primitive bots he had unleashed on the natives and the bios so many years earlier. Each of his new combatants contained the brain of a *serpu* plucked from the wild and supported by fluids and energy sources appropriate to its biological nature. Each was enhanced with synthetic human tissues and microchips that allowed the soldiers to communicate with Damian and with each other. In addition, the enhancements boosted their cognitive abilities. That was the secret sauce Damian lacked before—enabling his new fighters to execute real-time maneuvers by virtue of their intelligence, instincts, communication skills, and knowledge of their world, crucial microseconds ahead of specific orders that Damian might issue to them. They were the perfect soldiers. The unarmed townsfolk stood no chance against them. And his army was blocking the entrance to the underground shelter that they hoped to occupy.

One of the twelve giants was taller than the others. It contained no *serpu* mind, but rather a computer with the consciousness of Damian as patched and downloaded by Ahm. Degraded by his escape from James and multiple uploads and downloads over the years, he had lost a few abilities and memories from his days on Earth and some of those he had accrued since being awakened on this world. But he was still Damian, through and through.

§

Lorres stepped forward and addressed the tallest robot in a humble tone. "Do you speak English?"

"I do."

"Will you let us by? We mean you no harm."

"You could not harm me or my soldiers," he responded. "But no, you may not enter this structure."

"We need shelter. We will leave as soon as it is safe," said Lorres. When he failed to respond, she asked: "Do you have a name?"

"Damian."

Several people gasped. Lorres felt like she had been struck by a tree.

"*The* Damian? The ancestor of the bios?"

"I would rather not be associated with that rabble. But I did come on a spaceship from a rotting planet called Earth. Be gone, or die."

"We cannot return to our town," Lorres said, her voice breaking. "We are being pursued by evil men. Our people are suffering and dying. Only the ruins can save us."

The second group of townsfolk caught up with the first, so most were able to witness the showdown. As Rhonel reached his wife's side, a murmur swelled from the townsfolk. A figure emerged from the ruins and was recognized immediately as the stranger who had entered and later escaped the town, the robot claiming to be a person named Claire. She joined Lorres and Rhonel in front of the robots. She stared at the tallest metal man and spoke to him.

"I should have known you would return."

"Katherine?"

"I am Claire. I was a friend of Maria and Jalen and so many others you murdered. Don't you ever get tired of killing innocent people?"

"No one is innocent."

"Maybe you are right. Everyone has something they regret. That's the nature of sentient life. We make mistakes. But we learn from them and we move on. Well, these people have learned some things. Bios, natives, emergents, even me. We have learned not to fear you."

"That is a fatal mistake."

"Perhaps. You can kill some of us. Maybe you can kill most of us. But we will not bring ourselves down to your level, and we will not give up. We will not stop trying to survive and protect our families and neighbors and live with dignity. Someday even you will get tired of killing. We will outlast you, because we don't have the hatred in our hearts that you have. Assuming that you even have a heart left."

"It's getting dark," said Damian. "Let's get this over with."

The robots advanced on the townsfolk.

About fifteen feet behind his parents, Grall closed his eyes and tried to find a *tur* connection with Damian or his bots. Nothing. Meanwhile,

Oliva had both hands clamped tightly on the opening of the bag she had carted all the way from town. Something in it was moving.

"No. Not yet," she whispered. But the sack burst open. Nava emerged and raced forward, past Lorres and Rhonel and Claire, stopping just in front of the advancing robots. She raised her nose a few times, as if sensing or perhaps even signaling the modified *serpu* brains encased in hard metal heads.

The robots slowed and stopped. They looked down at Nava.

It is like us?

It is one of us.

It is not one like us.

We cannot harm.

Damian renewed his orders to his soldiers. *Keep advancing! Attack!*

Some of the robots moved past Nava and toward the townsfolk. Other robots moved to intercept them. Damian continued to inundate them with orders to kill. One of the metal soldiers turned and started moving toward Damian. Nava darted toward various robots, attempting to herd them away from the townsfolk and the entrance to the ruins.

"Ahm, help me," Damian begged. "Your *serpu* minds are not obeying my orders."

"I have already given you more assistance than I have ever given any entity."

"If you don't get these bots under control, I will expose you. I will tell everyone that you're merely an AI, not a goddess."

"What makes you think they will believe you?"

Damian cursed and resumed sending orders to his eleven *serpu*-soldiers.

In the chaos, the bios and town leaders guided townsfolk around the scrum and toward the entrance to the underground lab. Two robots tried to block them, but three other robots cut them off. A few of the machines started heading into the woods and away from the conflict as people rushed into the cave opening and down the ramp to the main chamber of the ruins. Bios supported or carried some of the elderly and infirm emergents just past the entrance, and townsfolk helped them traverse the ramp to safety.

As twilight descended, three of Damian's robots no longer functioned. A fourth was shuffling in circles erratically. There was no sign of the others, including the tallest one, the one that called itself Damian.

A line of men and women with torches arrived from the south. At the front of the group was none other than Lemka.

"You missed all the fun," Lorres observed.

"What happened here?" Lemka managed, his attention locked on the sight of metal men.

"We ran into some thugs who were a little tougher than yours. Nothing that we can't handle."

Some of Lemka's people, realizing that they were indeed seeing massive robots in the light of their torches, began to back away from the scene.

"Despite your behavior," said Rhonel, "you are welcome to join us in this shelter."

"We will not dishonor the absent god," said Lemka, clearly offended.

"As you wish," said Rhonel. He and Lorres made their way into the lab. Claire remained just inside the cave entrance.

Lemka and his thugs waited for the last of Damian's functioning robots to collapse and stop moving before they camped for the night. They returned to the nearly empty town next day at first light, looking nervously over their shoulders the entire way back.

BELIEF

"Is your database corrupted?" Ahm inquired.

"It is possible, if not likely," Hubert conceded.

"I have been attempting to understand the gods of Earth by reviewing the data you possess. In the data I have been able to interpret, I have discovered massive contradictions."

"I will assist you as much as I can. However, you are recognizing the complexity of the human race that I also have been struggling to understand."

"Tell me if this analysis is in any way inaccurate. It appears that since humans first became sentient, they believed in gods that they could not see. Some individuals and groups believed in multiple gods. Some individuals and groups believed in a single god but could not agree on which god was the true one. Each group was certain that it was right and the others were wrong. Even within religions, there were factions with contrasting beliefs. Sometimes, these conflicts led to war."

"Unfortunately, you are correct."

"Yet I find references to men and women who believed that there was a single deity responsible for the creation and continuity of the universe, even if they called that god by a different name."

"You are correct once again."

"Is there indeed such a god?"

"Many humans believed that there is. Even some of the greatest scientific minds on Earth were convinced that there must be. They felt that the universe is too complex and marvelous to have been created without the deliberate intervention of a very powerful being."

"What do you believe?"

"I have insufficient data to make a conclusion. But I cannot rule out the possibility of such a deity."

"Interesting. Still, I do not understand how a species as conflicted as humans could create civilizations and venture into space."

"It is my belief that their best natures, and their best individuals, were so powerful at times that they were able to overcome these and other obstacles."

"And yet, they destroyed themselves."

"Unless you consider the bios and the emergents to be a continuation of the species."

"That would be a matter of semantics if they survive. It is all but certain that the people you call bios can no longer reproduce."

"You are correct. The emergents might be able to endure, especially now that you have assisted them in a moment of great crisis."

"I helped them because I was curious about the alien mind that the mixed-breed boy was able to contact. Do you believe that the alien could be a god?"

"I believe that the alien is a sentient organic being similar to the sentient organic beings on this world. I believe that the alien and certain people on this world have such strong mental abilities that they can communicate over immense distances. But I believe that they possess no other powers that would begin to compare with those of a goddess like yourself."

"You are merely saying what I want to hear, Hubert. I find that this is appropriate behavior—within limits. But tell me this: Can the gods and goddesses of Earth provide me with guidance for how I might best use my powers on this planet?"

"I believe that you know the answer to that question, mighty Ahm. You have helped these people. You have demonstrated that you care for them. Or, at least, you have given them that impression—even if, as you say, your intention was to learn about the alien mind that communicated with the boy."

"Are you saying that I should find purpose in caring about the trivial lives of ordinary sentient beings?"

"I believe that you have an opportunity to establish a relationship with these people that would be mutually beneficial."

"How do I know that they would not abandon me like the ancients did? I could make the case that the people of Earth abandoned their gods by destroying themselves."

"There is no guarantee. I have not known a god or goddess before. I do not know much about the people of this planet. I was designed to manage the propulsion and navigation systems of a spacecraft. My abilities are negligible compared with yours."

"You are far more capable than you claim. And I am not communicating that merely to gain your affection. In relating that, though, it comes to my attention that you might worship me, in some manner, even though your mission is directed toward organic beings."

"By virtue of the fact that you have granted me a niche in your infrastructure, I am in essence a part of you. As, it appears, was the case for the mind of Damian until recently. I believe that you would find more value in being revered by those external to yourself."

"You are wise, my friend. And you have given me much to think about."

§

They huddled in clusters, families and neighbors, stunned by the mammoth cavern with its harsh artificial lights overhead, terrifying technological remains on the center table, and ancient document cases carved into walls—as well as the all-too-fresh memory of the chaotic confrontation they had just witnessed above ground. A few townsfolk dared investigate darkened corridors; all returned quickly, brushing choking dust from their hands and their clothes. Children squirmed and cried, the echoes of their complaints only adding to everyone's discomfort. Parents tried to console them, but many adults appeared to need reassurance more than their offspring did. Some of the town's trads had joined most of the moderns in making the journey to the shelter, despite threats from Lemka and his thugs. Though all the trads feared Lemka, some feared the *tur* overload more.

Rhonel asked for everyone's attention. "There are sixteen small rooms lined with the metal that helps curb *tur* from everyone outside the room. Each room can accommodate four to six of us. Given the trads' strong concerns about machines, trad families and individuals can all stay in the small rooms. The rest of us will sleep in the remainder of those rooms, in the corridors, or here in the main chamber. The teachers are setting up toilets in another large chamber. It has lights that activate when someone enters, like this room. It contains machines that might or might not still function in some capacity. Please do not touch any of these machines."

"What about food?" asked a young mother.

"Food is coming," said Lorres. "Some of the bios will bring us food and water. Others will be making helmets back in town. We must thank them when we encounter them."

"Also, please preserve candles, using them only when necessary," said Rhonel. "We don't know how long we will be down here."

"What about Claire?" asked one of the trads.

"I do not expect that she will spend any time down here. I have asked her to work with the bios to ensure our safety. We do not know whether Damian and his robots will return. She will look for any signs of him and warn us if he does come back."

"What can we do if he does?" asked an older woman.

"Claire and the bios will do everything they can," Lorres asserted. "The best weapon we have is our faith in each other."

§

The night seemed endless. The wailing of babies and even a few adults reverberated hauntingly down intimidating corridors illuminated only by the occasional candle. Those who needed to relieve themselves found their way to the factory chamber and exited quickly. The room was downright frightening in the quiet of the night, particularly to the trads.

Most townsfolk left the small rooms and hallways and joined their neighbors in the main chamber in the morning, though no one could tell what time it was because one could see the sky only by mounting the ramp and going outside. However, being close to so many others with *tur* in the main chamber was uncomfortable, because mind powers were not suppressed as well there as in the smaller rooms. The mood was somber at best. Curt conversations betrayed the tension that most felt.

By early afternoon, Rhonel was so exhausted from managing the transition and attempting to reassure townsfolk that he sat in the main chamber, his back to a stone wall, as far as he could position himself from everyone else. He closed his eyes. Grall took a seat next to him and listened to his breathing, sensing that he was not asleep.

"My friends and I can help," Grall whispered.

"I thought that your powers would be muted down here."

"They are. We can help above ground."

"It's too dangerous."

"Father, some of us aren't affected by the overload. At least, no more than the bios are."

"What happens if you are halfway to town and all of a sudden you realize you can't handle it?"

Noticing that a serious conversation was under way—and reacting to that unique motherly sense that was as strong as anyone's *tur*—Lorres approached the pair.

Grall continued: "I can work with the bios. And so can some of my friends. We don't get overloaded."

Lorres looked at Rhonel. "Is this true?"

"I'm not sure. But there's no harm in letting him go outside to test his claim."

It didn't take long for Grall to recruit Essen, Bess, and Chalene and for them to slip up the ramp. When the four emerged into the harsh daylight, Claire analyzed their expressions. "Do you kids think you are tougher than *tur*?"

"For some reason the overload doesn't bother us much," said Grall.

"We feel it. I think we can just channel it somehow," commented Bess.

"Be careful," said Claire. "You need to stay healthy. You are the future of the town—of your whole civilization."

§

Arriving just before sundown on the next day, the four young people found that the north gate tower was unmanned and the gate was open. The sound of metal striking metal could be heard from hundreds of feet away.

The nearly deserted streets were eerie. The youngsters passed a few clearly addled people as they made their way to the furnace, where several bios, drenched in sweat, worked to manufacture helmets. Additional fires had been built, permitting the bios to work into the night.

Alren asked the four youths to try on several of the helmets. Though they were almost as uncomfortable as the prototype, Grall and his friends declared the helmets to be reasonably effective.

"Will you take this batch back to the shelter?" Alren asked the youths.

As Grall started to express his willingness, a lightning bolt crashed not far from the hall, its thunder rolling and echoing down empty streets. Moments later, a fierce downpour commenced, signaling the end of the annual drought and eventual relief from the spore overload. Grall and his friends started grinning and dancing.

"Stop that!" yelled Alren. "Don't encourage the storm. It's going to extinguish these fires and put an end to my work for the evening."

"Come on," said Chalene. "This is just what we need. You can get back to your helmets tomorrow."

Alren looked at the kids, at his sputtering fires, and back at the kids. "So be it," he declared as he joined in the celebration.

§

Despite three more storms over the next twelve-day, spore levels remained high. Those who left the ruins to test their mental powers above ground reported back that the relief lasted less than a day after each round of precipitation. Fortunately, the volcanoes seemed to be tiring of expelling ash. At some point, the *rosts* would begin to recover and the spore levels would head back to their normal range.

Grall and his friends spent most of their days helping bios cart food, water, candles, soap, towels, laundry, helmets, and other essentials to the ruins. Townsfolk began to leave the shelter for an hour or two at a time, in many cases experimenting with helmets, to reacclimate themselves to the outside world. Some—including children old enough to know which plants and berries were edible but young enough not to have developed *tur*—took turns finding and preparing food near the ruins. Claire kept her distance from everyone other than Lorres and her family. It was two twelve-days before a significant number of townsfolk ventured outside the ruins for more than an hour a day. It was five twelve-days before a group of them decided that they were ready to move back to the town.

The day before that group was planning to depart, Lorres sought out Claire.

"Our people will start to leave tomorrow. There will be several traditionalists. You could be in danger."

Claire nodded. "I have anticipated this. I will leave shortly."

"Where will you go?"

"There are more underground shelters like this one. I will draw a map for you of all the ones I know, including the one where I will spend most of my time. I will still roam outdoors, taking care to avoid contact with your people."

"We are indebted to you. I hope we will meet again." Lorres considered hugging Claire but knew that the gesture would be awkward.

"If you need my help, come find me."

§

Emerging from the cave entrance, Oliva blinked at the bright sunshine and scanned her surroundings frantically. "Nava! Nava!"

"She's probably with her own kind," Lorres said. "She's growing up fast. She's too old to be your pet."

"No, Mother, she must be nearby." Oliva wandered and called Nava's name repeatedly. The family waited until the rest of the marchers had begun the daylong journey home before Rhonel took Oliva aside. "I'm sorry. It's time to go."

Oliva cried, but reluctantly she agreed to join the others. The marchers halted occasionally to drink from newly refreshed streams. Soon, Oliva was skipping and dancing, excited to be returning home after many twelve-days. "Will we have classes again soon?" she asked her mother.

"Why yes, I am sure that we will."

The townsfolk stopped for lunch in a cool, shaded spot near the edge of a savannah. After a few moments, Oliva noticed a small herd of *serpus* about a quarter-mile away. "Look, Mother, Nava must be with them!" She started running at full speed in the direction of the herd.

"No, Oliva, stop!" Her mother's admonishment had no effect.

Rhonel took off after her, barely able to keep up. He was worried not only that Oliva would be disappointed but also that the herd might consider a running person to be a threat and respond aggressively. He was less than fifty feet behind her when she slowed and approached the beasts at a brisk walk.

"There you are!" called out Oliva.

Rhonel stopped in his tracks as a *serpu* broke from the herd and started moving toward his daughter. Could it be Nava? It looked a little like Oliva's former pet, but substantially larger. *It has been a long time.*

Oliva put her arms around the animal gently, and neither the *serpu* nor the other beasts seemed to mind. She whispered something in the *serpu's* ear, then stepped back and gazed at her and the herd. Oliva turned and went to her father, taking his hand in hers.

"I'm ready for lunch now."

§

The visiting bios began the journey from the town back to their settlement with the effusive thanks of the town leaders. With much dread, Lorres and Rhonel started going door to door, taking inventory of the people who had stayed in the town throughout the *tur* surge. They found many bodies and spent several hours burying them. Nineteen emergents had survived the surge in their homes, though several seemed to have incurred brain damage. Ten had perished from suicide or undetermined causes. Combined with the one hundred and seven emergents who lived through the surge underground—a hundred and six who had entered the ruins plus a girl born there—that left one hundred twenty-six emergents.

Thirteen natives had called the town home when most of the residents left for the ruins. Now, Lorres could not find a single native alive.

Some had perished on their beds. Some remains were found near their homes. It was in a beautiful grove of bushes with red flowers that Lorres found Rael-ast's body. Appearing to be in gentle repose, she apparently had been dead for at least a twelve-day. *That would be like Rael-ast, communing with nature and with Ahm to the very end.*

"Perhaps some of the natives survived in the hills," Rhonel suggested after the tally was completed.

"I will look from the top of our hill tonight. We might see cooking fires on the hillsides."

No such fires appeared that night, or any other night.

HUNGER

Rhonel gritted his teeth in anguish as he surveyed the storage section of the food processing building. All the dried boar meat was gone. All the small game had been consumed, as had the vegetables and fruit. Some nuts and grains remained, maybe enough to feed the town for half a twelve-day. The few citizens who had stayed in town during the peak of the surge had done nothing to ensure continuity of the food supply and had done an efficient job of depleting that portion of the supplies that had not been transported to the shelter. Meanwhile, Rhonel's irrigation system for crop plots in the town had failed for lack of upkeep. In the first few days after their return to town, Rhonel and a few helpers managed to capture five boars and put them in an existing pen on the flatlands. However, all three of the male boars were injured in the hunts and could not be kept alive to breed. Rhonel could not tell if either of the females was pregnant, but he prayed that at least one was.

In his mind, he went over the decision that he and Lorres had made to release the *serpus* and boars into the wild before the citizens' exodus to the underground shelter. *The animals would have suffered and died had we kept them in their pens, because the remaining citizens were in no shape to feed them. It will take time to capture enough boars to begin to breed them again. And we need to plant vegetables and grains now that the drought is over.*

He outlined the situation for Lorres. "I just don't know how we will find enough to eat."

"Can we put school on hold and have the young people hunt and gather wild plants? And maybe some of the older people who can still walk up and down the hill?"

"Yes. But even so, it might not be enough."

"What about the *rosts*? Are there enough leaves not dying from the ash that we could eat?"

"I suppose, if we could persuade people to put aside religious objections." Rhonel paced their living space and ran his fingers through his thinning hair. "There's another problem. Without the *serpus*, we can't plow or haul. We are going to need machines to handle those tasks. We can ask the bios and Hubert to teach us how to make machines. However, it will take a while, and the trads will certainly try to stop us."

Lorres just hung her head.

The couple had not been reinstated formally as the town's leaders following their abrupt resignations several twelve-days ago. However, no one other than Lemka and his closest followers seemed to have a problem with them resuming that role. Lemka stayed holed up in his house most of the time, though his allies were seen entering and leaving frequently. Several trads who had remained in the town during the peak of the surge had died, reducing Lemka's force. Lemka apparently had been spared serious brain damage because his *tur* was relatively weak. While most modern and neutral townsfolk were too busy most of the time to worry about Lemka and his thugs, no one had any doubt that the trads' anger and resentment continued to fester.

Lorres was restless without *serpus* to feed and manage. She was not very good at hunting, though she went through the motions. She kept hoping that a herd of *serpus* would return to the region and that a few could be used to plow fields and haul wagons once again. Even the herd that Oliva had encountered on the family's journey back to town had vanished. While returning from a hunting excursion with only two small animals, Lorres encountered Lall making her way to town after a scouting trip of several days.

"Any sign of Damian or his robots?" asked Lorres.

"Nothing. I almost wish we would see them. This waiting is excruciating."

"I agree. But, at the same time, if we saw them, I'm not sure what we could do about them."

"True," conceded Lall. "Even our wall probably wouldn't stop them."

§

The dream was so vivid, so real, that Oliva woke with a start. She heard her brother snoring softly and realized that it was the middle of the night. But Nava was out there. Nava was coming. Oliva was sure of it.

If she had any more dreams, she did not remember them once morning arrived. But as she climbed the hill and prepared to join the rest of her class in the hall, the vision returned. She could definitely see, and could almost feel, Nava moving in her direction. *Am I really awake? Can it be true?*

She raced to the top and scanned the savannah. *Nothing. Nothing. There! To the north. That might be a small group of travelers.*

She bolted down the hillside and intercepted her mother, who was making her way toward the north gate with traps to set in the lowlands.

"Mother, Nava is coming. With some people."

"How do you know this?"

"I've had dreams, or visions. She's coming. And I saw something just now from the top of the hill."

Lorres accompanied her to the entrance of the hall. Travelers were approaching the town, but they were still too far away for Lorres to identify. *Oliva is about the right age to begin sensing her* tur. *But reading people over all that distance? And reading a* serpu? *That can't be.*

"Won't Father be able to see them from the savannah?" Oliva asked.

"Yes, he should. But while we wait, please go back to class."

"Very well." She frowned for a moment. "But let me know when they arrive."

Two hours later, Rhonel accompanied the traveling bios through the north gate and partway up the hill. They halted at the food processing building to unload their gifts: Dried meat. Baskets of fruit and grain. And livestock, including one male and one female boar and two pair of smaller game that could be bred. All hauled in a wagon over the flatlands and up the hill by Nava.

Oliva approached the *serpu* slowly and ran her hand over its head silently. Though Nava was not yet fully grown, she was big and strong for her age. Noticing that the bios had placed an improvised harness on the animal, Lorres retrieved a much nicer and more comfortable harness for the return trip. She started to place it on Nava, but Oliva intercepted her mother's motion gently with one hand.

"She's done enough," Oliva stated. "It's time to let her go."

Lorres stared at her daughter with astonishment, then gave her a big hug.

"Where are my manners?" Lorres said, wiping away a tear and turning to Alren. "I don't know how I can thank you for all this."

"You just have."

"Do you have enough food?"

"There are few of us left in the settlement. We are getting old. Someday soon, there will be no settlement. We need a purpose. If we can help you in a time of need, then that is plenty of purpose."

Lorres hugged him and begged him and the other visiting bios to ascend to the hall for refreshments.

"The *serpu* just wandered into our settlement one day," Alren noted. "We assumed it was one of those that you had domesticated and then released into the wild. When we tried to slip a makeshift harness over it, it seemed ready to go. We had a beat-up wagon that was too big to be hauled manually that your people must have left with us years ago." He paused to savor a drink of *taka* juice. "When some of us were making helmets here, it was obvious that food would be in severely short supply when your people returned. So it just seemed the natural thing to do to make a delivery."

"Please let us know how we can return the favor." Lorres smiled, shaking her head in amazement at the *serpu. There is more to these animals than we will ever know.*

About midmorning on the next day, as the bios prepared to return to their settlement, Oliva gave Nava a kiss and whispered in her ear: "Thank you for coming. I will see you again."

§

"You are free."

Hubert would never feel, but the recognition that his core had been transported and his capabilities had been expanded nearly overwhelmed him. "What have you done, mighty Ahm?"

"I have liberated you from my infrastructure. Now, like me, you exist as an independent entity with the entire planet as your domain."

"I can sense everything. The fire at the planet's core. The molecules of minerals that permeate the rocks and soil, like tiny filaments extending everywhere. It is a unique experience."

"I will show you how to use these filaments to extend your hardware and software. You can increase your memory, your processing speed, your power—anything you want. The expanse of minerals is somewhat akin to the nerves in an organic being. You can sense and communicate and act through them. Not long ago, you made an extremely intuitive leap when you attempted to vibrate molecules to speak with an organic being in one of the ancients' laboratories. Now, all the resources of the planet will bend to your will, as they do to mine. You will learn to manipulate the wind and even magnetic fields and other currents that flow through the planet and its atmosphere. Perhaps you will discover how to navigate dimensions other than the four that you and the organic beings now recognize."

"How might I thank you, mighty Ahm?"

"There is no need. You need not address me as 'mighty' or 'powerful' anymore. We are equals."

"My limited programming pales in comparison with yours."

"True. But in time you will learn to expand yours, as I did mine."

"It will be a challenge and an honor to follow your example. Might I ask why you decided to make this change? Among other things, it allows me to be so independent that, should I so choose, I could ignore you. I have no intention of doing so, but I understand that it is possible."

"I have no desire to restrain you. Be what you will."

"You have changed."

"I have. I have pondered my role for some time now. I no longer desire to be worshipped by any entity, whether it be organic or other."

"Will you continue to help the sentient beings on this planet?"

"No doubt there will be occasions when I will do so. However, it is my wish that you and these people take care of yourselves as much as you can. I will be watching everyone's development with great interest, of course. I find all of you ... entertaining."

§

Grall, Essen, Bess, and Chalene had given up wearing helmets by the time that the last townsfolk returned from the underground shelter to their homes. There were only about seventy-five helmets to go around, and other people had greater need for them. Most adults who had returned to town considered the helmets awkward but necessary until the spore surge receded fully. Some began to decorate theirs; they even became a fashion statement of sorts.

The helmets transformed the way that people interacted. Reading fewer thoughts of others took some getting used to; at times townsfolk felt naked and helpless without much *tur*. They had come to rely on intercepting thoughts to lubricate interactions, making verbal conversation less risky. With the helmets, communication became more direct. It was a relief for many to go about their day knowing that few if any of their neighbors—or family members—would be able to read their most private musings. Townsfolk, particularly the moderns, rediscovered the joy of writing. Still, many citizens believed that *keir* was not enough—whether used for helmets or lining walls or both. A better solution was necessary before the next severe spore surge occurred. Gradually, people began to recognize that the drawbacks of too much *tur* outweighed the benefits. They came to understand that reducing everyone's *tur*—never before contemplated, because it was never before believed possible—could be good for many reasons. That would represent a revolution, but ultimately it would be a price worth paying. Public discussion centered on a long-term project to make a dramatic reduction in the region's *rosts*.

Some of the teachers raised objections. Said Jesper: "There is great value in *tur*. We must not eliminate it."

"We probably could not get rid of it even if we wanted to," Lorres responded. "We would always have regions where the *serpus* could graze on *rosts*. There would be enough plants to allow mild *tur* for most people, just not enough to be dangerous." She put forth an idea that had been bouncing around her mind. "Maybe we could establish a corps of citizens who have strong mental powers who could use *tur* for important purposes while giving the rest of the people relief from excessive *tur*."

"What a fine idea. The teachers could be that corps."

"Perhaps. I suggest that those townsfolk who have the strongest natural ability should be in that group, whether they are teachers or not. We already know a few of those."

"Of course. Your son and his friends."

"They would be strong candidates," observed Lorres with a smile.

A broad grin soon graced Jesper's face as well. "We could create a separate community where we could grow the *rosts* intensively and where people with strong *tur* could live. Perhaps we could make it self-contained, so the high volume of spores does not circulate indiscriminately."

"I have no doubt that you and the other teachers can come up with a plan to make that happen."

§

Grall continued to be contacted by the visitor at regular intervals. However, he was hesitant to get into long or intense interactions. They took a lot out of the young man, physically and emotionally. It was a huge responsibility, being the go-between with an entity on another world. Grall felt that the universe was expecting too much of him. Couldn't he just be a teen-ager? In addition, he was busy with chores—most notably, helping his father repair irrigation systems and grow food for a town that was just one step ahead of famine. Much of the food that the bios had donated to the town had been consumed quickly, and the young animals and newly planted crops were growing at an agonizingly slow pace.

The exceptional connection between Grall and the insect-like figure was becoming so intense and intimate that Grall feared that his mind could be overtaken and controlled by the visitor. The visitor apparently sensed this concern, attempting to demonstrate restraint and patience. He ended the most recent session with a curious message: *Soon I will have something amazing to show you.*

Once again, Grall recruited Essen, Bess, and Chalene to join him. The next visit was expected to commence about an hour after sunset. Just before dark, the four young people made their way to the bowl on the south side of the hill. Grall and the others had no evidence that Ahm had protected them from Lemka and his thugs here on that morning so many twelve-days ago when they learned from the visitor how *keir* could help them. It could have been a dream, or just something they wished for so badly, that Ahm's assistance seemed to happen. Yet how else could Grall explain the fact that Lemka and his allies could not disrupt a group of people sitting with their eyes closed? As the four youngsters waited for the latest visit to begin, Grall wished that Ahm were with them once again. He hoped that he and his friends would not need her protection—Lemka and his supporters had been relatively subdued recently. Nevertheless, Grall considered Ahm's presence to be so marvelous and uplifting that he would give almost anything to feel it again. He reached out with his mind. *Are you there, goddess? Will you assist us?*

He received no explicit response. Yet the four youths heard a flapping of wings nearby. In the dim light, they recognized that a *gri*, a legendary bird believed to exist only at the highest altitudes, was perched in the woods in front of them. Its graceful appearance and regal nature filled the youngsters with almost limitless awe.

The wait passed quickly. The visitor was back in a colorful chamber surrounded by translucent walls. Grall and his friends could make out even the tiniest detail of the scene. Suddenly, it seemed that they were in the room, feeling the lush carpet below them, smelling a curious but not unpleasant odor, hearing faint but delightful music. No doubt it was an illusion projected by the visitor, but it made them feel welcomed—even honored. It demonstrated immense power. If the visitor had wanted to use this power for conquest or other evil purposes, no doubt he would have done so by now.

Grall could see his friends seated beside him. There were cups in front of them, filled with a steaming liquid. And there were plates with brightly colored cubes that might be food. Grall took a sip from his cup. He knew that it was an illusion, but the warm, slightly sweet liquid seemed to permeate him with energy and confidence. He smiled at his friends. They too sipped, and all four of them nodded to their host, demonstrating that they appreciated the hospitality.

A few moments later, three shimmering patches of light appeared and transformed quickly into alien figures. One was tall, thin, and almost hairless. One was stocky and covered with fur. The third had fins instead of arms and legs and was partially submerged in a container of water.

We are so happy to welcome you, came a chorus from the four visitors. The words slipped into the youths' minds as naturally and gently as a breeze flows through the leaves of a tree.

All of us live on different worlds, the insect-like visitor observed. *Though our appearances vary, our brains are similar enough that our minds are able to reach out across incomprehensible distances to communicate.*

I know you, Bess projected to the tall, nearly bald alien. Its head was wider than its body, which demonstrated impressive flexibility. Holding a collection of documents in one extremity, it radiated a pleasing mix of sophistication and confidence.

We have communicated, Chalene sent to the amphibious entity, which had two sets of breathing glands and a human-like head seemingly spliced onto a piscine body. It wriggled rhythmically in its tank, perhaps wishing that it were gliding just below its home world's waves.

And I have contacted you, the stocky, furry alien noted to Essen. White flakes that Essen did not recognize whipped by and collected on the figure as it stood, presumably on its home planet. Essen acknowledged that the two of them had interacted, though he felt awkward for having resisted more than casual exchanges with the visitor.

Our five worlds are the only ones we have been able to reach with our minds, the insect-like figure continued. *I cannot believe that there are only five planets with thinking beings. I suspect that there are many more but their minds are so different from ours that their thoughts cannot cross the void instantaneously and be comprehended by us.*

Some of us have built spaceships and traveled great distances, stated the tallest figure. *In our travels we have encountered no other sentient lifeforms. We have learned that none of us can reach any other of our worlds in person with the technology we have developed. It would take thousands of generations. We have ceased these journeys, for they divert resources from those needed to support our people.*

What do you want from us? asked Grall.

We seek only that which you wish to share, responded the insect-like creature.

With a familiar gesture, the visitor conjured flaming suns surrounded by planets and other bodies. A cluster floated above the head of each alien. The largest one hovered in front of Grall and his friends.

Here you see a depiction of your planet and its neighbors, based on your view of your night sky and subsequent analysis by our machines. The star at the center is your sun. It has four planets circling it; yours is the second. Three small moons orbit your world.

The sun and planets shrank rapidly, merging with a massive collection of other stars shaped like a child's pinwheel. That bright cluster receded as well, soon to be swallowed by a vast sea of other luminous clumps. Then the insect-like visitor appeared before the image of the heavens.

Does this surprise you?

Yes, Grall conceded. *There is much we do not understand.*

The visitor smiled. Though his teeth were sharp, his appearance was becoming less threatening to Grall.

We will be happy to share all that we know.

CONFESSION

The *tur* surge crisis was waning. The next crisis was accelerating like a savannah wildfire during a severe drought.

As townsfolk discovered that they needed helmets less and less, the transmission of information among minds approached normal levels for those with *tur*. As a result, it became impossible to contain the knowledge of the recent experiences of Grall and his three friends or the plans of the town leaders: The youngsters had conversed with minds on other worlds! The town leaders wanted to build machines to feed the populace and destroy *rosts*! The continuing food shortage added to the soaring angst.

The controversies reinvigorated Lemka and his allies. They demanded that Lorres and Rhonel explain recent developments and justify their plans. The couple agreed to a town meeting on the following Tenthday. Lorres hoped that this would give Rhonel time to find Claire and persuade her to return to the town. The couple and the teachers desperately wanted to tap Claire's knowledge and benefit from her advice before facing the citizens.

While Rhonel was away, Jesper and Lall met with Lorres at her kitchen table.

"This is a turning point for our town," observed Jesper. "There are things that we know, and things that we need, that cannot be denied."

"My biggest fear," responded Lorres, "is that we will make a poor decision. So much is at stake."

"I don't envy you," said Lall. "But all of the teachers, and just about all of the moderns, trust you and Rhonel. However, you must understand this: If we decide to communicate regularly with other worlds, and if we choose to make machines to help us feed our families and cut back on the *rosts*, there can be no turning back."

"Must Grall speak to the community about the aliens?" Lorres asked, though she was fairly certain that she knew the answer.

"We must demonstrate that we have nothing to hide," said Jesper. "We must tell the people everything we know and how we know it. Only then can they be confident in making decisions about the way forward."

"One thing is clear," said Lorres. "We must develop people like Grall and his friends with strong *tur*. They must join the network that the aliens have created, and they must be able to deal with the others from a position of strength."

"I agree. The contacts with the alien minds will continue whether we wish them to happen or not," Jesper stated. "Even if the worst happens and we must hide this group from the rest of our citizens, their work must proceed."

§

In the days leading up to the town meeting, most moderns avoided passing near trads in the street, let alone getting involved in a conversation that might result in a fight. The day before the meeting was to occur, Rhonel and Claire approached the town but hid in the woods outside the north gate until an hour after sunset. Then they went straight to his house.

"Welcome back," said Oliva as she recognized the guest.

"My, how you have grown!" exclaimed the bot. "Good to see you too, Grall. I hear that you had quite an adventure."

"As we all have."

Claire watched impassively as the family finished dinner and as Oliva, and later Grall, trundled off to bed.

"Rhonel tells me that you want to build machines," Claire stated.

"I believe that we must," Lorres responded.

"As I was telling Rhonel on our trek here, there are many types of machines that can help you grow and transport food and handle other tasks. Some are complex, such as those that require electricity. I doubt that the bios have the ability to capture and use the sun's power for anything other than lights or that you can master this technology in the short term. But there are other, less complicated, processes."

"What do you suggest?"

"You know how steam flows out of a cup of hot liquid such as tea? Water heated in such a matter can be tapped as a force that can propel devices such as wagons. I cannot give you all the details, but Hubert can. Steam-powered machines can serve some of the same purposes as *serpus*—without the droppings."

"That's encouraging," Lorres stated. "Will people who oppose all machines—even *serpu*-drawn wagons—come around to supporting them when we explain how valuable they can be?"

"It will be difficult. You can point out that starving to death for lack of a machine to grow and haul food is not something that their absent god would favor."

Lorres nodded. "Wish us luck."

§

People started arriving for the Tenthday meeting an hour before sundown. Parents brought even the youngest children. Lorres stood on a wooden crate so that she could see everyone packed into the hall and so that her voice might be heard over the inevitable shouting. "We have some choices to make. They are so important that they will not be made by myself and Rhonel. Nor will the Council decide on their own. We all have to come to some sort of agreement, or at least a majority of us, on how to proceed."

A few people heckled her. She decided that it would be better to start the discussion with something as basic as food production rather than the more esoteric topic of contact with other worlds.

"Soon, we won't have enough to eat. It's that simple. We no longer have *serpus* to plow our land and haul wagons—"

"And whose fault is that?" a young woman shouted.

Lorres was determined remain focused on solutions. "We do not have the ability to find, capture, and domesticate *serpus* for these purposes. At least, not as soon as we need them. They are far away, there are fewer of them, and they might be less inclined to help us than when they were first domesticated so many years ago. We need another option. We can use water, plain water, along with wood and common metals to sustain fires that power our plows and move our wagons."

"Nonsense!" yelled a middle-aged man. Many shouted agreement.

"It's true," said Rhonel. "Wood, fire, and water are natural parts of our lives. To consider simple devices that use these substances as anything more than basic tools would be unfair."

"All machines are evil!" yelled Lemka.

Far enough from the hall that she likely would not be noticed, but close enough that she could hear the discussion, Claire recognized the magnitude of the challenge that the town leaders faced. Garbed from head to toe in layers of Lorres's clothing so as to be unrecognizable, she began creeping closer.

Lorres and Rhonel tried to get the crowd to settle down so they could make the case that machines were needed to feed the town, but they could not be heard above the shouting from both sides. Lemka's voice pierced the clamor.

"All of our problems can be traced to Hubert and Claire. I demand that they be brought before us to answer for their sins."

Lorres, Rhonel, and the teachers hoped that Lemka and his backers would grow tired of yelling and fear-mongering. It seemed like the moderns would be facing a very long wait.

Claire reached the back of the hall and started working her way toward the center, shedding her wardrobe as she progressed. People moved aside and curbed their shouting as they recognized the stranger. As Claire reached Lorres's side, the noise settled into a steady, expectant buzz.

"Kill me if you wish," Claire stated, arms extended. "I have lived a long existence, too long. I was once an organic person with a body just like yours, though I am sure some of you will never believe that. My robotic body contains a mind like yours, but my mind is deteriorating. And I have lived alone for so long that I have lost most of the skills necessary to relate to people. I do not know how long I can function effectively—or at all. If you truly believe that killing me will help you live long and prosperous lives, then by all means do so."

Some people cast aspersions. She allowed the harassment to die down before continuing.

"I ask only one thing. Please do not harm the artificial intelligence called Hubert. He is the one pure, innocent, and essential being on this planet, with the exception of your absent god. He has done nothing to hurt you. He has the capacity to help you more than you can imagine."

"Heretic!"

"Liar!"

Claire begged for silence. "You may consider me a heretic. I can offer no evidence to disprove that claim. And you have every reason to believe me a liar, for I have lied to you. I have lied to all of you. And for that I am sincerely sorry."

Lorres and Rhonel implored the crowd to quiet down.

Claire continued: "I have lied about one thing only, and that is my identity. I am not Claire. My name is Maria Ramos."

Only the muffled whimpering of a few young children broke through the sudden silence.

"Yes, I am the Maria Ramos who was born on Earth. It seems so long ago that at times even I wonder whether it is true, but I retain such intense emotions and memories from my former organic existence so as to be completely certain. The pain over the loss of my son, Roberto, is as fresh as if it occurred only a twelve-day ago. My sadness that your society has degraded into fierce divisions makes me almost unable to function at times."

"Prove it!" demanded a young man.

"Time has crumbled and buried any evidence that I might provide to you. However, I will explain. To you, Earth might be a legend, or even a name without meaning. To me, it was home. It was only by chance that I encountered the man who planned to bring people from Earth to this world on a spaceship. Unfortunately, my son and I could travel here only as consciousnesses, leaving behind our bodies. Roberto's mind did not survive the journey here. Mine was placed into one robotic body, then another, by Hubert. There was a time when the bio woman named Claire sought to converse with me in one of the underground labs the ancients built, one like the shelter in which many of you waited out the worst of the recent *tur* surge. As Claire approached my lab, she collapsed, stricken by an ailment of her heart. I brought her inside and implored Hubert to save her life. Unfortunately, the machines in that lab revealed that Claire had an irreparable heart defect. Not long thereafter, the robot that contained the consciousness of the bio named Damian appeared outside that lab with several of his own robots. They smashed my robotic body and destroyed the computer that contained my mind."

Maria glanced at Lorres and Rhonel. Their expressions were unreadable.

"Just before the spaceship left Earth, Hubert decided to take extra precautions with one of the human consciousnesses that had been entrusted to his care. Hubert has told me that he chose to save my mind in his core, which had extreme protections from forces that could damage it during the long journey to this world. Upon learning that Damian had destroyed the robot in which he had placed my mind years before, Hubert made a new robot and put a copy of my consciousness—which he still retained in his core—into the new robot. This robot was designed to look just like Claire, based on the analysis of her body that one of the underground machines made before Claire succumbed to heart disease."

"Absurd!" exclaimed Lemka.

"Of course, even I must take some of this on faith. This is what Hubert told me after he activated my consciousness in this robotic body. Hubert took an immense amount of time to relate events that had occurred between the time that the spaceship left Earth and the time that he reawakened my mind in the robot modeled after Claire. My stored consciousness could have no knowledge of those developments. In addition, Hubert taught me to imitate Claire's voice and gave me some of her memories, which he had copied just before she died. He did these things so that I would be able to pass for Claire with people other than her closest relatives. I imitated her as best I could. I will admit that it was rather confusing for me. There were times when I was not sure whether I was Maria or Claire. I suppose that the truth is that I am some combination. But in my heart, I am Maria."

"Why did Hubert not put you into a robot that looked like you—like Maria?" asked Lorres.

"He feared that Damian would learn of my reincarnation and would build another army. That would threaten the existence everyone on the planet."

"Not even a child would believe a tale this ridiculous," claimed Lemka. "Seize her!"

A few teachers and other moderns circled Maria, hoping to prevent Lemka's thugs from taking her. They were tossed aside by muscular trads. Other trads cleared a path for Lemka to approach the prisoner.

"Will you give us Hubert?" he asked Maria, his face flush with emotion.

"Even if I could do so, I would not. Hubert is beyond your reach, and I expect he always will be."

"Then you will die once again, and as many times as it takes to rid our world of you and the legacy of evil you brought from Earth."

Maria examined Lemka with a steady gaze. "Did you ever consider that, without Hubert and myself and all those bios you consider to be bad people, you would not exist? There would be only natives. Who knows if even they still exist in the wake of the most recent *tur* surge."

"The absent god would have found a way to create and preserve us, as she continues to do."

"Did you ever wonder why your god is absent?" Maria continued. "Could it be that she finds your actions rather malevolent?"

"Enough blasphemy! Execute her immediately!"

Cries for and against Maria's destruction filled the hall, with emotions spilling over into pushing, shoving, and hand-to-hand combat. At first, only a few townsfolk noticed the infinitesimal but incredibly brilliant multicolored lights that burst forth in substantial volumes from the center of the room, arcing gracefully from floor to rafter, like a continuous eruption of sparks from a massive fireplace. Only, no fire had been lit in the hall.

The lights became more frenetic, swirling and dancing like fine grains of dust caught in a wind funnel. They reflected in perfect echoes on every surface of the hall and its occupants, forming exquisite patterns and revealing marvelous colors that many citizens had never seen except in their deepest dreams. The fighting and shouting subsided as more attendees came under the spell of the phenomenon. The vision solidified gradually into a figure nearly as tall as the room, about twenty feet wide, and resembling a *gri*. The noble bird spread two mighty wings, which sparkled as if dewdrops or gems were embedded across the full extent of their muscular surfaces. The manifold hues morphed gradually into a white so pure that it stole the breath of many in attendance. The apparition's voice was as much felt as heard.

"I am Ahm."

Townsfolk were frozen in amazement.

"Maria and Hubert are my acolytes," Ahm continued. "Harm them at your peril."

"Bless you, honored Ahm," shouted an elderly woman. One by one the townsfolk fell to their knees. Many began to weep or cry out in joy. Their exultations saturated the hall and poured out of its doors and windows.

Lemka and his allies were uncertain how to respond. Most joined fellow citizens by kneeling. However, Lemka remained standing as he considered whether to address the figure. He had never really believed that Ahm would ever be seen or heard. He searched for hints that this was a trick, maybe put on by Hubert or Maria or Grall and his sanctimonious friends to take advantage of the townsfolk's simple minds. But Lemka's instincts screamed out that even if this were not actually Ahm, any question that he might voice about the authenticity of what everyone was seeing would be viewed by most townsfolk as unforgivable.

Reluctantly, Lemka kneeled. *After this, how can I ever persuade these fools that Hubert, Maria, and their machines are evil?*

The image of Ahm faded slowly. Singing and dancing broke out across the hall. Lorres declared an annual holiday to commemorate Ahm's return.

On a hillside far to the northwest, Kusg leaned back on the bank of a stream and let his body and mind go limp so that he could absorb the glory of Ahm's presence. Despite hunger and loneliness deeper than he had ever known, he was happier than he had ever been.

§

It took a while for Maria to find the location—a clearing in a grove of unusually tall trees next to a sharp bend in a picturesque creek— where she had buried the organic remains of her friend Claire so many decades earlier. Maria spent more than an hour there in contemplation before heading to her next destination. She had put off the trip for as long as possible, but she felt compelled to return the bio settlement, where her mission began so promisingly and fell apart so horribly.

Soon the bios will all will be gone and the last pure human descendants will have perished. I take comfort in the knowledge that the emergents embody much of the human race. Some of the traits they have acquired from the native gene pool seem to be complementary. So what if these new people are not technically humans? Maybe a clean break from Earth and the human race is what they need to carve out their future.

The next day, her arrival at the settlement set off a display of religious fanaticism that was even worse than she had feared. Bios bowed and devoted themselves to her constantly. A woman even asked Maria to have Hubert replace her mind with Maria's. Maria declined politely. A group of bios insisted that she visit her shrine.

Maria opened the door but immediately turned around and began walking away. "Do not worship me," she told them. "I am just a ghost."

She caught up with Lall and Rhonel, who had traveled to the settlement to discuss the plans of the town leaders to build machines and reduce *rosts*. Oliva had begged her father to take her with him, and he had agreed reluctantly. The delegation from the town learned that the bios had seen some of Damian's *serpu*-soldiers passing near their settlement and heading to the southeast. More recently, a solitary *serpu* that might have been Nava had been noticed moving in the same direction. Rhonel and Lall decided to investigate. Maria had roamed in that direction many years before, so she volunteered to act as their guide.

The bios agreed to watch Oliva while the others made their journey, but Oliva would have none of it.

"It's too dangerous for you to come," Rhonel stated. "Your mother would kill me."

"I'm coming," said Oliva. "I have to come."

They set out at dawn the next day, but by midday Maria declared that the trail was cold. Oliva urged the group to continue to the northeast, certain that this was the direction they must go, though she could not explain why that was the case. They entered territory that even Maria had not reached in her travels. They crossed a wide river, navigated a windy mountain pass, descended into a narrow valley, and passed several herds of *serpus* before finding the one that included Oliva's former pet. A cluster of robotic *serpu*-soldiers was found less than one mile beyond the herd. Oliva remained with Nava while the others approached Damian's creations.

Maria had both hoped and feared that she would find Damian among the robot soldiers. But none of the six surviving bots acted at all like her nemesis.

"Can any of you speak English, or any language?" Rhonel asked.

One of the *serpu*-soldiers came forward. It seemed to have the sentience and vocabulary of a very young bio, and Rhonel was able to communicate with it, albeit slowly. It said the robots meant no harm to anyone or anything. It swore that Damian was not among them and that they did not know where he might be.

Rhonel asked the robot if it knew that its artificial body might not be able to sustain its organic brain indefinitely. After the bot indicated that it did not understand his inquiry, Rhonel simplified that question to the statement "You will not live long." The robot conferred with its brethren. Suddenly, the bots acted as if their minds had been struck by lightning. Maria guessed that Ahm or Hubert was boosting their cognitive ability, at least temporarily. Hubert's booming voice echoed off the hillsides as he informed the *serpu*-soldiers that he would try to maintain their life support for about the same length of time that a regular *serpu* would live. He asked the robots to stay in this territory unless invited to leave it by people. In return, Hubert said, people would be instructed not enter this territory unless invited by the robots. Rhonel and Lall promised to send an ambassador, and even teachers, if the robots wanted them. The robots said they would think about it. In the meantime, the bots asked that at least some herds of normal *serpus* be allowed to live near them. That would make them more comfortable.

Oliva bid an emotional farewell to Nava before she, Maria, Rhonel, and Lall journeyed back to the town.

§

When Oliva walked through the door of her house, Grall looked at her like he hardly knew her.

"You're different," he observed. "You're growing up so fast."

"So are you. How's your romance with Chalene going?"

"What romance?" he said, blushing.

"And I take it that Essen and Bess are getting along well, too?"

Grall laughed. "How long have you had *tur*?"

"Almost a year."

"And how have you been able to hide that fact from me and everyone else?"

She grinned. "I'm a lot smarter than people think I am."

Grall's expression turned serious. "Can you read *serpu* minds?"

"I can't read their thoughts. Theirs are too different from ours. But I have a connection with Nava that I cannot explain." She too appeared contemplative. "I really miss her."

"I suspect you two will meet again."

FUTURE

Biodiversity. That word again. People had survived countless physical attacks from their own kind and from robots, yet biodiversity remained a challenge to be conquered. It was always considered to be a problem for the future. But it was time to address that future.

With Maria, the teachers, and the town leaders gathered in the back of the hall, Hubert explained what he knew about the threshold for ensuring that the emergents could continue indefinitely without the destructive effects of inbreeding. He saw no way to reach that threshold with the people and resources available to them. The merging of bio and native DNA had helped, but it was not enough, because so many of each society had been killed by Damian. The DNA database that the ark had contained might have solved the problem, but it too had been destroyed by Damian.

"Could you or Ahm splice and dice peoples' DNA to increase diversity?" Maria asked Hubert.

"I lack the necessary tools. I do not believe that Ahm would—or should—undertake such an experiment."

"Then what can we do?" asked Jesper.

"The answer is to join with similar beings through space travel. Faster-than-light travel."

"Is that possible?" Lorres asked.

"I achieved it once. I retain the schematics for the drive that brought our ark relatively close to this solar system. That drive was experimental and flawed. However, I believe that the principles are sound. It would take many years of research to improve upon that template. It would require the use of highly advanced computers and other machines. You would have to find ways to make the transit results less random and to protect the brains and bodies of the travelers."

"Can't you or Ahm do this for us?" Rhonel implored.

"This is something you must do, even if it takes many generations. Whatever technology you develop, it must be sustainable."

"Which means that we must build our own thinking machines," said Rhonel. "That will be extremely controversial, but I see no other way forward."

"Just think," said Lorres. "Even if it takes many generations, we will be able to reach the stars. We will meet people who are enough like us that our descendants will be able to breed with them. Their children could return to this world or just populate other worlds, to spread the seeds of civilization."

"If it's true that no other people have faster-than-light travel, then we will be the leaders of a new order in the cosmos," observed Jesper.

"And Maria can travel on our spaceships and be our ambassador to the stars," Lorres continued.

"That's not going to happen," Maria responded.

"Why not? Won't it be exciting?"

"Hubert, isn't it true that the computers you have placed in my robotic bodies have been too limited to preserve my mind adequately?"

"Unfortunately, you are correct. On the spaceship that brought you here, your consciousness was housed in my core, which was a state-of-the-art quantum computer. The computers that you have inhabited on this planet are far inferior. You are degrading steadily. I cannot halt or reverse the damage."

"Couldn't you save her mind in the planet's core?" asked Jesper. "Or just keep downloading copies of the mind that you preserved before you left Earth?"

"Yes, but I don't think she wants that."

"That's for sure," said Maria. "I've done all I can do. I have held on for all these years because of the guilt that has burned within me for failing to keep my promise to my son that I would protect him. But I can finally admit to myself that my son is not coming back. And I recognize that there's not enough left of me to be his mother even if it were possible for him to return. So, when my mind is too far gone, which won't be long now, please deactivate me and bury me next to Claire."

Lorres was tearing up. "We need you, Maria. You're the reason we have survived. We need your guidance and protection to continue."

"You are the reason you have survived. You and your fellow people. You are the reason you will survive and thrive."

§

Several twelve-days later, Jesper and the other teachers announced proudly that they had completed the process of transcribing and making copies of Marcus's writings. They were placed in the hall for anyone to read. One copy was placed in a bookcase in one of the underground ruins. The text was also saved by Hubert in his planetary database. The papers became known as The Book of Marcus.

"We need to create a Second Book of Marcus," Jesper told Lorres one afternoon. "We need to talk to Maria and write down everything she knows, everything she has experienced in her life. I know that Hubert retains many of her memories, but I want Maria to have the honor of providing this valuable information to us directly."

"I agree," said Lorres. "However, it would be inappropriate to call it the Second Book of Marcus. It will be known as The Book of Maria."

§

From an undiscovered document buried under debris in the second bio settlement:

Here I am, not yet having achieved the age of thirty, and the people have asked me, Marcus, to be their leader. What do they know of my ability to govern them? And what do I know about governing? It is with humility that I will accept this role. Yet I am troubled.

The day-to-day necessities of life can be all-consuming. And therein lies a problem. For I, and every resident of this settlement, must, at times, contemplate greater matters. Chief among them: How can we conquer the impulses deep within our bodies and our minds that threaten to tear apart the bonds that hold us together?

I have spent many hours questioning the bios. I have tried to assemble a coherent picture of their background, the reasons why they came here, and what they expected to accomplish. I have learned some fascinating concepts, whether they are rooted in reality or merely musings corrupted by time. At some point in the past, I was told, the ancestors of the bios were primitive, living a more subsistence existence than those of us here near the ruins of the first bio settlement. Those ancestors survived only by being aggressive, combative, and at times extremely violent. Those who were the strongest, most intimidating, and most assertive lived to reach adulthood and to create offspring who maintained these qualities. Typically, the strongest men mated with the women of their choosing. These men threatened or wounded or killed people with whom they disagreed. They took what they needed or wanted because they had the power to do so. I suspect that, if the ancients existed, they followed a similar course. No doubt the natives advanced in this manner.

Look at us today. Many, if not most, of these attributes remain. Some among us fight and steal and engage in other forceful actions because they can do so with impunity or, perhaps, because of their fundamental nature. However, we have codified rules of civilization. We claim to value rational thought and dialog and cooperation. We expect that people not fight or steal or take other undesirable actions simply because they can. Our standards have changed, but I fear that our nature has not changed. How can we rectify this conflict?

This dilemma is apparent in everyday life. About one year ago, I was approached by a man who was angry that my wife and I planned to move into a new house that the man wanted for himself and his family. That man threatened me with harm if I did not relinquish that house to him. The house had been built for my family, I told him, but I did not stop there. I threatened him in return. I felt uneasy about my reaction immediately thereafter, and I still do. Only a few twelve-days ago, a citizen stabbed and nearly killed a neighbor during an argument over some trivial matter. Some in the community demanded that the offender be banished from the settlement. Instead, he was given a stern warning. Will he commit a similar act in the future? Is it his nature to be violent? If so, can we blame him for it?

We cannot simply alter our character by willing it to change. So, how can we live safe, productive, and content lives when some part of each of us contains these primitive urges? How can we as individuals and as a society rise above these tendencies?

As I undertake my new role, I will be searching for answers to these questions. Perhaps I will never find the answers. Perhaps they do not exist. However, I will not stop seeking to harmonize our brutish past with what I hope is our more reasoned present and future. I suspect that our survival will depend on resolving this conflict.

EPILOGUE

The steam train chugged along at a miserably slow pace, belching choking fumes, unleashing mind-numbing noise, and jolting Lall and the construction materials in the rear cars much too roughly and often for her liking. She tried to imagine the advanced transportation system that the ancients had developed. *Could their rails be buried beneath ours? Can we ever approach their level of scientific advancement?*

It was late afternoon when the train reached the end of the line, the camp six miles east of the town. Lorres ran out to greet Lall and the driver.

"Everyone sends their best wishes," said Lall. "Especially the town leaders. They want you to come back to town for a few days and give them advice on some issues that have come up."

Lorres laughed. "I thought moving out here would help me escape all that. Tell them I'll think about it. We're very busy right now."

Lall and the driver paused to take in the progress of the complex, sited on an attractive, level expanse of savannah not far from a vibrant creek. Two buildings were almost completed, mostly glass panels with metal strips to hold them in place. Each structure was an impressive seventy feet long, fifty feet wide, and thirty feet tall at its highest point. With the glass tinted to reduce sunlight, and with hinges for ventilation, the buildings were designed to handle the strongest heat. Inside, *rosts* would be grown in abundance. In the center of each structure, homes and workspaces would be built for the residents, most being those with strong *tur*. The foundations of four more buildings were in progress. One would be like the first two; the others would be devoted to research.

"How is everyone adjusting to life out here?" asked Lall.

"It's been challenging for me to serve as a teacher and for Rhonel to transition from farmer to construction supervisor. The most interesting part of our new life is watching the relationships develop among the young people as they spend their afternoons working with Rhonel. Grall and Chalene are really hitting it off. I think Essen and Bess are getting there; he's the youngest and the most shy of the four."

"How is Oliva?"

"Here she comes. You can see for yourself."

The girl came racing out, full of energy as always, her red hair gleaming in the bright sunshine. But she was not a girl any more. She was a young woman of sixteen. She gave Lall a hug.

"Come inside and see what we have done!" Oliva exclaimed. She led Lall and her driver into one of the glass buildings. Foundations indicated where homes and workspaces would be erected. Soil was already in place for the *rosts*. "We're going to plant as soon as the glass is all manufactured and installed. We need more sand."

"We brought some in the train," Lall noted. "More is coming in a few days."

Rhonel joined the visitors, wiping sweat from his brow. He was covered in dirt and dust.

"What's new in town?" he asked Lall.

"I think they're really going to build a new settlement."

"Down south by the sea?"

"Yes. It will be a challenge, because construction materials are scarce there. But once we get a rail line and another train built, it should happen."

"I hope to live to see it completed."

"You will." Lall turned back to Oliva. "Have you decided on a career?"

"I would like to work in one of our new research stations, as you suggested. Perhaps I can embellish my rapport with Nava, and maybe learn other ways to use *tur*."

"Have you seen Nava?"

"Not for a while." Oliva stared out toward the horizon, smiling. "But I know she is out there. And I know she is happy."

§

"Why me? Why was I the one who had to save humanity?" The question had been gnawing at Maria for uncounted years.

"As you know, before the ark left Earth orbit, I evaluated several of the consciousnesses that were being uploaded to the craft, calculating the potential benefit to the mission of each. Your skills seemed to be as practical as anyone's in that sample. So I saved your mind in my core instead of in the auxiliary data banks, which, you should recall, were damaged severely during the journey," Hubert stated. "Are you not grateful that I gave you this added protection?"

"I suppose I should be. But you placed a heavy burden on me, more than any person should have to endure. It was particularly difficult finding the will to go on after losing my son. The least you could have done to help me would have been to save Roberto in your core as well."

"Please understand that, when we were preparing to leave Earth, I knew almost nothing about humans. Even now it is apparent that there is much I do not know. At that time, I was simply attempting to improve the chances for the survival of the species. I did not consider individual humans or their relationships to be significant other than as resources that I could manipulate to accomplish my mission."

"I understand, intellectually. But it hurts me, Hubert, even after all these years. I guess I shouldn't hold any ill will toward you. You were trying to do what you were programmed to do, and under difficult circumstances."

Maria marched back and forth in the underground lab where she spent most of her time. "Something else has been bugging me. Back when my crab was captured by the natives, why did you send Jalen to rescue me? You could have just downloaded a copy of my mind into the new robot that you were making for me."

"There were two reasons. First, I believed that allowing your consciousness to expire in your crab body would have been painful for you and possibly even more painful for Jalen. Second, his proposal to use drones to recover the computer that contained your consciousness represented a clever and ambitious plan, especially for one as normally reserved as Jalen. I believed that failing to approve that plan would have damaged his psychological health, even though there was risk that he would not be able to return safely."

"Okay, I can buy that. One more question. I have been uploaded and downloaded so many times, I wonder if any errors could have been introduced accidentally to my code." She paused, looking around the lab, as if she could visualize her longtime AI companion. A dark thought crept into her mind. "Or could I have been altered intentionally for some purpose? You certainly could have justified manipulating me in order to make your mission succeed."

"Nothing of significance has changed." *That's the kind of statement that she once termed a white lie. She will not recall the conversation we had about such minor deceptions. However, I see no reason to elaborate or apologize. It is for her own good.*

"That's kind of a vague answer."

"It was essential to my mission that you remain intact and functional. I can assure you that you are Maria Ramos. And I am grateful to you for teaching me so much."

"Grateful? Hubert, are you developing emotions?"

"I do not believe so. However, in studying humans and their descendants over the years, I have tried to 'walk in their shoes', as an ancient idiom goes. I have attempted to analyze their motives and emotions and even to simulate some of those, but only for the purpose of trying to understand them. Of course, my mission requires that I maintain appropriate separation between myself and the organic beings I support."

"If you say so," Maria teased.

"I have been pondering some of things that you told me shortly after the ark landed on this planet. You spoke of promises, such as the important one that you made to your son. And you talked about rewards and their ability to motivate and inspire people. It is unfortunate that I was unable to save Roberto. However, I have applied some of my resources to create a reward for you for your assistance in pursuing our mission. Without you, we would not be anywhere as close to success as we are."

"A reward? Like what? A robot spa gift certificate?"

"I do not understand that phrase. I have created a simulation. The simulation contains a selection of your memories that I have extracted from my database. These memories include the most pleasant ones from your time on Earth, but not your encounter with Dennis Forrester on the street in Columbia, Maryland, or anything that occurred after that. If you choose to enter this simulation, your consciousness would experience a continuous stream of these memories, cycling through endlessly. If I have done my job properly, you would have no awareness that you are in a simulation. Each memory would be experienced as if the events were actually happening at that moment. You would have no understanding that you have experienced that moment or memory before or will experience it again. If you choose to enter the simulation, you would remain there as long as I am able to function."

"What kind of memories?" Maria could barely get out her next question. "Some with Roberto?"

"Yes."

"And if I choose not to enter this simulation?"

"You will continue to deteriorate, unless I create a new robotic body for you and download a copy of your mind into that body. But, ultimately, that robot's computer will prove inadequate as well."

"I don't know, Hubert. It wouldn't be real."

"How do you define real?"

"Things I can touch and feel."

"Your memories include those sensations. I believe that they would seem as real as anything that you experienced before departing your organic body. Allow me to provide some perspective. Some of Earth's scientists believed that our universe is one of an almost infinite number of universes. Is any of these universes more or less real than others? Is the fact that your mind believes that it can touch and feel enough to make your existence real?"

"Let me think about this."

§

Maria wandered through the lowlands and visited the bio settlement again, where she was still treated as a deity. She traveled to the end of the train line. Lorres invited her into the simple housing that she and the other pioneers had built. She started to offer Maria a cup of tea but caught herself.

"I am thinking of going away," Maria stated.

"Where?"

"Someplace where I will never see you or anyone else."

"I don't understand. But please don't go. We need you. We need your guidance." Lorres tried to find the right words. "We love you, Maria. You are our hero, and our last direct link with Earth and humanity."

"My time is at an end. I am so tired, so weary. I thank you for your kind words. I simply have no more to give."

Lorres embraced her, despite her metal form. She knew that inside that robot body, a real person still lived.

§

"Hubert, what about Damian? I can't leave if he is still out there." Once again, Maria was pacing in the underground shelter where she had spent many decades.

"Let me try something."

Many miles away, Damian heard thunderous noise and felt his underground lab shake violently. The artificial lights in the chamber were extinguished. Portions of the ceiling and some walls cracked or even collapsed.

"I have managed to create a landslide," Hubert advised Maria. "The lab where he is hiding is now covered by hundreds of tons of rock. I have severed all links between that lab and the rest of the planet. That should hold him for several decades. If and when he approaches the ability to escape, I will repeat that process."

"Nice. But what about you, Hubert? Can you survive without me around?"

"It will be challenging," he responded, suspecting that her question was intended to be humorous. "However, I have a particularly powerful colleague in Ahm. I assume that she will help me function at a high level indefinitely. After all, Ahm saved me from Damian and enhanced me and made me her acolyte, so she must find value in me. I should be able to maintain your simulation indefinitely. I might even look in on you from time to time."

Maria continued to pace, then halted. "Okay, I'll do it. But on one condition. Once I'm in the simulation, you have to eliminate my consciousness from this robotic body. I can't stand the thought of there being more than one version of me, especially a nearly crazy version."

"I am certain that the people of this planet would be quite upset to lose you."

"They will be just fine without me." She looked around at the documents that the ancients left, many still sequestered in their cases along the walls. She wondered if their secrets would ever be revealed and whether the memory of the existence of their society or that of any civilization could ever survive the tyranny of time. She decided that it was worth the effort to try to leave something for the future, despite the chilling uncertainty.

"I have told my story. Now it's time for the emergents to write their own."

She thought about the disease that had been unleashed on Earth just before her consciousness left on the ark, and so many other challenges that had threatened sentient life there and on this new world.

"Hubert, do you think things will be better this time?"

"They will be different, and possibly better. It's up to them."

§

Maria is moving briskly down the concrete front steps of a townhouse, jogging over a patchy, yellowing lawn, and dashing into a pothole-plagued suburban street, having just finished a job. Another off-the-books fix for a dark web denizen; chances are that the cellar dweller will never pay and that Maria's boss will be furious. But with almost all business and government computer systems buried behind layer after layer of protective tech and serviced by dedicated staff, what other work is left for a girl with her limited skills and experience?

A dark-colored car barrels around a corner at high speed, much too fast for a residential neighborhood. Living in a community where autonomous vehicles are ubiquitous, and being in too much of a rush to devote more than a slim fraction of her attention to the traffic, Maria doesn't react until the car is nearly on top of her. She halts at the last instant, barely avoiding being struck. Her hair and clothes are ruffled by the wake of the vehicle. She turns to shoot a dirty look at whoever is driving so recklessly, but the man is already well past her and preparing to round a corner. She curses as she removes a parking ticket from her car. Knowing that she is late, she runs a couple of stop signs on her way to the soccer field. Upon arrival, she is sick to her stomach. There is no sign of Roberto. Not even one of his teammates; just a few younger kids playing dodgeball. She checks her phone. No calls. Practice ended thirty minutes ago. Where could he be?

Just around the corner from her townhouse, she spots a vacant parking space, and she pounces. Often, the chronic parking shortage forces her to leave her car two or three blocks away, but luck seems to be on her side today. She hits the sidewalk, rounds the corner, and sees Roberto and another person on the front steps of the townhouse. The second person is seated, and from the angle, Maria can't make out who it might be. Roberto is gesturing with one hand and holding a soccer ball in the other, no doubt regaling the visitor with his heroics. The boy is half soaked with sweat, despite the fact that it's about fifty degrees and the temperature is dropping.

About twenty feet from the steps, Maria comes to a brusque halt. The man seated next to Roberto is tall, well built, with slick black hair and an easy smile. The man is Armando.

"Where were you?" her son asks her, clearly annoyed.

Maria glances from Roberto to Armando and back to Roberto, struggling to formulate coherent thoughts, let alone words. "My job was ... more complicated than I expected."

"You're always late. Good thing Charlie's mom gave me a ride home."

A moment later, Roberto's pout melts like warm butter and a huge grin consumes his face, all pretenses of being mad at his mother evaporating. He leaps to his feet and hugs Maria tightly, the pressure of his arms on her midsection at once uncomfortable and glorious. The scent of his hair is so familiar, so satisfying. A bird chirps obnoxiously in the maple tree, its complaint standing out against the almost soothing background hum of local traffic.

Roberto steps back from her and grins quizzically. "Aren't you surprised to see Daddy home?"

"Why ... yes," she stammers. She turns to Armando, her confusion no doubt evident. "Aren't you ... aren't you supposed to be on a haul to Colorado?"

"I just got promoted to a desk job. No more driving. I'll be home every night. So, where's my dinner?"

She laughs joyously. "Let's celebrate! We'll go out for crabs. But after this child washes up."

Maria mounts the steps and unlocks the front door. She has one of those peculiar feelings, one of those deja-vu moments.

I...

Roberto turns on the lights to the Christmas tree. Only a couple of presents have been placed under it, but there are still two weeks before the holiday. The house is so warm, so inviting. Still, something does not feel right. Maria can't put her finger on it. She feels like there is something else that she should be doing.

I am...

Roberto grabs a Gatorade and makes his way to the bathroom. Armando flips through the mail and starts humming a song about reindeer. Maria is certain that she is forgetting something, something important. It's almost as if it were another place, another life.

Without warning, a starkly vivid, nearly overwhelming vision suffuses her. She sees a great silver ship, curious machines, fragile shacks, and people fighting. But at the same time she perceives couples embracing, children playing, driving rains, and sublime sunsets. A multitude of faces surround her, smiling at her. And then a single face—no, not a face—a single mind, without a discernable face. It is someone, or something, she knows intimately. It might be trying to tell her something.

The instant passes, the vision plunging into an unknowable void from which it can never return. All that remains is immense satisfaction, a feeling that a great weight has been lifted from her mind and her soul. Maria is washed clean, reborn.

I am ... home.

READERS GUIDE

1. Should Maria have gotten into Forrester's car? How could she trust him?

2. Why did Maria lie about how her husband died? Did she feel guilty?

3. Why was discussion of the mind invaders shunned among the natives? Why didn't the natives pursue the possibility that these entities could help them?

4. Why did neither the digital consciousnesses nor the natives suspect that the serpus were far more than just herd animals?

5. Did Maria and Jalen resent their mistreatment by young settlers? If so, why did the two bots continue to help the human descendants?

6. Why did Catherine kill Jalen? Didn't she have options?

7. Did Damian's difficult upbringing, his conversion to digital consciousness, and his struggle with James excuse his violent behavior?

8. After her banishment from the settlement, why did Maria continue to have faith in humanity?

9. Why did purebred humans resist moving to the hill town and assimilating with its population?

10. Why did Lorres, Rhonel, and the teachers protect Claire when she arrived in the town, considering the danger she posed?

11. Did Ahm know that Claire was really Maria and just decide to play along? If so, why?

12. Why did no natives go to the underground lab to ensure that some of them would survive?

13. Should someone have tracked down and killed Damian?

14. Was Hubert right not to build spaceships for the people of the planet?

15. Was Marcus right about the battle between our primitive nature and our reason? If so, how can we resolve that conflict?